LUCKY CATCH

LUCKY O'TOOLE VEGAS ADVENTURE: BOOK 5

DEBORAH COONTS

Chestnut
Street
Press

For Bob

CHAPTER 1

*L*OVE AND lust—two four-letter words men often confuse.

More specifically, a certain man . . . the man standing in my doorway.

Teddie.

My heart tripped, then steadied.

Thinner than I remembered, he still had that tight ass, those broad shoulders, spiky blond hair, soulful baby-blues, and a sippin'-whiskey-smooth voice that could warm me to the core, despite my best efforts to douse the fire.

Teddie.

Despite serious reservations about turning a platonic friendship into something . . . not platonic . . . I had let him lead me into the deep, dark waters of love. And being an all-or-nothing kind of gal, I'd done a half gainer off the high dive and things had not gone swimmingly.

He left.

And now he was back.

As I looked at him and tried to compose myself—it just wouldn't do to let him see the splash his return made—I wondered how I'd ever get my heart back. The empty hole in my chest echoed with longing, leaving me winded.

My office phone jangled, giving me an excuse to avoid Teddie for a few moments longer. I grabbed the receiver. "Customer relations, Lucky O'Toole speaking. How may I help you?"

"We have a problem." Detective Romeo with the Las Vegas Metropolitan Police Department started in without preliminaries —not a good sign.

"What's this *we* shit, Kemosabe?" I tried to make light. Apparently, I failed miserably.

Romeo's tone hardened. "Dead body. Back lot. Somebody wrapped her head in plastic and killed her with a Saf-T-Smoke. You're going to want to see this one."

"She got smoked with a Saf-T-Smoke? Dang." I rubbed a hand over my face. "I never want to see that kind of thing. You know that." I looked up and locked eyes with Teddie, who stared at me, his eyes dark and troubled.

"Trust me on this one." Romeo took an audible breath, then let it out slowly.

"Okay. Give me fifteen minutes. I've got to take Christophe Bouclet back to his father."

"I'll meet you there. This one's bad."

As if they all aren't bad. "Meet me where?" My only answer was the hollow echo of a disconnected line. Romeo had hung up—he knew how much I hated that little bit of rudeness.

Men.

I narrowed my eyes at a prime example of the Y chromosome set standing in front of me.

Teddie knew me well enough to take a step back. "Romeo?" he asked with a forced lilt to his voice.

I set the receiver back in its cradle, but refused to let Romeo and Teddie get me all worked up. Problems, I could handle—as the vice president of Customer Relations at the Babylon, Las Vegas's most over-the-top Strip property, problems were my job. And, if I can say anything about myself, I'm good at my job.

Now, to the most immediate problem. "Teddie, why are you here?"

Ignoring my glower, he continued with the manner of an old friend stopping by to reminisce. "Your office door was open," he began in a casual tone, as if the earth still rotated on the same axis. "I expected to find you in your old office. What are you doing back here in this construction zone? Not VP digs. Congrats on the promotion, by the way." Teddie paused when his eyes came to rest on the young boy in my lap who clutched a crayon and concentrated on the drawing in front of him. I saw questions lurking in Teddie's eyes. Thankfully, he didn't voice them, choosing instead to give me a tentative grin.

A dagger to the heart.

A frown was the only response I could muster as my pulse pounded in my ears and I struggled to remain outwardly calm.

"This early in the morning, I expected to see your staff out front," he continued, oblivious to the fact this whole situation was fraught with possibilities of homicide. "But the desks were empty. Since you and I are . . . friends . . . I didn't think you'd mind me wandering back here to find you."

What was I going to say? "Get the hell out" seemed a bit extreme. And "no, we're not friends" would have been too hard to admit. Offering to shoot him the next time he wandered in unannounced also seemed a bit aggressive. Maybe. I opted to duck-and-weave. "If I minded, would it matter?"

Teddie's smile dimmed and he jammed his hands in his pockets as he shifted from one foot to the other, his shoulders hunched around his ears.

I took a deep breath and blew at a strand of hair that tickled my eyes. "To be honest, you were the last person I expected to darken my doorway this morning. Weren't you just in Prague or Moscow or someplace half a world away?"

3

"I quit the tour and jumped a plane."

Taking a step inside the doorway, he was brought up short by the look on my face. His arms wide, pleading, he said, "I had to see you."

I wasn't buying it. He always was a bit of a drama queen which, now that I thought about it, went with the whole female imper-sonator gig—I'd just never noticed it before—or it had never bothered me before.

Ever the performer, he adopted just the right tone—pleading without the whine. "You won't take my calls. You won't answer the messages I send you. You haven't even acknowledged the song. What did you expect me to do?" He let his arms fall to his sides.

"Expect?" My voice was flat, hard, pounded thin by the hammer of his insensitivity. And the song he mentioned? Every time I heard the thing, he bludgeoned me anew. Didn't he under-stand that? "Teddie, I expected you to stay gone."

Hurt flashed across his face as we stared at each other and time slowed to a crawl. He looked like he wanted to explore the subject further, but wisely altered course. "Got a new friend, I see." He nodded toward the boy.

Christophe squirmed under Teddie's scrutiny, then leaned back and looked up at me. While I counted to ten and prayed for self-control and a noninflammatory response, I bent down and gave the boy a kiss on the head. He smelled like baby soap, and with good reason—last night we'd used a gallon of the stuff.

That was before I'd spent the night with his father.

"Christophe Bouclet." My eyes found Teddie's, then skittered away and back again. Knowing me, I had "guilty as sin" written all over my face. But, he'd left. So why did I feel guilty?

Life had just gotten way more than complicated.

I had absolutely no idea where to start or what to do. To be honest, I wasn't 100 percent sure that, once started, I wouldn't finish by grabbing Teddie by the neck and squeezing the life out of him. As it turned out, I needn't have worried. My cell phone sang out at my hip, saving me from a long future making license plates at the invitation of the great state of Nevada. Actually, it was Teddie doing the singing. In a weak, masochistic moment, I'd installed as my ringtone a snippet of a song he'd written not only for me, but about me as well. Yes, *that* song . . . the one he'd mentioned and I'd avoided. He'd titled it "Lucky for Me."

Apparently, he loved irony.

At the first few notes, Teddie gave me a knowing look. I hastily reached for the device and silenced it with a stroke of my thumb. I gave him a steely stare, challenging the assumption I saw in his eyes. Never wavering, I pressed the phone to my ear. "O'Toole," I barked.

"How do you make a thousand turkeys disappear?"

"What?" I held the phone in front of me and squinted at the display, trying to bring into focus not only the tiny digits, but life as well. The number belonged to Jerry, the voice belonged to Jerry, but the question came out of left field—even from the Babylon's head of Security. "Jerry, this really isn't a good time."

"Tell me about it." He chuckled. "I got turkeys down here—the real things. A thousand of them." Chaos in the background filtered through the connection. "You know anything about them?"

I glanced up at Teddie—turkeys seemed to abound today. And to think, Thanksgiving was still a few days away.

"Lucky, girl, are you there? We could sure use your help."

As the Babylon's chief problem-solver, turkeys like the one standing in my office doorway were my specialty. However, my expertise did not necessarily extend to the feathered variety.

I put the phone back to my ear. "I'm here, but I'm confused. Where are you? And, just for clarification, what kind of turkeys are we talking about?"

Jerry replied in a rushed voice, "The basement, Level Two. Your mother . . ."

The light dawned. "Oh God, she didn't."

"She did." This time, he burst out laughing. "Mona, she is some piece of work. Better get that woman down here. And tell her, if she plans on feeding the hungry on Thanksgiving, she'd better bring her double barrel and a shitload of buckshot."

"Some people are alive solely because it's illegal to shoot them." Jerry laughed. "Your mother . . ."

". . . is their fearless leader," I said, finishing his thought. "But you aren't seriously considering turning a pregnant woman loose in the basement with a loaded shotgun, are you? Remember what she did to the sheriff?"

"Any other ideas?" Jerry's voice sobered a bit.

"Fresh out." I glanced up at Teddie—a frown creased the skin between his eyes as he watched Christophe, who was working intently on his drawing. "And since answers on this end seem to be in short supply, I'm invoking one of my three vice president lifelines and am phoning a friend. That would be you, by the way."

"But I called you," Jerry reminded me.

"A mere technicality. Mother is your problem. I'll get her down there. You figure out what happens next. If you kill her, just let me know where to send flowers." I terminated the call before he could guilt me into more. My vintage Versace suit and Loubous were hardly turkey-taming attire. And I didn't really trust myself around Mona right now, especially with a gun within easy reach.

Today was Monday . . . in every way.

My eyes met Teddie's and my heart tightened. Would I ever be over him? Christophe stilled in my lap.

"It's okay, sweetie." I gave the boy another hurried peck on the top of his head. "Ignore the man in the doorway. He's leaving." With both hands under Christophe's arms, I lifted him as I slithered out from under him, then deposited him back in the chair. "And so are we."

The boy wiggled his legs underneath him. Kneeling, he bent back over the picture he had been drawing when we'd been so rudely interrupted. "I'm drawing a picture of you and Papa and my happy-face pancakes." He gave me a look designed to melt my heart. God help womankind in another ten or twelve years. "See?" He pointed to one figure. "You have Papa's shirt on."

I sighed. Like I said, a Monday in every way. "That's wonderful, dear. It was fun, wasn't it?"

"Tomorrow we will make pancakes again?" A demand framed as a question—his father had the same habit.

Allergic to authority, real or implied, I don't know why it didn't irritate me. Maybe it was the French accent. Who knew? I smiled and ruffled his hair. "Of course. Now, I've got to take you to your father." I rounded up wayward crayons and stuffed them back in the box. Then I eased the paper from his grasp and carefully tucked it into a drawer. "Let's finish this later, okay?" Turning, I presented my back. "Climb aboard."

He jumped in exuberance, his legs encircling my waist. Holding a bit too tightly around my neck, he choked off the air. I loosened his arms and settled him on my hips. "Good?"

He nuzzled in, his mouth next to my ear. "*Oui!*"

"We're off, then." My eyes, full of challenge and probably a bit of hurt, met Teddie's as I moved to brush by him. I could see in his face the warning had registered. He opened his mouth to speak. I put a hand to the center of his chest to move him out of the doorway—the connection hit me like a sucker punch. I struggled to keep my composure. "Don't."

Clamping his mouth shut, Teddie did as I asked and stepped aside.

I let my hand drop. Why had I touched him? I knew every curve and angle of his body by heart. Closing my eyes, I could remember the feel of him, as real and immediate as if we'd never stopped. But we *had* stopped. Well, *he* had stopped. Apparently my heart, not to mention other parts, hadn't gotten the memo. Pulling air into my lungs in a vain hope that some would find its way to my head, I opened my eyes and gave a half-smile to the man who had stolen my heart. Then I eased past him, careful not to touch him again.

My old office, which was adjacent to my new one but lacked the whole construction zone motif, was empty, as was the outer office. The bird still slept under the nighttime cage cover. I'd never been so glad to find my staff absent and Newton, my foul-mouthed Macaw, muzzled for the moment.

Teddie followed me.

"Go away." I threw the words over my shoulder as I burst through the outer door, then turned and hurried down the hallway toward the elevator.

"Giddy-up!" Christophe shrieked.

Teddy was hard on my heels. "We need to talk." He reached for my elbow.

His hand fell away as I stopped. Taking a deep breath, I turned. Christophe fisted a hand in my hair.

"What do you want, Teddie?"

"Is that boy the new French chef's?"

"His son, yes."

An emotion, one that didn't look pleasant, pulled Teddie's lips into a thin line. "You didn't waste much time."

I rolled my eyes. "You know me, never let a warm bed cool." Turning, I resumed my stalk down the hall. Teddie knew me well enough to know that wasn't even close to being true. The sad truth was, he probably knew me better than I knew myself, which put me at a distinct disadvantage.

"Lucky, you shut me out." Teddie dogged my heels. "Would you stop for a minute?"

"Go away, Teddie. Leave me alone. I don't want to talk to you." I tossed the verbal arrows over my shoulder. "I have nothing to say." Okay, that was a lie—I had a ton to say, but now was not the time, especially with a five-year-old on my back. Besides, I didn't like to be ambushed.

Apparently, my verbal darts had finally penetrated his thick skull. When Teddie spoke again his voice held a quiet, plaintive tone. "I couldn't stay away."

"Pity." With Teddie I had never known where the act ended and sincerity began. I still didn't, but I'd built up immunity to the whole show. My phone rang at my hip, but with both arms full of little boy and my thoughts gyrating wildly, I had more than I could deal with already, so I ignored it. "Lucky for Me" jangled into the sudden silence. Thank God ringtones were only a few seconds long.

Christophe laid his head on my shoulder, his fingers entwined in my hair. The poor kid had traveled halfway around the world from his grandparents' farm in Provence, arriving last night, then had been too excited to sleep for long.

"I had to come home. Especially when your father called." With pitch-perfect comedic timing, Teddie could deliver a punch line better than Jerry Seinfeld.

I threw on the brakes mid-stride—Christophe didn't move. "What?"

Obviously taken by surprise, Teddie skidded to a stop. He stepped in front of me, then, at the look on my face, took a step back. Everyone in my sphere knew, when my eyes got all slitty it usually meant "run." Foolish man, he stood his ground. He even squared his shoulders. "Your father called."

"I heard you the first time." Teddie couldn't be lying, could he? That would be way too stupid, even for him. "Why did he call *you*?" I left the last word hanging, poised like a wrecking ball beginning its arc.

"He offered me my old job back."

"Really?" I tried not to let him see the effect of that low blow. Betrayed by my own father and blindsided by Teddie—could life get any better today? My father was the owner of the Babylon and, as such, complicated my life immeasurably, but usually not quite this boldly. I chewed on the inside of my cheek. "And?"

"We're working out the terms, but I think we have a deal. He made his offer contingent on your approval."

"So that's really why you're here, to get my blessing."

Careful not to upset the resting boy, I stepped around Teddie and strode to the elevators. I angrily poked the down button, even though I knew the speed with which the elevator would appear bore an inverse relationship to the fervor with which I punched. Teddie's perfect reflection eased in beside my rather ordinary one. Light brown hair, blue eyes, high cheekbones, angry scowl, a hint of hurt under a layer of homicide—not my best look.

"That's not why I'm here." Teddie's voice held a softer tone, inviting, cajoling.

Reeking of self-serving insincerity, his plea was too little, too late. I cocked a disbelieving eyebrow at his reflection.

He shrugged, apparently deciding that truth might be the salve to soothe the wound—he was wrong. "Okay, it's part of the reason I'm here. But you are the main reason."

"I can't tell you how happy that makes me." Sarcasm dripped from every word. "So, being a rock star wasn't enough? Now you have to come back here to mess with my magic?"

His voice dropped. "I love you."

"Low blow." Thankfully, the elevator doors eased open. I stepped inside, then turned and put a hand out, stopping him from following me. Unwilling to be singed again, I pulled my hand back before it made contact.

"Not now, Teddie. Maybe not ever."

Maybe? Where the hell had *that* come from?

The doors slid shut, saving me from further humiliation as tears welled in my eyes.

"Damn!" I shouted, the word echoing in the empty elevator. Christophe's head popped up and his body jerked in surprise. "Sorry, honey."

"I don't like that man. He made you mad."

I took a deep breath and calmed myself down as I dabbed at

the corners of my eyes with the knuckle of my forefinger and sniffed back further emotion. "He's a nice man, and he didn't make me angry. I had expectations he didn't live up to—my fault, not his." Saying the words was easy, believing them, not so much.

The boy's quizzical look reflected back to me in the polished metal doors. His face peering at me over my shoulder reminded me of an angel whispering in my ear. Stranded in the quicksand of my own confusion and ambivalence, I wished he had words of wisdom, but he was just a boy.

"Maybe he is like a puppy who has been scolded—he bites even though he is the one who has been bad."

Wow. That stopped me for a moment. My experience with children had been limited, but I guessed that whole out-of-the-mouths-of-babes thing had some truth to it. "You're probably right." I hitched him higher on my hips. "Teddie can be quite charming. You'll like him . . . everybody does."

"But you don't?"

"I like him, but with us, it's a bit more complicated." I rolled my eyes at myself. Relationships. I totally sucked at them. Pasting on a smile, I contemplated who to kill first—my father, Teddie, Mona—I wasn't sure the order mattered. Of course, I could line them up and rid myself of the lot of them all at once—a Thanksgiving Day Massacre. Tempting.

"Ms. O'Toole," a disembodied voice asked—the eye-in-the-sky, our omnipresent security system, "Mr. Jerry asked me to find you. He said you weren't answering your phone."

"One can run, but one can't hide?" I asked the voice.

"No, ma'am, I'm afraid you're screwed," the voice said, then paused awkwardly. "That probably isn't how I'm supposed to talk to a vice president, is it?"

"Well, since this vice president just yelled a not-so-nice word to an empty elevator in the presence of a youngster, I'd say you were well within propriety." The elevator stopped, and the doors eased open. A middle-aged couple stood there, waiting to enter.

I stayed where I was. "Now, did you want something?"

At first the couple looked taken aback, as if I were talking to them. Then they leaned forward slightly and glanced around the empty elevator.

"Yes," came the voice. "Mr. Jerry is apoplectic. He said to tell you that your mother is not answering her phone."

Stepping to the side and holding the door, I motioned the couple inside. At first they hesitated, but then they moved past, eyeing me as they did so. "What floor?" I asked them.

"Twelve," the lady responded.

I punched the appropriate button, then answered the voice. "Tell him I'll be on my way after I make a quick stop in the Bazaar, and I'll bring Mona if I have to shoot her with a tranquilizer dart and throw her over my shoulder."

"Yes, ma'am."

Letting loose the doors, I stepped out. As the elevator closed, I overheard the man say, "A tranquilizer dart. I wonder if she would do the same to Irene."

~

I PAUSED FOR A MOMENT STARING AT MYSELF IN THE ELEVATOR doors, gathering my wits, or what was left of them. Irene? The man's comment to his female companion certainly triggered an interesting visual.

Vegas, where two is a date and three is . . . an even better date.

Carefully, I shifted the boy on my back. Once again, Christophe's head had sagged onto my shoulder, his eyes fluttering, then remaining shut. The ability to sleep anywhere—if only I could bottle some of that.

Thanksgiving was three days away—an eternity in my world. The holidays were supposed to bring families together, to let bygones be bygones, giving us a chance to relax in the presence of folks who—short of homicide—couldn't get rid of us.

I wasn't feeling the magic.

Apparently, I was the lone lump of coal floating in a sea of the milk of human kindness—or I was the only sober one in a sea of well-oiled humanity. Excited voices swirled around me as I turned and strode through the lobby. As they waited for the next check-in clerk, travelers in their Bermuda shorts, sundresses, sandals, and goose bumps rubbed their bare arms, some cuddled against the chill. Most swilled the free Champagne passed by cocktail waitresses in their barely-there togas with gold braid belts, strappy gladiator footwear with five-inch heels, pearly smiles, and other Vegas assets properly displayed.

Vegas's location in the middle of the Mojave Desert fooled most folks into thinking summer was a year-round season. Not true. Winter could be windy and chilly. Today was a perfect example—a cool breeze wafted in each time someone pushed through one of the multiple sets of double-glass doors forming the Babylon's grand entry, letting in a taste of the out-of-doors. To be honest, I welcomed the change in the weather—while my life kept me teetering on the brink of insanity, twelve months of hundred-degree days would shove me right over.

For a moment, I let myself absorb some of the crowd's energy and enthusiasm. Glancing at the ceiling, I smiled at the Chihuly blown-glass hummingbirds and butterflies arcing in flight. A dozen skiers bombed down the indoor ski slope sheltered behind a wall of Lucite on the far side of the lobby. Multicolored cloth tented above Reception. Equally colorful mosaics decorated the white marble walls and floors, hinting at the Babylon's Persian motif. Unfortunately, I couldn't find a problem to solve—everything hummed with a well-timed precision. Darn.

Guess I had to deal with Mona and her turkeys.

Then a dead woman and a smoking thing, which sounded like the perfect recipe for a migraine.

I eased Christophe to one hip as he slumbered, freeing a hand. With a practiced motion, I grabbed my phone from its holster and flipped it open. My thumb found Mona's button. After the fifth ring, I started to ring off when she answered, her voice breathless.

"Lucky, honey. This isn't a good time. Your father and I . . ."

"TMI, Mother." I stifled a shiver of revulsion. No matter how old I got, how worldly I became, there was just something so . . . disturbing about picturing my parents inter-coitus. "And, come to think about it," I grimaced at the unintentional pun as I once again shifted the boy who clung to my back like a monkey, "are you supposed to be having S-E-X in your condition?"

"S-E-X? Why are you spelling? And what are you talking about? We're hanging pictures." She stifled a giggle.

"Right." I shifted the phone to my other ear, holding it with my shoulder, then put a hand on my hip, nearly taking out a cute Marine as he dodged around me.

"Sorry, ma'am," he said as he shot me a grin.

Even though the "ma'am" thing rankled, I allowed myself a moment to admire his ass as he hurried on. "Mother, Jerry needs you downstairs. Basement Level Two."

"Honey," her voice dropped to a conspiratorial whisper, "can't it wait?"

I tried to picture Jerry, his well-armed staff, and a thousand turkeys. "No, I don't think so. Jerry needs your help with the turkeys you ordered."

Mona's voice turned brusque. "Oh, well, I already had the staff clear enough room in several of the walk-ins. I don't see what he needs me for."

"I think he wants to blindfold you and stand you against a wall." I started laughing; I couldn't help it. "Seriously, Mother. I know your heart's in the right place. But couldn't you at least have ordered the turkeys already dressed?"

"But Chef Omer said he would make the dressing."

The sea of humanity in the lobby flowed around me as I let my head drop forward. My emotions, ragged and somewhat irrational, burbled up. I didn't fight them. Instead, I relinquished myself and laughed until I cried. It was the only non-self-destructive antidote to Mona and a day that, with Teddie's sudden reappearance and Romeo's little bombshell, had taken a hard turn toward abysmal. And to think, it had started so well. Warmth suffused me as I pictured my chef in his shorts and a smile. "Mother." I managed to squeeze the words out with what little air was left in my lungs. "'Dressed' means plucked, gutted, and ready to stuff."

There was a pause on the other end of the line, which gave me time to compose myself somewhat. I wiped my tears on the shoulder of my blouse—I never did like the color of this one anyway—then I bit my lip as I fought down another burble of laughter.

"You mean they're . . . alive?" Not the sharpest knife in the drawer, Mona apparently still had a bit of an edge.

"Mmmmm." That was the only sound I trusted myself to make.

"Oh, my!"

I took a deep breath. "Mother, at your behest, the press is coming tomorrow. And you've given the go-ahead to Crazy Carl to invite all of his fellow storm drain dwellers for the big feast on Thursday. The staff is ready to go, but I feel pretty sure they'll mutiny if you expect them to behead, gut, and pluck a thousand turkeys."

"But what should I do?" Her voice sounded small, imploring . . . like a child's.

Wise to her game, I refused to play. "You need to get down there ASAP. After that, I haven't a clue. You wanted to campaign for an appointment to the Paradise Town Advisory Board. You wanted to 'change the world one homeless person at a time,' which I believe were your exact words. You wanted to run this show. Well, run it."

"Lucky, you're not being very helpful," she harrumphed.

"I know." As I terminated the call, I couldn't wipe the gloat off my face.

CHAPTER 2

*A*FTER I reholstered my phone, then once again tucked an arm under one of Christophe's legs, I eased him into a more comfortable position on my back. A shiver hit me as I contemplated what awaited me on the back lot. Who was the dead girl? And why would someone kill her?

I so did not want to deal with death today . . . unless I inflicted it.

Apparently, the Fates didn't care—my day was galloping off without me, and unless I wanted to be left eating dust for the foreseeable future, I figured I'd better deposit the boy with his father and jump into the fray.

Jean-Charles Bouclet, Christophe's father, was a world-renowned chef who signed on to develop the signature restaurant in one of our new properties, Cielo. While he was tinkering with recipes and menus, he'd agreed to open a gourmet burger joint in the Babylon's shopping area, the Bazaar. Strictly for fun, the Burger Palais was an engaging trifle for a man of his abilities.

Let's hope he didn't view me in the same way.

Yes, I'd spent the night with Jean-Charles—a long, languorous, passion-filled rendezvous. Capped off by a pancake breakfast then a hot, hurried tryst in the bathroom behind closed doors, and obscured by the soundtrack from *Thomas the Tank Engine*. I was probably scarred for life, and most likely in need of serious chiropractic care, but my heart hummed and there was a spring in my step even Teddie, Mona, *and* my father couldn't flatten. Romeo? Now he just might. Murder made me twitchy.

But one problem at a time.

On the far side of the lobby, just past Reception, I angled to the right and entered our high-ceilinged temple to the Gods of Conspicuous Consumption—the Bazaar. The glistening white marble floors continued from the lobby, the intricate inlays in brightly colored stones beckoning like the yellow-brick road.

But the Bazaar was way better than the Emerald City.

Christophe still clung tightly, although he was awake now, as I dodged the window-shoppers eyeing all manner of goodies from French jeans, serious bling, and high-end shoes—my weakness—to the latest Ferrari—another weakness. Yes, even though I was immune to most of the city's vast array of excesses, I'd found it impossible to live in Vegas, the Consumption Capital of the World, and not get bitten by the bug. Samson's, our salon—billed as "the place where a woman's every need is met"—looked like it was doing a land-office business. Its double-wide, twenty-foot-high wooden doors thrown open, the beauty salon displayed some of its more obvious treasures—long-haired, beefy young men dressed in scanty togas and gladiator sandals who balanced trays of fluted crystal filled with Champagne and proffered them to the waiting patrons.

A couple waited outside the Temple of Love, the Babylon's wedding chapel. The woman was fittingly dressed in a white bikini topped with a fishnet cover-up that really didn't live up to its billing, six-inch white stilettos, and a red rose peeking out of the string bottom half of her swimsuit. Her platinum hair draped in a flowing wave, ending just above the backs of her thighs. The groom, fully a couple of decades older than his blushing bride, sported white tie and tails. Surrounded by a mismatched gaggle of people who I hoped had some relationship to the bride and groom, they chattered excitedly. Never one to judge, I hoped the happy couple wouldn't be looking for a lawyer and a bottle of aspirin in the morning. Weddings were easy in Vegas. Annulments? Not so much.

Vegas, we get you coming and going.

Now there's a tag line the city fathers could be proud of.

Jean-Charles's Burger Palais held a primo spot just past the Temple of Love. Perpetually open for business in this 24/7 Vegas world, the restaurant had yet to fill—the morning only now segueing toward the lunch hour. A lone hostess manned the station out front. Looking far too perky, she gave me a smile as I walked though the door heading to the kitchen in the back.

With exposed brick walls, drippy mortar, rich green leather upholstery, white tablecloths, and subdued lighting, the Burger Palais stood as testament to its proprietor's taste and savvy, and was so much more than a burger joint. In short order, the hungry hordes would descend. In preparation, the kitchen was up and running at full bore. Billowing water vapor hissed from the steam tables. Smoke rose from coals just reaching red-hot in the grill, then was quietly vacuumed into a huge hood and vented outside. Prep cooks . . . prepped. Everyone in clean whites danced to a silent, shared rhythm—the normal, pulsing tunes absent. That could mean only one thing: Jean-Charles was within hearing range.

Rinaldo, Jean-Charles's right-hand chef, a huge, towering mountain of a man with three chins, dark dancing eyes, and a mop of curly black hair, paused to give me a grin as he checked the coals. "Can't decide which of the Bouclet men to hang with?"

"Each has his particular charms." I tossed him a smile. "Jean-Charles in the back?"

"In his office." Rinaldo gave me a warning look. "But between you and me, I wouldn't go in there without a stun gun and a Taser."

"That bad?" My chef could be mercurial, but I'd never known his bad humor to faze Rinaldo.

As if on cue, voices escalated above the kitchen noise . . . French voices. Two of them. One male—*that* one I recognized. The other female. Rinaldo shrugged in response to my questioning glance.

Christophe provided the answer. "It is Aunt Desiree," he whispered in my ear, a hint of awe in his voice. His little legs beat against my sides as if spurring me forward.

"Hold on there, big guy. I'm not a pony." After a moment's hesitation, I followed the voices toward the far corner of the kitchen where Jean-Charles had partitioned a makeshift office.

As we rounded the corner, we caught Jean-Charles, his face crunched into an angry frown, and a woman who looked exactly like him, but for the obvious distinctions, in mid-tirade. Catching sight of us, both fell silent and whirled in our direction.

Neither of them smiled.

Walking into the middle of a fight always made me nervous. "I've interrupted." I glanced between the two of them. Tension clouded the small space like dense smoke from a fire. "I'm sorry."

Christophe didn't seem to feel the same. He squealed in delight and wriggled down my back. "Hang on. Hang on," I said as I bent my knees so he could safely dismount.

The second Christophe's feet hit the floor, his legs started churning, propelling him, arms open wide, toward the woman. *"Tante!"*

A look of love smoothed her scowl and bent her lips into a smile. Throwing her arms wide, she dropped to a squat. *"Mon petit chou!"*

The boy ran into her embrace, almost knocking her over. Jean-Charles placed a hand on her back, steadying her. Balance restored, he stepped back, then smiled at me, breaking the hardness in his eyes—although his cheeks remained flushed with emotion. As he moved to wrap me in his arms, I wasn't sure exactly which emotion.

His hugs were strong, infused with sincerity, which gave him a huge advantage . . . huge. Was there anything better than a heartfelt hug? At the moment, and considering the venue, I couldn't think of one. "Lucky, you have done something to me." He nibbled my earlobe, making rational thought impossible.

My arms encircled his waist. "I'm sorry to interrupt." That wasn't really the truth, but it sounded good as I sighed into his embrace. He felt good. *We* felt good.

I'd felt good with Teddie, too—a reality I didn't want to acknowledge. What had I missed? I pushed him from my mind, which was way easier than pushing him out of my heart.

Love . . . the slippery slope to self-destruction.

Jean-Charles must've felt me stiffen as he loosened his hold and stepped back. "I am sorry. I am being rude." With a sweeping motion, he gestured toward the woman who now stood, eyeing me with a cold yet quizzical gaze. "Lucky, may I introduce my sister, Desiree. We are twins. She is two minutes older, which makes her, how do you say it, a boss?"

"Bossy," I answered before thinking.

"This is it." Jean-Charles clapped as if he'd been given a present. "Bossy. She is bossy. Yes."

Desiree eyed me with a hint of amusement coupled with a dose of curiosity. Her eyes were blue like her brother's, perhaps a shade darker, but equally as expressive. The same high cheekbones and the same wavy brown hair, although hers held the light kiss of the summer sun. Thin and incredibly chic in her casual dark slacks, stiff white shirt with the collar turned up, and the perfect Hermès scarf knotted around her neck, she would be intimidating even to a woman much more self-assured than I. She rose out of her nephew's hug. With her hands on Christophe's shoulders, she held her nephew, his back against her legs.

"*Bonjour,*" she said in that perfect lilting accent that made everyday words transcendent.

I wanted to hate her. Actually, I wanted to turn and run, but neither was appropriate. Instead, I extended my hand. "I'm Lucky." At a loss as she raised one eyebrow, I stammered on. "I work here. I mean not *here* here. I work for the Babylon."

She smiled and took my hand in a firm grip. "Yes, my brother, my daughter, *and* my mother have told me about you."

"A legend in my own time." I shrugged as my cheeks reddened —I could only imagine the conversations. Chantal, Desiree's daughter, had also been witness to my morning attire and presence in her uncle's house. Being sixteen, she'd connected the dots.

"It is a pleasure." Desiree nodded as she let go of my hand.

"Likewise. I knew Jean-Charles had a sister, I just didn't know you were twins. You both are stunning—so much alike."

"Yes." Jean-Charles leaped off the sidelines and into the fray. "And we fight like animals—like we are one mind and one heart but two persons."

"That's not so bad." I looked first at him, then to her.

"You have brothers or sisters?" Desiree asked, cocking one eyebrow at me, her mouth turned down at the corners in mock amusement.

"Sort of. I have Mona."

She looked confused.

"My mother, fifteen years older than me. She is more trouble than I can handle."

"Ah." Desiree nodded. "This happens many times in my country as well."

I doubted anyone in France could rival Mona, but I kept that assessment to myself. "I didn't know you were coming to town; Jean-Charles didn't mention it."

Desiree glanced at the floor, then back to focus on something over my left shoulder. "He did not know. I had some . . . business . . . to take care of."

Jean-Charles explained. "Her company is providing the truffles for the Last Chef Standing competition. They are very special truffles, but there is a problem."

"I see. You will be ready for the competition, right?" I didn't know a truffle from a trifle, but I figured all my experience with problems might be of use. "Anything I can help with?"

Desiree muttered under her breath. Jean-Charles silenced her with a look. Ah, siblings. To be honest, I had no desire to get between the two of them—I could still sense their tempers, barely contained, like the flow of hot lava under a thin, cool surface.

"We can handle it. Thank you," Desiree answered.

Jean-Charles gave me a reassuring look, although I thought I caught a hint of waver in it.

At second glance, he looked confident. Relieved, I nodded. "Well, I'll let the two of you get back to your . . . conversation . . . as long as you promise there won't be any bloodshed." Then, turning to my chef, I explained with a shrug as a perfunctory apology. "As usual, life has gotten the better of me. Duty calls. I thought I could keep Christophe longer, but I've got to go. Detective Romeo . . ."

Jean-Charles's tentative smile dimmed.

I waved away his concern. "I've got to go."

"Thank you for delivering my son. Had you called, I would've been delighted to fetch him." A hint of worry flickered across his face, snapping his brows into a frown, and the conversation stumbled into an awkward pause.

These moments confounded me—I always felt like flinging an inanity into the empty air to keep the conversation going. Then there was the whole hug-or-not-to-hug question. To kiss or not to kiss. Mixing business with pleasure . . . . I shook my head and moved to go.

Luckily, a hurtling body flew into the room, saving me from myself. Even though I ducked out of his way, he still smacked into my shoulder.

Spiked black hair, tats, kohled eyes, dressed in all-black kitchen whites, a vaguely familiar young man skidded to a stop in between brother and sister. Neither Jean-Charles nor Desiree looked excited to see him. A moment of quiet, then a torrent of three raised French voices as each of them peppered the others, gesturing wildly.

Christophe abandoned his aunt and clutched his father's leg, his eyes wide and scared. I'm sure he followed the conversation. The odd man out, I caught about every fourth word, which made understanding a trifle *difficile*.

I reached for Christophe, pulling him to me, and frowned as the three of the nominal adults screamed and gestured, stomping a foot every now and again in emphasis. Jean-Charles should know better, but his anger had run away with him. Half of the kitchen staff had circled in behind me when Rinaldo entered the fray.

With his meat-hook-sized hands, he grabbed the newcomer by the arms, lifted him, then deposited him on the stool in front of Jean-Charles's desk. "Stay there," he ordered. "I ran your girlfriend off earlier. Didn't I tell you not to come back?"

Looking at the other two, he said, "Desiree, I told him you were coming into town, and he'd be wise to steer clear. I'm sorry." He shot Jean-Charles an I-told-you-so look.

Jean-Charles, his face crimson, his breathing labored, nodded as he visibly fought for self-control. His arms at his sides, clenching his hands, he was winning the battle.

His sister stilled for a moment, then launched herself at the seated interloper. Her fingers curled into wicked claws, she raked at him. The young man leaned to one side, avoiding the worst of the attack, although one fingernail left a reddening line down his forearm.

Rinaldo grabbed Desiree, preventing further bloodshed. He whispered in her ear and she quieted, although her eyes still threw daggers. She moved beside her brother, and the room fell quiet.

"Everybody back to work. Show's over." Rinaldo shooed away the gathered throng, leaving the five of us in the small office . . . well, the four of us adults, using the term loosely, and a small, wide-eyed child clinging to my leg.

Jean-Charles ruffled his son's hair, then bent and picked him up. He pressed the boy to his chest and whispered to him.

Desiree seethed in the corner, but had lost the look of murderous intent. The young man whose presence had been the catalyst hugged himself and pouted from his perch on the stool.

Rinaldo gave each of us a look, then settled on Jean-Charles. "I told you nothing good could come from this. But you had to go charming snakes. Well, this one is going to bite you in the ass." Before he drifted back toward the kitchen, Rinaldo said to me, "If I were you, I'd steer clear. When these three are together, only bad things happen."

No response sprang to mind, so I just looked at him wide-eyed.

"Told you a Taser would come in handy," he whispered as he turned, then headed back into the kitchen.

"Chicken," I whispered at his back. Well, so much for my quick exit stage left. I watched his retreating back for a moment, summoning courage, then I turned back to the group. On the theory that the best defense is a good offense, I clicked into corporate mode. "Would someone mind telling me what this is all about?"

Three raised voices started at once, only one in English—the newcomer had shifted continents. I held up my hands and closed my eyes until I had silence restored. "One at a time." Opening my eyes, I fixed them on the man on the stool. "Who are you?"

"Adone Giovanni."

"The young Adonis?" My voice rose with my surprise. I thought I'd recognized him—a young chef, a rebel. Unable to get legit work in an important kitchen, I'd heard he'd taken to the underground. "The pop-up guy?"

24

Adone gave me a slight bow and a rueful smile.

"Pop-up." Jean-Charles grimaced. "Such a demeaning name."

Desire jumped in. "Pop-up? Underground? What means this?"

"Illegal, unlicensed, with a changing location each week."

She gave a derisive snort as she rolled her eyes. "A new low."

"Maybe so," I said, "but he's all the rage in the underground foodie world. Word has it he is working with the backing of one of the big-name chefs in town."

Jean-Charles tossed a worried glance at his sister. He set his son back on his feet, holding the boy against his legs. I'd have thought he was using him as a shield if I didn't know better. Desiree's face reddened as she clenched her fists.

I ground to a halt. "You?" I whispered.

Jean-Charles tried to shrug it off. "It is nothing." He waved his hand with Gallic disdain. "Along with his own dishes, he is preparing some of mine in the food truck." Jean-Charles had bought a gourmet food truck, and was using it to try some recipes for his new restaurant at Cielo to see which blew folks out of the water, and which garnered only a tepid response. "He is truly a culinary genius—but alas, he is also an idiot." He shot Adone a withering look.

"You've given him your recipes?" Desiree's voice went cold and quiet. "What else have you shared?"

"*You* shared your bed with him." Jean-Charles's frustration boiled to the surface. He sliced the air with his hand as if striking red-hot iron with a hammer, banging it into shape.

Desiree bristled. "That is hardly your business."

"You have now made it my business, haven't you?" Jean-Charles lowered his voice to a menacing growl. "I can only think what the, how do you say it, bed talk was like."

"Pillow talk," I corrected before I thought about it. Jean-Charles and his trouble with American idioms. "Sorry," I added, when the two of them turned on me. A feeble attempt at placating, and one that was about as effective as trying to tame lions with a garden hose.

After glaring at me for a moment, both of them resumed peppering each other with rapid-fire French.

"Enough!" I guess I scared them, as they both swallowed their next comments and whirled to face me. Inserting my bulk between brother and sister, I put one hand on Jean-Charles's chest, holding him at bay. With the other hand, I grabbed Desiree's arm, anchoring her where she stood. When I was sure they'd stay rooted for the moment, I reached for Christophe, setting him on my hip as I shot his father a look telegraphing my displeasure. I kept a wary eye on his aunt—her thinly veiled lust for dismemberment didn't give me warm fuzzies, but I understood. My father's recent shenanigans with Teddie had my hand itching for something sharp . . . in well-honed surgical steel.

"Why don't you bring me up to speed . . . in English?" I directed the question to the happy little band assembled in front of me, hoping one of them could muster the control to answer.

Desiree took the bait. She gestured grandly toward Adone. "He is the Satan . . . the Devil. He will be my ruin." She placed her hands on her hips and leveled her gaze at her brother as if she was leveling a gun. "And now, my brother . . . . Men!"

"They should not be allowed to live." The words were out of my mouth before the filter of self-preservation had a chance to capture them.

Jean-Charles shot me a startled glance, which I answered with a benign smile.

Then, I studiously ignored him. "However, I haven't met a man yet who was worth jail time. So, what's your beef with Adone?" As I glanced at the young chef with his whole punk rock thing and the attitude to match, I figured he was probably pretty good at setting people's teeth on edge.

"He is stealing my business." Desiree spat the words, each one a bullet.

Adone huffed and answered with a sneer. "That is absurd."

"Why would he do that?"

Hatred etched her every feature as she glared at him. "He is my husband."

"Of *course* he is." Why was it that, lately, no matter what the problem was, I failed to see the final twist, the last turn of the knife?

Adone jumped in. "It is not *me*." As he shot his wife a wary glance, he pressed a hand to his chest in emphasis. "It is Fiona."

At the woman's name, Desiree made some feline, guttural sound.

I stilled her with a glare. "Fiona?" I asked her husband.

"His mistress," Desiree purred, which had me worried. "She is a stupid cow. Not only does she have poor taste in men, but she also thinks she knows truffles."

"She wants your husband and your business." I gave one of those half-smile snorts of appreciation. "I'll say this for her, she's got balls."

The room fell quiet.

I cringed. "I said that out loud, didn't I?"

Jean-Charles smiled a tight smile. "Yes. But you are right, the woman is brazen."

"A real bitch," Adone and Desiree said in unison, then glared at each other, refusing to be amused.

"And lately," Adone continued, "she is acting crazier than normal, making all kinds of threats."

"What kind of threats?"

"She is crazy. She is wishing us all to Hell, that sort of thing." Adone shrugged.

"Any idea why?"

The three of them looked at me, wide-eyed, as if I'd just disproven the old adage that there is no such thing as a stupid question.

"She wants what we have," Desiree added, saving me.

"Fiona," Jean-Charles said with a note of finality. A look passed between him and Adone.

"All want and no work," I summarized for myself, since no one else paid me any attention, caught as they were in their own battle.

Desiree put her hands on her hips and stared between the two men. "I will deal with you later," she said to Jean-Charles. "And that man, *salaud!*" She gestured dismissively toward her future former husband. "He is the ruin of me."

"Aren't they all?"

That got another interesting look from Jean-Charles. My cynicism was apparently peeking its ugly head through the thin "yes, dear" veneer.

Jean-Charles stepped toward Adone, prodding the young man's chest with his forefinger. "I have, how do you say, moved to the end of the branch . . ." He glanced at me.

"Gone out on a limb."

"This, yes." He turned back to Adone. "I have gone out on a limb for you, extending my reputation to you. And this is the thanks I get? You try to ruin my sister?"

"It's not me . . ." Adone wilted under his brother-in-law's frown.

"You must fix this," Jean-Charles growled, each word heavy with conviction. "I am giving you a chance when all others had turned their backs. Don't fuck it up."

He may have trouble with idioms, but he got that bit of American vernacular just right. Christophe clutched my neck so tightly I had to loosen his hold so blood trickled to brain and I could muster a thought or two.

"And if Fiona comes within shouting distance of my family, I will kill her myself."

"You wouldn't be referring to Fiona Richards, would you?" Detective Romeo pushed into the small space, followed by a couple of uniforms who crowded in behind him. Brusque and businesslike, the young detective focused on Jean-Charles.

"Romeo?" I blurted, startled at the intrusion. "I thought we were supposed to meet on the back lot."

He ignored me. Rumpled and stick thin, he wore a tired trench coat, dark slacks, his tie loose around the collar of a blue shirt, and a serious expression. His sandy hair was a bit mussed and longer than normal—I liked the look. Well, other than the cowlick that stood at the crown of his head like a flag in the wind.

Jean-Charles nodded. "Fiona Richards, yes. She—"

"Does not deserve to live," Desiree spat as she cut him off.

"Really?" Romeo cocked an eyebrow at her, then glanced around the group, his eyes coming to rest on mine. "Well, then, you'll be happy to know Ms. Richards was found dead . . ." His eyes shifted to Jean-Charles. ". . .in your food truck."

For a moment, the world stopped turning, I was sure of it, as my heart fell to my feet. Desiree's mouth hung open. Jean-Charles paled. Only Adone seemed nonplussed.

Christophe piped up. "A dead lady? Cool." The boy's fluency in English still surprised me—I kept forgetting he'd spent most of his life with his father in New York while he opened his restaurants there. At last count, he had three.

All the adults, using the term loosely, started talking at once. Jean-Charles plucked his son from my arms, swung him to his hip, and turned to leave.

Romeo stopped him with a hand on his arm. "We need to talk."

"*Oui.*" He drew in a deep breath, composing himself. "Not in front of my son, please."

Romeo nodded and let him go.

I watched him, holding his son tight and nuzzling him as he found Rinaldo in the kitchen. A few words passed between the two men, then Jean-Charles off-loaded the small boy into the waiting man's arms.

Jean-Charles returned, snaking an arm around my waist. I could feel him shaking. Murder could do that.

My pulse restarted, and I grabbed Romeo by the shoulder and pulled him around to face me. "The food truck? Where exactly?"

"On the Babylon's back lot." He kept his eyes roaming over our small group. "The door to the truck was open. Security checked it out, then called us."

"How long ago?"

"An hour, maybe a bit more." Romeo paused. "She hadn't been dead long. The body was still warm."

Three excited voices started babbling in French. Romeo raised his hand, silencing them. "In English, or I'll arrest all of you."

They fell silent.

"No cameras on the back lot," I muttered, thinking out loud. "Convenient."

Jean-Charles scowled his displeasure. I couldn't blame him—the situation wasn't exactly making my day, either.

Romeo turned to the other three, leaving me out. "I'm going to need to get statements from each of you."

Jean-Charles's feathers ruffled. "You cannot be serious. I have a restaurant to run."

"And I have a dead woman in your food truck." Romeo, with dark circles under his eyes and skin so sallow it appeared almost translucent, looked like the walking dead. He stuffed his note pad back where he'd found it. "We can do this the easy way, or the hard way. Your choice."

Jean-Charles flushed with barely controlled anger. As I turned to go, he grabbed my arm. "I am having some trouble with the new oven in Cielo. You will meet me there later?"

I fixed him with a steady gaze.

"Please," he added, perhaps remembering too late that I was not one of his minions who took orders. "I know it is not convenient, but I am meeting a friend there, and I would like you to take a look. You always know what to do."

I weighed his words as I mentally walked through my day—I had time, but not for a bit. "Give me a couple of hours." With a glance at Romeo, he nodded curtly. "I will be there."

~

I WAS NURSING MY THIRD DIET COKE AT THE BAR IN THE BURGER Palais when Romeo straddled the stool next to me. "About time you showed up," I said. "I'm practically floating away." I took a long pull through the straw until I exhausted the soda and pulled in air. The rude noise made me smile. Mona had always reprimanded me for doing the same thing when I was young—so, of course, I took delight in it. Still did.

"I needed time to separate the three of them and put an officer on each one to take a statement. I don't know anything about this Fiona Richards, but whatever she did to those folks, it runs deep."

"You don't really think . . ." I stopped him before he answered. I knew what he was going to say. "I know, it's not what we think, it's what we can prove . . . or disprove."

"You're worried about your chef." Romeo motioned for the bartender to give him one of what I was having. "You like him, then?"

"What's not to like?" I stared into my glass, trying to sort out my jumbled emotions, but that proved to be like capturing lightning bugs: when you opened the jar to trap another, those inside escaped and flew away.

Romeo eyed the bottles behind the bar as he swirled the Diet Coke in his glass. "You wouldn't have something with a bit more kick to it, would you?"

"Bourbon for breakfast? I'm not sure I could live with myself if I led you down the road to sin and perdition."

"Seriously?" Clearly, Romeo thought I was amusing.

Glancing at him, I realized he had aged a decade during our brief association, and he was developing some of my bad habits, which didn't make me feel good in the least. "I guess I'm not the best influence," I admitted grudgingly. To be honest, my recent comfort with the bottle had me a bit worried, not something I would readily admit. Heck, it was hard enough to admit it to myself. Delusion—sometimes desirous, sometimes disastrous. I knew I needed to be careful—while balance was a concept I understood, I found it next to impossible to apply.

Vegas and temptation, virtually synonymous . . .

"Wow, you've gone all quiet and pensive. I didn't know you had it in you," Romeo teased.

I knew he was trying to lighten my mood. "If you're trying to make me feel better, you suck at it."

"As I recall, we established that some time ago."

That got a grin out of me, despite my best efforts.

"Ha!" He pointed at me like a kid rubbing it in. "See, I *can* be taught new tricks."

"I think we established *that* some time ago as well."

His smile faded as he backed off his stool. "Save some of that firewater for later, okay?" he told the bartender.

"Sure thing, sir." The young lady shot me a questioning shrug.

"We'll be back." I pointed to a bottle on the top shelf. "And the 101 is ours."

Romeo put a hand on my shoulder. "Right now, I've got a crime scene to process. Care to join me?"

"For old time's sake?"

Romeo had been a greenhorn when we met chasing a weasel. We'd cemented our relationship tracking down a killer who had tossed an oddsmaker into the shark tank. Since then, we'd gone on to bigger and better things. Once the teacher, I'd now become the sidekick, and I actually liked it—expectations were lower.

In a perfect Columbo impersonation, Romeo patted his pockets as he tilted his head forward and looked at me from under his brows. "Don't let it go to your head. I'm just throwing you a bone to keep you from gnawing on my leg."

~

Jean-Charles's food truck was parked on the unpaved, sandy expanse at the rear of the parking lot behind the Babylon. Technically not part of our official lot, guests used it anyway. So did the hotel, parking extra corporate vehicles back there. The rub was that, since it wasn't an official public-use area, our video surveillance didn't cover it.

As Romeo and I pushed out the back doors of the hotel, I got a full view of the Presidio, my former home—one floor below Teddie's penthouse. The apartment building had been perfect, for a while. I could walk to work. Walk upstairs . . .

A tall cylinder of glass and steel, the Presidio was the finest place to live in town . . . at least, that's what the brochure said. Rectangles of dark and light formed a mosaic up the side of the building as various occupants opened their shades to welcome the sunlight or left them shuttered against the growing warmth of the day. My eyes followed the pattern to the top floor. I didn't want to look, but I couldn't resist.

The windows of the penthouse were uncovered—the shades that had blocked them for months now retracted. When Teddie had left, I'd turned the light out and moved into the hotel—I had a small apartment next to my parents'.

A place to sleep, it wasn't home.

Romeo followed my gaze. Looking up, he pursed his lips. "The top floor, that's Teddie's place, right?"

"Hmmm."

"Looks like somebody's home." The detective turned and looked at me.

A deer caught in the headlights of an onrushing life, I couldn't move, couldn't breathe. "Teddie."

Romeo let his gaze drift upwards. "I'm glad I don't have your problems."

"Thanks."

"It had to happen at some point. I mean, the guy couldn't stay gone forever."

"Why not?"

Romeo laughed as if I wasn't serious. He hooked his arm through mine. "Come on. Maybe giving me a hand with the dead girl will help."

"Homicide. Just what the doctor ordered."

CHAPTER 3

*T*HE FOOD truck was easy to find. Squatting in the middle of a circle of floodlights, surrounded by crime scene technicians, with the whole area cordoned off by the yellow tape used to delineate the boundaries of horror, the scene looked like a CSI location shoot.

Alas, no cameras. No make-believe. This was real.

Reality—not something most Las Vegans were equipped to deal with.

And it had happened in my backyard. Even worse, the noose of suspicion encircled people I cared about.

Romeo ducked under the tape, then held it up for me. He paused to talk with one of the technicians and I circumnavigated the truck, getting my bearings. A typical food truck, it was already several years old when Jean-Charles bought it a month ago. I knew that because I'd helped him find the thing.

My job offered me almost limitless pies to stick my fingers in. As a result, I was the go-to gal when anyone needed anything done—not as much fun as it sounds, but then again, I'd lost my smile.

Vegas boasted a cadre of gourmet food trucks serving every-

35

thing from fancy sliders to high-end tacos—which sounds like an oxymoron but isn't—to full-fledged creations by multi-starred chefs. Especially those chefs who, like Jean-Charles, used the trucks as platforms to not only attract a new and younger clientele, but also to try new recipes that might not please the palates of their established followers.

From time to time, the Babylon hired the food trucks and their cast of flamboyant culinary wunderkinder to provide an interesting twist to a promotional party or a fun slice of West Coast hip for patrons hailing from somewhere lacking a cool factor. Because of my love of food, I usually volunteered to ride herd on the truck vendors. Sometimes I even had to play my rung on the corporate ladder as a trump card to get the gig. When it came to food, I lost my ability to play well with others . . . sharing was not in my gastronomic repertoire. And when Jean-Charles had floated the idea of using the food truck as a combination billboard and test kitchen, I thought it brilliant.

Boy, had that idea backfired.

Like everything in Vegas, the truck had a light coating of dust. Here in the Mojave, we have such a problem with dust the city bought billboards to remind residents to refrain from off-roading. Of course, there wasn't much the city fathers could do about the wind, and it regularly blew hard enough to sandblast all in its path.

As I eased my way around the truck, I made mental notes: dented right fender, headlight rim also dented, the rear bumper had a scrape of black paint. Nothing stood out—and it would be impossible to tell when and how any of the bumps and bruises had happened. The tires, down to their last millimeter of tread, wore a halo of crusty mud. I couldn't remember the last time it rained . . . sometime in July, I thought. The monsoon season—a moniker that made me laugh. Monsoons conjured jungles—trees laden with vines, humidity, and man-eating felines. While Vegas had all three, all of them were kept indoors and had nothing to do with the amount of rainfall.

Coming full-circle, I paused at the steps leading into the truck and leaned in. Several technicians were wedged into the small space, hunched over the body, plucking, dusting, and bagging. I never got used to the indignity of death, which transformed a living, breathing being into a thing. I watched for a moment, not really thinking, trying not to feel. Although the techs blocked some of my view, I caught glimpses. The body contorted, the hands pulled behind and bound. The feet, also bound, were brought up to the hands and somehow trussed together, pulling the body into a backward bow. I couldn't see much more than that . . . and I didn't really want to. Death was never pretty.

Romeo stepped behind me and leaned over my shoulder. "What are you doing?"

"Trying not to look, but I can't help myself. How was she killed?"

"I told you, with a Saf-T-Smoke. It sorts looks like a gun thing that you use in cooking."

I shot Romeo a look. "If you have the smoking gun, then your job's done, right? Piece of cake."

He didn't smile. "I said *a* smoking gun-like thing, not *the* smoking gun, a subtle but important distinction. You've been watching too many old movies. Actually, the smoking thing didn't kill her, the plastic around her head did ."

After weighing my options for a nanosecond, I took the bait. "What, then, is *a* Saf-T-Smoke, exactly?"

"Apparently, it is a device that chefs use to impart smoky flavor to various foods, cheeses and the like. It looks like a large plastic handgun with a reservoir for the wood chips and a nozzle the smoke comes out of. You cover the food you want to smoke with plastic, then stick in the nozzle." He gave me a knowing look. "But this brings a whole new meaning to the concept of 'smoked.'"

I could picture the poor woman, her head wrapped in plastic, suffocating, while someone imparted a mesquite flavor to her flesh . . . or perhaps they preferred her apple-smoked. A shudder of revulsion rippled through me. Blinking rapidly, I shook off the visuals. Once again, I leaned in to catch another glimpse of poor Fiona—I don't care how awful she was or wasn't, suffocating was a terrible way to die . . . not that any of the options were all that great.

"Like Hannibal Lecter, but with a discerning palate," I said, instantly regretting the words . . . sort of.

"I'm going to pretend you didn't really say that." Romeo wasn't completely successful at keeping the grin out of his voice.

A daily dose of death required a morbid sense of humor for psychological survival. Cops had it, doctors, too. And, apparently, so did I, but mine was born from panic welling up inside me.

An odor caught my attention. Tentatively, I pulled in air through my nose, testing, identifying. "Smell that?"

Romeo leaned over my shoulder and sampled the air. "Death."

"Yes, but beyond that."

Like a lion testing the wind, he closed his eyes and sniffed. Breathing deeply, he ticked up a corner of his mouth in a half-smile. "Truffles."

"WE'VE GOT A PROBLEM," MISS P., MY SECOND-IN-COMMAND, SAID as I burst through the office door. As usual, she was sitting behind her old desk in the outer office instead of occupying her new digs in my former office—I'd been booted up to vice president, and Miss P. had filled my former Head of Customer Relations shoes— a game of corporate musical chairs that effectively changed nothing.

When I'd walked in, I'd caught her in the act of dialing the phone. Slowly, she replaced the receiver in its cradle as she blinked at me. As usual, her golden hair was spiked, her makeup subtle. Her eyes held the embers of after-glow—no doubt a gift from her much younger lover, the Beautiful Jeremy Whitlock, Las Vegas's primo PI.

The whole cougar thing had me a bit envious. But with my heart so recently splintered on the shoals of love, prudence dictated that I wait a bit before wading into the deep end again—not that prudence was one of my strong suits or anything.

I parked my butt on the corner of her old desk and reached for the pile of messages in my in-box. "Why are you sitting out here and not in your office?"

She leveled her gaze at me over the top of her cheaters. "Don't you want to know what the problem is?"

"Does it have anything to do with a homicide on our back lot?"

That stopped her. "No."

"Then not really." As I flipped through the notes, I pretended to be consumed. Like working a poker hand, I pulled a couple that I wanted to keep, then tossed the others.

"What homicide?"

I waved her question away. "Romeo's on it."

"I see," Miss P. said, although it was clear she didn't, which made me smile since I did the same thing all the time.

So I segued back to the original topic. "The way I figure it, you'll tell me what the problem is when you're ready. Until then, I'm happy with the whole ignorance-is-bliss thing."

"A kinder and gentler Lucky? Patience is a virtue and all of that?" Miss P. raised an eyebrow and fought a smile. "There wasn't really a homicide on property, was there?"

"Apparently." With a forefinger, I nudged my golden cockroach paperweight back from the edge of the desk. It had been a gift from the employees after dealing with a guest and his pests, and I was sorta attached to it. "What is this doing out here?"

"I have no idea." Miss P. looked like she was losing patience with my lack of interest in her problem—the one she desperately wanted to make mine. "I'll put it back on your desk."

I nodded, not really concerned. Everyone knew, if they took that paperweight I would consider it a capital crime. "For the record, I'm cultivating the talents necessary to move further up the corporate ladder."

"Passing the buck?"

"Please," I said, taking mock offense. "Delegating. Sloth, avarice, and a taste for three-martini lunches are next." I shot her a grin. "But I wouldn't hold my breath if I were you—the delegating thing is still a work-in-progress, although I'm warming to it. I just tossed a thousand live turkeys into Mona's lap. Well, not just, but a few hours ago."

A smile bloomed across her face. "Oh, I'd pay good money for a ticket to that!"

"To be honest, I'm feeling pretty proud of myself." I folded my messages and stuffed them in the tiny pocket in my suit. Versace wasn't known for his pockets. "Mother's driving me nuts with talk of testing the waters for a run at a seat on the Paradise Town Advisory Board. Now she's waxing poetic about the girls doing a bake sale to raise money for a possible campaign. How much can she possibly hope to raise with a bake sale?"

Miss P. looked at me over the top of her cheaters. "Well, when you're talking about a bunch of hookers from Pahrump selling their . . . buns . . . in the parking lot at Smokin' Joe's XXX Video Emporium, I'd say the sky's the limit."

My heart sank. She was right. If Mona took full rein, the bake sale would turn into a national news event. The same thing happened when she'd tried to auction off a young woman's virginity. She should've learned her lesson, but Mona wasn't big on lessons.

Mona had been my cross to bear, but recently she married my father, thereby terminating my illegitimacy and simplifying my life . . . in theory. Technically, my father, who is also my boss and the owner of the Babylon, was my mother's keeper now that she had given up her eponymous whorehouse in Pahrump, my childhood home, and moved into the Babylon. But unlike his daughter, my father was good at delegating. And when Mona made a mess, she still looked to me to show up with a broom.

But she was on her own with the turkeys. Proving once again I was more like my father than I thought. Maybe one day I'd believe it.

So, I shelved the bake sale—today's worry plate was full. "You can watch Mona leading the poultry parade for free. Basement Level Two, although the show is probably about over."

"And the homicide?"

"Romeo's problem." I didn't add that, given the players, it would most likely become my problem. At the moment, I lacked the fortitude to shoulder that little bit of fun. So, I feigned glibness and ignored the looming storms . . . all of them. "Now, what's the problem that's got your knickers in a twist?"

"We have a tiny trifle with a truffle." She delivered the words without even a hint of a smile. Impressive.

"I think that's redundant." I boosted myself off her desk. "Alliterative, but redundant."

She shrugged. "Actually, it's not a trifle with a truffle exactly." A hint of a smile tugged at one corner of her mouth. "It's really a problem with a pig."

"A pig?"

"Well, Chef Gregor . . ." Miss P. ground to a halt, raising my caution flag.

I probably didn't want to know, not really, but my Pavlovian response to all problems goaded me into hurling myself into the fire. "Chef Gregor." His name puckered my lips like a bad taste. For a moment in time, he had been the proprietor of the failed Italian restaurant occupying the space that now housed the Burger Palais. "He is a bit of a pig, but I'm not sure I'd be so cavalier as to call him that. I hear he has important friends and a bad habit of getting even."

41

Miss P. cocked an eyebrow at me. "Chef Gregor invited the truffler and the pig who found the prized truffle to the party."

I blinked at her for a moment, absorbing. "I need to sit down, I can tell." I sank into one of the chairs against the wall of glass overlooking the lobby below. I stretched my legs out in front of me and leaned back, fighting the feeling that I might tip and fall through the glass—I knew I wouldn't, but it made me nervous just the same. "The truffler?"

"The truffle pig handler."

"Truffle pig?"

"The pig that found the prized truffle."

"You said that already."

"Just making sure you're following all of this. It's important."

"I thought you said it was a trifle."

Over the top of her cheaters, she gave me the stink-eye. "You do remember we are holding a truffle worth a small fortune, and it is to be the key ingredient in the chef competition on Friday?"

"I have my shortcomings, but I usually don't forget televised affairs being hosted by the hotel, nor our participation in them." I shot her a narrow-eyed look. "I wasn't aware we were responsible for the care and feeding of the special truffle."

"Not technically."

"Then technically, it's not our problem. And, just to clarify, don't they use dogs to find truffles these days?"

"Yes, but a pig is just more . . . prosaic, don't you think?"

"Clearly it doesn't matter what I think, just don't tell me there is a four-legged pig in my hotel." I was well aware that, at any given time, there were several hundred of the two-legged, Y-chromosomed variety, hence the need to clarify.

"It's a very special pig." Miss P. sounded hopeful, as if that might make a difference.

"And where is this special pig . . . exactly?"

Her eyes skittered from mine as she developed a sudden interest in something over my shoulder. She worried with a button on her cashmere sweater as she chewed on her lip, which didn't make me feel very good. "Bungalow 7," she whispered.

I stared up at the ceiling as if praying for guidance from a higher power. My mother organizing a grassroots constituency of working girls. Turkeys running loose in the basement. My chef and his sister caught up in homicide and betrayal. The pig in the Kasbah was just the cherry on top of a real sundae of a Sunday.... At least I thought it was Sunday. Or was it Monday? In Vegas, day ran into night until one lost track of not only hours but also days and weeks and months. Some days, I couldn't even remember the season and if I should dress warmly or not. Looking outside never helped—it was always sunny.

Just another day in the asylum.

Miss P. seemed a bit stricken, maybe even contrite—an unusual state, so I thought it wise to milk it for all it was worth. I tried to look stern, but really, when I thought about it, all I could see was the humor . . . well, about the pig anyway, but I refused to let Miss P. see that. "You put the pig in the Kasbah." I used my best irritated-hotel-executive tone, and I focused on a spot on the ceiling, afraid that I would grin if I looked her in the eye.

The Kasbah was our high-roller compound—hidden, exclusive, decadent, it was a real feat to score a room there. I could just imagine what Cher would say if she got wind that we had given one of our most opulent bungalows to a pig. Last time she stayed with us, she had to settle for our largest suite on the twenty-ninth floor—the second most coveted location in the hotel.

I bit down on my lip, fighting another smile. To be honest, pigs weren't that worrisome. And they just declared miniature horses to be seeing-eye animals, requiring the hotel to accommodate them, so I'd better get used to handling a barnyard. Frankly, I was relieved it wasn't that horrible man with all the cockroaches . . . who had returned with an anaconda. The memory chased a shudder of revulsion down my spine.

"That means someone is walking on your grave."

"What?"

Miss P. nodded mater-of-factly as I struggled to keep my tenuous grasp on reality. "A shudder means someone is walking on your grave."

"I'm not dead, so I don't have a grave." I held up my hand, stopping her from interjecting. "Never mind. You're changing the subject. Back to the pigs . . . both of them." If she was going to drop a couple of pigs in my lap, I was bound and determined to make her pay for it, just a little. "You do know pigs will eat anything? Including prized truffles?"

Miss P. waved a hand at me. "The truffle is under lock and key, so don't worry about that."

"Whenever anyone says 'don't worry about that,' I get a really bad feeling. Sort of like when someone says 'I need to hook you up with my brother's college roommate.'" She started to take the bait, but I shut her down with a glare, although it failed to wipe the smug smirk from her face. "You know, you are not making my day easier. I need to find better staff."

"Good luck with that." Miss P. didn't seem bothered, which was understandable—she was as close to indispensable as anyone could be.

"Do you think I could fire family as well?"

"Yours?" She scoffed. "Not a chance. Even if you shot them, they'd come back to haunt you."

Now that was a scary thought. For a moment, I ran through the list of people I could pass off the pig to. It didn't take me long—the list was pretty short, just two names: mine and Jerry's, and Jerry was busy penning up poultry at the moment. He was also handling Mona, so I didn't feel right about dropping another farm animal in his lap. Although we were both well versed in farm animals . . . one of the perks of the job. "Just so you know, pigs will also eat thousand-dollar-per-yard damask for starters."

Ah, that shot down Miss P.'s smirk.

"Why don't you tell me what's wrong with the pig and exactly why it's in Bungalow 7?"

"Chef Gregor threatened to pull the truffle if we didn't cater to the pig. You know how he is, ranting and raving, threatening to go to the press. I thought it was easier to placate him than fight back."

"So, you left that for me," I added unnecessarily; after all, handling turkeys was within my job description. Some days, whining just felt good, and this was one of those days. I'd get over myself soon. "Apparently, Chef Gregor wants his fifteen minutes, let's give them to him."

"For the record, I'd like to shoot that man." Miss P. tossed that out as an afterthought.

"You'd have to stand in line. But patience, my friend, perhaps he'll choke on his dinner, get a bad piece of fish or something. It could happen." I fought the urge to give her Mona's double barrel when she was through with it—taking Chef Gregor out of the gene pool would be a huge favor to future generations. With half a mind, I wondered if that fact alone would be sufficient for an acquittal. I pulled my feet back toward me and leaned forward, my hands on my knees. Better not take that chance. "I'll handle Chef Gregor. But what's the problem with the pig?"

"She's depressed."

As I strode through the casino, I tried to get my mind around the idea of a depressed pig, but I was struggling with the concept. What did a pig have to be depressed about? Especially a pig ensconced in Bungalow 7, replete with hot-and-cold running foot servants and a twenty-four-hour chef.

Other than having to deal with a swine like Chef Gregor, of course.

The casino echoed the Persian theme of the lobby with palms, darkly hued walls dotted with open flames under glass, and leafy plants in the corners to add warmth. Cloth dyed in an array of bright colors tented above the rows of slot machines and sheltered Delilah's, a watering hole set in the center of the room on a raised platform. Guests crowded around the bar and the piano as I moved past. Teddie used to play that piano. My heart constricted. Teddie. He'd broken my heart. I'd patched it as best I could, but now he was back, breaking open the thin scab. The pain lingered. I wondered when it would go away, or if it ever would. With him underfoot, my chances at a cure were slim, that much I knew. But what to do?

Why did life always throw me a curveball just when I'd timed the fastball?

From the tables around me, the energy level rose on a crescendo of enthusiasm. Throngs two and three deep circled each game. Collective groans, occasionally offset by cheers, rolled through the room, overriding the thump of the energetic background music. Cocktail waitresses darted in and out of the crowd like hummingbirds testing the nectar of various flowers. The fact that the waitstaff could manage that dance on five-inch heels continually amazed me.

At the far side of the casino, tucked at the end of a long, nondescript corridor that, like the cave leading to Shangri-la, offered not one hint of the riches that lurked beyond: a world of opulence, decadence, and comfort.. The Kasbah, where a guest's every need would be met promptly and discreetly. Okay, perhaps not their *every* need. The crazy Russian who demanded we hang gilded swords from the Tsarist era over her bed had been a bit of a challenge, but our resourcefulness prevailed—one of our bellmen knew a guy in L.A. who collected the things. Another guest wanted a bed that Frank Sinatra had slept in. That one had been a bit easier. Vegas's history wasn't very old, and her fans were rabid.

With each new request came a new challenge. As the chief problem solver, I got to establish the boundaries of reason.

Although fairly understanding, I drew the line at farm animals ... for now.

After all, that Hollywood hunk who wanted a goat had left unsatisfied. So some overly inflated culinary bombast wasn't going to get his pig, either.

Huge double bronze doors folded back, open like an inviting embrace, marked the entrance to the Kasbah. Hieroglyphics of thin figures that looked suspiciously like ancient Egyptians had been pressed into the metal for that ever-important air of authenticity. Potted date palms softened the corners. I half expected to see a camel lurking to the side—I mean, that would sort of fit with the whole animal farm problem I had going on. I glanced around. Alas, no camel. I couldn't decide whether I was relieved or disappointed, which had me worried.

Every time I stepped into the Kasbah, I felt like Dorothy landing in Oz. Under a domed glass roof high above, the Kasbah nestled in a bath of natural sunlight—diffused and filtered for the perfect ambience, of course. Water burbled from the fountains and foliage lined the stream that pooled and meandered through the complex of separate bungalows. With private swimming pools, floor plans larger than most homes in the Valley, and a staff-to-guest ratio of five to one, our very private, *très chic* bungalows were the most sought after prizes in Vegas.

And we'd put a pig in one of them.

Bracing myself, I pulled the heavy cord hanging by the door to Bungalow 7. Chimes echoed inside and footfalls quickened to the door. Contemplating the pressed images on the door, which was a smaller replica of the large doors bracketing the entrance to the Kasbah, I half-expected a Nubian to swing the door open and usher me inside with a bow. Instead, a member of our solicitous staff greeted me with a nod and a pained expression.

Before I could say anything, he was muscled aside by the person I came to do battle with, Chef Gregor. With a pasty complexion flushed with exertion and misted with sweat, jowls that folded his skin like a venetian blind, beady dark eyes, and thin, mean lips, he looked one pat of butter shy of a heart attack. At just over six feet, he could almost carry the extra hundred pounds or so, but his stomach oozed over his belt, and his sleeves stretched over the flesh of his arms like casing around sausages. To add insult to injury, he wore his thin black hair greased back—completing the disgusting picture—which his personality perfectly complemented.

The chef pointed a thick forefinger at me. "You! What have you done with my truffle?"

"What truffle?" I stammered, blindsided once again—a recurring theme today. "I heard you have a problem with a pig."

He waved his hand as if shooing flies, then leveled a pitying look. "You are misinformed."

I felt like saying, *Honey, that's where I live,* but instead, I summoned years of practice to keep my voice steady and asked, "How so?"

"The problem is not with the pig. It is with the truffle." Turning on his heel, he stalked into the bowels of Bungalow 7.I had no alternative but to follow him.

The smell hit me first. Musty and ripe, it wasn't the normal potpourri of blended spices and exotic unguents used to fragrance the bungalows. As I entered the great room, the scene in front of me left me speechless—a rare and somewhat dangerous occurrence. The hand-knotted silk carpet had been casually rolled back, exposing the rough-cut oak flooring. Burnished to a dark, rich sheen, it was a work of art. I'd personally supervised the men on their hands and knees as they'd polished the wood with their little steel wool pads, then stained it so many times I'd lost count.

My eyes got all slitty.

Like some life-sized Erector set, a metal fenced enclosure grew from the middle of the wooden expanse. A puffy bedding of straw filled the pen. A metal trough completed the bucolic picture . . .

well, the trough *and* the huge black-and-white pig that stared into the filled feed bin, but didn't eat.

Chef Gregor stopped in front of the pig and turned to face me. With a superior look, he reached into a burlap sack on the floor and extracted a large, bulbous object that looked curiously like a white truffle. But it couldn't be, could it? Hadn't Miss P. said she had the thing under lock and key? After all, it was worth a small fortune to the proper culinary expert.

"Where did you get that?" I was getting a real bad feeling.

I watched him struggle with himself for a moment, then he looked me in the eye. "Fiona had it."

"Fiona Richards?" I tried to keep the shock off my face and out of my voice. If he knew she was dead, he hid it well. "Where did she get it?"

"She made a delivery to Burger Palais. She saw the box. When no one was watching, she took a look. When she saw the truffle, she pocketed it and brought it to me. She knew it was not my truffle, not the Alba." Gregor pulled out the same handkerchief I'd seen him use earlier, which I found a bit disgusting—or maybe that was just the chef's normal effect on me. This time, he blew his nose into it.

"Where did she give it to you?" I searched his face. If he was lying, I'd broil him myself.

"Right here in this bungalow." His eyes held mine.

"Was anybody else there?"

"No." His voice was firm.

"When?"

"Early this morning. Her call woke me up. It was around seven a.m., I think." He took a deep breath. "You can check the video feeds—they will confirm what I say."

"I will." I gave him my best steely stare. He didn't wilt. If he was that confident, I felt sure the tapes would jibe with his story. I'd ask Jerry to check, but I wouldn't red flag it. "So, I'm confused. You say this truffle isn't the real truffle? The one you bought?"

Stepping back, Gregor gave me a look that I couldn't read. He raised his hand.

The light dawned, but rooted to the floor, unable to raise even a hand to stop him, I stared in horror as the chef dropped the truffle into the pig's feed bin. It landed with a weighty thunk.

Adrenaline surged. Fear overrode inertia. I leaped toward the pen. "No!"

"The pig, she is not interested." The quiet words from the corner stopped me.

I whirled to face the man who had uttered them. Short and round, with a cherubic weathered face, gray curls, and a kerchief tied jauntily around his neck, he wrung his hands as he glanced at me, then cast a worried look at the pig. The fabric of his pants was shiny with wear, and his checkered shirt was faded on the shoulders as if from long days spent in the sun.

I'd guess this was the truffler.

"You see," he said, as he gestured toward the pig, who had turned up her nose at the proffered truffle, "she does not want that truffle." His voice was soft, heavily accented in that sexy French way. What was it about accents that turned normally smart American women all stupid?

As I struggled to understand, I felt my IQ plummet. "Why not?"

His mouth turned down at the corners, and he gave a shrug. "It is not a good truffle."

Totally adrift, I stood there with my mouth open. Clearly, my coping skills were at a low ebb. Finally, I managed to pull myself together, snapping my mouth shut and summoning a semblance of cogent thought. "Where is the good truffle?"

Chef Gregor looked like he was about to stroke out as he stepped into my space and pushed his face into mine. "Against my better judgment, I gave it to Chef Bouclet."

"Jean-Charles?" I squeaked.

"Hmmm. He is the only one with the proper refrigeration

controls to keep a truffle of that quality appropriately cooled. You do know that once truffles are harvested, they are at their peak for only a few days and must be cooled?"

I nodded, pretending I had a clue as to what he was talking about.

"Jean-Charles has stolen my truffle." Chef Gregor poked me in the chest, emphasizing each word as he growled. "You tell your chef he is a dead man."

CHAPTER 4

*J*EAN-CHARLES HAD not answered his phone, and I'd left a rather terse message. If our prized truffle had gone missing, he sure as hell better tell me about it. After all, since the buck stopped with me, my ass was on the line. Cleaning up after a pig, and now chasing a missing truffle, had me a bit testy when I burst into the kitchen at Tigris, the Babylon's high-end eatery and the toughest table in town.

"Tell me what you know about truffles." I had rescued the not-so-good truffle from the pig's bin and now plunked it down on the stainless prep table in front of Chef Omer.

Chef Omer was the chef de cuisine at Tigris, the Babylon's top eatery that had just been awarded its third Michelin star. My father had found him toiling away in the bowels of some Turkish eatery, had recognized greatness, and had moved the chef and his family to Vegas, where they all had not only taken root, but flourished. And Tigris had also blossomed under his careful grooming to rival the best restaurants in town . . . even Joël Robuchon, Picasso, and Guy Savoy. Omer gave me the twinkle-eye. "Sweetie, that would take more time than we both have."

He was probably the only man on the planet who could

address me as sweetie and live to tell about it—especially with sharp instruments within easy reach.

Short and round, with dark hair that had thinned considerably the last few years, Chef Omer was clearly amused, his smile folding the loose skin of his jowls and lighting his eyes. "What do you need to know about truffles?"

"I don't really know." I pointed to the mound of whitish-gray fungus on the table in front of us. With creases and nodules, weird discolorations, and an odd grayish hue, it looked like a brain drained of blood. "Why don't we start there?"

Chef Omer picked the thing up, holding it to the light and rotating it a few times. He pursed his lips as his eyes lost their light. "Where did you get this?"

I told him what I knew.

"This is not Chef Gregor's truffle," Chef Omer announced, his voice firm, ringing with conviction. "I would guess this is either a cheap Chinese version, or maybe even from Oregon, but it is not the prized Alba truffle." He pointed to some spots at various points on the thing. "And look here. Someone has loaded it with buckshot."

"Buckshot?"

"Increases the weight. And since the price is determined per gram . . ." Knowing I was smart enough to keep up, he let the thought hang there.

I sagged onto a stool. "There is nothing I hate more than cheaters."

"An old ploy." Omer paused. "Who sold this truffle to Chef Gregor?"

"To be honest, I have no idea where that truffle came from. Gregor said Fiona Richards gave it to him. Do you know her?"

He pursed his lips. "Hmmm." A rather noncommittal reply that spoke volumes.

"She was in the kitchen at Burger Palais, saw the truffle box, couldn't resist a peek . . . her story via Gregor. When she saw it was not the right truffle, she took it to Gregor."

His eyebrows shot up. "Interesting. What was she doing in the walk-in of Jean-Charles's place?"

"We'll never know exactly. I've got Fiona Richards laid out in Chef Bouclet's food truck with a smoking thing, and a truffle."

Chef Omer's face slackened, his eyes sad but not surprised. "Dead?"

I nodded.

He bowed his head for a moment, then proffered the truffle. "Now this is something she might try."

"I haven't met anyone yet who thought highly of her, but do you know anyone who would want her dead?"

"Run out of town, perhaps." He smiled a knowing smile. "But dead? That takes a special kind of hate."

"You do know the police will come around? Since the truffle was to be part of the Last Chef Standing competition, I'm sure they will want to talk to anyone associated."

Chef Omer looked surprised. "I am just one of the judges."

"Just the same, it's what the police do to make us think they are doing their job. Tell me about the other judges."

"You've not met them yet?" He gave me a steady, appraising stare. I shook my head, and he grinned. "Well, you've got a treat in store, then. Besides myself, there is one other chef, Viktor Gordon. He fancies himself quite the continental, but he was born to poor Ukrainian potato farmers. To his credit, though, he taught himself to cook, studied the techniques of the masters, then wrangled an apprenticeship with Ducasse in Paris."

"Brash?"

"Hmmm, we all are, to some degree. He has the talent to match."

"I've read his CV. Quite impressive."

"Yes, James Beard several times, Michelin stars, all the accolades, but well deserved." Chef Omer shot me a knowing look.

"Talented, yes, but mind you, he's a bit of a prima donna. He not only reads the glowing press, he takes it to heart."

"A peacock showing his feathers—he preens, but he gets down to business, so he shouldn't be too much of a problem."

Chef Omer didn't look convinced. "I shouldn't tell you, but Viktor Gordon is a sham."

"Meaning?"

"Gordon Ramsay, he will be the judge. The press is already sniffing a McGuffin." Omer shrugged. "Publicity. You'd think the great chefs and wonderful culinary creations would be enough."

"The dumbing-down influence of pop culture—look what it's done to music." I smiled and shook my head. "The ruse is actually quite clever—it'll go viral, and the chefs and this hotel, we will all have a wonderful platform to exploit."

"And our sponsors will be happy."

The marketer in me was impressed. "A win-win. And the other judge? Who is he?"

"Well, that's been a bit of an issue. The original one, I can't remember his name—some Hollywood luminary. He got stuck in Dubai or some such place. Heard he had a bad case of the clap."

I hit him on the arm. "The higher their K score, the stupider they get."

"What?"

"Klout score: a measure of one's ability to influence pop culture." I waved my hand, deflecting interest. "Have they found another judge?"

Chef Omer looked at me with big, dark eyes. "I heard your friend Jordan Marsh has agreed to sub for our fallen star."

I started to say something, but my phone singing out at my hip stopped me. Grabbing it to shut down Teddie and his song, I glanced at the number and smiled. If Chef Omer had anything to say about Teddie as my ringtone, he was smart enough to keep it to himself. I slid my finger across the face of the phone, then pressed it to the side of my face. "Jordan, we were just talking about you."

His warm, rich voice brightened my day. "Lucky, I'm counting on you to be at the airport."

"Just tell me when."

He gave me the particulars.

"Will Rudy be with you?" I asked.

A few months ago, Jordan, with my reluctant help, had broken the heart of every female on the planet when he had plighted his troth to his partner, Rudy Gillespie, an entertainment lawyer here in Vegas. I'd set them up. Thankfully, that was not a widely known bit of information, or I'd have had to go into hiding. As it was, although I had no proof, I still harbored a belief that somewhere depressed women in-the-know were sticking pins in my voodoo doll.

"Of course," Jordan said, adding jauntily, "and we are expecting our regular accommodations, please." With that, he hung up, squelching my objection.

His regular room was my guest room . . . in my apartment . . . at the Presidio . . . one floor below Teddie's digs. As I pocketed my phone, I tabled my worry. Why did it seem the whole world was conspiring to force me to face Teddie? I narrowed my eyes as I thought. . . . Why indeed? This had my parents' fingerprints all over it.

Some days, I wished I were an orphan. Today was one of them.

I turned my attention back to Chef Omer, who waited with amusement lighting his eyes. "So, are you comfortable with Jordan Marsh being a judge?"

"He has very refined taste. Besides, I think the audience will like having a nonculinary person on the panel—sort of someone like them."

I thought Jordan Marsh was as far from an average Joe as it was possible to get, but he'd shown he could play any role, and besides, presentation was everything, so I went with it and trusted Chef Omer's instincts. "So, back to Fiona."

Chef Omer's grin faded. "A truffle and a Saf-T-Smoke?"

"Someone was very specific."

As easy to read as a cook-by-the-numbers recipe, Chef Omer's thoughts marched across his face; he didn't even try to hide them. "Yes, whoever killed Fiona is sending a strong message."

"A message, yes. But to whom?"

Chef Omer stepped around the corner, then returned with a knife. He grabbed the truffle. He squinted at it as he turned it slowly in his hand. "Yes, this is the sort of truffle Fiona would try to sell."

"You knew her well?"

"We all did. She called on the top restaurants in town. Her partner apparently greased the way." He glanced at me, then refocused on the truffle.

"Partner?"

He shrugged as he rotated the truffle, analyzing it. "I don't know exactly who her partner was, but there was a rumor of some name behind her putting up the money, opening a door to the supply chain."

"You don't know who?" I pressed.

"Whoever it was stayed in the background." He glanced at me, his gaze holding mine. "But I know this, they had to be in the food world. Providers of the ingredients of the necessary quality and consistency are few, and in demand. So the competition for the most exclusive products is fierce. And Fiona's were some of the best from Central and South America."

"Explain."

"When a chef finds a purveyor, he or she will often agree to buy whatever the farm produces, which can run to tens of thousands of dollars a week."

"They buy it all? What if they don't want it?"

"If it is of the quality expected, we always want it. We can build a seasonal menu around whatever is available. We can change it daily, if we wish. That is the fun, and the intrigue that keeps the customers coming back and paying the higher prices."

Higher prices? Some bordered on the obscene, but I didn't say so. Of course, I wasn't a particularly discerning foodie, so perhaps my perspective was skewed. "Food acquisition has really changed since I had to cycle through the food prep side of the Big Boss's properties."

"Ah, this is the high end—very rarified air. Like haute couture."

"Haute cuisine . . . I can get behind that. But it sounds a bit cutthroat to me."

Chef Omer laughed. "True. And I must admit, when I heard someone else was in town to give Desiree Bouclet a run for her money, I was intrigued. It is never good to have only one supplier. They can try to put you over the barrel."

"Would Desiree do that?" My voice was tight.

Chef Omer gave a light, upward motion with one shoulder. "She is a good businesswoman . . . clever and resourceful, she drives a hard bargain. But her products are worth the price."

"And Fiona's?"

"I stopped taking her calls months ago. Some of her products —not the South American ones, but others, were not of a necessary quality or consistency." Lowering the truffle, he caught my eyes. "I have no proof, but I felt Fiona couldn't be trusted. I lost confidence in her. My reputation could be ruined by a bad batch of tuna, for instance. I am simplifying and probably being overly dramatic, but it is very important."

"What made you feel that way?"

"Just a feeling." His eyes avoided mine, sliding instead back to the truffle. "Maybe a little bit more. And once this"—he pointed to his gut—"tells me it is time to make a change, I listen."

"Maybe I ought to run my romantic choices through that bullshit meter."

Omer gave me a knowing, fatherly look of sympathy. "If I can help . . . my wife says I am very particular."

I didn't know whether we were talking about men, or still about food—I assumed the latter, as the male of the species was not a subject I wanted to delve into at the moment. "Maybe so. But to hear Desiree and Chef Gregor tell it, the original truffle that has now gone missing was of exceptional quality."

"Yes, I saw it." Chef Omer's face cleared. "It was a thing of beauty. I never saw one like it . . . never even heard of one matching it. Huge, it was the perfect Alba truffle. Very, very rare, not only because of its size, but also its quality." A wistful look softened his features. "Just like in the old days, a pig found it."

"A pig." I must've sounded less than pleased as Chef Omer returned from his trip down memory lane.

"Why this tone?"

"Until a little while ago, that pig was ensconced in Bungalow 7."

When he laughed his belly shook, reminding me of Santa Claus, well, without the beard—he did have a stomach like a bowlful of jelly . . . and a round, warm face and infectious laugh.

"You'd better not let your father know this," he warned, unnecessarily.

Personally, I didn't care what my father knew or didn't know —he was close to the top of my shit list. But I didn't need to air the family dirty laundry, so I shifted gears . . . again. I'd done more of that today than a NASCAR driver. "You are sure this is not the original truffle?"

"Lucky, girl, don't be insulting." Chef Omer softened the words with a smile. "Somebody substituted this one for the real thing." Using the knife, he began slicing the truffle.

Numbed by the day, I didn't even cringe.

"Why?"

With the point of the blade, Chef Omer popped out tiny beads of iron, which bounced, then rolled across the table.

I watched them for a moment, then looked up, locking the chef's eyes with mine. "And where is the real truffle?"

~

HUNGER GNAWED AT MY STOMACH—CHURNING ACID THAT I WAS certain would one day eat a hole in the lining, if it hadn't already. The pain propelled me to Nebuchadnezzar's, our award-winning, twenty-four-hour buffet-style feast. I'd told the Big Boss the name was too long, but he'd insisted on accuracy. Now, everyone called it simply Neb's. When I ate there with my father, I rubbed it in at every opportunity. I'm shallow like that.

For a regular glutton like me, the choices were immobilizing . . . almost. Today, I chose sushi and fruit. "I'm working on making better choices," I told the sushi guy behind the counter. He nodded and smiled, but gave me that glazed look as if he hadn't understood a word I'd said.

Grinning and nodding back, I reached for a plate with a little line of raw red meat curved over wads of rice. Unappealing and unappetizing, the identity of the fish remained a mystery. But, committed as I was to a moment of self-betterment, that didn't matter. I grabbed a few more things that looked like they would swim away if I tossed them in a bucket of water. Nothing like grazing from the tidal pool.

Waltzing by the fresh section, I grabbed some cantaloupe and honeydew melon, then a swing through the sugar section yielded a piece of chocolate layer cake. Everybody knew that some days, one required chocolate to keep the homicidal tendencies in check. Chocolate, the new health food—if not your own, then somebody else's.

A table by the window directly in the stream of sunlight called to me. Casino workers were like cave dwellers—no windows, no natural light, our vitamin D levels were probably nonexistent, so sunlight held the addictive allure of a psychotropic drug, and rounded out my health-laden meal.

One of the staff brought wine, half of which I downed in one pull. Then I settled in to tame the beast inside. I powered through some sushi and most of the fruit. A sense of peace and calm settled over me, and I let myself relax and unwind just a bit. Of course, the glass of wine—a nice Viognier they kept just for me—helped as well. The panic subsided. Life came into focus.

Stupid me. I knew better. Like a red cloth waving in front of a bull, letting my guard down tempted the Fates, goading them to take action.

Teddie caught me mired in indecision as I eyed the remainder of my sushi and the radiant delectableness of the cake. "Saint or sinner? Hard to choose, isn't it?" He leaned in, as if he needed to get my attention.

He didn't. My heart had felt a subtle change in the universe the minute he'd walked in. Feigning indifference to him took everything I had. Saint or sinner? Friend or foe? Good questions.

"A little of both, I should say. I'm trying to eliminate toxins."

He shot me a lopsided grin—the same one that used to make my insides go all gooey. It still did. "Not with that hunk of yellowfin tuna. The amount of mercury in the thing would probably make it glow in the dark."

My shoulders sagged. I just didn't have it in me to banter with Teddie. He was like an emotional black hole, sucking all the vim and vigor out of me until I was a sad, quivering mess of hurt and pain. "Please go away, Teddie. Leave me alone."

Lifting my face to the sunlight streaming through the glass, I closed my eyes and concentrated on the warmth, pulling peace and strength from it. Taking a few deep breaths, I settled myself, then opened my eyes, hoping to find myself alone. Instead, I was looking squarely at the man who had stolen my heart, then had gone gallivanting around the world with it. He'd parked himself in the seat across from me. Pain seared through me, singeing nerves as it flared, then subsided to a white-hot heat of betrayal in the pit of my stomach. Betrayal. I'd never learned how to deal with that, and life was rubbing my nose in the fact.

Pushing my tray away, I took a moment to feel. As Miss P. reminded me every day, I would have to face Teddie, to deal with the pain. I didn't want to. In fact, I'd gladly sacrifice a secondary body part to avoid it. But life had forced my hand.

A waiter appeared at my side. "Another glass of wine, Miss O'Toole?"

I shook my head, but didn't take my eyes off my dining companion. "Not today. Diet Coke, please." For some odd reason, I didn't want anything more to anesthetize the pain, to dull it so I wouldn't say what I needed to say. I waited until the waiter had drifted out of earshot. "Do you have the contract? I'll sign it, if that's what you want."

Surprise flashed in Teddie's eyes as he placed both hands palm-down on the table. "You would?" He seemed taken aback.

"My first obligation is to the Babylon. Your show was a big draw, but Christo just can't do the whole female impersonation thing like you can. Numbers are dwindling. I'll give you a shot, but if you don't get the attendance up, I'll shut you down."

"You'd like that, wouldn't you?" He leaned back, crossing his arms in a reflexive, defensive posture.

"Of course not." Pausing, I took a sip of the Diet Coke the waiter had slipped in front of me while I contemplated what to say. The day had defeated me. Teddie's appearance had cut me open like a laser—my emotions, held so tightly in check, spilled out. "I believed you. I trusted you. My trust was misplaced. You can only be yourself, Teddie. To ask more of you would be ridiculous . . . not to mention a recipe for disaster. I learned that the first time." *First time!* Where had that come from? Why did I open the door, even if it was just a crack?

"Would you like to give us another shot?"

How I wished I had a definitive answer to that. My head said no way in Hell, my heart wasn't so sure. On top of the fact that body parts often betrayed me, now they were fighting among themselves. Not only was I out of synch with the world, now I was out of step with myself. I felt manipulated, as if all those close to me didn't trust me to handle my own life, my own heart, my own hurt. Frustration and anger boiled over. "You know what I'd like? I'd like to turn back the clock. I want the life I had six months ago. The life we had before you left, before you told me you didn't love me anymore, before you chose a life on the road over a life with me." Oh, I know, probably a really stupid litany to hand him.

Everyone told me I should act indifferent, should play the game, but games just weren't my thing.

Teddie leaned forward, his eyes a dark, serious blue. He leaned on his hands, closing the distance between us. "We can have that back. I want it, too."

"We can never go back." I didn't even try to hide the defeat in my voice.

"Why not?"

"You lied." Simple words. Horrible reality.

"I promise you, I never lied to you."

How I wanted to believe him. "You told me you loved me, then you told me you didn't. One had to be a lie. Which one?"

"When I said them, I thought they were true."

I picked up my fork and poked at the raw fish. If he had a point, I didn't want to hear it. I chewed on my lip as I thought about how far I really wanted to go with this.

Teddie waited. He knew me so very well. I'd have to be more careful before I gave a man that kind of advantage again. A little cynicism for self-preservation purposes seemed highly advisable.

Decision made, I set the fork back on the table, carefully aligning it with the edge of the tray before I looked at Teddie. "Do you know what a broken heart feels like?" When he opened his mouth to speak, I silenced him with a shake of my head. "Let me tell you." Memories flooded through me as I opened myself, tore down the walls I'd hidden my heart behind. Every fiber of my soul vibrated under the assault. "First, you can't believe it's real, you go completely numb. You know your life is shattering—you can feel the shards as they rip through you—but you can't process it. You can't believe it's happening. Your heart dies." I swallowed hard, fighting the tears that, since Teddie had left, had taken up permanent residence behind my eyes, waiting to burst forth at the first hint of weakness.

Teddie reached a hand across the table. "Lucky . . ."

Before he touched me, I jerked my hand out of harm's way. "Don't." I crossed my arms, telegraphing my vulnerability, but I didn't care. I needed to do this, and he needed to hear it.

"Unable to feel, your brain takes over. Maybe it plays old tapes, maybe logic kicks in, I don't know. But reacting is rote." I paused, reading his expression. For a moment, I thought I saw my pain reflected there. "Remember after you told me you didn't love me, I took you to my office and cleaned you up—you'd had that horrible fight with your father?"

His eyebrows snapped into a frown. He remembered.

"Then I insisted on taking you to the plane and watching you go." I drew a ragged breath. "I don't even remember exactly what I did after that. I drove, I know that. But for how long or where I went . . ." I shrugged. "I do remember my father found me at that special place you and I used to go near Red Rock, but the rest of it is gone. If only it had stayed that way." I looked at him and tried for a sardonic grin. I don't know if I succeeded—his face remained stoic, passive, yet I could see the raw edges of pain, which made me feel a bit better. "Reality, it sorta sucks, you know?"

"It doesn't have to."

"No, and it really doesn't anymore. It sure did, though." I felt like picking up my knife, but I resisted—holding a sharp object in my hand at this juncture seemed a bit unwise. "You know what the worst part was?"

Teddie didn't say anything—he knew a rhetorical question when he heard one, he always had. I liked that about him, still did . . . despite my best efforts.

"I had to go home. I had to sleep in the bed we had made love in the night before."

"One last fuck before I left, I remember." Hurt resonated in his voice. "I didn't intend it to be that way."

I could tell he meant it, but that didn't lessen the betrayal. "But the sleeping part wasn't the worst part—I could take pills that made me sleep the sleep of the dead, no dreams, no memories. No, sleep was a welcome escape, but the waking up part?" I let out a ragged breath. There were no words to describe the pain, or if there were, I couldn't summon them. "Oh, yeah, the waking up part. First, just as you're shrugging off sleep, you remember the happiness, the unmitigated joy of the life you thought you had, the love you thought you shared, which brightened every moment, every thought. The warm blanket of joy, wrapping us both in the ecstasy of the present and the promise of the future. Then, you open your eyes, and reality hits you like a spear through your chest, opening a sucking, gaping hole. You can't breathe. And for a long time, breathing is all you concentrate on—it takes everything you've got."

"I know," Teddie whispered.

I narrowed my eyes. "You don't know." The words were hard and flat, angry. "You left. It was your choice. Don't play me, Teddie, don't ever play me again."

"I didn't . . ." He was wise enough to stop and let me continue.

I drew in a deep, refocusing breath. "So, you breathe. And you try not to feel. But you walk around a corner, you hear a song, a snippet of conversation,, and a memory assaults you. You try not to cry. Sometimes you do. Other times, you feel defeated. Then you have conversations with yourself, wondering, speculating as to what went wrong, where did the dream get lost? How could he say he loved you, then one day, he just didn't anymore? One night, you're planning the future, savoring the day. The next, it's all over. Who does that?" I looked at Teddie, and this time, my question wasn't rhetorical. "What kind of man makes that kind of decision without any discussion, without any attempt to figure things out?"

"I just thought it was the right thing for me." Teddie floundered. My question clearly had him back on his heels.

"I don't know what the word 'love' means to you, Teddie. Well, actually, right now, I have a pretty good idea. It meant you wanted me."

"That's not true." His expression held righteous indignation, but his words didn't pack the same punch.

"Whatever it meant, you didn't love me enough to even try. And that's what hurts the most." There, I'd said it. I'd finally admitted the truth not only to him, but to myself as well.

Lost in our own thoughts, neither one of us said anything for a bit. For me, saying these things out loud helped establish emotional order. For the first time in months, I felt the glimmer of hope, of possibilities, of strength . . . and it felt good.

"You know," I said, picking up the thread I'd abandoned. "After I got pretty good at breathing, I thought I'd be okay. But I wasn't. I kept believing that somehow, someway, you'd realize what a mistake you made, and you'd come home."

"I *am* home." Teddie's voice ached with my sadness. "If I could erase my leaving, my bad choices, I would."

"I know. But you can't."

"Why not? Let me show you, Lucky. Please?"

One of those carefully mended cracks in my heart opened just a little, letting loose a drop of hope, of misguided wishful thinking. "We can't go back. Words, once said, can never be unheard."

"Can you forgive me?"

"Of course. I did that a while back. But I don't know how to rebuild trust. As you know, overcoming disappointment, rising above betrayal to trust again, is not my best thing, Teddie. Besides, I don't think I can risk the pain again."

"You have to risk it, that's the only way to live."

This time, when he reached across the table, I didn't pull away. When his hand closed over mine, the connection blew through me.

I thought of Jean-Charles. "Maybe."

"Do you love him?" Teddie pressed, as if my thoughts were his.

I thought about that for a moment. The trust between Jean-Charles and me was still building—we were learning each other. With Teddie, the two of us had been best friends for so long that I knew him inside and out . . . or I thought I had. I'd warned him. Elevating friendship to romance risked leaving us with neither. And there we were.

Teddie waited for an answer. I could see the guardedness, the hint of fear in his expression.

"Jean-Charles?" I drew a deep breath. "I love him enough to try."

Even though right now the whole trust thing was a bit of a challenge . . . but I didn't voice that part.

What is love without trust?

CHAPTER 5

"*M*EN REALLY *are* pigs." I snorted.

Talking to myself, I drew a few bemused smiles as, battered and floundering in the aftermath of a storm of emotion, I wandered the lobby aimlessly.

God, sometimes I hated it when I was right. My theory had sort of begun as a tongue-in-cheek effort to get a laugh. Now, it wasn't so funny.

I'd abandoned Teddie sitting at the table in Neb's staring through the window.

Our confrontation had left me somewhat disconcerted, and oddly free. Unburdening myself had lightened the load for sure. Of course, I hadn't told him the whole story, not really. I hadn't told him that with him all my walls had come down; I fell fast and hard and completely for the first time in my life. So the hurt was immense. But, knowing him, he probably knew how I felt better than I did. Given that he was an expert on me, I'd sure like to ask him how I could've been so wrong.

But my men being pigs theory was proving oddly accurate. First Teddie, then Dane, another former friend with a secret, and my father . . . sort of. And now, Jean-Charles wasn't exactly stepping up to the plate.

Mona found me staring, mouth open, eyes raised, trying to get my bearings under the Chihuly hummingbirds and butterflies. At this time of the afternoon, the day usually quieted, with many of the guests choosing to nap or relax before going out—the calm before the chaos.

"Lucky! There you are." The woman was like a shark, able to sense the fresh blood of an open wound.

"I am so done with men." I didn't lower my gaze. Instead, I remained focused on the arced flight above me.

Not missing a beat, Mona stepped in next to me, her shoulder grazing mine. "Honey, have I taught you nothing? Take a lesson from their playbook: use them for sex and occasionally, if you find one who can think, an interesting dinner or two, but really, that's pushing their limits."

I gave her my attention. "Does Father know about this theory of yours?"

Mona puckered her lips as she gave me the that-is-such-a-stupid-question look. "Of course."

I had absolutely no response. None. Glibness had fled, fast on the heels of rational thought.

My mother gave me an accusatory frown. "Where have you been?" Her voice lost the bounce of banter, taking on a sharp edge.

I didn't even flinch. I was either numb or dead. Neither was optimal, so I tried not to think about it. "I am here, where I always am, just a rabbit in a cage."

"Don't be silly." Mona put a hand on my arm. "You're not in a cage. You can leave anytime you want to."

I swiveled my eyes to hers. "You really think so?"

She gave me a quizzical, distracted look. "You were supposed to go with me to the doctor."

The cloud lifted. My thoughts coalesced. Pulling out my

phone, I punched the button and glanced at the time. Way late. "I'm so sorry. I forgot." I gave her a quick once-over. To be honest, she didn't look herself. In fact, if I had to say, she looked a little off-kilter—unusual for my mother, the laser-guided human missile. "Did you go? Are you okay?"

"Why did you mention rabbits?" Her voice had gone all fluttery, never a good sign.

"What?" I tried to marshal my somewhat dissipated attention. Even if she wasn't acting totally in character, she sounded like my mother and looked like my mother, just bigger. I'd forgotten how far along in her pregnancy she was, but it seemed she was expanding before my eyes—sorta like someone had stuck an air hose up her ass . . . or like that fat girl who ate all the blueberries in *Willy Wonka*.

Pregnancy had an interesting effect on Mona, softening her features and the hard angles of her toned physique. Too bad it hadn't seemed to affect the sharp edges of her personality.

Today, she wore a flowing peach top that dipped off one shoulder, a pair of tan pencil pants, and gold ballet slippers. A gold leaf barrette at the nape of her neck caught her hair into a tail. Normally a shiny brown, the golden highlights were new. A touch of peach lip gloss, a little smoke and violet to make her eyes pop. No need for blush—she radiated a contentment I don't recall ever sensing before. As beautiful as ever.

A frown bunched the skin between her eyes, which were filled with worry. Glowing with health, she didn't look like she had bad news, so I relaxed a little. The whole day had me jumpy. I pulled free a feather that had become lodged in her hair. "Turkeys clipping your wings?"

She pouted, sticking out her lower lip just a bit for effect. "That's not funny."

"That depends on your perspective." I smoothed her hair as a parent would a child's. "I trust you and Jerry got the bird thing figured out?"

She worked the huge diamond on the ring finger of her left hand as she chewed on her lower lip and nodded. "For now. But what am I going to do with a thousand live turkeys?" She gripped my arm harder. "Do you know they bite?"

I bit down on a grin. "I really don't know what to say." I tried to block the visuals of Mona and Jerry herding angry birds. I was only partially successful. The whole thing made me want to laugh.

Mona's face crumpled into a frown, and she lasered me with the evil eye—it used to work. "You're mocking me."

"Mocking is one of my best things, along with chasing pipe dreams and kissing toads hoping for a prince."

Mona let go of my arm. "Sarcasm is a shield, Lucky."

I rubbed the spot she'd been gripping in an attempt to restore circulation. "Apparently, an ineffective one."

"I heard Teddie was back."

"Really?" I pretended not to care. "From whom?"

"Your father."

"Did he happen to tell you the whole story?"

She put her hands on her hips and tried to look fierce in the face of my waning good humor. She wasn't entirely successful. "For the record, I don't agree with what he did. But just the same, I'm glad he did it—you need to figure out the Teddie thing and move on."

Complicity. Betrayal, total and complete. And good intentions did little to soften the blow. I lowered my brows and gave her my best stern look. "You haven't talked to Jordan recently, have you?"

Her eyes drifted from mine as she pretended to be interested in the sparse crowd. With one finger, she looped and twisted the thick gold chain around her neck, tightening it until the flesh underneath whitened.

My fingers itched to help her. "You do know accomplices are considered just as guilty as the perpetrator of the crime?"

Mona switched to concerned-parent mode, as if that worked anymore. "Lucky, your father and I have your best interests at heart. We're worried about you. You've got to face Teddie, face yourself. You run around here solving everyone else's problems, doing what you should do. When are you going to do what you *want* to do? Figure out your own dreams, sweetheart, and follow them."

"It would be great if, just once, someone would leave me alone to solve my own problems, my own way, on my own time."

She rested her hand delicately on my arm. "We would, but you don't."

Just as I was adjusting to the truth in her statement, Mona snapped back to the Mona I knew. She waved her hand, slapping away our previous discussion. "Now, about those rabbits."

"What rabbits?" Floundering, I struggled to follow the flow of her conversation. I knew better—past experience taught me I'd end up at sea with a bad case of motion sickness.

"I went to the doctor today, and I killed two of them," Mona announced, tilting her chin just a hint higher.

All I could do was blink at her. "You killed two doctors?"

Mona sighed and looked at me with that patronizing parental look she was so good at. "No. Rabbits."

"You killed two rabbits at the doctor's office?"

She nodded, then raised her eyebrows as if willing me to understand.

We stood there, staring at each other. Clearly, I needed a Rosetta Stone.

"Rabbits . . . ," Mona prompted in a slightly louder voice, as if she were an ugly American willing a non–English speaker to understand.

"I got that, but why do they have rabbits at the doctor's office?"

She sighed dramatically. "It's an expression."

"Oh, well, that makes it so much clearer."

Mona rolled her eyes. "Twins," she said with a smile that didn't camouflage the panic in her eyes. "I'm having twins."

Time stopped. I stared at my mother. When I felt light-headed,

I gasped for air—that whole breathing thing again. "What?" I managed to gasp with the tiny bit of oxygen I had left. Clearly, none of it was reaching my brain.

"You're going to have a brother and a sister." She cocked her head upward and the corners of her mouth down. "Or maybe two brothers. Or two sisters." She looked at me. "Two more girls. I'd like that. I haven't a clue what to do with boys, do you?"

I felt pretty sure she had a real good handle on boys, but I didn't point that out—the context seemed a bit iffy. Recent history had proved I was the last person to offer advice on men, old or young . . . unless shooting them became an option.

"Which would you like?" She acted as if I had a choice. Finally, the light dawned. "Lucky, you're not saying anything. Why don't you say something?"

I opened my mouth, but words failed me. Vaguely, I was aware of a vibrating at my hip.

After a beat or two, Mona nodded in that direction. "Aren't you going to answer that?"

"What?"

"Your phone."

My hand shook as I grabbed my phone from its holster, swiped my thumb across the face, tapped the green button, then held the thing to my ear. "Yeah."

"Lucky?"

"Romeo?" I tried to gather my wits, but they drifted away like smoke in a strong breeze.

"Yeah, what's the matter? You sound weird."

"My family just . . ." I paused, searching for the words, but words were gone—not a good sign.

"No need to explain," Romeo filled the dead air. "Your family defies explanation, anyway."

"God love you, kid." Still struggling to find my sea legs, I cradled my forehead, massaging my temples with thumb and forefinger. I stared at the ground, willing my mother to disappear. "You wouldn't, by chance, be coming here to arrest my mother?"

The young detective had the audacity to laugh. "What for?"

"I don't know . . . intentional infliction of emotional distress?"

"That's not a crime, it's a civil tort." He didn't even try to hide his amusement—he'd been finding me pretty darn humorous lately.

I wasn't sure I appreciated his attitude. "I'll take that as a no." I blew at a lock of hair that tickled my eyes and tried to focus on a point across the lobby to stop my world from spinning. It didn't work. "Give me time, I'll think of some other reason. Maybe you could take her into protective custody?" My outlook brightened for a moment.

"From you?" This time, he laughed out loud. "Your bark is worse than your bite."

I crumpled under the weight of defeat. "You never know. One of these days . . ."

"Keep me posted. You know I'm always here to get you out of hot water. But until then, the help I need is yours."

"I figured as much. What can I do for you?"

"Fiona Richards's killer left a note . . . and it's addressed to you."

CHAPTER 6

ITH THE swipe of a hand, I brushed an arc through the dust on my desk—nothing like living in a construction zone. In the clean space, Romeo smoothed the note lightly until the message was legible. "We've already processed it for prints and whatnot."

I moved, taking my shadow with me, so the light from the exposed bulb on a wire above me illuminated the single sheet of paper, protected in plastic. Five lines long, the message had been scrawled in a generic blocked print using what looked to be a black Sharpie, medium tip. It read

Two chef, one chef,
Sous chef, done chef,
Smoke and air,
Cook with care,
Broil and baste, in your haste Lucky no more.

I read it three times. "Great, a psycho with a Theodor Geisel complex." Seated in my chair, with Romeo parked on the corner of my desk, I poked at the edges of the plastic, pushing the note away. I glanced up, catching Romeo looking at me.

He quickly looked away, hiding his worry, which didn't give me any warm fuzzies. "Theodor who?"

His question made me feel old, though I didn't know why. "Dr. Seuss."

Romeo's eyes widened. "No shit? That's his name?"

I shrugged him off. "Please, you know I only lie about serious things." I eyeballed the note like it was a rattler, coiled to strike. "Is this a threat, or am I being paranoid?"

"Seems like."

"Like what?"

He rolled his head side to side, waffling. "A threat."

"But why?"

"*Why* would be nice, but *who* would be a better place to start." Romeo dropped into one of the client chairs across from me. Glancing around, he let out his breath in a long sigh. "Are they working on this office at all?"

"Not that I can tell." As I leaned back, my desk chair groaned under the strain. With the toe of my left foot, I pulled out the lower drawer, then propped my feet on it. Steepling my fingers, I tried to remain calm. "The reference to smoke and air seems obvious."

"Fiona Richards." Romeo nodded as his gaze drifted from mine. He stared over my shoulder, but his eyes had the unfocused glaze of a man lost in his thoughts. "Somebody trussed her up like a turkey at Thanksgiving, then wrapped her head in plastic wrap, cut a slit for her mouth, then lit the reservoir on the smoking thing and stuck the nozzle through the slit." His focus returned, and his eyes caught mine.

"Sick son-of-a-bitch." Closing my eyes, I let my thoughts wander. My corner of Vegas was a magical place, most of the time. I hated it when someone felt the need to burst my little bubble of delusion and happiness. No matter Fiona Richards's sins, I felt sure she didn't deserve to be tortured and slowly suffocated. "But she wasn't a chef."

"I'm working on that. She was in the food service business—it is possible she started out in a kitchen somewhere and then made her move." Romeo jotted a note on a sticky pad on my desk, then peeled off the page, folded it, and stuck it in his pocket. "The coroner said Fiona didn't die easily."

"That much is evident."

"You should take this threat seriously."

"You know me better than that. Pinheads with Post-it notes don't slow me down. I can't let them—if they do, they win."

"You logic is as solid as Swiss cheese."

"I'm trying to think, and you're not helping." I opened one eye and shot Romeo a frown. When he didn't seem fazed, I leaned my head back and turned my thoughts loose, letting them freewheel —the strategy had worked before. Cook with care? Baste and broil? Something niggled at the edges of my consciousness, like a balloon lifted on the breeze floating just out of reach.

As I drifted, I was vaguely aware of the noises in the outer office: the door opening then closing softly, the rustling of papers, a drawer sliding open.

Newton, our adopted macaw, shouted, "Bitch, bitch. Filthy whore. Food now." A filthy bird with a filthy mouth—when he had landed on my balcony at the Presidio, I had been powerless to resist. Every day since, I'd rued that moment of weakness.

"Filthy whore" was Miss P.'s special term of endearment. She poked her head through the doorway, confirming my suspicion. "You guys want anything?"

"A new identity and a life somewhere far away." I assumed my former position and hoped that the next time I opened my eyes, all around me would be just a figment of my imagination.

"What? And give up all of this?"

Romeo slapped his thighs—at least that's what it sounded like. I didn't bother looking to see. "You got some 101 on the top shelf in the kitchen, right?" he asked. "I'm feeling the need."

"I'll get it for you." Miss P. sounded like she meant it.

"No." Romeo stopped her. "Not your job. Thanks, though."

I sneaked one eye open. Miss P. caught me and shot me a grin, then hooked her arm through Romeo's, and the two of them disappeared through the doorway, chattering as they moved out of earshot. Once again, my thoughts turned inward. Broil. Baste. Cook with care.

Suddenly, like leaves caught in an eddy, my thoughts coalesced.

Oh, my God! I bolted upright, my feet slamming to the floor. I tried his cell phone—hitting redial several times. He didn't answer. In a fluid motion, I pushed myself out of the chair and launched myself through the makeshift doorway into the hallway, and ran.

Jean-Charles had said he was having trouble with the oven.

~

WHAT IF JEAN-CHARLES WAS THE NEXT COURSE ON THE murderer's menu?

The wind buffeted me through the open top of the Ferrari. My hair whipped, stinging my face. Ignoring it all, I stomped on the accelerator and cranked the wheel over, just missing one of the gate supports as I raced onto the construction site at Cielo. The trip here had been a blur—I hoped I hadn't killed anyone. With two feet on the brake pedal and one hand fisted around the hand-brake, I locked the wheels and slid to a stop, spewing a cloud of sand.

Jean-Charles, the next victim—the thought weakened my knees and made the bile rise in my stomach.

Oh, God, let him be all right. I threw open the car door, levered myself out, and ran.

Cielo, our new property, was a hard-hat area. A few men moved to greet me as I raced through the gate in the chain-link fence, grabbed a hard hat, and bolted into the building. I shouted at them. "Jean-Charles? Have you seen Chef Bouclet?"

Blank stares answered me.

Slapping the hard hat on my head, I ran for the stairs. Time waiting for the construction elevator would be wasted. The stairs would be much faster. Of course, Jean-Charles's restaurant was on the top floor.

∿

THIRTY FLOORS, TWO STAIRS AT A TIME, HAD ME ON THE VERGE OF apoplexy as I burst through the fire door at the top. Breathing hard, with sweat trickling down my sides wilting my shirt, I was cold, despite the exertion. Propelled by fear and running on pure adrenaline, I slammed through the entrance to Jean-Charles's restaurant —we still hadn't agreed on a name. He wanted J. C. Prime. I told him that sounded a bit like Jesus Christ had opened a bistro—Jean-Charles didn't understand why that would be a problem.

As I ran, the smell registered first. Roasting meat. Pork? It smelled good enough to eat. Maybe he was working. Oh, please let him be preparing some incredible feast. I could picture him in his chef whites, his brows creased in concentration, whistling "La Vie En Rose."

Raking the hard hat from my head with an angry swipe of my forearm, I targeted the kitchens behind the double swinging doors in the back. Past the walls of windows, across the tasteful distressed-wood floors, under the million-dollar chandelier that would be the focal point . . . in addition to the Van Gogh hanging in the entrance, and the food, of course.

But without Chef Bouclet, without its beating heart, the restaurant would just be a hollow shell with fancy window dressing.

"Jean-Charles?" I shouted. "Jean-Charles!" I felt tears well in the corners of my eyes, then one broke and trickled down my cheek. I didn't bother wiping it away.

Hitting the doors with my shoulder, I barreled through, then stopped in my tracks. The kitchen was a mess: pots and pans and broken plates littered the floor. Smoke pushed its way through the gap where the oven door met the frame and billowed toward the ceiling. The contents of a pot steamed on the stove, water boiling over in an ominous hiss.

A man stood in the center, his back to me.

He turned slowly, as if not alarmed by my sudden presence.

I squinted my eyes, trying to focus understanding. "Teddie?"

"You shouldn't be here." His voice sounded dead, his eyes looked haunted.

"*I* shouldn't be here? What about you?" Doubled over with my hands on my knees, I sucked in as much air as I could. This was the last place I expected to find Teddie. He'd been showing up unexpectedly lately, so I don't know why I was so surprised. Actually, I wasn't surprised as much as I was angry. Finally, I stopped seeing stars as oxygen flooded my brain and adrenaline spurted into my bloodstream. Clarity hit me like an ax to the head. "Oh, my God! What happened here? Where is Jean-Charles? What is that in the oven?" Terror squeezed my heart. I couldn't breathe.

As I made a staggering step toward the oven, Teddie reached out and grabbed my arm. "Don't." He didn't look quite himself. In his Harvard sweatshirt, the one with the neck cut out that I used to wear, and his faded, threadbare jeans that were just tight enough, he looked good enough to be a featured dish on the menu.

I jerked my arm out of his grasp. Fear kept me rooted to the same spot. "Why not? Jean-Charles must've been preparing something."

Teddie said nothing.

If he didn't start staying out of my way and my life, I'd roast him on a spit myself.

"For some reason, I keep tripping over you today." I tried to make sense of him being here, but I was having trouble. "It's like I've really pissed off some minor deity, and she is now having fun at my expense."

"Your lucky day?" He soft-served the comment with a weak smile, even though he knew I hated that sort of word play.

I narrowed my eyes at him. "Don't push your luck. What are you doing here? And where is Jean-Charles?"

He ran a hand through his hair, making the spikes stand up. He seemed sort of shell-shocked as he slowly shook his head and looked around the kitchen. "I don't know."

"Where is he?" I advanced on him, stopping a stride short.

His eyes flicked to the oven, then back to me. "I told you, I don't know."

"How long have you been here?"

"A bit before you. Five minutes? Ten? I don't really know."

"Is there anything you *do* know?"

He looked at me for a beat before answering. "I know there is a man in the oven."

"What?" My heart stopped. Silence. Then it started beating again. "A man?" I croaked, my throat constricted by emotion. I whirled toward the oven. The smell . . . oh, God.

Teddie grabbed my arm, stopping me. "Lucky, don't." He looked green.

"Broiled and basted," I whispered as I stared at the steam escaping from the oven and rising toward the ceiling. The smell . . . it hadn't been pork. . . . "Broil and baste . . ." I felt my knees buckle as the world faded.

Teddie caught me as I fell.

THE SMELL OF AMMONIA. STRONG. STINGING MY SINUSES. I GAGGED and choked, then gulped air. My eyes fluttered open. I stared up

81

into Teddie's, dark and deep with concern. I slapped away his hand waving the ammonia capsule under my nose. "Christ. That stuff could bring back the dead." With the back of my hand, I swiped at my eyes as the fog in my head cleared.

Crumpled on the ground, I was half cradled in Teddie's lap. As the ammonia odor dissipated, the smell of cooking meat replaced it, jump-starting my memory. "Jean-Charles?" I whispered, fearful of the answer, but driven by a need to know.

Teddie looked up, his eyes traversing the kitchen. "I don't know. Not yet."

With a hand on his shoulder, I pushed myself out of his lap until I was seated on the kitchen floor. Before I could ask anything else, the door swung open as Romeo burst through, then skidded to a stop. His eyes raked around the room, then swiveled back to the oven. He closed the distance in two strides. "Did you turn it off?" He threw the question over his shoulder as he reached for the handkerchief in his pocket, then shook it out. He covered his hand with the thin cloth, then grabbed the handle to the oven door.

"Don't . . . ," Teddie and I said in unison, but Romeo didn't listen.

He threw back the latch, pulled the oven door open, then staggered back, letting it bounce once or twice on its hinges before slamming it shut. "Whoa." He threw his forearm up, covering his face. "Was this thing on broil?"

"Yeah." Teddie sounded tired. "I turned it off, but the guy . . . well, he was already overdone." He must've seen the stricken look on my face because he followed that comment quickly with, "Sorry. I'm not myself."

I shot him a pained look—I didn't even try to hide my fear. What if it was Jean-Charles in the oven? And Christophe? My heart broke for the little boy. Losing two parents would be so . . . I hadn't the right word . . . if there even was one. My hand shook as

I swiped at a lock of hair that fell into my eyes. And his sister? I cradled my head in my arms for a moment. And what about me? A wave of heat washed over us when Romeo eased opened the oven door, allowing it to rest on its hinges. His eyes traversed the kitchen, then settled on Teddie and me once again—they were old eyes, lacking his original youthful idealism, and I felt a pang of guilt, I didn't really know why.

"Looks like there was a bit of a fight in here," he said, understated as always.

I looked at the mess of pots and pans and broken plates. Jean-Charles putting up the fight of his life?

Romeo locked his eyes on Teddie, who had pushed himself to his feet and now seemed overly interested in brushing down his jeans, ridding them of invisible dust. "Anything you can add here?" Romeo asked.

"This is how I found it." Teddie stuffed his hands in his pockets and hunched his shoulders around his ears. " Nobody was here . . . well, except for the guy in the oven."

Romeo stared at him for a moment, a visual litmus test.

A numbness washed over me—a self-protective disbelief cooling the burning residue of panic. I hugged myself. "What if that's Jean-Charles?"

Romeo's eyes snapped to mine. "Call him. See if he answers."

"I tried earlier." I struggled for air. "He didn't."

With a sense of impending doom, I pulled my phone from its hip holster and flicked my thumb across the screen—I had to repeat it three times before I got it right. I tapped my chef's number in the list of favorites. "He shouldn't be too hard to find." When you were responsible for a twenty-four-hour restaurant, your tether was tight. I knew—I was responsible for a twenty-four-hour hotel. My call rang once, then rolled to voice mail. I tried again. Same result. I looked at Romeo. I opened my mouth, but words wouldn't come. I shook my head.

"He doesn't answer?" Teddie asked, his voice flat, devoid of emotion.

Why was he here? The question kept echoing in my head.

I found my voice. "No." I dialed the Burger Palais. The hostess picked up on the first ring. "Chef Bouclet, please. This is Lucky O'Toole."

"Oh, Ms. O'Toole, I'm sorry, but he left a little while ago. I thought he was going to meet you."

"When did he tell you that?" My voice was hard. Fear tempered it thin, and my tone sharp.

"As he was walking out."

"When was that? Tell me exactly."

"A couple of hours, I think. I don't know exactly. He said he was going to meet you at Cielo." The girl had that breathy way of speaking that young women the world over seemed to think sounded grown-up in a Marilyn Monroe sort of way. To me, it just sounded like they were auditioning for a porn movie. "To be honest, we're getting a bit worried. He left Christophe here. Rinaldo was sure he'd be back by now."

Dread won out in my heart. I hung up, as if doing so would sever the channel to bad news. Enough "me" remained to think I would have to apologize later.

As I ended the call and replaced the phone at my hip, I locked eyes with Romeo. "According to his staff, Jean-Charles said he was coming here to meet me."

Teddie looked a little twitchy. "It's going to be okay, you know. I'm sure the guy in the oven isn't him." Despite his effort to placate me, he could no longer calm my fears or make me feel better. In fact, as living proof that things didn't always turn out okay, he made me feel worse.

"Right. And, if I'm a good girl, Santa will give me everything I want for Christmas." I pushed myself to my feet, then staggered over to Romeo. "I need to know."

As if sensing my hurt and fear, the detective circled an arm around my shoulders and pulled me against him. "Lucky, this isn't a good idea."

Teddie stepped in next to me, his hand gripping my arm. "I agree."

Jerking my arm from his grasp, I shut them both down with a glare. Romeo finally nodded, but held on to me, not letting go.

The three of us peered into the oven. The body curled away from us, the skin bright pink, all the hair burned away. Charred bits of clothing hung from the body—a collar, it had been white. I stepped on my rising panic. The broad expanse of his back faced outward, the top of his shoulder a crispy, burned dark crust. Bile rose in my throat. I pressed my hand over my mouth, fighting the urge.

Romeo must've felt the tremor of revulsion. He tightened his arm around my shoulders and tried to steer me away. "The crime scene folks are on their way. Let's give them some room."

I shrugged out of his embrace and focused anew on the body. My eyes traversed down his spine, looking for something I'd recognize, something . . . identifying. The skin next to the bone actually looked . . . uncooked, but not unique. Under the man's haunches, the soles of his feet peeked through some sort of green goo. "What is that?"

Romeo leaned in, waving away the heat. He pulled a pencil out of his coat pocket and poked at the green slime. When he removed the pencil, he pulled thin threads of the stuff with it, sticky and gooey like a spider's web. "Looks like plastic."

"Plastic," I whispered. I dropped my head and let loose a reedy, nervous laugh. My legs weakened with relief, but my knees held. I squeezed Romeo's arm.

"What?" The young detective looked at me as if I'd finally gone 'round the bend, as I been threatening to do for so long.

"Crocs." I pointed to the green goo. "Jean-Charles wouldn't be caught dead wearing a pair of Crocs."

~

TEDDIE AND I RECONVENED IN THE CORNER OF THE KITCHEN AS THE macabre work continued silently in front of the oven. Side-by-side we now sat on stools, leaning against the wall, watching the techs work the rest of the crime scene, dusting and photographing, plucking and bagging trace—mind-numbing work, but part of the thrill of the chase. No tiny speck of lint remained untouched, unexamined.

The cops had separated us and had taken their time. I didn't know about Teddie, but I was bone-weary, angry, and scared. The smell of seared flesh lingered.

"It'll be a long time before I can face roast pork." Teddie pulled one knee up, lacing his fingers together to hold it.

"Your jocularity is a bit overdone, Mr. Kowalski." I gritted my teeth. Panic. It did it to me every time. I never missed an opportunity to say something inappropriate—like a joke at a dead guy's expense. At the moment, food in general held no appeal, but I didn't feel the need to share that tidbit. So to speak. I squirmed on my stool, angling for the best view of the body, which the techs had laid out inside a body-bag. "Do they have an ID yet?"

Teddie didn't answer—he was good that way, letting me sort of babble my way back to logical thinking. The sizzle of fear still arced through me, jolting me at the touch of the memory. "Thank God it wasn't Jean-Charles. But I wonder who, and why, and why here?"

"All good questions."

"And where is Jean-Charles?" I'd tried his cell repeatedly, each with the same result. "What if the killer has him?" Crossing my arms, I hugged myself—suddenly, I felt very cold.

"What if he is the killer?" Teddie sounded almost as if he'd like that outcome.

"Why would he leave Christophe at the restaurant, then?"

"A trip to the scene of an impending murder doesn't sound like a family outing to me," Romeo added as he joined us, taking the third stool.

"But I know him, he wouldn't . . ." I trailed off. They had a point. Not one I would accept, but without more facts, I couldn't argue . . . yet.

Romeo pulled a square of cloth out of his front pocket and blotted his forehead. He didn't refold the bit of linen, preferring to stuff it back where he'd found it. "We're looking for him, if that makes you feel better."

Two officers muscled their way through the single swinging door, forcing me to bite off my reply. The larger of the two, who looked like he was a NFL lineman moonlighting to make ends meet, glanced around the room, his eyes finally finding who he was looking for. "Detective Romeo, sir, we found this guy hanging around outside."

Reaching behind him, the officer grabbed the man lurking there and pushed him to the front.

Adone Giovanni.

Romeo raised an eyebrow. "Thank you officer. I'll take it from here."

"Sir." The two cops touched the brims of their hats, then left as quickly as they'd come.

"That's not Jean-Charles, is it?" Adone's dark eyes danced wildly, his gaze darting between each of us and the body on the floor half-hidden by the surrounding techs.

"Why are you here?" Romeo asked, his voice serious, even a bit hard.

"I was looking for Jean." Adone's voice wavered, then steadied, as he took a deep breath. "The hostess at the burger place told me he would be here." Still in all-black chef attire, tattoos, kohled eyes, his hair spiked, he looked out of place in Jean-Charles's kitchen.

"And what did you want with Chef Bouclet?" Romeo pressed.

Adone grabbed one elbow, holding his arm to his side and

looking like a kid who needed a hug but was afraid to ask for one, or a kid stilling himself because he had something to hide.

I narrowed my eyes. Pulling my phone out, I once again dialed the Burger Palais. The same voice answered. "Yes, this is Lucky O'Toole again. Sorry to bother you, but are you the only hostess on duty?" I locked eyes with Adone. He swallowed hard. "You are. And how long have you been on duty? All day. Did you tell anyone besides me where Chef Bouclet had gone?" I chewed on my lip and waited a second or two before repeating her answer. "No. Yes, you're right, Chef Bouclet would not like you telling anyone his business. Thank you." I rang off and reholstered the phone without a word.

Romeo looked at Adone. "So?"

The rebel chef deflated. "Look, I was supposed to meet Jean-Charles here. They're releasing the food truck, so I'm back in business. He had some new recipes we needed to work on." He looked at me, his arms open, pleading.

I shot a questioning look at Romeo. He nodded. "Coroner's done with the truck."

"When did you and Jean-Charles arrange this meeting?" I asked Adone.

"Earlier. I called him."

I thought back. Something Jean-Charles had said the last time I saw him—in the kitchen at Burger Palais. He was to meet a friend here. I looked around and the carnage. Some friend.

"Why did you lie?" Teddie asked the obvious next question.

Romeo frowned at his intrusion—as a detective, he treated questioning as his sole province.

"I walked right into the middle of a police investigation." Adone's eyes skittered to the body, then back to Romeo's. "I'm assuming this is the second dead body. The last thing I wanted was for you to think I had something to do with it."

I rolled my eyes. "Well, *that* strategy backfired."

One of the techs called to Romeo. He gave me a look that was easy to interpret, then excused himself.

I motioned to the stool Romeo vacated. "Join us?" I said to Adone in a tone that made it clear there was only one answer.

The chef did as he was ordered, straddling the stool. Keeping his legs wide, he gripped the slice of seat between them with both hands. His wide-eyed gaze lingered on the body before turning to me. "Is that Jean?"

"No."

He straightened as the answer hit him like a slap.

"Aren't you relieved?"

Teddie thrust a beer at Adone and one at me, then took a deep pull of his own as he retook his stool. I never saw him leave.

Adone drank deeply, then rested the bottle atop one thigh while he bounced his foot.

I waited for the jiggled beer to overflow, but that would be his problem . . . probably the least of his problems, so I didn't mention it.

"Of course I am happy . . . for Desiree. There is not so much love lost between us, to be honest, but I wouldn't wish that"—he jerked his head toward the body—"on anybody. Why would someone put a body to broil like that?"

"To make a point."

"What's the bad blood between you and Jean-Charles? Besides the way you're treating his sister."

I saw an excuse in his eyes, but he thought better than fighting that fight. "Jean, he is very classical in his culinary approach. Very French. I like to shake things up a bit. There's a group of us, younger chefs, we are trying different fusions, different techniques."

"The anti-Ducasse and his 'quality restaurant' label," Teddie said. I guess he'd picked up a thing or two on his whirlwind world tour.

Adone's eyes lit with zeal. "Exactly. Collège Culinaire de France took a dislike to us."

"You were blackballed." Not wanting any more of my beer, I handed it to Teddie, who had drained his.

"What is this? My balls are sometimes blue . . . women!" Adone shook his head. "But they are not black."

I did not smile. I didn't know, but I had a strong feeling he was patronizing me and I was the butt of a subtle joke. "You couldn't get a job in a legitimate kitchen in France."

He looked chagrined that his joke didn't elicit the expected response. "This is so."

"You blame Jean."

Adone shrugged.

"And then." I leaned forward, pressing home my point. "When you came crawling, he put you in a food truck."

Adone pulled himself out of his slouch, pressing his shoulders back. "He told me I would not work in any of the best kitchens."

"Not ever? Or not yet?"

Adone's face shut down. "It is a small difference."

Teddie and I exchanged glances.

The hate ran deep between these two.

Deep enough for murder?

CHAPTER 7

*T*HE MINUTE I strode through the front entrance to the Babylon, Flash Gordon, my best friend and Las Vegas's primo investigative reporter, hit me like a killer whale hitting a baby seal. She fell into step beside me, which was good—I had no intention of slowing down . . . I knew what she wanted.

"Girl," she said. "I've been cooling my heels here for, like, forever. Where you been?" She gave me the once-over. "You got the look on you. Give it up."

I flicked a glance in her direction. Refusing to meet her stare. She was like the Devil—if she looked into your eyes she could see into your soul—or so it seemed, anyway. Today, I didn't want to fall under the spell of her particular form of black magic.

The lobby was packed with people strolling, looking, cuddling, or just enjoying the ambience. Many took advantage of the moment and paused to snap photos against the wall sectioning off the indoor ski slope, or while sitting on the railing of one of the arcing bridges across our version of the Euphrates as it meandered through the lobby. Some even pointed their lenses skyward to capture the Chihuly rainbow of blown-glass hummingbirds and butterflies. All of that should have warmed my heart, but with Flash in full barracuda mode, I wasn't feeling the joy. Somebody roasting a man in "my" oven, and a missing chef, had put a serious damper on my day.

Even with Flash in heels and me in flats, my six-foot frame gave me a huge advantage . . . almost a foot. Today, as every day, Flash's clothes looked painted on: tight jeans, a hot-pink tee shirt stretched well past the point of good taste. Not that taste was ever Flash's goal. Riotous curls of red hair cascaded down her back from the clip that caught them at the nape of her neck. Gold diamond hoops, way too large for her heart-shaped face and diminutive stature, looped from her ears and banged against her neck as she took two strides to my every one. Hot pink lips pressed into a thin line and large doe eyes that belied her killer instinct completed the picture. I ignored all of it as, deterred by the line in front of the elevator, I motored toward the stairs.

Flash reached for my arm, but I shifted it out of her reach. I might not outlast her, but I could outrun her, or at least stay out of her grasp.

"Come on, Lucky. Throw me a morsel," she gasped as she struggled to keep up. "Even a tidbit would keep me ahead of the pack."

When the alarm tone on my phone sounded at my hip, I changed directions. I didn't even need to look at the thing. The prep meeting for the Last Chef Standing competition was scheduled to begin ten minutes from now in the Golden Fleece Room. Since I was in charge, I figured I probably ought to show up.

Flash grabbed me hard and whirled me around, despite my serious size and weight advantage. There was a leverage lesson in there somewhere, but I was too scattered to glom onto it. "That look. Yup, you got it, and I want to hear about it. You got bodies being fricasseed all over town. A recipe for disaster."

"Isn't that my line? If it isn't, it sure sounds like something I might say." I yanked my arm from hers. "Regardless, it's an ongoing police investigation." The woman was amazing—she must have a direct tap into the information superhighway. The bodies weren't even cold yet. I cringed at the visual of the baked guy and wondered how long they could leave him out of the cooler before he started to rot. Of course, he was half-cooked, so that might help. I let my head drop forward—Christ, I was one sick puppy.

After making sure I had Flash's attention, I gave her a stern look. "You really should leave this alone."

She made a rude noise. "Honey, you know 'should' ain't in my vocabulary."

I continued walking. "Yeah, well it should be." Was that like a tautology? I couldn't remember. Unable to come up with a better pithy reply, I left the whatever-it-was hanging between us. Then a thought hit me. I stopped, catching her off-guard. She galloped a few strides before adjusting and coming back. I gave her a serious look. "Our normal agreement, right?"

She nodded and switched gears seamlessly. Faster than I could say Siegfried and Roy, a pencil and pad materialized in her hands. "I help you. You give me the exclusive, but I don't print a word until you say so."

"Don't even breathe a word until I give you the go-ahead." She nodded once, which was enough. With Flash, a nod was a bond. "I need all the info you can gather on Fiona Richards. Apparently, she was a purveyor of gourmet foodstuffs."

She had me spell the name, even though I couldn't imagine how else one would spell Fiona Richards besides the obvious way, then I gave her all the background I knew, which took all of ten seconds, fifteen at the outside.

Flash flipped her pad closed, then stuffed it in her back pocket, surprising me—the fabric looked stretched beyond imagination as it was. The pencil, she stuffed in the crevice of her ample rack.

"Why do you put that there?"

"It's the best place to keep pencils." She managed to say that with a perfectly straight face, but buried under two murders, my sense of humor couldn't rise to the innuendo.

I glanced down at my own inadequate chest. "I wouldn't know."

"Not much to work with."

I gave her a stunned, wide-eyed look. "For your sake, I'm hoping we've shifted back to the business at hand and are not waxing poetic about my inadequacies."

She shot me an equivocating grin.

"Cute. Anyway, that's all I got. You've worked miracles with less." I started again toward the elevators, the line had dissipated. "I need to start making connections. I'll have the name of the other victim as soon as Romeo figures out who he is . . . was. Then I want you to dig until you can connect the dots."

"Isn't this the sort of thing the Beautiful Jeremy Whitlock is better at? After all, he's the city's best PI, and you got him in your back pocket."

I stared over Flash's head. "Yeah, but I need him for something else."

I wasn't ready to tell her I needed him to find my missing chef.

FLASH LEFT ME TO RIDE THE ELEVATOR UP ONE FLOOR TO THE mezzanine on my own. A precious moment of solitude to gather myself. Unfortunately, it wasn't nearly enough. When the doors opened and I stepped out, I still felt shaken and out of synch with the universe. Heading down the hall, I made a half-hearted attempt to pat my hair into place, then smooth my skirt and adjust my jacket. I swiped a finger under my eyes—with all the tears, I could only imagine what my makeup looked like—and tried to pull myself together. Catching a quick glance in a wall mirror, I was surprised to see a calm and collected outward appearance that perfectly hid the tumult inside.

Smoke and mirrors kept me together. Abject fear propelled me forward.

My favorite venue for meetings, the Golden Fleece Room appealed to my cynical side, or maybe it was my sarcastic side . . . sometimes, the two blended. Regardless, the name usually suited the gatherings, and this one was no exception. The folks at the top of the gourmet world were notoriously . . . difficult.

The murmur of voices through the closed doors sounded like a swarm of bees, excited and ready to sting. Oh, joy. I paused, tucking in my shirt one more time, fortifying my resolve. Pasting on a smile, I threw back my shoulders and strode into the room with conjured confidence.

No one noticed me.

The contestants and staff clustered in the middle of the room, talking animatedly, their voices rising with their tempers. Everyone gestured, emphasizing points that no one listened to as everyone talked at once. I was used to this fire drill, so I took a moment to size up my challenges. Scanning the room, I noticed Jean-Charles was absent. Of course, I hadn't expected him to be there, not really, but his absence extinguished the last, tiny glimmer of hope.

Something was terribly wrong.

And the killer could be in this room right now . . . or not.

Again, I tried to focus on the gathered throng. Curiously, Adone was there, as was Chef Gregor. The other two contestants besides Jean-Charles were Christian Wexler, a young chef riding a high after winning one of those Food Network shows, and Chitza DeStefano, a tatted, whippet-thin, rising local star.

I'd first met Chef Wexler when he had wanted to rent the space formerly occupied by Gregor's Italian place and currently home to the Burger Palais. I'd accepted Gregor's bid. In retrospect, not the right choice, but I'd had good reasons at the time. One being that Wexler had wanted a huge amount of participation from the hotel. Gregor came with money in hand. I knew better than to make a choice based totally on dollars and cents, but I did it anyway, and lived to regret it.

After we turned him down, Chef Wexler had opened an eatery in Summerlin to much fanfare and continued success. I'd snuck away to eat there a couple of times. While his dishes were innovative, they were still accessible to culinary neophytes like me . . . I could identify everything on my plate, which was big with me. Even in an obscure location, his restaurant was filled each night with Vegas foodies.

Shorter and rounder than average, Chef Wexler wore his dishwater-blond hair pulled back and up into one of those ratty, samurai-looking man-buns. While the younger women apparently liked the look, it was totally lost on me—not that Chef Wexler cared. With his dark eyes, smooth skin unmarred by even the hint of facial hair, and an oversized mouth with thick lips, he was the human equivalent of a room decorated in contrasting styles—somehow, the odd combination worked. In addition to his obvious skills, Christian Wexler also exhibited that elusive, intangible it-factor of a true celebrity.

Spying me, Wexler separated himself from the others, who continued to worry the topic at hand like a pack of wolves tearing at a downed deer. "Miss Lucky, might I have a word?"

"If it's quick."

"Yes, ma'am." His eyes flicked to mine, then returned to their lowered position, as if my covered belly button held an incredible appeal. "It's about the ingredients for the competition. You will be providing them, correct? And they will be the same for each of the contestants?"

The answer was easy, but I had a question of my own. "Why?"

"Some of us can get the products we need more easily than others. And consistent quality can be an issue." This time, when his eyes met mine, they held a hard look.

"We will provide each contestant with the same ingredients, in amount and quality."

He looked relieved. "I've been struggling with the quality issue with my supplier, but it is hard to find a replacement—the hotels and top chefs get first crack at the good stuff. I can't serve good food without good ingredients."

"A dog-eat-dog world, is it?"

That got a hint of a smile out of him. "Yes, ma'am. Thank you." He dipped his head and stepped away.

I returned my attention to the gathered throng.

While Christian had a shy, Southern manner, Chitza was the opposite. Half Venezuelan, half French, she had heat and distinction. Her deft culinary creativity, coupled with brash beauty and an exuberant personality, made her a hit with the moneyed thirty-somethings. Of course, she knew most of them—they'd all grown up with Vegas. Born to a Venezuelan exotic dancer, who had turned her back on her family of hardworking farmers, fleeing to Vegas to take up with a French gymnast whose specialties included a particular skill with a unicycle—I couldn't recall exactly what—Chitza was a local girl made good.

She's studied at the Culinary Institute, then had apprenticed to first the local chefs, then moved up the ranks of the celebrity chefs. Her entire training had been in Vegas, giving her the local knowledge and local association to put her at the forefront of the off-Strip Vegas dining scene. She'd gained a bit of national attention by making the finals of the *Best Chef Test*—one of the more popular contest shows on the Food Channel. Many chefs appeared on the show, including Jean-Charles—it was a feather in one's toque to be asked.

Chitza opened her own place on the west side last spring and, by all accounts, it was a success. Although, I had that on hearsay alone. I'd yet to break away to eat there—but soon . . .

I clapped my hands. "Everyone, if I may have your attention?"

They turned on me like a pack of rabid wolves caught briefly in a flare of lights. A moment of silence, then they pounced, shouldering each other aside, jockeying for my attention, shouting questions.

Everyone, that is, except for Chitza, who stood casually off to one side, one arm crossed across her stomach, her other elbow resting on her forearm, a cigarette nipped between the fingers of her raised hand. Periodically, she would take a drag, then tilt her chin and blow a stream of smoke toward the ceiling. Then she would return to look with disdain on the pack of circling dogs. Her black eyes tilted up at the corners, giving her an exotic Elvira, Queen of the Night, kind of look. She wore her jet-black hair in a short, severe, hip style, like Rooney Mara in that *Dragon Tattoo* movie. With the sharp angles of her face, and a jaw that looked cut from granite, it would be easy to picture her as the high priestess of some select foo-doo cult. Cool and aloof, Chitza brought heat to the kitchen, and the world was finding a path to her door.

"One at a time." I lowered my voice, not even trying to raise it above the ambient noise—competing to be heard only added to the cacophony and encouraged the others to shout louder.

Everyone settled down.

"Better." I took a deep breath.

Chef Gregor muscled his way to stand in front of me. "Where is my truffle?" Underneath his bluster, he looked white as a ghost.

The truffle—I'd forgotten. Two bodies had sort of pushed it down my priority list. "I'm working on it."

He stepped into me, his face inches from mine. "That's not good enough."

I could smell his fear. "That's all I got."

The other chefs murmured and shifted, like caribou sensing a wolf, but they didn't press me. The fact was, there were plenty of nice white Alba truffles to be had. Maybe not one the size of Chef Gregor's, but whether we found his or substituted a smaller one, the chefs would have a truffle for their creations.

Chef Gregor grabbed my arm. At my scowl, he let his hand drop. "You don't understand. If I don't have that truffle, I'm a dead man."

Considering I already had two dead bodies, I paid a bit more attention than I normally would have. "Why?" Mona always said bad things came in threes. Why that didn't work with good things as well was an enduring mystery.

Chef Gregor stepped back, out of my space. "It is worth much money—I am to auction it after the competition. Surely you remember?"

I remembered, but my priorities had shifted. Like I said, two dead bodies sort of trumped a missing truffle. "Are you going to have all the participants autograph it first?"

A dangerous shade of red colored his jowls. "You are not taking this seriously."

"I'm sorry." And I really was, too. He was being a jerk, but he also seemed truly scared. I made a mental note to try to catch him when he was feeling vulnerable, and we weren't on stage, to see what I might get out of him . . . if anything. We weren't exactly on the best of terms since I was responsible for closing him down. But, as they say, business is business. "I just don't understand how this is my problem." I had to play dumb, at least for now—given that the Bouclets were up their eyeballs in this whole truffle thing. Pulling their cojones out of the fire was at the top of my to-do list —if I only knew where to begin.

"The truffle, it was under the care of your kitchen staff, Jean-Charles assured me of its safety personally. And now it is gone." Chef Gregor raised his voice. "Perhaps we should notify the Babylon's insurance company?"

"Don't you have to wait twenty-four hours before filing a

missing persons report?" My snark was showing. "Perhaps you can give me as long?"

Gregor eyed me coldly. "My truffle. Or your company can pay."

I'd give my eyeteeth to see the look on the insurance guy's face when he took that claim—not your run-of-the-mill slip and fall. "I will try to find your truffle. And if you wish to file a claim, please do so through our legal department."

Chef Wexler elbowed Gregor aside, with moxie. He had the look of someone who wanted to try his hand at besting the best. Or maybe I had read that in his profile, I couldn't remember. "Where is Jean-Charles?"

Good question. My chef owed me some answers. Okay, he owed me a whole lot more, and his answers, or the lack of them, would support or refute my all-men-are-pigs theory. Right now, the man was punching all of my buttons. But, being the mouthpiece for the Babylon, I swallowed that and segued into party-line mode. "Chef Bouclet is unavoidably detained." My eyes met Adone's and held for a moment. He didn't look away. I thought I saw a flash of fear, and then it was gone.

"Adone has been telling us about Fiona Richards." A man I didn't know stepped into the conversation. He mopped his brow with a stained handkerchief—the stains looked like fresh blood, but I hoped they were tomato sauce. He stuffed the piece of cloth back into the rear pocket of his chef's pants before I could ask, stilling my overactive imagination.

"And you are?" I arched a questioning eyebrow at him.

"Baker. Brett Baker." He licked his lips as he glanced nervously around the group. "I have one of the local food trucks. One Fish, Two Fish, perhaps you've heard of it? Voted Best of Vegas in the *Review-Journal*?"

"The sushi truck, sure." I nodded as my stomach growled, getting smiles from the group. "Been meaning to try your stuff.

But why are you here? I wasn't aware of your participation in the competition."

"Chef Bouclet, he asked me to be his sous chef." The young Mr. Baker wrung his hat in his hands and shot a sideways glance at Adone, who glowered. "I'm also the point man for the food-truck fest the day before the competition."

"Got it." I looked at him for a moment longer than necessary. He seemed sort of twitchy, but maybe I was imagining it. This whole event had everyone on edge, and now with the murders . . . well, they were a match to dry tinder.

"Sort of intriguing, don't you think?" Chitza purred from the periphery. "The young gladiators, with the truck guy elevated to the kitchen and the chef stuck in a food truck. Leave it to Jean-Charles to stir the pot, eh? It's not the first time someone close to him has died." When she looked at me, I could've sworn the temperature in the room dropped.

Not only what she said, but also the way she said it, left little doubt as to the implications riding the undercurrent, which left me feeling a bit off-center. Was she telling me something, or was I reading something that wasn't there? Should I show my hand or keep it close? Unfortunately, these days, everyone was guilty until proven innocent, tried and convicted in the media practically overnight. The truth got buried under heaping piles of misinformation and conjecture, if not outright lies.

"Let's get started. I know you all have preparations to make." Amazingly, everyone settled down and at least pretended to listen as I went over the basic rules of the upcoming competition. Basically, Friday, the day after Thanksgiving, the three chefs, assuming we found Jean-Charles, would assemble in Teddie's theatre. They would be given the same ingredients, the white truffle being the final one—I'd been told it was something you put *on* the final dish, not in it. I had no idea one didn't cook with white truffles. Of course, the array of things I didn't know was so vast, I'm surprised it wasn't listed on the register of national landmarks.

Then, they would have an hour to prepare a three-course meal. The judging panel,Chef Omer, Gordon Ramsay, whom I had yet to meet, and Jordan Marsh, as the amateur gourmand, would chose the winner and most likely add to the fireworks. The whole thing was actually a huge fundraiser, part of the Vegas Feast for Famine, a cringe-worthy name in my opinion, to raise money for Three Square, a local charity that provided food to the disadvantaged.

The food-truck fest would be a prelude to the main event and a more wallet-friendly affair to bring the locals into the fun. One of the main attractions I'd managed to score was a White Castle burger truck. The original sliders, those little White Castle gems, inspired foodie lust bordering on the absurd. Last year, the line had stretched for over three hours. And still, no plans for a Vegas location. The White Castle folks were either brilliant or stupid beyond belief, I couldn't figure out which.

Addressing the throng, I hit the high points. When I'd finished my spiel, I fielded a few questions, then the gathering disbanded.

One question they had asked lingered: where was Chef Bouclet?

The Burger Palais had been the last place I'd seen him. Seemed like as good a place as any to start.

∾

ROMEO HAD BEATEN ME TO THE PUNCH. "YOU'RE LATE." HE glanced at me, but didn't smile.

"I made some calls." I sidled in next to him, taking a stool at the bar of the Burger Palais, which was now absorbing the full brunt of dinnertime. "Was I supposed to meet you?"

"No, but I knew where to find you."

"Then could you tell me where to find me? I seem to be having trouble getting a handle." I encircled his shoulders and gave him a quick squeeze—he just looked so down-in-the-mouth. "Have you found Jean-Charles?"

He shook his head. "Next time you run off on me, take me with you, okay?"

"Is that even possible?" I motioned to the bartender for a glass. Having made good on his promise to return for the Wild Turkey 101, Romeo had already laid claim to the bottle. "I hope you saved a drop or two for me."

"Could you stifle the glibness? You know what I mean."

"Glibness is my last defense against reality." Reaching across him, I grabbed the bottle by the neck and poured two fingers' worth into the double old-fashioned glass the bartender slid in front of me. She knew me well enough to have forgone the ice—my father had taught me ice just bruises good bourbon. I had no idea what that meant, but sometimes I took his advice on the off chance I might be missing some subtlety. Although, in my experience, Wild Turkey 101 was designed to hit you over the head, not sneak up on you. "Shouldn't you be slaving over a hot crime scene?"

"I left it in capable hands—the coroner and his staff are doing their thing. I figured my time would be better spent looking for answers."

"In the bottom of a bottle of bourbon?"

To his credit, he didn't hit me. Instead, he jiggled the ice in his glass. "Your Chef Bouclet is riding to the top of the suspect list. Don't you think it's odd that he is nowhere to be found?"

I refused to agree on principle, although he was right. "So, what do you think?"

"Like I said, we put an APB out on him. But, other than that, I haven't a clue. I was hoping you might have some insight."

While digesting that for a moment, I stood on the foot rail. Leaning over the bar, I snagged a dish of cashews. My stomach growled as I popped a few in my mouth, then slid the dish toward Romeo. "Not offhand."

"What about the note?" Romeo tossed that line in front of me like a kid with a cane pole hoping to catch a crappie.

I arched an eyebrow at him. "That's an over-broad question. *What* about the note?"

"Why do you think it said 'Lucky no more'?"

"Well, the two victims certainly ran though their allotment of luck. Getting smoked, the other broiled." I shivered—I couldn't help myself.

"You're deflecting. 'Lucky' was capitalized. . . ."

"We're back to that, are we?" I stared into my glass, but it was fresh out of tea leaves. "What beef would the killer have with me?" Romeo opened his mouth—I saw a quip lurking there, so I shut him down with a glare. "It must've been a typo."

"A typo?"

"Yeah, well." I swirled my drink around in my glass, careful not to spill even one small drop. "A writer is his own worst editor."

"Really?" He looked at me like I'd lost my mind. "Where'd you hear that?"

"Everybody knows it." I waved away any more on that topic. "Do you have an ID on the second body?"

"Yeah, that's why I texted you."

"You did?" I snatched my phone and squinted at the screen. Sure enough, his text was one of many I had missed. None from Jean-Charles. Nor any calls. "I didn't hear anything." I checked the switch on the side of the phone—it had flipped to silent mode. "Every time I stuff this thing into the holder, it flips to silent. Can't get used to it." I scrolled through the messages quickly—nothing that couldn't wait, even the half dozen from Mona—if it was really important, she would've found me. This time, I put the phone in my shirt pocket, even though the weight of it gapped the thin fabric away from my skin. Showing my cleavage, such as it was, wouldn't even cause a ripple in Silicone City, so I didn't worry about it. "Who was it?"

"Some guy named Richard Peccorino."

I caught myself before I snorted bourbon—been there, done that, hurt like hell. "Dick Peccorino? Sounds like a porn star. With that name, nobody'd have to kill me, I'd do the deed myself."

Romeo looked at me wide-eyed, blinking furiously. "Inappropriate." He tried to sound serious, but I heard the hint of a smile.

"Don't look so shocked. You know when under stress I have no filter." My hand shook as I raised the glass to my lips. The first hit of stout bourbon was the best, burning a fiery path down my throat, then exploding in a welcomed ball of fire in my stomach. Warmth shot through me—I found it relaxing. That should worry me, which it did—I just didn't have time to dwell on it. Finally, I sighed and lowered the shield. I could trust Romeo, and I was tired of being brave. "I'm scared. I don't know where Jean-Charles is. He could be in trouble."

"There's another way of looking at that."

Romeo soft-served his accusation but, although I'd pondered the possibility, coming from a member of the police, it hit me with all the subtlety of a sledgehammer. I raised my voice; I couldn't help it. "You really think he's a suspect? Why would he leave Christophe in the Burger Palais, a temporary babysitting arrangement to say the least?" Heads turned in our direction, and Romeo shushed me, which I only half-complied with. Words tumbled over each other, fighting to be formed and heard. "He'd have to be the dumbest killer on record to put two bodies in his kitchens."

"Or the smartest." Romeo blew out through his mouth. "Think about it—if you want to make yourself look innocent, make it look like someone is setting you up, why not do something people would be sure you wouldn't? It's brilliant, really. And the foreman saw Peccorino go up the elevator with Chef Bouclet."

"What?" This time, all I could manage was a choked whisper.

Romeo nodded and gave me a little shrug of helplessness.

"What about anybody else? Did the foreman mention anybody else going up to the restaurant?"

Romeo shook his head, which gave me steam.

"What about Teddie? He was there when I got there. Did the foreman mention him?"

"No, he said he was busy—no one really checks who's coming and going. It's a huge project, as you know . . . since you're the boss." Romeo took another sip of his hooch. The stuff was having an effect—I could see the red flush rising in his cheeks.

"Not the boss exactly, more of a nominal figurehead . . . none of the authority, all of the blame."

Romeo didn't buy it. "Why don't you have people sign in and such?"

I gave him a disbelieving look. "There're hundreds of people working there on a daily basis, and probably as many delivering products, consulting, inspecting. If we checked everyone, the logjam would be worse than the TSA line at McCarran on a Sunday."

"Still—anybody can come and go." Romeo insisted on whipping that dead horse.

"My point exactly." I tried to quell my rising panic. "Did Teddie give you a good reason why he was in Jean-Charles's kitchen in the first place? I would've asked him, but I don't trust him to tell me the truth anymore."

"Has it dawned on you that Teddie may have told you the truth from the beginning, and the truth just changed?" Romeo kept his eyes lowered, as if conjuring wisdom from a glass of serious joy-juice.

"I'm not willing to admit that possibility yet."

"Why?"

Defeat forced the air out of my lungs in a long, heavy sigh. "Because then I couldn't be mad anymore. I want to be mad."

"Anger only hurts you." When Romeo finally looked at me, I could see the concern there. Everyone close to me had been shoveling the same shit my way . . . perhaps it was time I listened.

Not yet ready to completely concede, I squeezed his arm.

"He told me he wanted to clear the air with the Frenchman," Romeo said. "To make sure his intentions were honorable."

That poked a hole in the thin veneer over my anger. "Just my knight-in-shining-armor. Am I lucky or what?"

Romeo glanced at me, then ground to a halt when he ran headlong into my not-so-happy face. "Look, I don't like this any more than you do. It's my job to chase all the leads. I ask the questions and write down the answers, until they lead me to the truth."

I jumped all over that. "So you don't believe Teddie either?"

"I didn't say that." Romeo looked like he wanted to run. Instead, he shook his glass, bringing to my attention that it was empty. "Rein it in, Lucky."

I ignored him. "Surely, somebody saw someone other than Mr. Peccorino and Jean-Charles?"

"I've got half the force on it. We're having a hard time just trying to determine who was at the site legitimately. Once we narrow that down, we'll go through them one by one. You know how it goes—and it's going to take time."

"I got a feeling time is something we don't have with two bodies already and not even a whisper as to what's going on. Much less any leads." I took another sip of the bourbon, hoping for some clarity.

Romeo reached for the bottle to refill his glass. I nudged it out of his reach. He didn't complain. "I still can't get past the fact that you appear to be in the middle of this somehow." He seemed genuinely concerned.

Having no real answer and not wanting to speculate, I ignored him. "Any note with this guy?"

"Not that I found."

"So why a note at the first murder, and not at the second?"

"We got one smoked food service person and one broiled tech guy and no connection between the two, yet you're assuming we have one killer."

That sobered me right up. "I think that's a safe assumption."

"Based on what?"

"Fear." I took a couple of nice, large sips of bourbon as my brain freewheeled. Was a large sip still a sip? Or was it called something else—like the first sign of a drinking problem? "The idea of two killers running loose in my hotel is too horrible to think about. Isn't one enough?" I shot him a questioning look, but he knew me well enough to know a rhetorical question when he heard one. "Let's start looking for connections—it'll make me feel better. Tell me about Mr. Peccorino. You said he was a tech guy?"

Romeo glanced at the bottle of Wild Turkey, but didn't reach for it. Instead, he reached for the cashews and popped a couple in his mouth. "Mr. Peccorino . . ." Romeo pulled his note pad out of his inside coat pocket. After dabbing his thumb on his tongue, he used it to flip through the pages until he found the one he wanted. He began reading. "Richard Joseph Peccorino, born in . . ."

I waved him quiet. "If where he is born is relevant, I'll pay attention. If not, spare me that sort of thing and cut to the chase."

He shot me a scowl. "He was born right here, in Henderson. And at this point, I don't know what's important and what's not. He was here with the techie group that's just ramping up their little get-together at your hotel."

"Techie group? The Babylon? You mean the guys from UC-Berkeley?" It was my job to at least be aware of every group meeting at the Babylon, whether they were my personal responsibility or not. My young assistant, Brandy, had handled the scientists, as I recalled. The topic of their meeting escaped me—I'd probably read it at some point, but hadn't understood. Not at all unusual—most technology was beyond my meager geek skills.

Romeo nodded.

"How did a geek end up basted and broiled in the kitchen of a restaurant in a hotel that isn't even open yet? And why was he with Jean-Charles?"

"Both good questions," Romeo said quietly.

I couldn't disagree, so I searched for benign possibilities. "Far from prying eyes?"

"Maybe. But it's an awful long way to go, and a fairly dramatic presentation, don't you think?"

"A message in the method." I deflated. Of course, he was right. This would have to play out to its logical conclusion—and Jean-Charles would be under suspicion until he stopped acting guilty.

I threw a pleading look at the young detective. "What else can you tell me about Richard Peccorino? Anything you can give me, any possible connection, would sure help."

"That's all I got. At the time of his murder, all of his colleagues were in a meeting, one that he was supposed to attend. None of them are suspects, so, I've made an appointment to talk to them all tomorrow—I spoke with one on the phone just a bit ago, and he's already pretty oiled, along with all his cohorts, so I thought tomorrow would be better." Romeo flipped his note pad shut and put it away. "Do you have any idea how long it's going to take just to bring Peccorino down to room temperature?"

I didn't know what that had to do with anything, and I didn't ask—I have a delicate stomach.

"The coroner can't even touch him yet. He said putting a scalpel to him would be like sticking an overheated sausage."

"I could've done without that visual, thank you." I threw back the rest of my bourbon, hoping it held the bile down where it belonged.

Romeo motored on as if he hadn't heard a word. "Hell, it was hard enough putting a name to him. I'm just getting into the meat of it." He cringed.

I tried not to smile, I really did.

Romeo rubbed his eyes and refused to smile. "God, the more I'm around you . . ."

"Your goose is cooked." I nudged his shoulder with mine.

"You are seriously sick—if you see any guys in white jackets, you better head the other way." This time, he couldn't hide his grin.

"Everybody in Vegas is running from something. Why should I be any different?"

Romeo turned so I could see his look of wonder. "What? Cynicism from you, the head acolyte in the Order of the Perpetually Cheerful?"

"Cynicism? No. Reality. Whether it is cold winter weather or a last name that ends in a vowel, everyone here has left something behind."

"Maybe so." Romeo sipped his drink more slowly now. His eyes held a glassy look—Wild Turkey was pretty high-octane for Romeo's four-stroke engine. "I'd sure like to know what Ms. Richards and Mr. Peccorino left behind."

I deferred my emotion to his reason. "Maybe that would shed some light on how they got caught in a killer's crosshairs."

"I'll do the background stuff, work the databases, if you'll help me figure out some of this, connect the dots. These casino folks only want to talk to one of their own. They open up to you."

"It must be my special charm."

"No doubt."

"I did find out an interesting tidbit from Chef Gregor." I told Romeo about the truffle.

"So Fiona took a look, here in the kitchen, saw the truffle was not as advertised, then took it to Gregor?"

"That's what Gregor said."

"Can you check the video feeds to confirm?"

"On my way over here, I called Jerry. It only took him a few minutes, since I had the location and the time. Gregor's story checks out."

"And Fiona. Why'd she run to Gregor?"

I took a stab at an answer although I was flying blind. "She knew he'd have a cow, and the missing truffle put the Bouclets on the hotseat. She wanted Desiree's husband and her business. People have killed for less."

"Good point. Let's try to prove that, although with her dead, we may never know why she did what she did. Where'd she go after meeting Gregor?"

"Out the back to a rendezvous with her killer."

"Well, we tie up the time of death pretty tight then. I'm checking alibis. That's the best I can do right now." Romeo backed off his stool. "Keep poking around, okay? But stay out of any kitchens. They can be bad for your health."

CHAPTER 8

*A*FTER I sent Romeo home with a full-blown hug right there in front of everybody, which made me feel better but embarrassed him, I cleared our tab, then wandered back to the kitchen, which was firing on all cylinders to feed the crowd out front. I didn't know what I was looking for. Comfort? Answers? A thread to follow? Some hint of the deadly game being played.

Seeing Rinaldo at the grill hurt my heart. Every member of the staff moved with shared syncopation—calculated efficiency, their tasks ingrained, their movements by rote. I watched for a moment, trying to learn the steps to a dance I didn't know, set to music I couldn't hear. Finally, I gave up, judged the flow, then picked my time to ease into the fray, making my way toward the back and Jean-Charles's office.

Expecting it to be deserted, I paused in surprise to see Desiree and Christophe sitting on the floor. Desiree faced me, her attention on her nephew.

The boy, on all fours, his rear pointing skyward in my direction, hunched over a drawing. Sensing my presence, she raised her eyes to mine. Christophe must've felt his aunt's attention shift.

"Papa?" He whirled around.

The hope in his eyes fled when he saw me. His smile turned down and his lips quivered. Pushing himself to his feet, he rushed to me and clung to my legs.

Reaching down, I grabbed him under his arms and lifted him into mine. He settled nicely on my hips, his hand fisting in my hair. "Oh, Lucky, where is Papa?"

I stroked his hair—I could still smell the baby soap from last night's bath and giggles. Life—it could turn on a dime. "I wish I knew, baby. We'll find him."

Desiree stood and brushed down her slacks. Of course, being French, she still looked impeccable—except for the worried crinkle between her eyes, and her shoulders, which bowed, her posture sagging like a clothesline holding too much laundry.

"You're staying at Jean-Charles's?" I confirmed.

She nodded once. "I have arrived so suddenly, I have not been there yet, so I don't know where his house is. I've spoken with my daughter, Chantal. She said she can direct me, but of this, I am not so confident."

"I'll take you there. Do you have a suitcase?"

"In Jean's car." She shrugged and tried to smile.

"Too bad you don't have a tracking device in the thing." With the boy clutching my neck, I gave a nod toward the front of the restaurant. "Let's go. You two must be beat."

A look of confusion flashed in the Frenchwoman's eyes—she suffered from the same idiom affliction as her brother—but I didn't feel the need to explain. "We'll take one of the limos."

THE BABYLON'S VALETS WERE UNCTUOUS, IF THEY WERE ANYTHING. I should know, I'm their boss, and as such, I tended to get a bit more bowing and scraping than the average Joe, which didn't make me happy. As many times as I'd told them it should be the other way around, they still dropped everything to meet my needs. Tonight was no exception. The head valet caught sight of me before we'd had a chance to walk out the front doors and made a beeline in my direction.

I turned to Desiree, who clutched her nephew's hand. The boy had just a light polo shirt on. And his aunt's cotton one wouldn't provide much warmth in the cool wind, either. "It's chilly outside. Neither of you are dressed warmly enough for the cold desert nights this time of year. Let me go see about a limo." I glanced at the tangle of cars out front. "It may take a few moments to maneuver through the traffic. When it is out front, I'll come get you."

When I stepped through the door, the head valet gave a signal like a conductor cuing the symphony. In the darkness, a pair of headlights blinked on. The car couldn't move, though, it would have to wait for the running valets to clear a path.

"I'm going back inside to wait with my friends."

The head valet nodded, his eyes watching the limo. "Yes, ma'am. It shouldn't be but a few minutes. A busy time right now."

I didn't feel the need to engage in further obvious observations. As I turned, my eyes searched through the glass doors for Desiree and Christophe. They waited where I'd left them, but someone else had joined them. A trim figure in chef whites, with short dark hair, knelt down in front of the boy. Chitza DeStefano reached out and touched his cheek. The boy ducked his head but didn't cower back—he didn't seem afraid. Of course, Christophe Bouclet was a resilient spirit; at least, what I'd seen of him so far indicated as much. The chef said something to the boy, then pushed to her feet. With a nod to his aunt, Chitza eased into the crowd and disappeared from sight.

Pushing through the door, I smiled when Christophe caught sight of me and a grin split his face. He pulled away from his aunt and launched himself into my arms. As I cradled him against me, it occurred to me that he gave me comfort and strength when I intended the opposite. "Did you know that lady talking to you?"

"No."

"What did she say?"

"She told me I look like my mother." He pulled his head back and eased his hold around my neck so he could look at me. "Did you know my mother?"

"I would have liked to."

He gave me a sweet smile as he laid his head on my shoulder. "Me, too."

My heart cracked a little. "Do you want to ride in a big car?"

Christophe nodded against my cheek.

"I'll take you home."

"To papa?"

"I don't know. But your aunt will be there until your father comes home."

"And you." Even though his voice was small and tired, the statement was clear—he wasn't asking.

I didn't think sleep was in my near future, but I also didn't think it appropriate to say so. Nevertheless, the thought made me tired.

Out of the darkness, one of the Babylon's limos eased into to view, then settled at the curb in front of me. With a tilt of my head, I motioned Desiree to follow me outside. The valet bowed and, with a glistening white smile, brandished the door. "Please, Ms. O'Toole, allow me."

"Thank you." At my nod, Desiree preceded me into the car, disappearing into the cavernous interior. Once settled, she reached for her nephew. I passed the boy to his aunt. As I bent to lower myself into the car, Paolo, the Babylon's head chauffeur, bounded around the front of the car, muscling the valet off the door handle.

A short, dapper man with jet-black hair combed straight back, smiling dark eyes, and a thousand candlepower grin, Paolo bowed dramatically. "Ms. O'Toole, allow Paolo."

I slipped the valet a twenty and turned my tired smile on Paolo. Even at this hour, his pants held a sharp crease, his shirt and jacket were unrumpled. A twenty-five-year service pin, his only accessory, sparkled in his lapel. Just standing there, he oozed so much energy, I felt that if I grabbed his hand, my hair would stand on end. "Are you driving us tonight?"

"But of course!" He gave a smart, efficient nod, which, due to the frequency with which he trotted it out, had probably become a learned tic.

"Great," I said, as I lowered myself into the car. I loved Paolo, I really did, but in anything other than small doses, he wore me out. Somewhere in his DNA lurked the solution to the world's energy crisis.

The door closed with a thunk, plunging us into relative darkness. Window tinting dark enough to attract attention from even the most casual passersby was de rigueur in Vegas. The whole thing made me feel foolish—an impostor dashing the expectations of those hoping to catch a glimpse of someone important.

I sat facing forward and Desiree sat across from me, with her nephew sprawled across her lap.

Once ensconced behind the wheel, Paolo slid down the dividing glass and waited. I gave him the address and general directions. They were probably an insult: he prided himself on knowing the city better than the hordes of rats that infested the suburbs. Yes, we have rats, thousands and thousands of them, as large as toy poodles—some of the local wildlife *not* touted in the visitor guides. When I was a kid, I used to sit on the back porch at dusk and pick them off with my air rifle. Alas, with the growing human population, that was a magical childhood that my children would never know—assuming I ever had any children, which was in serious doubt at this point.

As we started rolling, I leaned my head back and closed my

eyes, savoring the first peace of the day. With the lights of the Strip fading to a glow behind us, I felt myself relax. After taking a few deep breaths and marshaling my panic-scattered thoughts, I felt the prod of unanswered questions. Raising my head, I focused on Jean-Charles's sister—the resemblance was striking, of course; after all, they were twins. "Do you feel up to helping me out a bit?"

"But of course." A perfunctory response—outward willingness covering Gallic coolness.

While we glided in comfort through the quiet residential streets of Vegas, I asked her all the questions I could think of, and all that were appropriate in the presence of a five-year-old. Desiree answered with a strong voice that didn't sound at all like prevarication—and I'd had a lot of recent experience with that, so I should have been able to recognize it when I heard it. As I wound down, defeated, she relaxed back into the comfortable seat cushions.

"I am so sorry, but I cannot think of anything about my brother that seemed unusual or stressed lately. He can handle very much, so for him to be upset would be very much out of the ordinary—I would've heard the tension in his voice. We are twins."

"A special bond, a connection the rest of us don't have. Or so I've been told." As I talked and thought, a miracle at this hour, I pulled my phone from its place at my hip and punched the screen to life. No messages, no calls. No joy. I put the thing back where I'd found it.

"We can finish each other's thoughts."

"I wish you could conjure each other's location." Glancing out the window, I recognized the neighborhood as Paolo eased the big car down the off-ramp of Summerlin Parkway, then stopped at the red light at Town Center Drive. We were close. "Did you know the chef who was talking with Christophe?"

"No." She shifted under the boy, who had fallen asleep across her lap. "She said her name, but it was not familiar to me. Why?"

I looked out the window, staring up at the stars. I felt like wishing on one of them, but I wouldn't know what to wish for first. "Just curious. None of my business, really. So, tell me about Adone."

She let out a long sigh. "He is impossible, brilliant, arrogant, a wizard in the kitchen."

"A bad boy." I nodded. I had one of my own. "You loathe each other."

"Loathe, what is this?"

I could see the pain on her face as the car passed under the street lamps. "Hate."

"Oh, no, I love him."

"Even worse." What was it with strong, smart women and the stupid romantic choices they made? Christ, it was almost a bad joke . . . almost."Adone was happy being Jean-Charles's second?" I raised my voice at the end in question.

"He knows how this business is. I am sure he was thankful for the chance—no one else would give him that, not after he spat on the Escoffier, especially on U.S. television."

"Change, it always makes some uncomfortable."

"In France, cooking is a religion."

"So, spitting on the Escoffier is like crucifying Christ a second time?"

Although she seemed a bit taken aback at my crude metaphor, she gave a curt nod and a wisp of a smile that dissipated quickly under the worry in her eyes. "This is so."

I could only imagine the bloodshed in this country that a change of such magnitude would bring. For an uncultured American, it was hard to imagine food enflaming such passion, but I took her word for it—the French were odd that way.

"And what was Fiona Richards's angle, if you don't mind me asking?"

Desiree looked out the side window. In the muted glow of distant lights, her expression was impassive, but she didn't look happy. The French may embrace a European freedom when it came to monogamy, but women were women, no matter their nationality. And sexual freedom always exacted an emotional toll —a piece of one's soul. When the one you loved chose another . . . that pain, I knew.

"Men, they are always thinking that having sex with a woman is a sign they are still wanted, they are still attractive." Her eyes sought mine. "But men do not understand, if the woman is not worthy, they have gained nothing."

Other than a good time, I thought, which might have been the sole goal, but I thought better of trotting that little observation out. "Some women will prostitute themselves for what a man can give—money, power, prestige, knowledge. But accepting the trade does not make a man a better man."

She nodded once. "But just because a man is weak does not mean he is not worthy of your love."

My personal jury had reached a different verdict, so I didn't offer a response. "So, what did Fiona want with Adone?"

"I am not sure." Desiree turned once again to stare out the side window, but I doubted she was admiring the passing landscape. "He is good in the bed." She gave me a half-grin, then glanced quickly down at her nephew—he was asleep, so she needn't have worried, but her concern was nice to see, nonetheless. "But it was something more—it does not take a special man to fulfill one's physical appetites."

Personally, I thought divorcing the physical from the emotional was a recipe for disaster, but, for once, my mouth obeyed my brain and the words remained unspoken. "More?"

"Yes, I thought it was the truffles. And when Jean told me there was some trouble with some of my shipments, I came immediately. Mine is a business built on reputation and an ability to deliver."

"You suspected Fiona Richards?"

Desiree's eyes flicked to mine, then back out the window. "She seemed the most obvious one to consider."

"Did you have a chance to talk to her?"

Again, the flick of a glance. "No."

A chill washed over me. For the first time tonight, my gut told me she was lying.

~

PAOLO EASED THE LIMO NEXT TO THE GUARD SHACK AT JEAN-Charles's gated community—I didn't remember the entrance being quite so grand. The guard had to step out of the hut and walk the length of the car to talk to me through the back window. I told him my name—luckily Jean-Charles had put me on his permanent list of allowed guests. "Have you heard from Chef Bouclet?"

The guard's gaze rose from his clipboard and held mine as he gave me a hard stare. "Not since he put you on this here list. You want I should call him?"

I almost said no, then I reconsidered. "Yes, yes, please. Try his cell. You have the number?" If Jean-Charles was avoiding my calls, which the fact that when I dialed his number it rang once, then flipped to voicemail, would indicate, perhaps he wouldn't be so cavalier when it came to a call from the security guard assigned to guard his house . . . and his child.

"Yes, ma'am."

As the guard turned his back and ducked into his little shack, I urged Paolo to move forward so I could watch and hear. He eased the car forward, the front bumper almost touching the closed gates, but he managed to maneuver me close enough as the guard picked up the phone and dialed.

Desiree met my eyes as we waited through one ring, two, three . . . We both whirled when the guard said, "Chef Bouclet? Yessir, yessir, your family's fine. No, your house isn't burning down, no one has broken in. Why? There's this lady . . ."

I launched myself through the open window. Hanging half out

of the car, I grabbed the phone from the guard and pressed it to my ear. "Jean-Charles? Are you okay?"

The guard tried to reclaim the phone. Desiree shut him down with a sharp *non.* He recoiled, snatching his hand back as if a viper had bitten him.

"Lucky? Oh, Lucky." Jean-Charles's voice hitched. "I am okay. You will know all soon. Christophe?"

I calmed down and tried to wiggle back into the car, tough to do with one hand. "He is safe. Where are you? Are you okay?"

"I cannot say." He sounded tired, scared, a bit exasperated. "You must watch behind you."

"Look over my shoulder?"

"This is it." When he got like this, his English deserted him. "Do not trust anyone."

"Jean-Charles, what the hell is going on?" I glanced at Desiree. Her stoic stare stopped me cold. "How can I keep everyone safe? How can I help, if I don't know what's going on? I don't understand any of this."

"You will. I can't say more. Somebody might be listening. I must go."

"Listening? Who?" I was having trouble keeping up.

"I will find a way to show you. I am only figuring it out myself."

I tried to wiggle more fully into the back of the car, but the phone cord brought me up short. "You need to tell Romeo what happened."

"He would not believe me. I must fix this."

"Fix what?" My head spun, my thoughts whirled. Desiree looked at me, and her stoic façade slipped into an intense look I couldn't read. She didn't reach for the phone.

"Please keep Christophe safe, and Chantal. Desiree, she is difficult, but she is my sister. You be safe. Keep looking over your shoulder. People are not what they seem."

"Jean-Charles, don't . . ." The line went dead.

Holding the receiver to my ear, I waited, willing his voice to return. When the dial tone sounded, I thrust the receiver back to the guard. "Thank you," I said, my manners in place, but my wits gone.

His brows lowered, he took the instrument, then backed away from the car. "Anything I should know?"

He would be horrified at all the things he didn't know. But I tried to smile as I shook my head. "Perhaps if you could alert the patrol to be on the lookout for anything unusual, that would help. There have been some . . . threats. The police are on it, but their manpower is stretched thin. They would appreciate your help, I know."

The guard nodded. "Yes, ma'am. The police are already here." He eyed the card I handed him, then punched a hidden button, and the gate eased open. With a wave, he motioned us through.

As we wound through the neighborhood, the trees shrouding the street, deepening the night gloom, my heart beat faster with the irrational hope we would find Jean-Charles at home. Stupid, I know, but hope springs eternal—I'm foolish that way.

I scanned the driveway for a car, the front of the house for signs of life, but hope fled as quickly as it had risen. Except for one lone light in an upstairs window, the house was dark, the driveway empty. A Metro cruiser lurked in the shadows on the opposite side of the street and down a bit. I didn't know whether that was a good thing or a bad thing, but I did take some comfort in the protection for the kids.

Using her cell phone, Desiree called her daughter, whispering a few hushed words. Lights sprang on, and within a few moments the front door flew open and the girl bounded out—brown curls like her uncle's, a guarded look like her mother's. With thin-limbed teenage energy, she took a few strides, then grabbed her mother in a bear hug. It was a good thing I had taken Christophe, who now was dead weight in my arms, his head on my shoulder as he slumbered. Kids could succumb to the siren call of sleep with singular speed anytime, anywhere. A skill that adulthood, with its worries and demands, banished. I felt sleep niggling at me, but with frazzled emotions and tangled thoughts, that so wasn't going to happen.

Chantal looked at me over her mother's shoulder, her eyes wide with confusion. "The police were here. They had a piece of paper. Did Mother tell you?"

Desiree glanced at me, then her gaze slid from mine with a guilty look. Jean-Charles implied I could trust her, but she wasn't making it easy. "No, what did they say?"

"They looked in Uncle's office and through his room and the kitchen."

"I'm sorry you were here alone." I smoothed a curl from her forehead. "Did they take anything?"

"Nothing." Her voice cracked as her brave front crumbled. "Where is Uncle? What is going on? Something is wrong, no?"

"Have you heard from your uncle?"

Before the girl had a chance to answer, her mother cut her off. "Come," Desiree announced. "We should get inside."

Their arms looped around each other in the casual yet fierce embrace of parent and child, Desiree and Chantal turned in unison and ambled toward the light streaming though the open door. Heads bent together, Desiree talked to her daughter in hushed, somber tones. The glow in the dark reminded me of the light at the end of the tunnel. If only it were so. . . . Given recent events, the glow was more likely from the headlight of an onrushing train.

Desiree's voice was so low, I could barely hear. French such a beautiful language it made even death sound melodic. I strained to capture the words and to translate, but couldn't do much of either. Of course, I knew the story, or at least some of it. The rest, I'd have to discover when I could get Chantal alone and put the thumbscrews to her.

We trouped in tandem up the walkway. In the front hall, we

parted company. The two of them disappeared through the kitchen toward the family room in the back of the house, while I turned and headed up the stairs with Christophe still slumbering in my arms. I welcomed the growing silence as the sound of their voices dimmed with the distance.

Christophe's bedroom was the second right at the top of the stairs—if I remembered correctly. When I flipped on the overhead light, the pile of stuffed animals looking at me with their vacant stares confirmed my memory was indeed accurate.

Memories. I felt the echo of last night as I laid Christophe in bed, gently taking off his shoes and pulling the covers over him. Removing his clothes wasn't going to happen. He looked so peaceful—I didn't have the heart to awaken him. As I tucked the blanket around his chin, I smoothed the hair back from his eyes. He blinked to a moment of consciousness and gave me a smile that pierced my heart. I bent and kissed his forehead. "Sweet dreams, sweetie."

His lids closed. "Pancakes? With happy faces?"

I had shown him how to make a smile out of chocolate drops. Had it only been this morning? It seemed like a lifetime ago. "Happy-faced pancakes, of course."

"With Papa," he whispered as his lids fluttered closed.

Turning the light off, I left the door open. If Christophe had a bad dream, I wanted to hear him. My hand trailed along the bannister as I retraced my steps down the stairs, the memories of last night echoing around me. Laughter as Jean-Charles tickled his son. Shouts of joy and competition during a hotly contested game of Wii tennis. Chantal, a curious mix of child and young adult, trying to remain above the childishness, but giving in eventually. A vigorous bath time for Christophe . . . with bubbles.

Then adult time. With a different kind of bubbles.

At the foot of the stairs, I turned right, pushing open the double louvered doors to Jean-Charles's suite. The smells of the night lingered—the scented candles; his cologne, sensual and earthy; the musk of sex. I breathed them in. Savoring, absorbing, remembering . . . dreaming.

A dangerous game, and I knew it. I was hurt, needy, reaching for hope, hoping for love. So willing to buy into the fantasy.

Leaving myself open, raw . . . had I misjudged?

How well did I really know Jean-Charles? He'd told me people are not what they seem. Who? Who had something to hide or a grudge worth killing for? Adone? He'd already voiced his lack of affection for Jean-Charles. And I couldn't say I blamed him. When folks climbed on high horses, I got testy, so I understood the young chef's frustration. But kill?

Who else had a bone to pick? Desiree? The others? The killer could be any of them. And Jean-Charles, could I trust him? *Should* I trust him? My track record proved I was way too trusting. And now, was I grasping at straws, desperate for someone to be who they said they were?

God, I couldn't even trust myself.

I sat at the foot of the bed and lay back. Staring up at the ceiling, I ran my hands over the beautiful fabric as if making a snow angel. The textures, the smells, the sounds, all hit my heart and opened me wide.

Why was life so . . . confusing, upsetting, hard? It wasn't supposed to be this way, was it? Being a grown-up really could suck.

And here I had thought that when I became a grown-up, I would have all the answers. But all I seemed to have right now were questions. What was going on with Jean-Charles, Fiona, Desiree, Adone, Chef Gregor, and a scientist from UC-Berkeley? And with two murders, this certainly seemed to be about far more than a truffle, no matter the uniqueness. But if it wasn't about a truffle, then what?

A world-renowned chef, I seriously doubted Jean-Charles could be some closet murderer. Although Romeo had certainly seemed open to the idea, which I both understood and resented. I had to admit that each of us has murder in us—even me. My mother pushed me tantalizingly close so many times. Okay, that was a bit of hyperbole, but still, I could envision pointing the gun at someone and pulling the trigger. But it would take something incredible—protection of life and limb, of family.

Unwilling to resort to snooping through drawers and closets— the police had already looked, anyway—I closed my eyes.

What would push Jean-Charles to take matters into his own hands?

And why was I being drawn into the middle of this dangerous game? A tickle of fear prodded what was left of my rather spotty good sense. I squelched it.

Could Jean-Charles be protecting his sister's reputation? Possible, but would he sacrifice his own in the process? Doubtful. No, there was something else going on—a high-stakes game I could just catch a faint scent of. Desiree's circumspection didn't make me feel any better.

She knew something; I could feel it. Where were the thumb-screws when I needed them?

Torture was something the French would understand.

CHAPTER 9

I PUSHED myself to a seated position, swiping the hair out of my face. Worry about the future only wasted the present. Time to pull on the big-girl panties and get to work.

Launching myself to my feet, I strode out of the room, leaving behind my trip down memory lane . . . and the whiny pansy-ass I'd become. What had happened to the gal who shot first and asked questions later?

When I hit the family room, I felt the old piss and vinegar flowing through my veins. It felt good to have me back.

Chantal and Desiree huddled together on the couch, a nice, warm flame burning brightly in the fireplace. Desiree looked up as I walked in. "Christophe, he is okay?"

"For the moment. He wants his father." I parked myself in front of the blaze. The warmth enveloped me—I hadn't realized how cold I was. Chilled to the bone by too little food, too much emotion, and a lethal dose of worry.

"Yes, with no mother, his father is most important." Desiree glanced at her own daughter. "Jean and I, we have not made the best choices for our children." She brushed back the hair from Chantal's forehead.

"You both do the work of two," Chantal whispered.

"I thought Jean-Charles's wife died in childbirth."

"Oui." Desiree's face clouded. "It was horrible. So sudden, she died in Jean's arms. Her mother, none of her family, got to say good-bye."

"They weren't there for the birth?" Warmer now, I eased a bit further from the fire.

"They live very far away, several hours outside of Caracas. They'd made plans to come the following week. We had not met them before—Jean's courtship and wedding, it was very fast. All fire and heat."

"That didn't burn out fast," I finished the thought.

"No. They were very much in love." Desiree paused as she gave me an appraising look, then nodded. "I am glad Jean found you. We have been worried. He has not had another since his wife died."

"The heart can take a long time to heal."

"I think it was not so much the heart, but the pain. So much loss." Desiree brushed a curl out of her daughter's eyes. "Christophe was very early. We almost lost him, too. Jean was frantic. I think my brother has been afraid to love again."

That made perfect sense to me.

"It was all over so fast."

My heart felt heavy for all of them—and I needed to explore a painful present on top of a horrid past. "We need to talk." I caught Chantal's attention. "Could you leave us alone for a bit?"

The girl eyed me, then shot a questioning glance at her mother. At Desiree's nod, she pushed herself slowly to her feet, then sauntered out of the room with slouchy indifference, telegraphing her irritation at not being included in the grown-up discussion. Teenagers. The fact that the human race hadn't died out years ago bore testament to a parent's boundless love and endless patience.

I watched her until she was out of earshot, then I hit her

mother with both barrels. "Your brother is a suspect in a double murder investigation, and you are not being honest with me." I kept my voice low, but I couldn't keep it from shaking with worry, anger, and probably a host of other emotions I didn't want to think about.

"Double?" Through her fatigue, she looked genuinely shocked.

"Mmmm, a scientist from a premier university."

Her brows crinkled. "What could he have to do with this?"

"I haven't a clue. This whole thing is a mystery, but your brother is in more than a bit of trouble."

To her credit, Desiree didn't try to deflect. She didn't even deny my accusation; she just looked tired. She rose and stepped around the bar. I warmed myself by the fire and cooled my heels while she found a suitable wine and uncorked it. Dispensing with pretense, she chose two of the largest glasses, filling each to within a millimeter of the brim. Sort of the French version of doing shots, I guessed.

Handing me a glass, she stepped in beside me, absorbing the warmth. "Truly, I do not know what is going on." She took a sip of her wine and practically groaned. "Jean, he has impeccable tastes."

I wasn't going to be sidetracked by Jean-Charles's likes and dislikes. "You have your suspicions, though."

"*Oui*." She narrowed her eyes, staring steely-eyed into the past or the future—it was hard to tell which. "How do I know I can trust you?"

I fixed her with a blank stare. "Jean-Charles has impeccable taste."

Her head swiveled in my direction. She shot me a sardonic grin. "Touché."

"I make good happy-face pancakes as well."

Her brows crinkled. "What is this?"

"Deflection." When the confused look remained, I waved it away. "A poor attempt at humor to break the tension. Never mind.

Why don't you tell me what you know, and what you suspect, and we'll try to put some pieces of this puzzle together."

She weighed my suggestion for a moment, then gave in. "About a month ago, some of my clients started complaining. I did not know what to do with this. I have never had an unhappy customer."

"Never even one dissatisfied customer?" My voice rose in admiration. "You wouldn't be looking to change careers, would you? Perhaps to hotel management?"

She smiled thinly. "When your products are few, and your suppliers are your friends, keeping customers happy is not difficult." She pressed her nose into the bowl of the wineglass and inhaled deeply. An ingrained ritual I wasn't even sure she was aware of doing. "So, when I hear complaints, I am confused. I call Jean. He asks some questions for me. It seems that my shipments are being tampered with. I don't know where or how."

"And what did your brother suggest?" I tried to keep my sinking heart out of my voice.

"He wanted to track the shipments."

"How?"

Desiree looked like she was mulling over exactly how to explain it, so I waited.

"What do you know about cold-chain tracking?" She smiled at my blank stare. "Okay, well, it's actually technology that has been around for a while. You have a corporate ID badge, correct? One that you hold in front of a scanner?"

I nodded.

"That's the same technology. It's called RFID and involves radio waves. When the tag is read by a reader, information can not only be read, but imprinted as well. So, if I put a tag on one of my shipments, every point at which it is within one hundred feet of a reader, that information will show up on the tag." She signed and shook her head. "I am making this very simplistic, but you understand, *non?*"

I picked up the train of thought. "So, when the package arrives at its ultimate destination, all of the waypoints along the way can be discerned from the RFID chip."

"In theory." She swirled the wine in her glass while she talked. "The United States government is very interested in using the technology to keep the food supply in this country safe from terrorist tampering. They have installed readers almost everywhere."

That sounded very scary—like the cameras on the city streets watching us all. "So your original shipments weren't tracked?"

"It is an extra expense." Filling her mouth with wine, she swished it around before swallowing. She gave an almost imperceptible gesture of appreciation. "And there was no need, at least for most of them."

"How much information can be stored on the chips?"

Desiree took another sip of wine. "It depends on the type of chip. Most of it is out of my ability to understand. But I know that the chips can be read from a hundred meters or more and can be read through the packaging." She looked at me, pausing. "They can even be implanted in humans."

"Scary."

"Much of life is like that, *non?*" She held up her glass, the fire lighting the blood-red wine. "Good things can be used for bad purposes."

I couldn't argue—the line between good and bad was razor-thin.

"My brother, he suggested his new chip, so we could see exactly where the packages went. Maybe this way we could determine who was altering them."

"And in doing so, you stumbled into something a bit bigger." I swirled the wine in my glass—carefully, as Desiree had overfilled it.

Desiree acknowledged the obvious with a quick shrug, which I caught out of the corner of my eye.

"So," I continued. "Which shipment was the first to be chipped?"

"We started with the truffle."

"Chef Gregor's? The white Alba?" I thought perhaps that was redundant, but she sidestepped my ignorance, which I thought nice.

"This is the one." A look of disgust pinched her face. "Truffles, especially one like that, must be kept cool and used within days of their harvest. And it was of exceptional quality, so I thought the chip a good thing." Her Gallic shrug and pursed lips, turned down at the corners, exaggerated and expressive, reminded me of her brother, which hit my heart.

I slammed the lid on my emotions—they never facilitated logic. "And what about Fiona? When did you speak with her last?" As I raised my glass to my lips, I kept my eyes fastened on her over the rim.

Desiree left my side in front of the fire and stepped behind the bar to refill her glass—and stall for time. Her inner struggle marched across her face as she concentrated on the task at hand. Finally, she apparently reached some conclusion. When she looked at me, her face was calm, her eyes clear.

"I arrived only this morning, early."

I lowered my glass without taking a sip. Apparently, I had been holding it there poised, wondering, waiting, and forgetting about the wine.

"I was angry to begin, and I'd had many hours to get even angrier—it is a long flight from Provence."

I sensed she was a woman who didn't like to be prodded, so I didn't.

"I went looking for Fiona." She stopped for a moment. I thought I saw her shiver. She rubbed her arm with her free hand. "I found her." Desiree's voice dropped to a whisper. "In the food truck." When she looked up at me, her eyes were haunted. "She died before I could get a knife and cut her loose."

"You were there?"

"*Oui.*" A tear trickled from the corner of her eye. She wiped it away with an angry swipe.

"Did you see anyone?"

She shook her head.

"Who knows about this?"

"My brother. That's what we were talking about when you brought Christophe."

Desiree's hand shook as she lifted her glass to her lips and drank deeply. She dabbed at her lips with a napkin as she set her glass down. "The box the truffle had been in was there."

"With Fiona?"

She nodded once, her curls bouncing, then recoiling. Why I noticed that, I don't know. "The Alba was not. The box Jean had stored it in was open, the truffle gone. I took the box and gave it to him."

"What did he say?"

"Nothing, really."

"Was the tracking chip with the box?" I didn't know enough to even sound intelligent.

"No, but the truffle had been in Jean's refrigerator—at least that's what he told me. I assumed he had taken the chip already." She looked at me, her eyes large and unblinking. "I am in trouble, *non?*"

"Did you kill Fiona?"

Desiree's head whipped back as if I'd slapped her. Her anger flared and then was gone—like touching a flame to gunpowder. She answered me with a word in her native tongue, not one I was familiar with. However, delivered with force, her meaning was clear. "Of course not! But I feel responsible. I tried to save her."

"Then you don't have much to worry about." I glossed right over the fact that the police would take a dim view of removing evidence from the scene of a homicide. And they wouldn't like the fact Desiree did sort of a hit and run by leaving the scene and not reporting the death. I had no idea how to spin all that with Romeo, not that it was my problem. But if I wanted her help, keeping her out of jail seemed like a good place to start. Assuming I trusted her in the first place. Which, at this point, wasn't a given.

As I thought, I remembered the wine in my hand. My thoughts elsewhere, I swirled the liquid, sloshing a bit on my hand. Ignoring it, I stuck my nose in the bowl of the glass and sniffed. The full bouquet, fruity and bold with hints of spice and smoke, captured my attention. I sniffed again, then took a sip. "My God, what is this?"

"A very nice Bordeaux." She eyed me blandly—so much like her brother.

"No, not a Bordeaux . . . a Burgundy. But, not that, either. Too smooth. Rounded edges. Not the *terroir* you folks in France are so hung up on." I shook my head as I took another sip, moving the liquid around in my mouth before swallowing. Holding the glass to the light, I swirled it to give the wine some air, then stuck my nose in the bowl and breathed deeply one more time. "A California pinot. Sonoma Coast?"

Desiree smiled. "Adobe Road, 2009. You have the nose."

I didn't gloat—unusual for me. To be honest, my ability to distinguish wines came more from a lifetime of consumption than a talented nose—not something I thought gloat-worthy.

And sniffing a connection between newfangled technology, Jean-Charles, and a dead UC-Berkeley geek in his oven, didn't take a brilliant nose, either.

WHEN I STRODE THROUGH THE FRONT ENTRANCE LOST IN THOUGHT, the tumult of the Babylon firing on all cylinders sucker punched me with the here-and-now. While I'd been off searching for pieces to a puzzle, life had gone on. As I struggled to catch up, I stepped to the side out of the fray and scrolled through the messages on my phone. Slowly, the music piped through the overhead sound system filtered into my consciousness. Teddie's song. The one about me. I made a mental note to find the person responsible for putting it in the playlist and have them shot at dawn.

I blew at a lock of hair that tickled my eyes. There was that murder reflex again. I probably should worry about my escalating homicidal imaginings, but they were so far down on my current list of unimaginables, I just couldn't work myself into much of a lather.

"Ms. O'Toole? Excuse me, please."

I looked up into the dancing black eyes of Sergio Fabiano, our front desk manager. Dark and Mediterranean, he had the good looks of a movie star and the body to match. He also had the irritating habit of flicking the hair out of his eyes with an exaggerated toss of his head. In addition, he was a bit too fastidious for my taste, not that he cared—he always had a bevy of women swooning around him like a parlor-full of Victorian ladies with the vapors.

"Sure. What can I do for you?"

He leaned in close to me as if he feared someone could overhear a word we uttered. The chaos swirling around us took care of that possibility, but still he leaned closer, his hand on my arm, squeezing in a conspiratorial way. "There was a beautiful young lady"—he gave me a knowing look— "asking at the desk for the Sodom and Gomorrah Suite—if you understand my meaning. The guests in the suite also are wanting a case of duct tape, a twenty-foot ladder, a nail gun with a variety of nails in differing lengths, a radar speed detector, a timer accurate to within a thousandth of a second, and a HD video camera, with high-speed capabilities." He ticked those items off on his fingers, apparently from memory, impressing the heck out of me. After this day, I couldn't remember what I'd had for lunch, or if I'd even *had* lunch. Sergio stopped and looked at me, wide-eyed, a confused look on his face. "What should we do?"

I could smell peppermint on his breath, which reeked of a premeditated personal space violation—a total turn-off. "Who's in the suite?"

"A Dr. Phelps is the registered guest."

"Doctor? Of what?" I learned not too long ago that an appellation didn't always come with the integrity and class it implied.

"He's a computer engineer." Sergio shrugged.

"My condolences. How much is his run-through? And what games is he partial to?" I switched my thoughts to the computation of his theoretical loss—an algorithm based on average bet and the game's particular odds. What I would spend on keeping him happy would be a fairly small percentage of what I could reasonably expect to make off him—that's the way the game was played. I cocked an eyebrow at Sergio. "I'm assuming he doesn't play blackjack with a group of friends? We don't need another group of MIT wannabes with a dream of cheating Vegas." The math geeks were always card-counters—we did our best to ferret them out and rescind their invitation to play at our establishment, or we put them under contract not to play blackjack if they had another game they liked, such as poker. Most folks thought gambling in a casino was a god-given right. Not so. And disabusing them of that notion usually fell to me. Am I lucky, or what?

"He's from UC-Berkeley, and we have no record of his gaming activities."

UC-Berkeley—way too coincidental. I bet he knew Richard Peccorino. This was the perfect opportunity for a little bit of casual sleuthing. "I'll take this one. You keep manning the desk."

Sergio looked relieved as he leaned back, leaving me alone in my personal space.

If Dr. Phelps didn't play in my sandbox, I wasn't inclined to play in his. His desires would go unfulfilled—a message I intended to deliver personally.

~

My father caught me waiting for the elevator to whisk me to the penthouse floor and the Sodom and Gomorrah Suite. "We need to talk." He sounded beleaguered, which didn't bother me like it normally would.

I snuck a glance at him—he wasn't looking at me, so he didn't catch it. "I'm not talking to you . . . not yet. First, I need to think of appropriate words longer than four letters."

Normally well pressed and impeccably put-together, with an air of confidence, tonight my father looked faded . . . almost human. The starch had not only abandoned his shirt, but his posture as well. A short man—I had him by nearly six inches, although at six feet, I was on the tall side—he normally walked with shoulders back and chin cocked, inviting a challenge and making him appear taller. Tonight, he carried none of that attitude, looking not only his size but also his age. Worry deepened the creases that bracketed his mouth and the laugh lines around his eyes. Had his salt and pepper hair suddenly sprouted more salt, or was I imagining that? For a moment, my defenses weakened.

He must've sensed my wavering. "Look, I know you've got a bone to pick with me. And I have an explanation—not sure you'll like it, but I can offer it, if you'd like. But can we do that later? I don't have the stomach for it now."

I relented. "To be honest, me either." I looped an arm through his. Someone had told me once I shouldn't let the employees see me being casual with my boss, but the Big Boss was also my father, and sometimes I just needed the connection . . . so, sue me. "You look like life is putting you through the wringer."

"Not life . . . your mother." He hitched up his pants—he'd been losing a bit of weight recently. I'd heard stress could do that— unfortunately not to me, or I'd be small enough to wear on a chain by now.

"With two dead bodies, I'd forgotten about twins and turkeys." Funny how murder could put other problems into proper perspective.

"Twins and turkeys?" My father shot me a harried look—one I could say I had never seen on his handsome, in-control, I-dare-you visage.

"Mother hasn't told you about her adventures today?" I tried to keep my voice steady. If my mother hadn't told him he was going to be the proud father of twins, there was no way I was going to step in front of the firing squad—and it was just like her to maneuver me into position to take the bullet.

My father looked confused and panicked. Inciting those emotions in others was Mona's best thing. I should know—I'd lived with her for, well, forever. I almost felt sorry for my father, but he chose her . . . he should've run before she threw the noose around his neck. "That woman hasn't told me anything. She keeps dropping hints. I tell you, there are days . . ." He shook his head.

"Tell me about it." I blew at some hair that tickled my eyes.

For the first time, he looked up and really gave me a hard stare. "Care to share? I've always been a willing shoulder." And he had. To muster anger toward the man who had always been my rock, even before I had been told of our family ties, took energy I didn't have. To be honest, I couldn't remember staying mad at him for long.

"You're part of the problems today." As the elevator doors dinged open, I stepped inside and held them for my father, who followed me in. "But we agreed to table it for now. Besides, I've got a problem that needs my attention on the penthouse level. Where can I drop you off?" I had been holding the doors, awaiting his response. I released them, letting them slide shut but keeping my finger poised over the buttons.

"It doesn't matter." He raked his hands through his hair, then rolled his head as if loosening his shoulder muscles. "Just killing time, avoiding Mona. I'm along for the ride.

"Along for the ride—that should be our theme song." I stuck my card in the slot and punched the button marked ph. "I'm thinking a long soak in the hot tub, a stint in the steam room, then a good massage might do wonders for your mood."

That got a hint of a grin out of him. "I don't think I'd be let off my leash for that long. Your mother is hell-bent on raising money for her bid for the open seat on the advisory board—I'm not entirely sure she understands it's an appointed position. Anyway, there was no talking sense into her, so I said I'd just write her a check." When he turned and looked at me, he had a hint of homicide in his eyes. "Do you know what she told me?"

I bit down on my smile. "I can hardly wait."

"She told me there was no way she was going to accept a bribe from one of the fat cats who had a vested interest in this city."

This time, I let my grin loose. I was pretty sure Mona had no idea what the term "vested" meant. "No saint like a former sinner."

"But that's like biting the hand that feeds you."

"Or shooting the goose who laid the golden egg." I almost felt sorry for him. "Now, we can continue trading clichés, or are you going to tell me what really has you all hot and bothered?"

"That's it, I don't know. I was hoping you could fill in some of the blanks."

While I thought through my options, I bought some time. This was like having "the talk" with your kid—I weighed how much to say and what I could skate past. "Can you give me a hint?"

"It involves Teddie." My father stepped to the side, putting some distance between us.

He needn't have worried. Relief flooded through me—I wasn't going to have to take a bullet for Mother today . . . at least, not yet. "Of course it does." I laughed as I fought the urge to run. "All you people will be the death of me. What do they say? Family, just a bunch of folks you wouldn't invite to dinner if you had the choice? Up to this point, I thought that a bit harsh, cynical even."

My father placed a hand on his chest. "Child, you wound me to the core."

"If you want my sympathy, I'd tone down the oversell." I glanced up at the floor numbers as they flashed by. The elevator slowed for arrival. "I believe it was your idea to offer Teddie his old job back. You turn loose the snake, you shouldn't be surprised when you get bitten."

"Point taken." He looked at me with "guilty" written in every feature. "Any suggestions?"

When the doors opened, I stepped through. "Why don't you come with me? I'm going to meet a UC-Berkeley engineer. Should be entertaining." I kept my voice passive, my face devoid of even a hint of what I knew would be waiting in the Sodom and Gomorrah Suite.

If I couldn't get mad at my father, at least I could get even.

CHAPTER 10

O/*N* OISE ASSAULTED us halfway between the elevators and the suite—music pulsing, male voices raised above it punctuated by excited shouts. Gales of female laughter. My father frowned in a worried sort of way.

I shot him a benign look as I raised my hand, fisted it, and pounded on the thick wooden door. We waited and, as I raised my hand to bang again, the handle turned and the door swung open. Quickly, I pushed the door further open and came face-to-face with a completely naked young woman.

"Hey." She waggled her fingers at me. Long blond hair, not a wrinkle in sight, and a figure so long and lean if she turned sideways she'd be hard to see, well, except for the requisite Vegas enhancements, those stood out like flags in a gale-force wind. She had the face of an angel and a body built for sin—a combination that could command at least a thousand a night. "Do you have the duct tape?" The way she asked made me think duct tape was part of her normal fun and games. Probably more than I needed to imagine.

"On the way," I lied. Leaning in, I looked over her shoulder.

The furniture had been moved to the sides, piles of priceless antiques stacked to make room for the crowd gathered in the middle of the large room. I counted ten young men, shaggy-maned, ubiquitous facial hair carefully trimmed in a variety of coverages, wearing trim designer jeans and stylish collared shirts —they didn't look like nerds. In fact, not one of them looked like they'd had enough time on this planet to have graduated from high school, much less earned the title "doctor"—the oldest looked to be barely thirty. They had convened in a knot in the middle of the large room, their heads pressed together. Bent over a laptop, the ones in the back of the pack on their toes, craning to see the screen, they all tried to outshout each other and the thumping music.

The naked girl shivered and rubbed her arms briskly—I didn't feel sorry for her.

"There's a nice robe in the bathroom." She gave me a blank look, and I pointed her in the right direction. I watched her walk away, her perfect, perky, tight little ass taunting me with its lack of jiggle and cellulite. The only way my ass would look like that would be to take a picture and Photoshop the hell out of it.

"What is going on here?" my father growled, his face flushing red.

I put a hand on his arm and my mouth next to his ear. I still had to raise my voice. "Let me handle this." Amazingly, he stepped to the side, crossed his arms, and relinquished the floor.

The boys had yet to acknowledge our presence. Turning down the music did the trick. The sudden silence hit them with the subtlety of a cattle prod to the butt. They bolted upright, heads swiveling, eyes searching, their expressions confused as if they'd just landed in a parallel universe.

"Is there . . . ?" My voice still raised, I stopped—without the music, I didn't need to shout. I regrouped and modulated my rising irritation. "Is there a Dr. Phelps here?" I asked in a normal tone.

The youngest-looking of the group separated himself from the gaggle. "That would be me." He wore huge, dark-rimmed, square-framed glasses in the current style. They slipped down his nose, and he looked at me over the top of them. Shaggy hair, goatee, and bedroom eyes, he looked cute enough to be accustomed to having his every demand met. "Do you have the things I requested? I called down to the front desk hours ago. I can't imagine what is taking so long."

Yes, every demand . . .

He had the glassy-eyed look of too much firewater. In fact, the whole group looked over-amped, not that that came as any surprise.

"Your list was rather . . . unusual. Would you mind telling me what you need all of that for?"

Before he could answer, two separate screams split the air—a female one from the direction of the bathroom, and a male one from high above. While the men turned and charged en masse toward the female in distress, my eyes turned upward . . . just in time to see a body peel away from the twenty-foot ceiling and plummet to the floor with a thud.

Dr. Phelps paused his charge and turned. Gesturing to his fallen comrade writhing on the floor, he gave me the look a brilliant man saves for fools. "The duct tape," he said, as if that was sufficient explanation.

My eyes grew slitty, but he didn't see the warning—he had turned and bolted after his friends.

I dropped to my knees next to the man on the floor, my father dropped in next to me. "Where's Mona's shotgun when you need it?" he growled.

"Shooting the guests would be a bit of a disincentive, don't you think?" Before I touched him, I let my eyes wander over the man who had landed in front of me. No odd angles to his limbs. His ribs expanded and contracted—I took breathing as a positive sign. I felt my father watching me. "Would you go check on the woman in the bathroom? And, just don't hit anybody, okay?"

"I'm not sure you should touch him," my father offered, as if he had experience with this sort of thing, which I doubted. He was like most of his Y-chromosomed brethren: the less they knew, the more positive they sounded.

The man had landed face first—his back covered with long strips of duct tape. I was afraid to roll him over.

My father gave me a condescending look as he pushed himself to his feet—apparently, there was an epidemic of stupidity going around. "For the record, I would never hit one of our guests." He retreated toward the bathroom before I could offer an opinion. While he sounded confident, I wasn't so sure—experience had taught me that if there was a scream-worthy problem in a bathroom it usually involved rodents, insects, or wild animals. How my father would handle that was anybody's guess, but it would be entertaining for sure. Hey, I'm shallow that way—I take my jollies where I can find them.

On my knees, trying to decide whether my father was right about not touching the fallen man, I called for the paramedics, then set my phone on the floor.

The man in front of me groaned. As he rolled over onto his back, he clutched his stomach and started laughing. His lip was bloodied and he'd lost at least two teeth, pieces of which he spit out with a wad of bloodied spit that dribbled down his right cheek as he turned to look at me. He blinked rapidly, then squinted, working to bring me into focus. "You're pretty. Are you the one they bought for me?"

"If I am, you got robbed."

He reached up and curled a strand of my hair around his finger, then gave me a shy smile. "You're my prize."

"For this little stunt?" I tugged at the duct tape. A short nail stuck through the end of one of the pieces. I pulled on a few other strands; they, too, held nails.

Letting go of my hair, he looked around and seemed confused to see the room empty. "Did they get it?"

"Get what?"

Before he could answer, shouts echoed through the room. My father's voice. Livid, with a hint of hysteria . . . not good. Perhaps I had overplayed my hand.

"Stay right there," I ordered the duct-taped man as I pushed myself to my feet, grabbed my phone, and bolted toward the bathroom. The lists of felonies already committed was long enough to land us all on *Nancy Grace.*

As I rounded the corner, I skidded to a halt.

The scientists huddled in the corner next to a shower stall large enough to rain on a serious parade. Dr. Phelps had a bloody lip, a hurt expression, and a growing red welt on his jaw, which he massaged tenderly. "He hit me." He nodded toward my father.

I was batting a thousand, which didn't make me happy. Turning, I growled at the donor of half of my DNA—a fact I wasn't too thrilled about right at the moment. "The one thing I told you not to do."

He glared at me thorough narrow slits as he cradled two white tiger cubs in his arms. Blood oozed from a line of scratches on one cheek, and he looked a bit shell-shocked. And pissed as hell.

When he took a menacing step toward the scientists, I put myself in his path. "Let me handle this." I turned to Dr. Phelps, stepping on my own urge to get physical with the twit. "Consider yourself lucky, I would've broken your nose."

I took a deep breath and counted to twenty. Then I counted to twenty again for good measure. I turned to my father. "I told you not to hit anybody." Like *that* was really going to help.

"He asked for it." When his eyes met my slitty ones, he backed down a bit, the red flush in his cheeks pinkening. He had the good sense to look remorseful as he proffered the cubs. "What should I do with these?"

"Just tell me their mother isn't within striking distance."

He shot a worried glance at the closed door to the steam room. A low, threatening growl answered my question.

"Great." I pulled my phone and hit Jerry's speed-dial. As it rang, a thought hit me and my heart jump-started. "Where's the girl?"

All the men in the room looked at the closed door to the steam room.

Still holding the phone to my ear as it rang, with two strides, I crossed the marbled expanse, then grabbed the handle and tugged open the door.

"Yo, girlfriend. Whatcha got?" Jerry said when he picked up— he sounded bored.

I tried to answer, but words failed as I stared at the young woman, now wrapped in a robe, cradling a large, white tiger across her lap.

The woman cast a beatific smile at me. "Isn't she sweet? Look, she loves to be rubbed behind her ears." Like an overgrown housecat, the tiger tilted her head and leaned into the scratching.

"Lucky? You there? What's the story?" This time, Jerry's voice held a bit of a worried edge.

As the wave of emotion receded, carrying my panic with it, I let out a huff. "Ah, Jerry. Where to start? To begin, I need an exotic animal vet to the S and G suite, probably a tranquilizer gun with enough juice to tame a wild tiger, although she's looking pretty happy at the moment."

Jerry started laughing. "If she's hungry, I got a thousand turkeys we could feed her."

I almost said a thousand and one as Teddie flashed through my mind, but I resisted. "That's a thought. Why don't you suggest that when you call the Secret Garden and see if they are missing some mammals?" Siegfried and Roy kept a full animal farm behind the public version of the Secret Garden at the Mirage. Replete with in-house vets and special organic food prepared on the premises, the huge building housed a multitude of white variants of several species—tiger, lion, and jaguar among them. The last time I was there, I thought there was also a bear, but it'd been a while. "And, since I'm sure they'll be grateful to get their man-eaters back with no public fanfare, see what you can get in trade." I couldn't imagine how the idiots broke in to steal the felines, but to be honest, I didn't really want to know.

"You got it, girl."

"And send the doc up here. We got a guy who took a nasty fall. Luckily, he's so shellacked, I think he just bounced, but I'd like him checked out, anyway. I've scrambled the paramedics."

"Sounds serious. Where'd he fall from?"

"The ceiling."

Silence greeted that admission. When he'd collected himself, Jerry added, "I'm not going to ask."

"Probably better that way. But you might want to let Sergio know we won't be needing the duct tape, nail gun, nor probably the radar gun." I rang off at his stunned silence, reholstered the phone, then addressed my father. Pointing to the shower stall, which was roomy enough to accommodate a large party, I ordered, "Put the cubs in there, but make sure the mama tiger can still see them. And if you cause me any more trouble, I'll give Mother another explanation as to how you came by those scratches."

My father shot me a grin and let me have my bit of fun—we both knew he deserved it . . . and that while I might have the bark, when it came to him, I lacked the bite. He rushed to the shower, set the cubs inside, and closed the glass door as he shot the mother tiger a glance.

My anger spiked as I turned on the huddled group of geeks. "Explanation? And it had better be good. You do not even want to think about how much jail time you're facing, not to mention a nice little bill for damages."

Dr. Phelps stepped forward. "My lip and my jaw."

I stepped in close to him—I had him by a couple of inches, which I could see made him nervous, so I went with it. "You don't want to call my bluff, really you don't."

As realization dawned, guilty school kids replaced the smug eggheads. "It's all really innocent. Really," one of the guys started.

Dr. Phelps shut him down with a stare. "This is my fault."

"Amazingly, that much I figured out all by myself." My anger fled as quickly as it had come—and to be honest, I doubted it had much to do with this whole silly scenario. I could handle this sort of thing in my sleep, and had hundreds of times. No, Teddie's reappearance and my family's complicity had me hard-wired to pissed off. Then that simmering murder thing and Jean-Charles on the lam. At least the goods doctors gave me a problem I could solve. I crossed my arms and fought back a derisive snort.. Just to make sure my father wasn't going to complicate things now that I was getting them under control, I snuck a glance at him. From the look on his face, he didn't see the humor, but he no longer looked ready to take a chunk out of someone. "What were you going to do with these animals?" I asked the assembled group.

"Chip 'em."

"Explain."

He vacillated a bit, but then gave me most of what I wanted. "I developed some new chip technology. Actually, it's been around for decades—I've just refined it a bit. It's used to track animals, shipments, that kind of stuff."

"RFID?" I said as if I knew what I was talking about.

"Yeah." A look of respect lit in his eyes, which was different. "I've developed a way to make it more economical while making it more useful, incorporating different kinds of data. It's all a bit esoteric."

I agreed with him—he had just exceeded my knowledge base by many multiples, but I faked it. "Impressive. Did you happen to know a Richard Peccorino?"

"Pecker? Sure. He's supposed to be here." All of a sudden, reality broke through his haze, and he looked wildly around the small room. "Where is he?"

I stepped closer to him and put a reassuring hand on his arm. "Dr. Phelps, you and I need to have a chat."

∾

TELLING SOMEBODY HIS FRIEND AND COLLEAGUE WAS DEAD, EVEN though I spared him the specifics, had me feeling drained and my stomach queasy—of course, no food and too much firewater didn't help. All things considered, he was coping pretty well, although he looked a little green. We had left the others under the direction of my father, to sort things out while we repaired to the living room and parked ourselves in facing wing-backed chairs, a good distance from where the paramedics and the doctor tended to Dr. Phelps's fallen comrade.

When Dr. Phelps leaned back, the two rear legs of the very expensive chair holding his weight, I didn't even cringe. But I leaned forward, and when he moved to put a booted foot on a delicate antique table, I eased it to the side. Dr. Phelps gave me a distracted look.

"Do you have any idea what Mr. Peccorino might have been doing in Chef Bouclet's kitchen at a hotel that isn't even open yet?" I put my elbows on my knees and rested my forehead in my hands.

"Not sure, exactly." Dr. Phelps pushed off with one foot, rocking further back in the chair. When he returned forward, he caught himself with the same foot and pushed off again. One hand clutched the arm of the chair. The other hand shook as he rubbed his eyes, then ran his fingers through his hair. The effects of the alcohol evaporated quickly under the assault of reality. Shell shock replaced the arrogance I'd seen in his eyes earlier.

Conjuring control I didn't know I had, I resisted making him stop rocking—if the chair broke, we'd add it to his tab.

"Pecker was working with JC . . . Chef Bouclet. . . . They were testing our new RFID chip."

149

"Testing?"

"Yeah, tracking various shipments, see how the chip held up, especially the power source." Dr. Phelps laced his fingers behind his head as he stared up at the ceiling and continued his rocking, like a kid with ADHD.

"Any idea why?"

That stopped his rocking—the front legs of the chair banged on the hardwood. Placing his hands on his knees, the kid leveled his stare at me. "To see if it works." He gave me one of those you-can't-be-that-stupid looks, which I chose to ignore, primarily because he was wrong—I could indeed be that stupid.

"And how did they hold up?"

He shrugged. "I don't know. I sure wish I did—the project is expensive, and our research funding hangs in the balance. Pecker was over at JC's to collect the chips and grab the data off them. God, I can't believe somebody killed him." With the back of his hand, he swiped at the tear that trickled out of the inner corner of one eye. "The guy wouldn't hurt anybody." He looked at me with haunted eyes. "He's really dead?"

I reached over and squeezed his knee. Stupid, I know, I just couldn't think of anything else to do or say. "How do you guys know Chef Bouclet?"

"I introduced them."

I whirled at the female voice. "Chitza?"

The chef moved with the grace and subtlety of a feline hunting dinner as she stepped over to Dr. Phelps, looking as if she wanted to bend down and give him a kiss. The almost imperceptible shake of his head stopped her and she recovered nicely with a hand on his shoulder. "I heard about Pecker. Are you okay?"

"Me? How about you? The two of you go way back." Dr. Phelps patted her hand on his shoulder.

"It's a shock."

"I can't believe he's gone," Dr. Phelps continued. "What could he possibly have done to deserve this?"

Chitza turned her cold eyes in my direction. "Do the police have the killer?"

"Not that I know of. They're working on it. I assure you they will do everything possible . . ."

She cut me short with a curt gesture. "Right. If there is a way to screw up an investigation, Metro will find it."

Even though I harbored an equally low opinion of the bulk of the police department, I didn't think trotting it out now would be a good idea. "Do you mind me asking how you two know each other?" I couldn't fathom how a chef would cross paths with science guys.

Chitza gave me a flat stare—she could probably turn me to stone if she wanted. She let a couple of beats pass before answering, as if to tell me she did in fact mind my asking. "I have taught some courses at Berkeley. The new science of food preparation has a basis in chemistry."

"Acids and alkalines and all of that?"

"To put it simply," she purred.

If the cooking gig went south, she could get a job writing thinly veiled insults.

"And you knew Jean-Charles?" I arced a questioning eyebrow at her.

She shrugged in a nonchalant sort of way. "The culinary world is small."

SADNESS OVERRODE ANY LINGERING SIZZLES OF ANGER AS I RODE the elevator down to the lobby, changed wings, then rode the elevator back to the penthouse floor, this time in the west wing, the private wing. With all current crises dealt with, or at least tamed for the moment, Dr. Phelps and his gang itched like a burr under my saddle. Boys will be boys and all of that. Personally, I thought that little maxim provided an excuse for the male of the species to continue acting like idiots long past the single-digit years, the only acceptable age range for idiocy, but nobody had consulted me and apparently, my opinion wasn't widely held.

My small, temporary abode was halfway down the hall on the right. The double doors at the end guarded the entrance to my parents' permanent address—they also had an elevator entrance inside, so they rarely used the hall past my place, unless they came for a visit.

The door to my apartment stood open, which didn't alarm me. Access to the floor was limited, and Mona and the Big Boss regularly availed themselves of my stocked bar while waiting for me to share news of the day. Although, since her pregnancy Mona had limited herself to club soda, amazing me with her selflessness. However, I didn't allow my guard to drop—I knew her newfound virtue would expire when those babies took their first breaths.

Today, my father and I had already shared enough, so I expected I'd find Mona curled on the couch, wanting to hear my side of the adventure.

I was wrong.

CHAPTER 11

A MAN stood at the wall of windows, his back to me, his hands clasped behind him. Although silhouetted by the lights of the Strip below, his shape gave him away. Every inch had been branded on my soul.

Teddie.

I paused in the doorway. One hand on the jamb, I bent and pulled off one shoe, then shifted feet and shucked the other one. I must've sighed as Teddie turned.

He acted like he wanted to say something. I beat him to the punch. "You take a lot of liberties, Mr. Kowalski, and you are trying my patience."

"What? We used to wander in and out of each other's places all the time." Amazingly, he sounded somewhat taken aback.

"Yes, but we are not the 'we' we used to be." I shook my head at the tortured syntax, but it was the best I could do.

"We could be that 'we.'" Teddie picked up the syntax baton. Oh, joy. He was trying to make nice. I wasn't ready to be friends. I was still trying to get over being a jilted lover and I thought "angry" was one of the steps along the healing path—right before homicide.

I tossed my shoes toward the couch, then stepped to the bar. Pulling a double old-fashioned glass from the shelf, I poured myself what most would describe as a healthy dose of Wild Turkey, although I doubted it had anything to do with my health —Teddie's health maybe, since he was within pistol range. Closing my eyes, I savored the hit as jangling nerves settled. Only then did I did I open my eyes and face Teddie. "Is that really what you came here to talk about?"

"It's burning a hole in my heart." When I started to fire off a retort, he stopped me with a raised hand. "Not the time. I know that. And—" He reached into his pocket as he walked toward me. Stopping barely short of too close, he pulled his hand from his pocket and showed me what was in his fist. "I found this in Chef Bouclet's restaurant." He extended an envelope—white, legal size, it looked normal, except for my name in an angry red scrawl— Jean-Charles's handwriting. Distinctive and practically illegible, his was the scribble of a doctor, not a chef.

"Where did you get that?" Apparently, all my smart brain cells had either been killed or had vacated, leaving only the stupid ones.

Teddy repeated, "In Jean-Charles's restaurant, before you came. Before Romeo showed up."

"You didn't tell the police?"

"I thought it better if we read it first."

"Better? Like bringing us closer to incarceration will bring us closer together?" My voice escalated, but then, just as quickly, I curbed it—Mona and my father would come running if they thought something was wrong. Of course, something *was* wrong, a whole lot of somethings, as a matter of fact, but they couldn't help—not unless they'd assist in burying the body, which I doubted. Parents could be so straitlaced that way, even mine.

"I am trying to help." Teddie actually sounded like he believed it.

"Yeah, helping me right into jail." Curiosity overrode good sense, not that I had much sense, good or bad, at this point. I took the envelope and stuck my finger under the flap, working it loose. "There's something in here." I looked up into Teddie's eyes, dark blue pinpoints. "Hold out your hands."

He cupped his hands, palms up, in front of me, and I placed a sheet of newsprint I grabbed from the coffee table over them. I shook the object out of the envelope.

A plastic, rectangular tag dropped onto the paper. The chip from the missing truffle, if I could hazard a guess, but I kept that tidbit to myself.

"What is it?" He poked at the chip.

I ignored his question as I bent over, inspecting the chip, then raised my eyes to his. "I can't believe you took evidence from the scene of a homicide."

"Now, we're both in this together. Is there anything else in the envelope?"

"A note." Using two fingers, I clamped one corner and worked the letter loose, ignoring the whole in-this-together thing. What had he meant by that? Come to think of it, Teddie had been pretty cavalier about handling the envelope—not worrying about disturbing any prints or adding his own. The Teddie I used to know would've been more careful. After all, hanging with me gave him at least rudimentary knowledge of evidence preservation techniques. Not that I was proud of that, but a hotel like the Babylon was a cauldron where alcohol distilled life to the elemental.

Murder had knocked on my door before.

Leaving Teddie standing there, I stepped to the couch in front of the windows. Lowering myself to the cushions, I stared out at the lights and wondered where in that vast sea Jean-Charles had hidden himself. Was he all right? Scared? Angry? Guilty? That last thought stuck in my craw—I just couldn't believe it. He'd sent me the RFID chip. What did he want me to do with it? Who could I trust?

The last person with an interest in this chip had gotten himself broiled.

Curling my legs underneath me, I pressed myself into the embrace of the deep cushions. I almost didn't notice Teddie as he joined me. His Old Spice cologne enveloped me like the hug of a warm memory. Lingering for a moment, I then shook myself loose of the past and lay the folded sheet gently in my lap, thinking, feeling. Jean-Charles. I knew he was safe. I don't know how, but I just knew. I also knew Romeo was going to be beating every bush looking for him. And the police tended to get pissy when you made them work hard to find you.

"You love him?" Teddie's pitch rose at the end, making the statement a question—it was a good one.

"You've asked me that before." My voice cracked a little—life was getting to me. And the alcohol overrode my defenses, letting loose emotions too long held in check.

When he put an arm around my shoulders and pulled me close, I didn't resist. Instead, I put my head on his shoulder.

"I can see that you do." He sounded sad. And clearly, he saw more than I did, but I didn't point that out. I was so done with giving everyone what they wanted. At some point, there needed to be some quid pro quo. "Let me help." He sounded sincere.

But I was too tired and too scared to detect any subterfuge, which wasn't my best thing, anyway. "With what, exactly?"

"Why don't you read the letter, then maybe we'll both know."

Why did his arm around me have to feel so nice? Raising my head from his shoulder, I looked at the folded paper on my lap, buying time. Did I really want to know what it said?

Teddie nodded toward the note. "Read it."

I took a deep breath, then carefully unfolded the paper and let my eyes wander over the words. Jean Charles's scrawl took a couple of passes to decipher.

"What does it say?" Teddie asked.

I scanned the lines one more time to be sure, then carefully refolded the page and put it in my pocket. Lifting my eyes, I caught Teddie's gaze and held it. "He said that chip is the first. There are others—more pieces to the puzzle. He is being watched, but he will tell me where the other chips are."

"How?"

"He didn't say." I stared out the window. "He's scared. Although he didn't say so, I get the sense he was doing something benign, working on a new, more economical, high-level food-tracking system. And somehow he stumbled into something far more sinister than you or I can imagine."

"We've got two gruesome deaths. Imagining is not necessary."

I turned to Teddie. "That's the problem. Jean-Charles felt the killer was only getting started. Knotting the threads, he said."

"Knotting the threads?"

"Tying up loose ends." I smiled, but not from joy. "He's not too good with American idioms. Especially when he's scared."

Teddie's eyes held the sadness I felt.

I needed a hug. I could tell Teddie wanted to comfort me. But Jean-Charles stood between us, as effective a barrier as if he'd truly been standing there.

"How many loose ends do you think there might be?" Teddie asked, knowing I would have no clue.

"More. I think the ante just got upped." Propelled by stifled frustration, I whipped my feet from underneath me, propelled myself off the couch and out of his embrace, and retook my position in front of the window. Unable to still my thoughts or my body, I paced in front of the window as I tried to calm down and corral a coherent thought or two. What had been an amorphous threat had now coalesced into a race to stop a killer before he eliminated all the threads. We only needed one . . . a place to start. "If we could just find some connections." I wanted to run through theories, bat some possible scenarios around, but for the first time ever, doubt seeped through the fracture between me and Teddie. Could I really trust him? What had he really been doing at Jean-Charles's restaurant? Was my distrust founded on his personal betrayal, or something more?

Again, the question for which I had no answer confronted me: how did one rebuild trust once it was broken? I hadn't a clue.

Until I had an epiphany, I decided to keep my own counsel—at least I'd never let me down . . . well, not intentionally, anyway, and I'd never hidden my betrayal from myself. Oh boy, I was losing it. I needed sleep . . . in the worst way.

"Any ideas?" Teddie asked, his voice flat, his face a mask.

Closing in on myself, I didn't answer—I had nothing to say, not to Teddie, anyway. Too tired, scared, and hurt for any more civility, I crossed my arms and kept my mouth shut.

"Let me help you," Teddie implored, his tone just a hair short of begging.

Stopping, I turned and stared him down. "You need to go. Safer that way . . . for both of us."

"Lucky." He rose and moved toward me.

I turned my back. "I don't need you, and I don't need your help. Please go."

He didn't touch me, thank God. After a few moments, the sound of the door closing echoed, then reverberated in my heart.

I had doubts, so many unanswered questions, but I was certain of one thing:

Everybody was right—it was time for me to go home.

AFTER A FITFUL NIGHT, I FINALLY ABANDONED HOPE OF TRUE REST and staggered into the day. Yesterday had defeated me a bit, and I was in need of some serious attitude. Formfitting skinny black jeans ending above some Jimmy Choo sparkle and a silver sweater slipping off one shoulder did the trick. Grabbing my Birkin, I hooked it onto an elbow and headed out.

I gave myself a last once-over in the metal doors to the elevator while I rode down, and I felt some sass filtering in. I'd phoned Romeo and then left the note and the chip downstairs for him. He hadn't been pleased, taking a bite out of my ass over taking stuff from the crime scene. Although Teddie was the culprit, I didn't begrudge Romeo his venting. The messenger always took the brunt, so I shrugged it off.

Today started the same as most days—too many questions with too few answers—but I had learned one thing in the past twenty-four hours: I was tired of getting kicked around by life, by men. My own fault really, too often I fell in love with a man's potential, overlooking his limitations to actually reach the heights I perceived. Done in by my own optimism, I vowed to rein in the horses and take a long, hard look before jumping into the game of love once more. Yes, a bit cynical for me, but in the interest of self-preservation I adopted the new plan, realizing, of course, that putting it into effect was the impossible part.

I needed to grow some balls. To solve some problems. To move on before I could look back.

And I needed to catch a killer, before somebody else got fricasseed.

∾

"MR. LIVERMORE IS PACING BACK AND FORTH IN YOUR OFFICE," MISS P. announced when I walked through the office door.

Stopping in front of her desk, I traced the new gold stenciling on the corner—maintenance had finally found time to do as I asked. Of course, they couldn't finish my office, but they could letter the Beautiful Jeremy Whitlock's name—minus the beautiful part, that would be too ego-gratifying for him—on the corner of

Miss P's desk across the exact bit of real estate his butt usually occupied. I bit my lip to keep from smiling as I looked up into Miss P's stern countenance.

"Proud of yourself?" She tried to sound unhappy, but failed miserably. Giving into the grin, she pressed a mug of steaming coffee into my hand. With the day already amped to full wattage, I found myself dangerously undercaffeinated. Holding the mug under my nose, I breathed deep. "Ah, Don Francisco Vanilla Nut, the best." I gave her a look through the steam before I took a sip. "You're treating me awfully well for a Monday morning."

"Tuesday."

"Tuesday?" I took a sip of the coffee, savoring the hit. Caffeine and alcohol kept me functional—obviously not optimal, but I no longer cared.

Miss P. nodded. I thought I saw a flash of sympathy, but I might have imagined it. We all were overworked; thank God we weren't underpaid.

Something was missing. It took me a moment to figure it out. "Why is the bird still covered? I'm not sure how to start a day without being called a filthy whore."

"That would be me."

"Right." I took another slug of coffee and felt a hint of my smile. It hadn't been so hard to find after all. "What am I, I forget?"

"Effin' bitch."

"Right." I eyed her over the mug. "You said that with a bit too much relish for my taste."

"You asked."

"I asked for information. The enthusiasm was all yours." Needing the caffeine jolt, I downed half the mug of coffee as quickly as the heat would allow. "I need a favor. It's time for me to go home. Could you make it happen, please?"

Miss P. paused and gave me a penetrating stare. I didn't wilt.

With an exaggerated sigh, she caved. "Cleaning crew first, then pack you up and move?"

"Whatever it takes." I sipped my coffee a bit more sedately now as I wandered to the glass wall and concentrated on the lobby below.

"And your time frame?"

"Cleaned, fresh linens, stocked fridge and bar . . . by tonight." Before she could verbally carve off a chunk of my flesh, I added, "For Jordan. He'll be here later or tomorrow, I forget. Regardless, he is expecting his 'regular accommodations': his words, not mine."

Tossing a Hollywood hunk, even a gay one, to her was a sure-fire way to mollify.

"Jordan Marsh?" Miss P. whispered like a lovesick schoolgirl, which made me grin. News of his sexual orientation had done little to cool her ardor. Granted, Jordan Marsh was the absolute pinnacle of male pulchritude.

Even in my all-men-are-pigs mode, I pretty much got it. "Yes, and we don't want to disappoint Jordan, do we?"

Miss P. switched gears. As she reached for the phone, I could see her brain whirling, planning. This delegating thing really had its moments.

"Power has its privileges," I announced as if I believed it. However, it was simply a bluff, a comment carefully crafted to elicit a response, except I don't think it even registered. If it did, Miss P. ignored me, which wasn't unusual.

My mug dangerously low, I wandered toward the little kitchen cubby, raising my voice as I did. "So, you said there is a Mr. Livermore burning off steam in my office? Guess he's not a happy camper?"

"I most certainly am not!" A disembodied, unfamiliar male voice, pitched on the high side, answered me.

Guess my voice carried further than I thought. For some reason, I didn't feel the need to apologize.

"Well, then. May I offer you some coffee? It's been known to cure all manner of ills."

"I don't partake of stimulants. I consider them a sign of weakness."

Holding the coffee pot poised in mid-air, I peered around the corner, eyeballing him.

A small man, he lurked in the makeshift doorway to my office. A splash of dust decorated the shoulder of his dark jacket—he should have known better than to wear a dark suit in a construction zone. His round face and squinty eyes reminded me of a cave-dwelling rodent, if there was such a thing. With pasty skin and thinning hair highlighted by an ill-fitting, coarse toupee that missed his real hair color by several shades, Mr. Livermore had the look of terminal middle management about him. The fact that the hair bolting from his head had apparently migrated and taken root in his eyebrows completed the expectation. He couldn't have looked any more nondescript had he planned it.

"A sign of weakness? Most assuredly," I said in a chatty tone as I poured myself another mugful. Tasting the witch's brew, I sighed, then replaced the pot on the warmer. Thus fortified, I felt capable of dealing with the Mr. Livermores of the world. "Let's go into my office, and you can tell me how I may be of assistance."

"Nelson Livermore." He pressed one of his cards into my hand. "No, we've not met. I've been sitting in there for the better part of an hour."

"Did we have an appointment?" I asked, knowing full well we didn't.

He wilted under my steady gaze and my five-inch height advantage. "No."

With my coffee mug, I motioned through the door into my office, such as it was. He turned and slithered thorough the doorway. Following him, I moved around my desk as I eyeballed his card.

Mr. Livermore sought refuge on the couch, eschewing the chairs in front of me.

Stepping to my chair, I set the coffee mug on my desk. "Insurance investigation? How may I help you?" I asked, but my thoughts were elsewhere. My desk had been tampered with—it didn't look right. The piles of paper looked the same, even the layer of fine dust. Through the lingering morning haze, I tried to focus.

"As my card indicates, I'm with the hotel's insurance carrier." Mr. Livermore sounded officious and dull—of course, he *was* a claims adjuster.

I paid him only half a mind, which was all I had, anyway. "Shouldn't you be talking to the legal department?"

"They sent me to you."

I glanced up at him, still trying to identify what was wrong. "Why?"

The little man nervously worried the watch on his left wrist—it looked like a Timex. "I'm here about a truffle. You see," he started in, as if his story was riveting, "the truffle did not go where it was supposed to go."

All of a sudden, it hit me. "Miss P.!" I shouted. "Get in here!"

Both Miss P. and Brandy, my other assistant, or now actually Miss P.'s assistant—I had trouble keeping the pecking order straight—dashed into the room. The bird shouted, "Fuck, fuck," in the background.

"Did somebody die?" Miss P. asked in a glacial tone. I guess she liked to be summoned by a shout as much as I did.

I pointed to my desk, the surface of which was curiously empty. "My cockroach. Where is it?"

Mr. Livermore pulled his knees to his chest, raising his feet off the floor.

I didn't even smile. I pointed to the round mark in the dust. "It's gone."

Miss P. and Brandy stood there, dumbfounded. Miss P. said, "Last time I saw it, it was on my desk, remember?" She shot me a worried glance. "I put it back on your desk as you asked."

"You have a cockroach," Mr. Livermore squeaked.

I pawed through the papers littering my desk. "It's a paper-weight. A gold cockroach encased in Lucite with a green felt bottom."

"It's dead?" His voice still quivered.

I shot him a look.

Mr. Livermore replaced his feet on the floor with a thud. He straightened his tie and, with a hand on top of his head, mashed his toupee down, wiggling it into place. "Was this item valuable?"

Simultaneously, Miss P. said no and I said yes.

Mr. Livermore glanced between the two of us. "Which is it?"

"Only sentimental value," I admitted.

"But everyone knows about it," Miss P. added. "It's Lucky's signature item, like a totem."

I opened my mouth to argue, then snapped it shut. What was the point, anyway? "It was like a good luck charm," I said to Mr. Livermore, refusing to accept that my staff associated a roach with me.

"But iconic?" Mr. Livermore pressed.

Miss P. and Brandy both nodded.

Terrific.

Mr. Livermore made a tsking sound. "We've been getting a rash of these sorts of claims. Kids think it's sort of funny. Some-body stole a garden gnome from the Conservatory and took it on a tour of Paris. It's harmless, really."

I could only blink at him in incomprehension. "But it's steal-ing," I managed to mumble.

"Technically," he agreed. "But they usually return the item when they've had their fun, so no harm, really." Mr. Livermore motioned Brandy over to the computer behind my desk, the one I never turned on if I could help it. "Why don't you do a quick search, see what you find?" He frowned and added what sounded like an afterthought. "There was also the case of a Mr. Potato Head who someone brought, I believe, here to Vegas for a tour, taking pictures of it in iconic places."

Brandy perched on the edge of my desk chair, which I had relinquished, stepping to the side, out of the way but still able to see the screen. She booted up the computer, then let her fingers fly over the keyboard. As I watched her, I felt woefully anachronistic—sort of like a dinosaur staring up at the asteroid as it hurtled earthward through the atmosphere.

I sipped my coffee, and the others remained glued to the screen as Brandy searched the ether.

"Ah-ha!" Brandy settled back into the chair, her mouth turned up at the corners in a self-satisfied smirk. "He was right!"

She caught me mid-swallow. I gagged as the coffee went down the wrong pipe.

Miss P. banged on my back. "Raise your hands."

I glared at her as I fought for air.

Lowering her head, she looked at me over her cheaters in a show of maternal patience. "If you raise your hands it opens your windpipe."

Thankfully, I got some air without sticking my hands in the air like a fool.

Mr. Livermore didn't look surprised. "See? You'll get it back when the show is over. Now, about my truffle . . ."

I pointed to him. "I'll get to that." I must've sounded harsher than I intended. Mr. Livermore curled up in his chair and clamped his mouth shut. I turned back to Brandy. "This is absurd. Let me see."

She angled the monitor, focusing the picture on the screen. And there it was. My cockroach paperweight . . . okay, a photo of it. I leaned closer and squinted, concentrating on the background. "Where is that?" I mused out loud.

Miss P. moved in next to me. The three of us, heads together, focused on the image on the screen.

"My truffle?" Mr. Livermore's voice lacked strength.

"Shush." The three of us females said in unison, then refocused as one on the image of the Lucite-encased cockroach. It sat on a table of mosaic tiles, a white napkin underneath it. In red ink and a scrawl I recognized was the single word: Max.

Miss P. pointed to a blurred, triangular image in the background. "What's that?"

"Looks like a lantern," Brandy said. "You know, like one of those stained glass things they hang on patios."

I pushed myself to my feet, shocking everyone, myself included. My head sort of swum—it was going to be that kind of day. "Grab your stuff," I said to my assistants.

"You know where that is?" Miss P. looked dubious.

"Call for a Ferrari." I fingered the delicate fabric of my off-the-shoulder sweater—pretty thin for November temps. The black jeans were great, but I'd forgotten a jacket.

Miss P. must've read my thoughts as she disappeared, then returned quickly with a light jacket from the closet in my former office. She thrust it at me without a word.

"Thanks."

Brandy vacated my chair and moved to stand by the door.

"My truffle?" Mr. Livermore trailed off under my gaze.

"Process the claim. I don't know what else to tell you."

"Where are you going?" Mr. Livermore sprang to his feet. "Do you know where Chef Bouclet is?"

I stopped, leveling a gaze at him, my voice calm. "I should think he's in his kitchen, where he always is. Has he gone missing?"

Mr. Livermore blanched, if that was possible with his sickeningly white skin. "How would I know? The legal department sent me to you. They said you would help coordinate with the Bouclets."

I gave him a curt nod. "And we will do our best."

Miss P. addressed Brandy. "You go with Lucky. The car only holds two, and someone needs to stay here and actually work." She retreated to her office with a grin. I heard her pick up the phone and ask for the Ferrari dealership.

I stayed where I was, but I used the moment I had to draw out Mr. Livermore a bit more. "Okay, you said the truffle didn't go where it was supposed to go. Could you explain?"

Uncurling, he sat up straight, his knees pressed together like a schoolgirl's in church. His hands on his knees, he took his time before he answered, which I sort of deserved, so I waited. "The truffle, it was supposed to come here."

God, I just love it when people try to beat me into submission with the obvious. I cocked an eyebrow at him, which, amazingly enough, he read properly.

Sensing my impatience, he cut to the chase. "The shipment should've come here directly, but it didn't. The shipper routed it through a facility in Kansas."

"Kansas? I don't know much about very expensive food products, but routing them through Kansas seems . . . wrong. It's not like Kansas is the epicenter of the gourmet world." I was pretty sure it fell on the opposite end of the spectrum, but I didn't say so. Miss P. grew up on a farm in Iowa, which I thought was close to Kansas, in every way, and I knew she was listening.

Mr. Livermore actually smiled. "That's why the legal department sent me here."

"Because they think I have a Kansas connection?"

This time Mr. Livermore laughed. I couldn't shake the feeling he was playing me . . . something about him seemed a bit forced. "I don't think so. I need to talk to"—he consulted a note he pulled from his inside coat pocket—"Jean-Charles Bouclet and Desiree Bouclet, his sister, I believe. I've been led to believe they are both here at the hotel. My search for them has yielded nothing. The legal department told me you could help."

"Really? Well, they overstate, but I'll see what I can do."

I stepped around my desk and headed toward the door. Grabbing Brandy by her elbow, I pushed her ahead of me into the outer office. "Change in plans," I whispered so Mr. Livermore couldn't eavesdrop. I handed her Mr. Livermore's card, then gave her quick instructions and sent her on her way. Returning to my office and the insurance guy, I conjured a smile. "I've sent my assistant to try to find the Bouclets. Perhaps you'll let us know where we can find you when we have things arranged?"

Mr. Livermore settled back in his chair. "Oh, I'll wait."

I stepped to the side and extended my arm. "Okay then, but I'd prefer you wait in our vestibule."

"Fine." He seemed unconcerned as he moved by me into the outer office.

As I grabbed my Birkin from Miss P.'s bottom desk drawer, I said in a conversational tone, "Why don't you call the Beautiful Jeremy Whitlock, ask him to get his butt over here . . . now."

Her eyes widened a tad, but she did as I asked. After a hushed conversation, she recradled the phone. "Five minutes."

Mr. Livermore stood with his back to us as he looked through the wall of glass to the lobby below—he didn't seem to be paying us much attention.

"Great. I'm just going to step down the hall to powder my nose. I'll be right back, but have Jeremy wait for me, okay?"

I didn't say good-bye to Mr. Livermore. Of course, he thought I'd be right back.

Jeremy was as good as his word—I'd only cooled my heels for a minute or two in the hallway when the elevator dinged and he pushed through the doors before they had fully opened—which was a feat as his shoulders were at least an ax handle wide. "Hey." I caught him by the elbow before he'd gotten up a head of steam.

He whirled around and took my breath. Several inches taller than my six feet, with golden hair matched by gold flecks in his brown eyes, and dimples to top it off, Jeremy was two hundred and twenty-five pounds of solid Aussie muscle—a total dream . . . and he belonged to Miss P. Fifteen years her junior, he was also the prefect example of cougar bait—a fact I used to get her goat on occasion. "She used our secret word. She's okay, right?"

Purposefully, I had chosen my position in the hallway to be

able to see both office doors. No one had come or gone. "Would I be standing here if she weren't?" He took a deep breath and the concern that had bunched his shoulders fled, allowing them to drop into a somewhat normal position.

"Here's the deal. There's this guy in my office, he claims to be from our insurance company. A rather major truffle has gone missing." I waved away the questions I saw clouding into Jeremy's eyes. "Not important right now, but here's what's interesting. First, the guy said the legal department sent him to me, so I could find two employees he wants to question. That would never happen in a million years."

"The legal beagles don't trust you to find a couple of blokes who work here?"

I gave him a withering look. "They would never let anyone question any of our employees regarding a claim against this hotel without one of the legal staff present."

"Ah." Jeremy piped down and let me continue.

"Second, the guy said the legal department sent him to me to find Jean-Charles, but also Desiree."

"Desiree?"

"Jean-Charles's sister, just off the plane from France. Our lawyers wouldn't have any idea who she was or why she would be here. So, those two anomalies raised my antennae. I've sent Brandy off to question the legal staff, and then to query our insurance provider regarding Mr. Livermore."

Jeremy looked pretty impressed. "And you want me to hang around and keep the staff safe, is that it?"

"For now." I put a hand on his arm and wiped the gloat off my face—it's not often I can impress Vegas's primo private investigator. "Be careful. I know this seems silly at the moment, but we've got two dead bodies already."

With that, he bolted down the hall and disappeared into my office.

Ah, love . . .

I paused for a fraction of a second, bound by the rope of a perfect memory . . . Teddie.

If only.

CHAPTER 12

$\mathcal{A}$S REQUESTED, the Ferrari waited, engine warming, at the curb in front of the Babylon. After handing the valet who held the door a twenty, I folded myself into the car. When I was settled, he carefully eased the car door shut, not even trying to hide the drool in the corner of his mouth. Men and fast cars . . . If keeping them interested was only as simple as taking them for a ride.

Before I had time to ease the car in gear, the passenger door flew open and a body fell into the seat. My heart rate spiked. Then my blood boiled.

Teddie.

"Get out," I growled.

Ignoring me, he pulled the door closed. His Old Spice washed over me, weakening my defenses. I was beginning to believe he knew the effect and wore the cologne on purpose. He looked at me and motioned forward. "Let's go."

Today, he still sported his just-tight-enough 501s, but a collarless white cotton shirt replaced the Harvard sweatshirt. He'd knotted a sweater around his neck against the cold—on anyone else that would have looked a bit too *GQ*. Fresh-faced, clean-shaven, his hair gelled and spiked, he looked . . . wonderful. Damn him. "What are you waiting for?" He acted all innocent, which he was darn good at.

"For you to get out of the car."

He eased his shoulders around—hard to do in the tight space. "Look, I get it. You don't want to see me, talk to me, touch me, listen to me. So, how about you let me help you?"

"With what?"

"Whatever it is you're in such a hurry for."

I cocked my head. "To find Jean-Charles."

"That's cool." He reached to put a hand on mine, but when I flinched, he pulled his hand back. "Look, truce, okay? Can we at least try to be friends?"

"I told you when we opened this can of worms, we could never go back."

"I know you did. I didn't believe you then, and I don't believe you now. So, let's give it a go, see who's right. What do you say? I got a ten-spot says you're wrong." He looked at me with a penetrating, challenging, clear-blue gaze.

I tickled the paddle shifter, putting the car in the appropriate gear; checked that my path to the Strip was clear; and hit the gas.

Teddie didn't say another word until we'd flown up the 15, taken the overpass to the 95 at speeds not normally seen on the highest ramp of the Spaghetti Bowl, then accelerated toward the exit to the Summerlin Parkway. To his credit, he didn't hold on—of course, he was pretty familiar with my need for speed. "Where's your buddy, Dane? I haven't seen him around."

I let my breath out in a long exhale between my lips. "He went home for a bit."

"Really?" Teddie pursed his lips, presumably while he processed that. "I thought he was kind of sweet on you."

I wasn't in the mood to tell him the whole sordid, sad story, so I concentrated on driving, which he should've been happy about. Speeds over a hundred mph deserved at least a modicum of focus.

He let the Dane matter go. "I've been doing a bit of research on that chip."

"The RFID chip?" I tossed that between us with feigned confidence.

He took the bait, snorting and shaking his head. "Staying ahead of you is going to take my A-game, and I'm a bit rusty." Leaning his head back, with a smile curling his lips, he said softly, but loud enough to be heard over the steady thrum of the engine, "God, I've missed you."

I'd missed him, too—the easy camaraderie, the closeness, but I'd never tell him, not in a million years.

I didn't even want to admit it to myself.

THE GRAPE SPOT OCCUPIED THE TOP RUNG OF THE LOCAL CULINARY ladder on Vegas's northwest side. Great food, great atmosphere, special wine list, and cool vibe, what was not to like? And, this time of year, the fire pit on the patio would be wonderfully warm and welcoming—the lanterns in the trees providing the perfect ambience. Of course, we were a bit early for the whole romantic ambience thing . . . thankfully. Lunch would be the next meal on the schedule—and the only thing that made lunch romantic was Champagne. I wasn't going there today.

Tucked into a nondescript office park on the north side of Charleston, The Spot, as the locals referred to it, was difficult to find, even for those of us in the know. I almost blew by the turn but spied the tiny sign tucked low next to the busy street. Cranking the wheel over hard, the Ferrari nimbly following, I just made it without leaving too much rubber on the road . . . or Teddie in my lap. He managed to grab the handhold at the last minute. Easing down the short street, then into the parking lot, I smiled at the disappointment on the valet's face as I rumbled by and selected my own space far from the maddening crowd.

As we walked up the steps toward the entrance, Teddie trailed a step or two behind. Before going through the doors, I looked to my left. The perfect patio was just as I remembered—an oasis sheltered from the sun in the lee of the building, beautifully designed with several subtle levels and nooks and crannies hidden by flowering shrubs. Individual tents shaded several larger tables, like private dining grottos worthy of the most exalted Sultan. Above it all, trees provided a cooling canopy and an inviting playground for a variety of birds.

Woven in the branches, providing a warm ambience and subtle light when the glow of the sunset receded, were a series of lanterns, each hanging at a different height, and each unique in its design.

All of them made from stained glass.

A young woman stepped out to greet us. Impossibly thin and undeniably beautiful, she wore her long, black hair straight, her dress tight, her eyes blue, and her lips pink. "May I help you?"

"Is Max here?"

Her eyebrows lowered, but her frown didn't even crinkle her flawless skin. "I'm sorry?"

"Max Danzer, your executive chef."

Her yes widened with understanding. "Of course. I'll check. And you're Ms. O'Toole from the Babylon, right?"

I nodded. "We'll be waiting right over there." I pointed to a cozy two-top with a white tablecloth and a candle that had yet to be lighted. "Could you send a waiter over?"

She disappeared and I turned to Teddie. "I'm feeling the need for a Viognier. Wine, the new breakfast beverage." My empty stomach growled in protest, but I ignored it.

"Works for me." He held the chair for me. "However, I'm feeling the need for something with a bit more kick than that."

My favorite server, Marcello, with his ready grin and dancing eyes, greeted us. After we gave him our order and he rushed off to do our bidding, I settled back, lifting my face to the sun's caress. I jumped a little when Teddie's hand closed over mine as it rested on the table between us. The effect he had on me was undeniable, and something I was going to have to learn to deal with . . . or reconcile myself to.

"Remember when we used to come here? The fire pit in the winter, a blanket covering us, my arms around you?"

I didn't want to remember, or at least I didn't want him to know how often my thoughts drifted back, or what they did to me. "Of course I do." Like I said, I'm not a game player.

"Yeah, me, too." His voice sounded wistful and sad, which matched my sentiments exactly. The mad was gone.

I sneaked one eye open a crack. Teddie also lifted his face to the sun, eyes closed, drinking it in. Absorbing, embracing the pain, I let my eyes traverse his face. For a brief moment in time, I'd had it all . . . then it was gone . . . he was gone.

Now, he was back. I looked at our hands overlapping—our hearts had been like that. Could we go back? Was it possible to regain trust? To recapture the joy? Yes, it would be different, but could it be as good? Or better? Could we be friends? That was the part I missed the most.

I snapped my eyes shut, closing out the glimmer of hope.

Right now, I had simpler problems, like a double homicide and a missing lover.

I heard a chair scrape back and pulled my hand from under Teddie's. Opening my eyes, I caught Chef Danzer glancing at me with a concerned but semi-bemused expression. "Hey, Max." I gestured toward Teddie. "This is Ted Kowalski."

He shook Teddie's outstretched hand and gave him a nod, then his eyes flicked to mine. "I sure hope you're looking to hit me up for a job. I could use someone with your skills to work on some PR and branding stuff for me right now. The restaurants are on the uptick, and I'd like to keep that momentum going," he said to me.

"How's the new location?" The Spot had just opened a hip little place at the Fashion Show Mall. I think they called it the Spot on the Strip. With windows overlooking the Strip, it was a regenerative respite to ease the pain of power retail therapy. But it was also hard to lure the locals to the chaos of that stretch of road that defined the city.

"Catching on, and with this thing Jean-Charles is planning, well, it's got me enthused."

Without a word, Marcello set a glass of wine in front of me, a shot of Patrón in front of Teddie, and a bottle of Pellegrino with a glass and a plate of lime wedges in front of his boss, then backed away.

"What thing?" I scooted my chair closer to the table.

Max leaned back, his hands in front of him, palm-down on the table. "We were working on a promotional thing. Some off-menu items that those in the know could ask for by name. Sort of a hidden menu tour."

"Like a foodie treasure hunt?"

"Exactly." He gave a rueful laugh. "You know how Vegas folks are—they're so used to the lure of the new on the Strip, that us local guys have to work to keep their attention."

"You're an institution around here. Heck, the happy hours here are legendary."

He smiled. "Gotta innovate to stay ahead."

"The treasure hunt for only those who know is a great idea." I glanced at Teddie, who was trying to be patient, let this play out. Turning back to Max, I continued my casual questioning. "And your menu items, did Jean-Charles ask for anything specific?"

Max shrugged. "The choice of dish was mine, but he asked that we order our ingredients through his sister, which was fine. I used her for the high-end stuff, anyway. She's the best in the business."

I leaned back. It was a brilliant idea, actually. "How many restaurants were involved?"

"I'm not really sure." Max poured himself a dose of Pellegrino, then squeezed a lime, dropping the wedge into the glass. "A few names had been bandied about, but it was Jean's project. I trusted his taste—we have the same objective."

"And that would be?" I sipped the Viognier—it didn't disappoint. The Grape Spot had an amazing wine list—great quality, yet good value.

"Raise awareness of the fine dining options off the Strip." Max took a sip of his Pellegrino, then added a few drops more of lime juice—chefs and their penchant for perfection.

"Have you received any orders from Desiree Bouclet recently?"

Max nodded. "Just this morning."

"They wouldn't happen to have had a tracking chip in them, would they?"

"Curious you should ask." The chef's eyes fixed on mine. "They did, actually. Why?"

I brushed his question aside. "Could I have the tracking thing?"

Max pushed himself to his feet. "Hang on just a sec, I think there were two shipments, each with its own chip. I'm sure we haven't thrown them away yet."

Teddie and I sat lost in our own thoughts and the beautiful day. A slight breeze tickled the leaves, making them dance. Pretty soon, they'd succumb to winter and would fall, but they would bloom anew in short order—that was one of the great things about Vegas: winter passed in a blink.

Max returned quickly. He extended his hand. "Here."

In his palm were two rectangular plastic tags.

With an index finger I poked at them, then picked one up and looked at it from both sides. "RFID?"

He didn't appear surprised that I could trot out that nomenclature. "You'd be surprised what kind of info can be saved on those little things. Way beyond my level of comprehension, but they work. Jean-Charles was telling me about a new technology he was working with that makes these things economical even for us little guys. They can even get power from the reading wave and then transmit info from another sensor such as a thermometer. Pretty amazing stuff, really."

I felt a grin lift the corner of my mouth. "May I keep these?"

The chef shrugged. "Sure. I didn't read the things—I have no need for any data on them—the shipments weren't particularly expensive or temperature sensitive. I just did it for Jean."

I took a last sip of wine, leaving half of it. Somehow, that made me feel a little less . . . alcoholic. "Oh, one more thing. Were your shipments okay? Nothing out of the ordinary?"

His brows crinkled as he once again fixed me with a stare. "They were short. I figured stuff was on backorder, although the invoice was for the complete shipment." He narrowed his eyes and hit me with a pointed look. "What is all this about?"

I feigned a cavalier attitude. "I have no idea. Teddie and I were out here on another mission, and Jean-Charles asked us to stop by to pick these up." The lie slipped so easily off my tongue.

I seemed to be picking up all sorts of bad habits.

~

WITH THE TAGS BURNING A HOLE IN MY POCKET AND TEDDIE'S presence scratching the scab off the hole in my heart, I drove more sedately on the way back to the hotel. Even though the temps were a bit chilly, I put the top down on the Ferrari, discouraging conversation. Fragments of thoughts flew across my synapses with dizzying speed facilitated by fatigue and fueled by worry. The liquid diet wasn't making matters any better.

Solid food was next on my list. Right after getting rid of Teddie.

Teddie stared straight ahead, one hand holding tight to the armrest, his face pinched in thought. I'd ask him what he was thinking, but men hated that question . . . or so I'd been told, more than once. Besides, I'd lost faith in his veracity of late, so even if I asked, I wouldn't learn anything I didn't already know. Asking would just make me seem interested, which was a weakness Teddie would exploit.

Games. How I hated games. Heck, even in the game of Life, people felt compelled to cheat. Seemed to me to be not only self-defeating, but also a quick slide toward self-loathing.

While we had been away, the Strip had started to stir. Couples wandered the sidewalks hand-in-hand. Most of them older—the day was still way too new for the kids who generally partied until night thinned toward dawn, they'd still be sleeping. Vegas was a bit like school that way, the older kids started earlier, the young-sters finished out the day.

The queue of cars lined up for the valets warmed my heart. Business was good—I'd be employed for at least one more day.

But another day was another opportunity for a killer to kill again.

With the specter of death at my shoulder, I couldn't hurry fast enough.

The valet jumped to take the car. I let him, levering myself out, then heading toward the lobby with Teddie behind. His blue-blood manners in place, he stepped around, pulling open the heavy glass door, and held it for me, then followed me inside. The energy level in the lobby hummed but had yet to reach full bore, which allowed me to throttle back and take my time to get up to speed.

Ignoring Teddie, I turned for the elevator as a man stepped into my path. "Ms. O'Toole?"

Tall, broad, fit, and fair, he had "cop" written all over him. I stopped and looked up into his impossibly green eyes, and out of nowhere a memory daggered my heart.

Dane had impossibly green eyes.

Dane, a friend gone missing. Well, not missing, exactly.

He'd sent me a note recently. It read simply GTT—gone to Texas. Home to heal his heart.

Another disappointment. Curiously, the fact that I was the

only common denominator in these unsatisfying relationships wasn't lost on me.

The man standing in front of me adopted a serious expression as he reached for his inside pocket, extracted a leather bifold, and flipped it open. I glanced at the badge. I'd been partially right—a cop, but not local, federal.

"I'm Special Agent Joe Stokes, Homeland Security. May I have a word with you?"

"Don't tell me you guys are running another preparedness drill. Now would not be a good time."

"No, ma'am." His eyes flicked to Teddie, who had stopped within earshot. "I just need a moment of your time . . . in private."

Teddie took the cue. "I'll see you later."

I didn't watch him as he walked away.

"Friend of yours?" Special Agent Stokes asked.

"Nope."

"More than friend?"

I raised one eyebrow. "Is my personal life under federal investigation?" When men and women met, the initial sizing up always had a frisson of sexual sizzle. Usually, I found that jolt a great jump start, but not today. Although I was flattered.

"No, ma'am." Embarrassment reddened the agent's cheeks, and he actually looked a bit chagrined, which was quite endearing. I felt the tug of attraction. Fighting it, I clamped down on my libido. I had more trouble than I could handle as it was. Why was the grass always greener?

Men—each one a royal pain in the ass in his own unique way.

I had no doubt the calm, cool Special Agent Stokes would be no different. Oh, many had some redeeming qualities, but lately, I'd committed to developing a blind eye—life just seemed to be less painful that way. Gesturing toward the casino, I adopted a conciliatory tone—the best way to get the feds out of my hotel was to play nice. I'd learned that one the hard way. "Let's go sit, and you can tell me what it is you want from me."

Once seated in Delilah's, I leaned back in the club chair and took a deep breath as I steadied myself—the day had already knocked me off-center. I felt like one of those blow-up clowns we played with as kids—the ones with sand in the base that would rock when punched, then snap back for the next blow. The analogy was a little too perfect for my liking. I asked my table-mate, "Want something to wet your whistle? Even this time of year, the desert sucks the water right out of you."

His attention, captured by a couple of sweet young things in barely-there dresses at the bar, swiveled back to me. "Pellegrino with lime, please."

I liked it that he didn't defer, that he accepted my offer. I wondered where that was listed in the Federal Guidelines for Disarming Women. And why was I still climbing on that mental jungle gym? The seeds of my own destruction were of my own making—a cruel quirk of life.

The minute I glanced in her direction, a waitress stepped to the table. I gave her the agent's order then said, "A Diet Coke and an order of sliders for the table, please."

She made a couple of notes with a fleeting grin at me and a longing look at Agent Stokes.

He seemed oblivious to the attention he attracted as we engaged in idle chitchat while waiting for our orders—apparently, he didn't want to be interrupted again by the waitress returning. Settled in, the weather fully discussed, I lapsed into silence and waited. The silence hadn't even stretched to awkward before the waitress returned. After arranging our food and beverages on the table, she drifted back to the bar, out of earshot.

I turned my attention to the sliders, each one a drippy mess of perfection. After quickly consuming one, I powered into the second. "Want one?"

Special Agent Stokes had yet to tell me why he'd called this meeting. Instead, he watched me as he took a long drink of his fizzy water, then set the glass back down, squaring the napkin, and shook his head.

Recognizing the stalling tactic, I took the opportunity to admire the line of his jaw, the crinkles around his eyes. Although all business, he looked like he could be nice—not that I was a good judge of character or anything.

And I realized something else: it had been far too long since I had seriously ogled any men. Far too fun a game, I'd have to rectify that, starting now. Although, since this wasn't fun and games, I'd have to be discreet.

The special agent cleared his throat as his eyes found mine. "I wasn't completely honest with you earlier. I'm with the department of Homeland Security—specifically, I'm the federal liaison with the Southern Nevada Joint Terrorism Task Force. I need to speak with Jean-Charles Bouclet—I understand you have intimate knowledge of his possible whereabouts."

Intimate. I wondered why he chose that word. "Really?" I feigned surprise. "What makes you think that?" I set the last third of my second slider down, wiping my fingers on the linen napkin. As I sipped my Diet Coke, I gave him a calm, steady stare. Amazingly, my voice followed suit . . . it didn't even hitch, not once.

His discomfort showed in the pinkening of his cheeks and his inability to keep steady eye contact. Fiddling with his lime slices, he squeezed enough juice into his Pellegrino to dissolve enamel.

"Surely, our chef can't have an impact on national security. Are you sure this isn't one of your training things?"

Special Agent Stokes's voice hardened into serious. "You have two murders so far, I hardly think that indicates a drill."

He had a point. "What can I do for you, then?" I picked up the remainder of my slider, eyeing it, turning it for just the perfect bite.

"My job involves analyzing all the possible means of terrorist attack on our soil, including adulterating our food supply." He let those words make the obvious impact.

My hand froze, the slider suspended in mid-air. "Food? You mean poison?" My voice squeaked—it'd been doing that a lot lately. Leaning forward, I replaced the slider on my plate, shoving it away with a forefinger. "My appetite just disappeared." I glanced around to see if anyone was paying attention to our conversation. No one looked alarmed or interested, for that matter. I lowered my voice when I recovered my composure. "You think all this is about poisoning a whole bunch of folks?" Crowds were gathering for the chef competition as well as all the attendant events, not to mention Thanksgiving. If some wacko wanted to cause a big stir, this would be a good opportunity. Christ! Thankfully, I kept the panic out of my voice, and its volume modulated.

He shrugged, and his confidence sagged a little. "That's where I'm not sure. We picked up a scent of something odd going on, some shipments routed through an odd location . . ."

"Kansas."

He stopped and shot me a quizzical look. "No, we're not exactly sure where they get derailed. We think they arrive in Vegas . . . somewhere."

"Really?" So my instincts weren't completely on the fritz. Livermore, the little weasel. And I was pretty sure I had part of the answer in my pocket. The RFID chips would give us routing information. But if I gave them to Stokes, he'd bury the info and I'd have one heck of a time catching a killer. Okay, maybe that was a bit harsh, but the feds were notoriously bad about sharing their information with local agencies—Romeo and I would be out in the dark. And while Homeland Security rode off chasing some imagined terrorists, a killer would still be roaming the halls of my hotel.

There I was, justifying again, and championship level stuff at that. And I had little doubt that, if I wasn't careful, I was justifying myself right into an invitation for an extended stay at the behest of the federal government.

"Why did you think Kansas?"

His question startled me, lost as I was sowing the seeds of my own incarceration. "What?" I waved his question away. "Just being flip, sorry," I lied, stalling for time. There were just too many folks in this game playing their own angles. Before I trusted anyone, I needed to get some facts, something concrete. And I sure wasn't going to sic the feds on Livermore—not before I got my hands around his neck, anyway. Nothing like the feds to scare the rats back into the sewers.

"I assure you, Ms. O'Toole, this is very serious." The look he gave me could strip paint. "Withholding information is a federal offense."

I wanted to correct him—there was more than a bit of bluff in his statement—that so far we had no federal crime, at least, not one I was aware of. But I decided to play along. . . . As Mona used to tell me, "Be nice until you squeeze the trigger."

"Understood, Special Agent. My humor is a way to off-load some panic." I gave him a self-deprecating shrug as I took my scolding like a man. "Most of your guys call me Lucky. As you probably know, I work closely with Metro and Homeland Security, although Jerry, our head of Security is the point man."

"I was told you were the one to entrust this to." He extended his hand. "Since we're practically partners and all, you can call me Joe."

We shook hands in a silly, now-we've-met-for-real way that did little to lighten the mood.

"You are working with Metro and rolling in our kitchen and banquet staffs?" I asked, clicking into corporate mode. "I assure you this hotel will help you in any way, all I ask is that you be discreet until you have all your ducks in a row." I waited for his nod, then continued. "Okay, Joe. Give me what you got, and I'll try to help you put together the puzzle pieces. Trust me, I want widespread panic even less than you do." I'd walked the Strip after 9/11. The tourists gone, the cars absent, Vegas had turned into a ghost town overnight. The only thing that had moved, other than me, was trash swirling on silent breezes. The only noise had been the pounding silence. I'd never fully overcome the fear, the incredible creepiness, the anger, the horror. I fingered the RIFD tags in my pocket and wondered how they played into this whole thing. And when I figured it out, and I faced the responsible person, I'd have no problem squeezing the trigger, and smiling as I did so.

"Chef Bouclet started tagging a bunch of shipments—I won't burden you with the tech aspects and all."

My eyes narrowed, but my smile didn't dim—he was dangerously close to patronizing. I'd shot men for less.

Apparently unaware of the dangerous waters he'd waded into, Special Agent Stokes . . . Joe . . . continued: "Curious as to what he was doing, we intercepted a couple of shipments and scanned the tags, then sent them on. Some of the data was gibberish. Besides, we really didn't know what we were looking for."

"And here I thought you guys had all the answers." I chewed on my lip. "Is Chef Bouclet working with you?"

"You know I'm not at liberty to say." He paused, perusing my face—looking for a hint of guilt about something, I suspected. "We need to find Chef Bouclet. He's the key to all of this."

Special Agent Joe Stokes had that part wrong. Jean-Charles wasn't the key.

But I knew who was.

CHAPTER 13

LASH CAUGHT me as I was scribbling my name on the check. She nodded at the retreating back of Special Agent Stokes. "Yummy." She flounced into the chair he had abandoned and fastened her Elvira eyes on me. "Girl, you gotta tell me your man-catching secret."

"My secret?" I put the pen down and gave her the once-over. "Disinterest."

Still looking like she stole her wardrobe from the punk-rock preteen section of a second-rate outlet store, her face painted in varying shades of pink—darker on the cheeks, lighter on the lips —her red hair unfettered, cascading in a riot of ringlets, Flash was the one constant in my life.

"Seriously. How do you do it?" She looked sincere.

"I told you."

That got me a dirty look. "Fine, be that way. But really, you get Captain America, and I get Captain Save-A-Ho."

"What?" The word tumbled out on a laugh. "Captain Save-A-Ho?"

Flash motioned to a cocktail girl. "Bring me some of that pink stuff with all the bubbles," she said when the girl approached.

The girl's eyes widened into a look of impending panic—she must have been a new hire.

"Rosé Champagne," I clarified, and the girl disappeared, presumably to do our bidding, although Flash may have scared her off.

I leaned back, waiting. Flash moved forward, keeping the same space between us. "So, the other night I met this guy from L.A., well-heeled, older, important friends—in the film business."

"That should've been a huge red flag."

Flash gave me a fleeting scowl. "Who am I to judge? Anyway, a mutual friend introduced us. So, this guy acts all interested, telling me how he's tired of rescuing women who can't hold their own, you know what I mean?"

I nodded, not even trying to hide my amusement—this was a train wreck anyone could see coming.

"He's relationship ready, wants something profound and meaningful. And he can tell right off I don't need him for his money, and I don't need to be saved."

"Quite the opposite." I waved off the cocktail waitress's offer of a glass for me and watched while she poured a flute for Flash. "With you in his life, he'd need a body guard."

"Not if he played straight." Flash grinned and puffed out her prodigious chest. "So, this dude comes on, says all the right stuff, and I'm thinking this could really be interesting—maybe, for once, I meet a guy who has some substance. Know what I mean?"

"By reputation only. Solid guys are an endangered species." I thought for a moment. "If not wholly extinct."

She sipped her Champagne, then groaned and giggled. Bubbles had that effect on me, too. With her free hand, she tapped her pink-tipped talons on the table as she got into the meat of the story. "Here's where the train goes off the rails . . ."

"Stay on the high side, I shock easily."

"Right." She huffed. "Anyway, he takes me out to dinner. We're swapping stories, having a fine time. After dinner, he takes me to the Foundation Room."

"Impressive."

"Yeah?" Flash throws back her Champagne and motions for another glass. "So, we order some bubbly and he says, 'Here's my deal.' I thought, uh-oh. I didn't know there was a deal—maybe he had me all wrong or something."

"Wouldn't be the first time." I felt compelled to toss that in, just for fun.

Flash gave me a dirty look, which I countered with a benign smile. "Anyway," Flash continued, warming to her story. "I let him talk, and he tells me he's not sure if he wants a relationship, really. Maybe he wants many, or none. He didn't know."

"Poor baby." I frowned. "What an ass."

"Oh, honey, it gets better." Flash scooched her behind farther back in the chair, settling in and cradling her flute. "The guy tells me that for the first time in a long time, he's dating a bunch of women, and they actually like him."

"Poor taste on their part," I added, enjoying the tale.

Flash settled me with a disbelieving look. "Do you know what he said next?"

"I'm afraid to hazard a guess."

"He had the audacity to tell me he didn't want to disappoint any of those adoring females."

"By giving you exclusive rights?" In disbelief, I had to ask for clarification. Men had said some stupid stuff to me, but this ranked right up there.

Flash drained her flute, then, leaning forward, she set it on the table, a glint in her eye. "Here's the kicker."

"It gets better?"

She nodded. "So, after dropping that little stink bomb, he tells me that I must surely understand that he's working through what he really wants." Her eyes dance with murderous delight. "Oh, I understood all right, but before I could rip him a new one, he pulls out a hotel key and says, 'How long do we have to stay here in the bar? Let's go to my room and see where this goes.'" Flash shot me an evil look. "I can tell you where it went . . . *it* marched right down the stairs, got in a cab, and went home."

"The man is lucky to be alive."

"Sorta sorry I didn't take him out of the gene pool—or at least keep him from swimming for a bit. But I let him live to prey upon another unsuspecting female."

"Noble," I said, although he really deserved a go-direct-to-dating-jail card. "He'll find someone who's willing to put up with his put-downs. We pair up based on our need states." Now, *that* was a can of worms, wasn't it?

"Thank you, Dr. Phil." She eyed me coolly. "The whole thing was nothing but a booty call—a Champagne and Kobe steak booty call, but that didn't make it easier to swallow. Turns out the guy has a history of dating women inappropriately younger who appeal to his hero complex. He thinks they actually like him when all they're doing is circling, biding their time to swoop in and take a bite out of his bank account."

"Captain Save-A-Ho." I chuckled. "Did you come up with that?"

"Wish I had. Pretty brilliant, actually, but apparently the stereotype is so prevalent the moniker is in the dictionary."

"Seriously? The dictionary? I guess Oxford has lost some of its stuffiness. I never thought that possible."

"Not *that* dictionary—the Urban Dictionary."

I'd never heard of it. Not surprising—corporate executives are a cloistered lot, even in Vegas. "Apparently I need to crawl out of my hole a bit more." Flash and her dating woes. But who was I to laugh? "Ego coupled with insecurity—a deadly combination."

"Aw, he wasn't worth shootin'." Her face sobered. "But, that's not why I came looking for you. I got some news."

Banter fled as my voice turned serious. "We've got a killer

itching to kill again, and we are no closer to his identity. If you could help make some sense of this, I'd be forever in your debt."

"Just hook me up with Captain America, there." Flash mooned in the direction Agent Stokes had taken. "If you don't have designs on him, that is. I don't poach from my friends."

"I'll make the introduction. The rest is up to you." The combination was just so wrong, it might work.

Flash settled back, her glass of bubbly in one hand and a satisfied look on her face. "I did some digging on Fiona Richards, as you asked,, and the more rocks I turned over, the more snakes I found." Her face shut down into a frown. "Some of this, you won't like."

I blew a short breath of air, lifting my bangs. "I don't like *any* of this. Tell me about Fiona."

Flash flipped to recitation mode as she did a memory dump. "Most of it, you know. She kicked around as a sous chef, hit some of the TV cooking shows, worked under a lot of chefs."

The way she said that made me look at her.

She gave me a knowing grin. "Sort of the casting-couch method of culinary ladder-climbing."

"Everybody's looking for an easy in." How I kept a straight face, I don't know.

Flash rewarded me with the hoped-for laugh—a big, bawdy one. "She got around, for sure." Flash sobered. "I checked the Secretary of State, and Fiona's business docs seem fine, but minimal. She's the only listed member in her limited liability company. She's got a moneyman, I know, but I'm still rooting that one out. Whoever it is, they've buried the evidence pretty deep."

"Makes you wonder why all the precautions," I said, thinking out loud. I knew Flash was already way ahead of me and didn't need my help.

She gave me a serious, rather pained look. "How much do you know about Jean-Charles?"

"Don't tell me Fiona slept with Jean-Charles."

"Are you letting your jealousy show?" Flash chided.

I snorted. "I'm never jealous of the past. If they had been intimate, that might just have been a bit too incestuous, don't you think? She and Adone Giovanni were lovers. And Adone is Desiree Bouclet's estranged husband."

"You know those French." Flash shook her head. "I'm gonna need to get me one of those."

"Yes, a lover with a mistress. Sounds chummy."

"Threesomes are . . ."

". . . out of the question," I said before she could horrify me with her take on it. "Now, back to Jean-Charles?"

Flash took a sip of bubbly, then set her glass down with a bit more attention than normal. She was stalling. Finally, she looked at me. "He has the reputation of being a real cut-throat."

I shrugged. "The higher you climb, the more enemies you make."

Flash drained her bubbly, then looked at me from under her brows. "Apparently, he likes to bed the help."

"Back to that, are we?" My voice held the hint of a snarl. Clearly, I wasn't the one to throw the first stone—Teddie and Jean-Charles technically both worked for me. "Not wise, but not a crime, either." When I said it, I thought maybe that wasn't entirely accurate. Using your position to gain sexual favors was certainly actionable. But to think I had any power when it came to the two men in my life was laughable.

"I guess that would depend on who he slept with and why." Flash had a point, and she made it.

"So what's the punch line?"

"Chitza DeStefano. Apparently, they had quite a dustup in Paris. Word is, they had an intense affair and then it blew up."

I pursed my lips and nodded. "Chitza said she knew Jean-Charles. How long ago?"

"Three years. I haven't found anyone who had firsthand knowledge, but it was quite the topic of conversation." Flash motioned for more Champagne, and we waited while the cocktail waitress refilled her glass. Flash took a sip, then continued. "Chitza came back here and opened her place."

"Interesting, but hardly condemning."

"Grist for the mill. But the rest of the info on your dead girl is a bit more compelling."

"Saving the best for last, are we?" I leaned forward, my interest piqued. "I hope it's good."

"Did you know she trained at Le Cordon Bleu?"

"You said she was a sous chef, so she must've trained somewhere."

Flash nodded.

Two chef, one chef . . . A shiver chased up my spine. "Le Cordon Bleu here in the States?"

"No, in Paris. Then she apprenticed with one of the important dudes, I can't pronounce his name, but"—she dropped her voice as she glanced quickly around—"the other apprentice? Chef Wexler."

THE BEAUTIFUL JEREMY WHITLOCK, ONE BUTT CHEEK PROPPED ON the stenciled corner of Miss P.'s desk, jumped when I burst through the office door.

I smiled at him benignly. "Did I scare you?"

"I'm a man. If I wasn't scared of you, I'd be a fool." He shot me those damn dimples.

The bird was the only one happy to see me. He sidestepped from one end of his perch to the other as he sang, "Fucking bitch! Fucking bitch!"

"As greetings go, I'd say that one needs work."

Miss P. stared in rapt attention at Jeremy, ignoring me entirely. Mr. Livermore was nowhere to be seen. I rewarded the bird for his affection with a slice of browned apple from the dish beside his cage.

Before he grabbed it, he rewarded me with a heartfelt expletive. "Asshole!" He delivered his best word with feeling, which helped me rediscover my smile.

"Good bird." I grabbed the messages in my box, then motioned for Jeremy to follow me. "Bring me up to speed."

Jeremy pulled out his phone as he trailed me into my office. "The guy, Livermore, struck me as a no-hopper, you know."

I sorted my remaining messages, discarding most of them as I took my chair. The springs groaned, which did nothing to improve my mood. "A no-hopper. There are so many meanings my imagination can attribute to that phrase. Do me a favor, save me from myself."

"A fool."

"Why didn't you say that?"

"I did," Jeremy deadpanned.

I gave him a look that had sent lesser men running.

"Okay." Jeremy took a spot on the sofa. Leaning back, he crossed one leg over the other, one ankle resting on the opposite knee, his hands holding his shin while his foot bounced with barely contained energy. "After you left, the guy got all twitchy, like a bucket of prawns in the sun. He didn't wait long, then he made some excuse and ran."

I looked up. "That's it?"

Jeremy scrolled through his phone. When he found what he wanted, he rose and stepped to my desk. Extending the phone, he handed it to me. "The wanker made straight for that guy." He pointed toward his phone in my hand.

Glancing down, I came face-to-photo with Adone Giovanni. "Well, that's certainly an interesting twist." He was popping up enough to garner some attention.

"You know him?" Jeremy actually sounded surprised . . . for a moment. "Silly me, of course you do."

I told Jeremy what I knew.

"Families." Jeremy's comment begged a few questions, but I

didn't indulge. "Seems like you know a lot about the guy, but, want me to run some background stuff, see if I can dig up anything odd?"

Personally, I'd have liked to know his definition of odd—this whole mess qualified, if you asked me. "That would be great. But concentrate on Livermore . . . we need to know his angle. If you bring me some good info, I will personally arrange a special spot in Babylon heaven with your name on it." I crinkled my brows, unsure as to what I might have just promised . . . Vegas had a weird effect on expectations. Trust me on that one.

"Miss P.?" I called without raising my voice—I knew she was within easy earshot.

She stuck her head through the doorway. "Your wish . . ."

"Could you see if you can find the UC-Berkeley guys, specifically Dr. Phelps? Last time I saw them, they were sobering up in the Sodom and Gomorrah Suite."

Her head disappeared—I took that as a yes. Jeremy wandered after her, hopefully to do my bidding, a hazy, lost-in-thought look on his face. She mumbled something, presumably to Jeremy, then the office door opened and closed.

The bird sang out, "Pretty girl! Pretty girl."

Brandy had returned. She materialized in my doorway, then, responding to my smile, stepped inside.

"Does that bird realize how very close to being slow-roasted on a spit he is?" I growled, half-pretending to be irritated.

Brandy, aka Pretty Girl, gave me a thousand-candlepower grin, confirming the bird's impeccable taste. "I checked with legal. As you suspected, they'd never talked with Mr. Livermore." She paused for my gloat. "The insurance company is equally at sea— they've never heard of the guy. However—" She paused until I gave her my full attention. "Chef Gregor filed a claim on the missing truffle just this morning. Apparently, he's making quite a stink about it."

"Interesting. But that's one less problem we have to deal with

—the insurance guys can take it from here. I sure would like to know what Livermore is after." I worked through the possible angles he could be working, which didn't take too long—with little concrete to go on, I was throwing darts in the dark.

"What do you think he might be after?" Brandy's eyes danced as her voice dropped to a conspiratorial whisper. "Do you think he could be the killer?"

I pictured the nervous little man with the thick, coarse, poorly cut gray hair poking from under his hideous toupee and the bushy dark eyebrows. "If he is, then he would've needed help to stuff Mr. Peccorino into that oven—the good doctor wasn't a small man." Rehydrated, he would probably top two hundred pounds, but I kept that little tidbit to myself—Brandy still had the easily bruised sensibilities of an early-twenty-something. And she hid a big heart under that feigned toughness. So much about her reminded me of myself at that age. I wasn't sure I appreciated that little insight—I'd always been the up-and-comer. Guess it was high time to pass that baton.

"I wonder why he came here," Brandy continued her musings out loud. "Since he felt the need to lie, I assume whatever his reasons were, they weren't aboveboard."

"Safe assumption." How I hated people who tried to maneuver me. Recently, there had been a lot of that going around, making manipulation my new hot button. I reached for my cockroach paperweight, then remembered it was gone—a fact that accelerated my mood's slide. The little trinkets of life around me helped keep me centered. "We can't do anything about him now, so let's concentrate on things we can have an impact on. How're all the ingredients for the rest of the week gelling?"

Brandy got that sort of weird look that meant her focus had rolled to an internal checklist. I used to be able to keep all the balls in the air, but lately, I'd fallen in love with the note-taking app on my iPhone, which probably would've bothered a lesser me. The new me was trying to embrace her limitations.

Brandy ticked off the items. "The press conference your mother had called?" She looked at me for some sign I was following. I gave her a nod. "Your mother postponed it."

A shot of cold adrenaline to the heart. "Why?"

Brandy looked nervous—as well she should, sitting smack in the center of the crosshairs. "Mona wouldn't say, exactly, but something about a bigger announcement."

"Which will be a bigger problem. Oh, joy." With my plate overflowing, I refused to worry about Mona's scheme, whatever it was. "Go on."

"The turkeys . . ." Brandy's focus switched to me, probably just an instinctive bit of self-preservation. Apparently feeling that death wasn't imminent, Brandy hit the list again. "The turkeys are caged in the motor pool, which . . ."

". . . is a very short-term solution," I said, narrowing my eyes as if training a sight on an invisible Mona. "Can't wait to see how Mother handles it."

That got a smirk from Pretty Girl. "The set for the cook-off is pretty much set up—the chefs have the rest of the day and tomorrow to familiarize themselves with the available equipment. I shouldn't think there will be any complaints—they have no idea what they'll be cooking."

Brandy had never dealt with the creative culinary wiz-kids, so I let her naïveté go—although I did offer a veiled warning. "Just in case, I would keep the knives locked up until the show, if I were you."

She looked for my smile. When she didn't find one, she made a note—or at least, she looked like she'd file it in her mental in-box. "Chitza said she might not make it down until tomorrow—the Sodom and Gomorrah Suite hired her as their private chef."

"Really?"

"I got the impression it was sort of a setup, an inside job, if you will."

"How so?"

The girl looked at me like I'd been living under a rock or something. "She and Dr. Phelps are tight. When Chitza was in the chef thing on TV, every day, he was in the front row cheering her on. It was *sooo* great. Guys can be so wonderful." Her smile dimmed when it ran headlong into my skepticism. "Don't you watch TV or read the rags?" She didn't really expect an answer—I knew that, so I just raised an eyebrow. "Oh, right. You don't, like .. . have a life or anything."

"Anything else?" I asked blandly, unable to pull off huffy. Her little tidbit did explain the comfortable pull I had detected between Chitza and the young scientist.

"Just the normal craziness." She paused and returned from mental gyrations. A sly smile ticked up one corner of her perfect, pouty lips. "So, what's up with the Teddie thing?"

"There is no Teddie thing. And it would behoove you to focus on the problems you can solve." What do you know, I *could* do huffy today.

She nodded and gave me a knowing look. "Ah, not so good, then. Interesting." With that, she tossed a pitying look at me and strolled out of the office.

Could today get any better?

Filled with questions and riding on a wave of unspent energy and emotion, I needed to move. When I stepped into the outer office, the bird sang out like a bo'sun whistling arrivals on deck, "Bite me! Bite me!"

"Enough out of you. If you don't learn some manners, I'll pluck you one feather at a time."

"Asshole!"

"I mean it!"

The bird glared at me and stopped hurling invectives. Instead, he let loose a wolf whistle and shifted his charm to another. "Pretty girl, pretty girl," he cooed, making me laugh out loud.

Hunched over some papers on her desk, Brandy pretended to ignore both of us, but her smile gave her away.

Miss P. was on the phone. Flinging a hand over the mouth-piece, she gave me a glare.

I raised my arms and mouthed, "What? I just walked in here."

While she finished the call I waited, shifting from one foot to the other in front of her desk.

"Yes, yes. I see. Could you give me the address again?" Holding the receiver in place with her shoulder, she jotted notes. "Got it. Thank you." Lowering her shoulder, she let the receiver fall, catching it in a deft move, then dropping it in its cradle. She tore off the top sheet of paper and handed it to me, giving me a look over the top of her cheaters. "Here."

I tried to decipher her scrawl, with only marginal success. "The big what?"

"Hole."

"The heavy equipment experience?" A very creative entrepreneur had bought a vacant lot way south on the Strip and leased some heavy equipment. For a fairly hefty fee, anyone could don a hard hat and move some serious dirt or dig a tunnel to China with a Caterpillar. Admittedly, that kind of mechanical power had its appeal—I'd been tempted more than once. Of course, there'd usually been a body I'd been fantasizing about tossing in a hole and covering.

Fantasy, the alternative to life without parole.

Miss P. nodded and gave me a look usually reserved by the insensitive for the slowest kid in the class. "Apparently, your good doctor and his friends are putting on a show for the press. It starts in forty minutes. If you hurry, you can just make it."

I'd MADE IT ALL THE WAY DOWNSTAIRS BEFORE MY PHONE VIBRATED at my hip—probably a record of some kind. Rotating it, I glanced at the caller ID. Romeo had run out of patience.

Grabbing the thing, I confirmed it was the young detective—

he'd caught me striding across the lobby. As I caressed the face of my phone with my thumb, I made a beeline toward the entrance. The noise of day was quickly escalating toward nighttime and its promises of fun, frivolity, and a dose of debauchery. The Ferrari slid to the curb as I pushed through the doors and pressed the phone to my ear, hoping I could hear. "Whatcha got?"

"Not the good news you're hoping for." The voice had a weird echo—like it came through the phone and yet it sounded like he was standing in front of me.

In crumpled overcoat, slouched stance, messy hair, and a scowl, he blocked my path, bringing me up short. Okay, so he was in front of me. A dribble of mustard trickled down his tie, which I thought I remembered seeing yesterday.

Face-to-face with the young detective, I terminated the call, replaced the phone at my hip, and switched to conversation mode. "Have you had any sleep?"

"A couple of hours last night on the couch in your office. Why?" He stepped out of my way and followed me to the car. Pausing with his hand on the passenger side handle, he looked at me over the top of the car. "Forget that last question, we need to talk . . . and you are so not going to like it."

"If longevity is your goal, you might want to let me arrive at that conclusion myself—you know what they do to the messenger."

I didn't even get a smile. Not a good sign.

"We have another note."

CHAPTER 14

"WHERE DID you get this?" I asked Romeo.

The young detective swallowed hard. "You don't want to know."

"Of course not. That's why I asked."

Huddled together, the crowd streaming around us into the hotel, Romeo and I examined a small piece of foil he had carefully unfolded and spread on the top of the car. The foil looked slightly off-color, and it was easy to tell it had been crumpled.

I read the words aloud. "Pigs to find a feast so rare. But eat a morsel taking care. A bit is fine but take heed. Death will come to those with greed." The little ditty had been scrawled on the foil in black ink—the writing looked familiar, but I was no expert. "Is that the same handwriting as the first note?"

He nodded. "That's not official, of course. The analysts are looking at both notes right now, but off the cuff, they said it sure looks like the same perp wrote them both."

"Have you compared the handwriting to examples from any of the potential killers?" My brain was spinning, but thoughts whirled just out of reach of reason. Stress—it'd either send me off the deep end or run me out of town if I didn't learn to handle it better.

"The notes are printed using block letters. Most people don't write that way." Romeo ran a hand through his hair, making it worse. Amazingly, the kid looked worse than I felt.

"Loosely translated, that would mean you're working on it, but don't hold out much hope the comparisons will tell you anything. Guess my wish to remove Jean-Charles from the suspect list isn't going to happen."

Romeo gave me a tired smile and a shrug. "That's how these things usually go. These days, a clever killer can run on a long leash."

"We'll pop him when he hits the end." I gave him a reassuring smile that I didn't feel. My personal take on that whole if-you-build-it-they-will-come thing was, if you believe it, it will happen, so I went with it. And if Jean-Charles turned out to be in this up to his *toque blanche*? I'd deal with it—but I would totally swear off men for a while. Could my picker be that far off? Oh yeah, it sure could. That was my MO in the dating game. "I got something for you." I rooted in my pocket, then deposited the chips from The Grape Spot into Romeo's hand.

"Where'd you get these?"

I gave him the short version. Satisfied he didn't need to preserve any fingerprints, Romeo dropped the chips into his pocket. "You know we're having some trouble reading the first chip you gave us. I've got forensics working on it."

"You'd better hurry, my ass is on the line. I lied by omission to Homeland Security. You've got my back, right?"

Romeo gave me a half-hurt look. "Of course. What did the feds want?"

"They're wise to some of this rerouting game and are worried about the continued safety of the food supply."

Romeo's eye shot up. "First I've heard. I'm low on the totem pole, but normally, that sort of thing would cross my desk."

"The feds are your problem," I said, although I wasn't entirely sure that was true. Agent Stokes had knocked on my door—I wouldn't be able to shrug him off that easily. "They have even fewer answers than we have, so help from that quarter probably won't be forthcoming . . . not that they ever play nice with us peons."

Romeo rubbed his eyes. "I don't know about you, but I'll take all the help I can get."

"I'm on my way to get Dr. Phelps and his geek squad on board right now. Somebody has to know how to read those damn chips."

"Right." Romeo looked like his thoughts weren't exactly tracking today. I knew the drill. "So, Brandy told me somebody stole your paperweight thing, and is taking pictures and posting them on the Internet?"

"Apparently."

"Who?" Romeo actually looked like he expected a real answer.

"I'm pretty sure it's Jean-Charles. I spoke to him briefly, and he told me he would tell me how to find the chips. I followed the first photo to the Grape Spot."

"Pretty oblique." Romeo frowned. "When did you talk to him?"

I told him.

"And you didn't tell me because?"

"He didn't tell me anything you needed to know."

Romeo narrowed his eyes at me as he thought, then he shrugged.

I'd won that round. What I told him was true . . . technically. But the same argument didn't quite cover the fact that I hadn't told Romeo about the note Jean-Charles had sent me with the first chip, and I didn't feel like explaining why at the moment— none of it would matter, anyway. We needed proof, not protestations of innocence. "Jean-Charles or whomever, right now, it doesn't matter. The only thing that does is that they are leading me to the chips. I have a feeling once we have them all, and we can read them, a key bit of this sordid tale will be in there."

"I can buy your theory that your chef might be the one helping you. That doesn't get him off the hook, though."

"That pesky little proof thing, I know." I opened the driver's side door. "Get in. You can tell me the rest of the story about that note on the way. That way, I don't have to look at you while you tell me which orifice you had to probe to find it."

Traffic flowed at a snail's pace, then got hung up entirely in the ever-present knot in front of the Bellagio, which was okay since the fountains fired off every fifteen minutes at this time of day—so at least we'd be entertained. "Okay, I think I'm ready."

"Actually, it's not as bad as you think. The note was wadded up and stuffed down Richard Peccorino's throat."

I swallowed hard and fought a shiver of revulsion. What kind of person would do that? The kind of person who would stuff a guy in an oven, I guessed in answer to my own question. "Not as bad as I think? I'm sure that depends on perspective."

"I should arrest you and Teddie for tampering with evidence. You do know that, don't you?" Romeo stared at the fountains and sighed heavily.

"Teddie, maybe. I gave you the chip as soon as it came into my possession, remember?" I shot him a serious look. "But I'll let you handcuff me if it would make you feel better."

That didn't lighten Romeo's sad face even a little. He turned and stared out the side window. "This job is getting to me."

I wanted to wrap him in a hug and protect him from the world —a surprising reaction, actually. Impossible, and it would most likely be unappreciated, so instead, I let his statement go without a response. "Let's think about this. Read the note again."

"Pigs to find a feast so rare. But eat a morsel taking care. A bit is fine but take heed. Death will come to those with greed." Romeo recited the lines, his voice a monotone, like a child trotting out a hastily memorized poem, the words correct, the meaning all but lost.

"These things make my brain hurt. And I'm getting really tired of this little game." I inched the car forward, then jumped at the opening salvo of the fountains—the noise always reminded me of a cannon shot.

"Jumpy, are we?" Romeo leaned to the side and turned to get a better look.

"Just running on fumes, as usual. I need a vacation."

"Considering our lives lately, a staycation is about the best you can hope for."

"We live in Vegas, how bad could that be?" I drummed my fingers on the steering wheel as I glanced at the time on the newly erected neon monstrosity in front of Planet Hollywood. The sign was so bright, I felt sure the astronauts could read every word from the International Space Station.

"Not for most people, but you have two bodies in your hotel, a lover who has disappeared, and another who has reappeared, and a mother who . . ."

"Stop, you're making me want to hurt myself."—I pointed to the note in Romeo's lap—"I'm assuming no prints on any of these things?"

"None that shed any light."

"You'd think, just once, we'd get a break," I groused.

"Wasn't it you that used to quote that female baseball movie? What was it you said?"

"It's the hard that makes it good. From *A League of Their Own*. A great flick, by the way." For our Tuesday movie nights, Teddie and I had watched that movie . . . several times. I flipped on my blinker to move to the left. Why did I always forget that driving in the right lanes along the Strip was impossible—cars inevitably wanted to turn, but the constant flow of humanity on the sidewalks rarely ceded an opening.

"You know, taken out of context, there's some innuendo there . . ." Romeo trailed off when he caught my glare.

"Those are my lines. I'll thank you not to poach." I didn't worry about telling him I was kidding.

"I've been spending too much time around you. Apparently, I'm turning into you."

"God help you." Finally a guy in a white Prius let me move over, but not without a wolf whistle. With an upstanding member of the police department ready to defend my virtue, I smiled and waved. "Okay, what I want to know is why the killer seems to think I'm in the know."

"I'm curious about that as well." To Romeo's credit, he didn't act like I was hiding anything.

Feeling slightly guilty, I mentally ran through what I knew. No secrets. Then a thought dawned. "If you didn't send Homeland Security to play in my sandbox . . ." I looked at him for confirmation.

"Nope, I'm too low on the totem pole for them to give me much attention."

"Then I wonder how they singled me out," I mused out loud.

"You mean since you're so low profile and all."

"It's just odd. They usually work through Jerry and Security."

"They had some story about tampering with the food supply?" Romeo pulled out his crumpled note pad and pencil, jotting notes as I recapped my conversation with Detective Stokes. "That does seem odd, poisoning the food supply? In Vegas? Hardly the large-scale kind of thing the terrorists go for. You'd think they'd be more interested in the water supply or something. I take it you can't offer any clarity on this new note?"

"Give me time. I've never been all that great at these word puzzle things." Finally, the light changed and the crowds clustered on the sidewalks, freeing a path for the cars. When my turn to move came, I took full advantage, whipping around the cars in front of me and accelerating down the Strip. The traffic always eased south of Flamingo—bunching briefly at Trop, then opening completely south of the intersection.

"Where are we going, by the way?" Romeo asked, but didn't seem too concerned.

"I'm feeling the need to play with heavy equipment."

"You know, at any other time, I would take a cut at that curve ball." Romeo tried to banter, but he came off sounding defeated.

I joined the innuendo game. "Probably something along the lines of look no farther, you're the complete package."

"Always one step ahead." Romeo leaned his head back.

"I play to my strengths." Letting the horses run, I tried to let my brain freewheel.

Pigs to find a feast so rare.

∼

THE MOJAVE DESERT.

Most folks forgot, or perhaps never knew, that Vegas was a carefully cultivated and nurtured oasis in a vast sea of land unsuitable to human life. And once one ventured beyond the watered environs, the landscape changed. Scrubby plants barely eking out an existence, sand and dirt, maybe a cactus or two, but little else—the perfect place to pretend to be a dirt mover.

The Big Hole wasn't too hard to find—just navigate toward the cloud of dust. With next to no moisture anywhere, the sand became airborne with the slightest movement, and usually remained so for some time, carried on the ever-present breezes. This often had interesting results: while the rest of the world had rainstorms, we had sand storms. Just the other day, I was less than a quarter of a mile from Mandalay Bay Hotel and I couldn't see it —a Vegas brownout, as it were.

Cars packed the parking lot, an unlined dirt square cordoned off with rope and cones. With no painted lines to supply order, there was none. Reluctant to toss the Ferrari into the melee, I reached across in front of Romeo, my hand open.

With a cockeyed grin, he put his badge in my open palm.

The parking attendant didn't look at me—instead, he drooled with thinly veiled car lust as he let his eyes rake its length. If I'd been the Ferrari, I would've slapped him. When he finally looked at me, he seemed only slightly chagrined, and I waved the badge under his nose.

"Man, guess it really pays to be on the public payroll. Glad you guys are living the good life on the backs of us working stiffs." Lifting the rope, he slid the low-slung car underneath, then motioned me to a safe spot behind the food trucks.

As Romeo extricated himself from his "ride," he shot me a quip. "You do so much for Metro's public image."

"Just doing my part. You know, increase recruitment . . . maybe attract a higher-class crowd." My disdain for the local cops was no secret. As he usually did, Romeo ignored me, but I caught a smile before he covered it with an important look.

Romeo—an iconoclast in a conformist's uniform—a sista by a different mista, if you ignored the whole gender thing.

I threw my arm around his shoulders as we met in front of the car and turned to take in the spectacle. Normally a fairly straightforward, sedate affair, today the Big Hole had the look of a sideshow. Crowds packed the hastily erected grandstands on two sides of the big pit where the heavy equipment crawled on giant treads. No expert, I tried to identify the major pieces—a grader, a huge backhoe, a front-end loader, and a new addition—a crane swinging a wrecking ball, presumably against the triple-thick cinder-block wall bisecting the pit. Today, a shaky-looking platform had been erected atop the wall.

One side of the pit lay open, a gentle grade rising from the floor to accommodate the passage of the equipment to and from the storage shed fronting the road and protecting the casual passersby from the slight chance of runaway machinery. A conglomeration of several food trucks and a mobile reporting van from each of the major television stations pressed together, forming a perimeter on the fourth side, completing the whole stadium effect. One station had even brought the boom truck with a bucket, which now dangled out over the pit, the hapless reporter crouching inside and a cameraman looming over him, his camera pointed down.

Shielding my eyes against the low-angled sunlight from the west, I scanned the crowd looking for someone familiar . . . anyone . . . Jean-Charles. Not seeing that particular someone, nor anyone of pertinence, my mood plummeted. "Man, all we're missing is the marching band."

"I'm taking it something special is happening today," Romeo remarked.

I felt no need to dignify the obvious with a response. Instead, finally spying a friend, I galvanized myself into action. Stepping to the window of the farthest food truck, I feigned interest in the menu. "Give me a number seven, extra hot."

Without looking up from his grill, the chef began a perfunctory answer. "There's no number . . ." He stopped and looked up, recognition lighting his face. Quick as a cat, he bolted down the steps and caught me in a bear hug. Holding tight, he rocked me back and forth until I laughed. Then he held me at arm's length.

I let him have his look while I did the same.

As always, Beanie Savoy looked good enough to eat. Mocha skin, a wicked wide smile, short dreads, and a hard body covered in a loose Hawaiian shirt, khakis tied at the waist with a rope, and Tevas: he had a Lenny Kravitz mojo. Under that shirt, he sported some of the most perfect abs in the business—no, I will not tell you how I know that.

"Don't you eat?" I asked. "You do know skinny chefs do not inspire confidence."

He rewarded me with a wider grin. Letting his arms fall to his sides, he took a step back. "Where they been keepin' you, girl? Why haven't you come ridin' with me? Remember that time the cops chased us damn near to the California line? Man, that was wild. Who knew those hookers . . ."

I cleared my throat, stopping him as I threw a glance over my shoulder. "This is Detective Romeo with Metro. Romeo, this is

Beanie, the very best gourmet taco maker this side of Montego Bay."

The two men shook hands.

"Tacos and Jamaica?" Romeo looked skeptical.

"Food-doo, voodoo, mon. Lucky, she gave me that name a long time ago." With that, Beanie raised a finger, then bolted back into the truck, where he stirred and flipped and mashed the ingredients cooking on his grill. He stuck his head out the window: "You want your special?" His eyes locked onto mine.

"Extra hot."

A moment later, he handed me a plastic bowl lined with white wax paper. Nestled inside were two of what I knew to be the most succulent, sublime, spicy pulled pork tacos. He gave a bowl to Romeo as well, but his eyes stayed on me. "Soft and tasty, just like you like it."

Romeo took his food. "You guys are doing a great job of ruining my appetite." But one bite, and I could see his attitude change. "Oh, man," was all he managed through a full mouth.

Beanie and I exchanged knowing smiles.

"It's so good to see you, girl."

"You, too." I took a dainty bite, anticipating the firepower inside the tiny taco. "Even better than I remember—and I remember it all."

Beanie gave me a lopsided grin and a cock of his head as he waggled his eyebrows in silent appreciation of the memory of "it all."

"How'd you get wrangled into this little soiree?" I asked as I blinked back the tears of appreciation for the Jamaican spice. My game had gotten rusty—I used to be able to eat Beanie's stuff until I couldn't feel my lips, and I was sure I'd lost at least the first couple of layers of skin from the inside of my mouth.

"Girl, all high and mighty you've become—lost your toughness." Beanie handed me a paper napkin. While I was struggling, Romeo silently powered through, popping a taco at a time into his mouth and then groaning with happiness. Age, or lack thereof, sometimes created a chasm.

Beanie looked at me as if he could read my thoughts. "The word went out there was some kind of show. You know me, I never miss a party—I was the first one here. Well, except for that guy over there." He nodded toward Brett Baker, the sushi truck guy and Jean-Charles's second in the cook-off.

A school of painted fish in different shapes, sizes, and colors swam across the rear and the side of the food truck. The large, open mouth of a grouper encircled the order window. The words one fish, two fish were stenciled above the window in bright red, childlike letters—like the cover of a kid's book. Dr. Seuss. One fish, two fish, red fish, blue fish . . . Two chef, one chef . . .

Chills chased down my spine. "Cute." I tried to be flip, act like nothing had creeped me out. From the looks of Beanie and Romeo, I pulled it off, although Romeo eyed me a bit more intently. I watched Brett Baker, using his wide, white smile and easy manner to lure the passersby, mostly women. "What's his story?"

Beanie leaned on his arms, resting his elbows on the shelf of the order window. "Don't really know—he keeps to himself mostly. But I can tell you he showed up here out of the blue— none of us had even seen him around or nothing. He's got serious shit though, top quality. And I heard people say he's trained with the best in Japan, learned his sushi skills from masters."

"Wonder why he's driving a food truck then, if he's so good," Romeo added, making me fight the urge to dive out of the line of fire.

Beanie bristled. Pushing himself up off his elbows, he glared down at the detective. "You just ate my food, yet you still think we're all glorified burger-flippers."

Romeo shot a look of distress my way.

"Nothing like a faux pas to get a friendship off on the right foot, eh?" I teased, knowing Beanie wouldn't take offense. "Kid, I love you, but I'm not falling on your sword."

Putting on his most hangdog look, Romeo returned his attention to the guy he'd just stuck a knife in. "I'm sorry. You're right, I'm afraid. I don't know what I was thinking." The kid actually looked contrite..

I'd lost that ability decades ago. "Not thinking at all, I should think," I added just for fun.

Beanie beamed—he had that wonderful Caribbean ability to laugh insults away. "No worries, mon."

"If you say 'be happy' I'll slap you," I added, stopping him before he could trot out that overused lyric—one of his favorites. "He showed up with good shit, you say? I sure would like to know more."

Beanie gave me a sage nod. "I'll ask around." Inclining his head, he directed my attention behind me. The line had been growing while we chatted.

I stepped to the side, motioning the man behind me to the front. "Sorry."

Beanie gave me another full-wattage grin. "Been doing some interesting things with exotic fish lately that's been going over pretty good. Great to see you, girl. Don't stay away so long next time. Like I said, my ceviche tacos are killer."

ROMEO AND I WANDERED THROUGH THE CROWD. THE SHOW, whatever it was, had drawn quite a crowd, one that was still arriving. In a space designed to hold far fewer, the swelling throng pressed tightly together, making movement difficult. A cool breeze wafted through carrying smoke and tantalizing smells from the gathered food trucks, making the crush bearable and my mouth water.

We ambled a bit, absorbing the atmosphere. Romeo dogged

my heels chivalrously, allowing me to cut a path as I turned back toward the food trucks.

"Care to go for Round Two?" I asked him as we ambled, angling my head toward Brett Baker's truck, which held the primo spot closest to the action. Personally, I thought Romeo was way too thin, but I'd already commented on that and I didn't think I needed to hit it again.. "Want some sushi?"

"Can't stomach the stuff." He tossed off the line like the true burger man I knew him to be. "So, what did you get from your friend? Whatever it was, I missed it, but I can see your wheels grinding."

"Nothing concrete, just a hunch." I kept my eyes scanning over the crowd as I talked. "One of the frustrating things about a tourist town like Vegas is, the local restaurants often can't get the quality products they'd like. All the top-end stuff is reserved by the big-name chefs and the hotels."

Romeo caught on quickly. "That must make it doubly hard for these truck guys."

"And Brett Baker breezes into town with 'good shit,' taking the street food world by storm."

"And?"

"Wonder where he gets his good shit."

A second person poked her head out of Brett Baker's food truck window. Chitza DeStefano.

Romeo and I glanced at each other. "Interesting," we both said.

Chitza caught me looking at her. She held my gaze for a moment. She didn't smile. Breaking eye contact, she ducked back inside the truck, out of sight.

On my second pass over the crowd, my eyes hit on another familiar face. "Wonder what Chef Gregor is doing here."

Apparently unaware he was being watched, the chef pulled a handkerchief from his back pocket and mopped his face. He stepped back into the cover of a shadow.

Romeo followed my gaze. "Gregor looks pretty hot around the collar, especially on such a cool day."

As we watched, another man joined him, smaller, bald, twitchy. Chef Gregor bent down to hear what the man was saying —the chef didn't look happy.

I narrowed my eyes. The shorter guy looked familiar—something in the way he moved, his mannerisms. It took me a moment, but I finally placed him—Mr. Livermore, without the bad toupee.

"You know that guy?"

"He came snooping around the office. He wasn't who he said he was." Romeo started to speak, but I raised a hand, stopping him. "Let's give him some rope just yet—I've got my people working on it."

Romeo didn't argue—he was well aware that sometimes my network worked much more efficiently than the rusty cogs of the ponderous Metro bureaucracy.

Both men stayed in the shadow.

"Guess the crowd is big enough to draw the paramedics." Romeo nodded toward an ambulance that had backed to the festivities, its rear doors folded back. One of the EMTs sat on the bumper. "Isn't that . . . ?" Romeo trailed off as if he'd forgotten the paramedic's name.

This was a weak ploy to draw me out, so I cut him off at the pass. "Nick. His name is Nick, and yes, he's cute. Yes, he asked me out. Yes, it's none of your business."

Romeo seemed happy with that. "Are you going to tell me what this circus is about, or am I supposed to be surprised?"

"I don't know, and I'm not sure I care, although with all the interesting people gathered in the crowd, I am curious. But, right now, my goal is to find Dr. Phelps, he's running this show." Shielding my eyes, I scanned the crowd. On my third scan across the crowd, I spied another one of our chefs. "Look over there." I pointed for Romeo's benefit. Christian Wexler seemed to be angling toward Chef Gregor and Livermore, still arguing in the shadows. Time to see what they were up to. "Follow me."

Wexler paused in front of Gregor, stepping into the larger man's face. He spat some words, punctuating them with pokes to the chest. Gregor looked incensed, his face an angry red. I moved faster, trying to get closer but losing sight of the three of them as the crowd moved and surged around me.

By the time we reached the spot where the men had been standing, the little party had broken up. "Damn." I scanned the crowd anew.

"There!" Romeo's hand appeared over my shoulder, pointing in front of me.

I followed the line of sight and spied Dr. Phelps climbing up a thin metal ladder that shook with each rung he took. At the top, he stepped off to the side and onto the platform over the cinderblock wall. Grabbing a wireless mike, he tapped it with his finger. The thing was on, the volume up. He held it pressed close to his lips at a ninety-degree angle—he'd done this before. "Hello, I'd like to thank you all for coming to see our little demonstration. Frankly, I'm a bit amazed there are so many of you interested in the obscure construct of RFID technology."

The crowd, including me, waited in rapt attention. When the crane engine cranked to life, belching black smoke, I think we jumped collectively. Once the engine had settled into a smooth thrum, Dr. Phelps continued. "Refining and miniaturizing existing technology, my team at Cal has added some economically viable, industry-needed features that are quite impressive."

He raised his shirt, showing the world his washboard abs—a geek god. A black band encircled his chest. He raised his hand and shook a white tag dangling on a chain. "This chip contains our new technology. It will monitor my heart rate, my temperature, and my position via GPS. The power source is supplied through the radio beam of the reader, and all of this for less than a penny a tag, readable using readily available RFID readers."

Dr. Phelps gave a cue to the technician working the sound-board. He flipped a few switches, and the rhythmic sound of Dr. Phelps's slightly elevated heartbeat reverberated through the speakers placed around the pit.

"See and believe." Dr. Phelps thumbed off the mike. Bending, he handed it to a young man who stepped to the platform—I thought I recognized him as one of the UC-Berkeley guys from last night.

A flexible banner unscrolled behind him. The crowd collectively gasped when the white sheet sprang to life, revealing that it was in fact a video screen. Dr. Phelps' heart rate, temperature, and latitude and longitude coordinates appeared in large numbers.

Romeo fidgeted at my shoulder, glancing at his watch—thankfully, he resisted adding an exaggerated sigh. "What are we here for, exactly?"

"Haven't a clue."

A tall man standing in front of me turned and gave me a disdainful stare. "You are watching history being made. This will revolutionize the food industry and save this country from contaminated food products."

I smiled in return. "Thereby saving Fast Food Nation and its contribution to the exalted tradition of Escoffier and its fellow *artistes gastronomiques*."

To my delight, his face softened into a grin. "Our lasting legacy."

The sound of the crane's engine deepened and grew louder, forestalling more banter and grabbing our attention. I could see a figure in the glass cage at the base of the crane's arm working the levers, but I couldn't make out his features or any identifying trait —I assumed he was another of Dr. Phelps's colleagues.

The arm, from which the chain and wrecking ball dangled, extended high above us, then eased the iron ball over to Dr. Phelps, who stepped on the ball and grabbed the chain. After testing his footing for a moment, he gave the thumbs-up sign to the operator. Lifted from the platform, he soared over the crowd. I shaded my eyes against the ever-lowering angle of the sun, trying to follow his path arcing above our heads.

The staccato rhythm of his heartbeat sounded through the speakers, which I found vaguely disconcerting—the audible manifestation of Dr. Phelps's increasing fear, which did little to allay mine. In an instinctive, sympathetic response, my heart rate accelerated.

"Holy shit." Romeo sounded awestruck.

Glancing at the large screen, I realized the readout of Dr. Phelps's vital signs was updating, the page scrolling as new information accumulated.

"How's he doing that?" Romeo asked as we both watched the crane swinging him in what looked to be a defined pattern.

"It seems new info is added at the apex of each arc. Other than that, you got me."

The guy in front of us was no help, either.

After watching a few more passes, which I suspected was the entire show, I decided to heed the lure of all the whiffs of delicious foods wafting through the crowd while I waited for Dr. Phelps to finish. As I turned to go, I caught the ball as it reached yet another apex. The young scientist hung on with one hand, waving to the crowd with the other.

At the high point, the ball suddenly dropped, a jerky hitch to the fluidity.

Slack in the chain. The crowd gasped. I probably did as well, which was a challenge, considering I was holding my breath.

Startled, Dr. Phelps clutched the chain with both hands. His heart rate zoomed. A pulsing rhythm booming through the speakers, it pounded through my chest until my heart syncopated.

The ball hit the bottom of the new length chain with a jolt. Dr. Phelps had bent his knees to absorb the impact, but it wasn't enough. One foot lost its grip. He swung wildly as he tried to regain his footing. After a few failed attempts, he worked his foot back under him, but he stayed crouched.

The crane moved, pulling the ball, increasing the arc. As the ball started down, slowly at first, then building speed . . . it headed straight for the cinder-block wall in the center of the pit. Mesmerized, I watched in growing horror.

Finally, with pulsing certainty of the scene unfolding, adrenaline freed me, propelling me forward. Pushing people aside, I moved, driven by the need to stop the disaster unfolding in slow motion in front of me. I sensed Romeo behind me, but I didn't look.

As I ran, I shouted, "Jump!" to Dr. Phelps as he accelerated overhead in a downward arc. I knew he probably couldn't hear me. And even if he could, he was most likely too scared to let go, but I still had to try. At the edge of the pit, I launched myself in the air. Hitting the sand, my feet sank a bit, stopping my momentum. Putting my hands out, I rolled, letting the momentum carry me until I hit my feet again and ran.

The ball was coming down hard and fast now. I could see the terror on the young doctor's face as he curled up, putting his back to the wall, cringing for impact.

I had no idea what I was going to do. It didn't matter.

I was too slow.

The ball, with its precious human cargo, hit the wall.

The wall crumbled. Dr. Phelps disappeared in a cloud of dust.

The world went quiet.

Without thinking, I hit the hole in the wall. Grabbing at pieces of blocks, digging, scraping, I followed the chain into the pile of rumble. Romeo pushed in next to me. Together, we fought like panicked rescuers in a collapsed mine.

"His heartbeat has stopped," Romeo gasped through labored breathing.

"No. It can't have. Just the sound has stopped."

Romeo didn't argue. I grabbed a huge chunk of stone, struggling with the weight. Romeo grabbed the other side. We turned to toss it behind us. Other hands grabbed it. Like a bucket brigade, others joined, helping to move the stones and clear a path for the paramedics, I hoped.

The next time I reached, my hand hit cloth, then flesh. "I got him."

Romeo and I increased our pace—working as fast as we could, as quickly as we dared. First, we uncovered his legs; one was badly broken. Bone protruded from his thigh. Blood had pooled underneath his leg, staining the light sand a dark, ugly reddish brown. The wound only oozed now . . . not a good sign. Romeo shucked off his shirt, ripping off a strip. Feverishly, I tied it tight above the wound, then kept working. It seemed like an eternity, but we finally cleared his chest, then his head.

Two fingers against his neck, I felt for a pulse. Nothing. With a hand, I stilled Romeo and concentrated. Still nothing.

Someone pressed in behind us. A hand squeezed my shoulder and a gentle, calm voice said, "Lucky, we'll take it from here."

Turning, I met the blue eyes of Nick the paramedic. He'd ridden to my rescue several times before.

Pressing to the side, I eased out past him—a very tight squeeze. It was funny how desperate need facilitated the normally impossible. On the other side, Romeo also flattened himself, allowing Nick's colleague to join him. The path now clear, we backed out on our hands and knees, first Romeo, then me.

The crowd huddled around, silent, round-eyed. Several of the men were dusty and bloodied. Glancing down, I realized I was the same. Several fingernails ripped and torn, the skin on my hands and arms scored with ugly bright red gashes as if I'd been mauled by an otherworldly beast—the clothes I stood in soiled and torn beyond repair. Thought stalled as I floundered in the aftermath of the adrenaline rush. Without a word, Romeo reached out, pulling me into a hug. Putting my head on his shoulder, I tried to breathe.

An eerie silence enveloped us.

Absorbing his strength, I finally pulled away. Holding vigil, we all waited.

Raking my hand through my hair, I scanned the crowd. Christian Wexler stood above me on the other side of the pit, staring at me. We locked eyes. He tilted his chin in challenge, then stepped back, and the crowd swallowed him.

Romeo filtered through the crowd, wandering, searching. Casually, I kept track of him as he talked with random folks, questioning the media people in the crowd. Occasionally, he pulled out his pad to jot a note. Other Metro officers arrived. Romeo directed them, and I watched as they fanned out through the crowd. I let Romeo do his thing—if I tried to help, I'd only be in the way—he'd told me that several times before.

Distracted, I let my eyes wander over the crowd—they couldn't find anyone else familiar to settle on. I struggled through the loose sand, clambering up to the edge of the pit. Putting a hand down, I sat on the edge, my lower legs dangling. I concentrated on keeping myself still, quieting my mind, and slowing the hammering of my heart. The needling pain of each shallow cut and scrape was a sharp reminder of the fine line between life and death and comforting evidence of which side I fell on.

Romeo returned, looming over me as he stuffed his note pad back in his pocket. Dropping down beside me, his mouth was set in a hard line, his face closed and angry.

"From the looks of you, I'm guessing nobody saw who was in the cab of that crane."

Romeo snorted. "With our luck? Nobody saw anything. None of the camera crews had any footage, either—everyone focused on the drama."

"Figured."

"It coulda been an accident." Romeo sounded hopeful.

"Right." I looked him in the eye.

His hope deflated. "But you don't think so."

I turned my attention back to the pit and the hole Dr. Phelps had disappeared into. "Kid, there're a lot of things I don't believe in, even though I'd like to: Santa Claus, Cupid, the Tooth Fairy. It's a long list that includes coincidence and easy answers."

He mulled that over for a moment. "You don't believe Cupid is flapping around piercing us all with arrows tipped with the elixir of true love?"

"Hell, no—the little fairy is long gone. Some dissatisfied customer strangled the life out of him centuries ago."

"That's not like you at all."

"Someday, I had to grow up." I shot him a hopeful smile. "I'm done looking to anyone else, real or imaginary, for my happiness."

He returned my smile. It was still his turn to dole out the hugs —I took it like a man.

A figure behind us cast a shadow, blocking the heat of the sun as it dropped lower toward the west. The sudden coolness tickled the nape of my neck. A shiver chased through me as I turned, shielding my eyes with one hand.

Brett Baker gave us a tight, worried smile. "May I join you?" He motioned to the spot next to me.

"Sure."

He crouched, levering himself with one hand as he dropped his feet over the edge and settled in. "What's going on?" he whispered.

I brought him up to speed.

"Wow. You think they can bring that dude back.?."

"Right now would be a great time for a miracle." I took a deep breath, marshaling my thoughts. Romeo glanced at me, but didn't say anything. The floor was mine. "Brett, I know this is an awkward time, but would you mind if I asked you some questions?"

"Questions?" He glanced at me, his expression open. "I guess so."

"How do you know Jean-Charles?"

"He recruited me to work for him in New York. I'd just finished training in Japan, and really had few contacts in the States." As he talked, Brett stared into the pit, watching the paramedics work. "I interviewed with Chef Bouclet. He hired me. I rotated between his three restaurants refining the fish preparation, adding some sushi where appropriate. He has been a wonderful mentor."

"And Adone Giovanni? Any bad blood between you two?"

His eyes flicked to me. "Not for me. I can't speak for Adone. He is a great chef, very talented. But he's an ass."

Romeo nudged me—I got the hint. "How so?"

"Too much ego. Too much anger. This is a tough business—we all have put in many years of long, hard days. He thinks it is his time."

"Is it?"

Brett gave me a knowing look. "That is for time to decide."

"Ah yes, timing is everything." I trotted out this little banality as I watched the paramedics working around the hole where Nick and Dr. Phelps were hidden from view. Talking helped. "Do you still do any work with Jean-Charles in New York?"

"No. I left about a year ago. Moved to L.A." He rubbed his thighs with both hands—the evening had turned a bit cool for shorts. "Loved the restaurant I worked for there, but I fell in love with the whole idea of this food truck thing. You know it's really big on the West Coast."

"And here as well." I tucked my hands under my thighs. Mr. Baker had made me aware of the chill. "Of course, trends travel the short distance between Southern California and here pretty quickly."

"I bought a truck, and here I am." Brett seemed amused by that fact.

"Who is your supplier here?"

His smile faded. "Not sure now. It was Fiona Richards."

"How was her quality?"

If he thought the question odd, he didn't let on. "The best. She could get anything, even the most rare stuff."

"And Chitza? Where did you meet her?"

"I'd never heard of her until I came here. I met her at the meeting earlier, the one you held." He must've sensed my next question, or he saw it in my eyes, I don't know which. "She came by today. Wanted to see my truck. Just curious is all."

Silence enveloped us once again, and time slowed to a crawl. To be with this many people with no sound other than the passing of the traffic sorta creeped me out a bit. And worry was making me twitchy. Metro had set up a perimeter, moving the crowd back farther so the paramedics could work. Nick was taking an awful lot of time—I didn't know whether that was good or bad. I chose the former on the theory that manifesting, or "wishful thinking," as I liked to call it, really worked.

After a seeming eternity, I heard a sound. Cocking my head, I waited. It came again. One beat, then two. Then a steady rhythm pulsed through the speakers.

The crowd cheered. We all reached for those within hugging distance to share the joy.

Romeo jumped down and began giving orders. He pointed to a couple of officers, young guys with strong backs and large arms. "You two, come here."

Nick had left a metal cage stretcher next to the opening Romeo and I had cleared. Romeo nodded toward it. The young men bent and eased it into the hole, one of them carrying the front, the other guiding the rear.

Romeo returned to his spot next to me. We both continued our vigil.

"You okay?" I asked.

"Yeah, you?"

"I'll be better when I know he's okay."

With nothing else to do, I silently bartered with the universe, offering anything if he could just come through this whole.

Glancing around, I noticed others doing the same thing, their lips moving in silent prayer or incantation. Beanie's food truck sat open yet abandoned—I assumed he was waiting somewhere in the crowd.

Everything looked pretty normal. Except for one noticeable exception:

Brett Baker and his truck were gone.

CHAPTER 15

"WE'VE BEEN worried sick!" Miss P. jumped from behind her desk and rushed to greet me when I pushed through the office door. "We heard what happened."

Obviously feeling the emotion, the bird flapped his wings as he yelled, "Fucking bitch. Fucking bitch. Bad, bad girl. Smack you bad."

I would've smiled, except I wondered where exactly he had learned to say that . . . and what had happened to the "bad, bad girl." The thought made me sad, angry, and afraid.

Miss P. took both of my hands, one in each of hers, then stood back. "Look at you." She turned my hands over—bloody and torn, they weren't pretty. "Oh, baby."

"Have you heard anything on Dr. Phelps's condition?" I wandered back to my former office and looked in the closet. As luck would have it, some of my clothes I kept there for just this sort of thing were back from the cleaner's. I pawed through them, trying to ignore the increasing pain in my hands—and trying not to get blood on any of the newly clean clothes.

"I pulled rank with the hospital operator, told her I was you."

I snorted as I pulled an outfit out—jeans and a warm sweater. "That'll get you a cup of bad coffee and a spot at the end of the line."

"It got me through to the attending physician. He said somebody got to the young man just in time. His heart, already under strain from losing blood from his compound fracture, had stopped under the weight of the rocks on his chest. Quick thinking and a tourniquet stabilized him, the paramedics did the rest."

Relief washed through me. My legs went all wobbly, and I sank onto the toilet in the small bathroom and set about shucking my clothes, replacing them with a cleaner, more hearty set. The shoes, too. Flats were definitely in order.

When I returned, somewhat cleaned up—I hadn't the nerve to do much with my hands other than run them under cold water—Miss P. waited where I'd left her. "We tried to call, but you didn't answer your phone."

I let her help me to one of the chairs by the window. "Really?" Once seated, she backed off and I reached for the thing, but the holster was empty. "Better order me a new one—apparently, I've lost this one."

Brandy waltzed through the door with an air of efficiency, until she saw me. "Whoa. What happened to you?"

The bird let out a piercing wolf whistle.

I pointed to him. "Enough out of you."

To my amazement, he sidled to the corner, pulled his head down low, and ruffled his feathers.

"Okay." I nodded, feeling a bit like the man behind the curtain in *The Wizard of Oz*, but I rolled with it. Between the report on Dr. Phelps and my momentary magic over the bird, I was feeling a bit more bucked with life as I brought her up to speed.

"Too coincidental to be an accident." Her face clouded. "Romeo? He's okay, right?"

I pressed a hand to my chest, which I tried to puff out with feigned indignity. "You wound me to the core. Of course he's okay. Do you really think I'd let anything happen to him?"

"Well, you did let Jeremy get shot."

"Grazed. Thank you very much." I gave her a haughty look.

"Whatever." Like so many of her age group, Brandy tossed that word out with the obligatory eye roll when she couldn't think of a clever retort.

I chose to ignore it—engaging in verbal thrust and parry with one of the under-twenty-five crowd would be like challenging Olive Oyl to an arm-wrestling match.

"Proving, once again, inches matter." Miss P. said that with a straight face, earning my grudging respect, as she proffered a glass of amber liquid, Wild Turkey 101. "For medicinal purposes."

As I grabbed the glass, my respect was complete and total. I threw back the whole thing in one gulp, then winced as the jolt of heat traced a path to my stomach, bringing tears to my eyes. "I dropped Romeo at his car. He wanted to head home to clean up, and get another shirt—the one he had he donated to the cause."

"You good?" The young woman eyed me as if convinced of my invincibility.

I wasn't about to disappoint. "Just in need of a new uniform and a manicure, then I'll be good to go."

As she turned away, she said, "I just saw Mona in the lobby. She was looking for you, and she had that look."

"What look?" I eyed my assistant warily.

"Like a lion stalking a gazelle." With one hand, Brandy batted away my concern. "Don't worry. I told her you were off-property."

That wouldn't put Mona completely off the scent, but it would buy me some time, so I relaxed a bit. "Dr. Phelps had sure set up quite the circus act. You wouldn't believe who all was there."

Both heads swiveled my direction as my staff said in unison, "Who?"

Holding up my hand, I ticked them off, one finger at a time, "Gregor, Mr. Livermore, Chitza, Brett Baker, Chef Wexler—the whole cast of characters, well, almost. But a curious little bunch, and I wouldn't think any of them would be that interested in some new RFID technology."

Brandy held up a finger. "I just thought of something." Stepping to her desk, she returned with a magazine, folded open, which she handed to me. When I took it, she reached over and pointed to a picture and short blurb. The column was titled "We Came. We Saw. We Consumed," and the byline read *The Phantom Phoodie.*

I glanced up at my young assistant. "The Phantom Phoodie? Really?"

"No one knows who he is. He's like this hip, cool food critic. Last week, he broiled Chef Wexler's entrails, really eviscerated his menu, his preparation . . . everything. Don't you remember?" She paused. Clearly, she expected a response.

"If it doesn't concern this hotel or Cielo, in all likelihood, I wouldn't give it more than a passing interest—my brain is full, if I add new information, old stuff spills out the back, so I have to be careful."

Watching me for a moment, weighing my words, she acted like she believed me. "I noticed that." She lifted her chin toward the column, refocusing my attention. "Anyway. It just goes to motive, since we're plucking at straws. If Wexler is on the ropes financially, and now his rep gets totally ripped, well, he just might be looking for a fight."

"Good thinking." I made a mental note to keep Brandy out of the murder game from here on out. Although she seemed to have a nose for it, she also had that youthful air of invincibility that had gotten her in trouble and damn near killed last time. And I didn't want her blood on my hands . . . unless I wrung her neck myself.

She seemed pleased. "And there's something else."

My eyes followed her as she stepped to her desk, then returned with an iPad mini. "Where'd you get that?"

"They were issued to all the C-level staff last month."

C-level, that would be me, unless I'd gotten fired and was now slaving away for free. It struck me, since the whole Teddie thing, I'd just let the details of my life go while I remained mired in self-pity. Boring. I was so done with that! I lowered my head and looked at Miss P. from under my eyebrows. "And mine would be?"

She gave me a flat look that conveyed her feelings perfectly, along with the deadpan delivery. "Under the stack of papers you haven't touched on the left side of your desk . . . held there by the phone you don't answer."

I shot her a tight little smile lacking in appreciation for her sarcasm. "Thanks." I turned to Brandy. "Show me what you got." When she kneeled next to me, I didn't object.

She folded back the cover and brought the screen to life. "We have another picture of the cockroach thing." She rotated the device and handed it to me.

And there it was, in full color, sitting on the corner of a black-and-white photo of a man. I looked more closely. Then I smiled and shook my head.

Brandy piped up. "Do you know something I don't? I haven't a clue who that old dude is. And why would anyone take a picture like that—no one looking at it would know what it meant."

"Except the person it was meant for."

Brandy's eyes widened. "You?"

My smugness evaporated just a bit. "Well, I don't know for certain. But I suspect Jean-Charles is sending me these pictures. He knows I like old movies." I pointed to the screen, then touched it when it went dark, bringing it back to life. "And that is John Barrymore."

Brandy snatched the iPad, looked at it for a moment, then clutched it to her chest. "This is so romantic!"

Miss P. and I both looked at the girl like there was no way we could imagine ever having said anything that inane. Although, truth be told, we both probably had had our swooning moments —I mean Miss P. was a Dead Head back in the day. And she still wouldn't tell me if she'd slept with Jerry Garcia—a fact that rankled a bit. I'd get it out of her if I had to resort to torture . . . but not today. I tentatively flexed my fingers, but couldn't get them to move much. The scrapes were drying out, the skin stiffening until it felt like a leather glove that had been soaked in water, then dried in the sun.

Finally, shot down by our lack of giddiness, Brandy returned to earth. "John Barrymore. Should I know him?"

"No." I sighed. When people no longer knew who John Barrymore was, well, the world just seemed less kind somehow. "But you know of his granddaughter, Drew." I waved silent her burgeoning excitement. "But that's irrelevant. There's a restaurant called The Barrymore. It's in a refurbished hipster joint just north of the Riviera called the Royal."

"I've heard of that," Brandy's voice held a hint of awe. "Romeo has been saving money to take me there. He thought maybe by New Year's. It's supposed to be fabulous."

"It is. And here's your chance. Call Romeo. Tell him you both can have dinner on me—tonight. Tell him about the photo; he'll know what to do."

Brandy dropped the iPad to her thighs—thankfully, she still held tight with both hands. "Seriously?"

"Order the foie gras appetizer. And tell Romeo he needs to have the burger, but it's not on the menu."

Brandy gave me a quizzical look.

"It's a secret. Kobe beef, special buns—they only order enough each day to serve twelve of them. But you have to be in-the-know."

"And one of the first twelve," Miss P. felt compelled to point out.

"It's early in the week. A holiday week as well. You should be okay." I made a sweeping motion with my hand as if moving her along. "You better hurry, though."

She bolted to her desk, set the iPad down, then grabbed the phone.

After that, I stopped paying attention. Leaning my head back, I closed my eyes and breathed deeply, letting the day seep out of me. Before my thoughts could coalesce, the office door burst open and Mona barreled in, scattering them once again. When her eyes landed on me, she stopped, mouth open . . . apparently unable to throw the mental switch so she could change tracks. "What happened to you?" She bent over me, brushing the hair off my forehead.

Not wanting to relive each moment one more time, I deflected. "It's a long story."

"I have a long time," she said in a businesslike tone. When she grabbed one of my hands and I winced, her eyes softened, but the tone remained. "You're coming with me. Those hands need some attention. I'll clean them up while you tell me all about it."

ENSCONCED ON A STOOL NEXT TO THE KITCHEN SINK, I TRIED TO BE brave as Mona dabbed at me with a wet cloth. What is it about being ministered to by your mother that causes instant regression? Memories flooded over me, and once again I was a child. Despite her shortcomings, Mona had cared, although her mothering skills deviated drastically from societal norms. Still, she had done her best, which was all any of us could do.

Before she'd hauled me up here, I'd called the Barrymore and set up dinner for Brandy and Romeo—even reserving one of the last two hamburgers. Now, if I could just catch a killer. I needed to think.

Mona jumped into the silence, a reverberating gong echoing,

rippling like waves on a wavetable until chaos killed the calm and quiet in my mind. "Do you remember when you fell off that motorcycle?" She stepped to the sink, rinsed the cloth—the water ran red, which surprised me—then started gently wiping down my hands again.

"What?" Keeping up was proving difficult, as usual.

"Billy Lane's." She didn't look up. Her eyebrows pinched together, she focused on her work.

"That was a minibike." Reflexively, I jerked my hand back a little as she hit an especially tender spot.

Entwining her fingers around my wrist, she retook possession of my hand. "Regardless. I'd forbidden you to ride the thing, so you did it anyway. That's when I knew you'd be okay."

"Really?" I scoffed.

She shrugged. "Well, either okay, or dead."

My family, so warm and fuzzy. "As I recall, you beat the tar out of me with a mesquite switch. Stung like hell."

"Well, I had to act like I was in charge, but I appreciated that you had some guts, a willingness to tackle life."

That was an interesting revelation, one I had no idea what to do with. "What made you think of that?"

She looked up and narrowed her eyes. "You'd lost that for a bit, but I see you're back. Don't ever let anyone take that from you again."

What could I say? She was right.

Mona went back to work on my cuts as she chattered, once again in a light tone. "When Billy laid that bike over your leg got caught underneath, remember?"

I shivered. I really hadn't until she mentioned it. "I left a bunch of skin on that blacktop."

"And we both picked rocks out of your legs for a couple of days." Mona turned my hands over so the palms faced up. "You did almost as good a job today on these hands."

"It was important."

She paused and gave me a long look. "So I understand." Her voice held the hint of an attaboy. "But don't let the scrapes dim the spirit."

"I got it. No need to rub it in."

Mona raised one eyebrow, then hit my open wounds with the iodine.

"Damn," I hissed as I sucked air in through gritted teeth and winced against the pain.

"Honey, I know it hurts." She sounded like she was sort of enjoying the whole thing, but I might have imagined it.

I took a deep breath as the piercing sting turned to numbness. After taking several more hits, I beat back the blur of pain. "Have you told him yet?" I asked, deciding it was time to go on the offense.

Mother scowled, and her lips got all pinched.

"I didn't think so." I was warming to the task of rubbing it in when my father's voice sounded behind us.

"Told who what?"

Mother and I both jumped. Mona turned and graced him with a loving look, which seemed a bit pained to me. My look, I'm sure, was completely pained.

Looking every inch the casino owner in his steel-gray power suit with a faint pink pinstripe, white shirt, pink tie, diamond collar bar, and lingering summer tan, my father rifled through some papers in his hand as he ambled into the kitchen. Pausing, he stomped on the waste can, popping the lid, then eighty-sixed the whole lot of them. He beamed as he kissed Mona with meaning, then gave me a paternal grin. "Are you two plotting the overthrow of a small nation?"

Mona looked nervous, and her normally powerful voice tightened to a reedy shrill. "What makes you think that?"

My father started to fire off a retort—I could see it in his eyes—but his mirth fled when he caught sight of my hands. Standing next to me, he reached to touch them, then thought better of it. Instead, he squeezed my shoulder. "Looks like you lost the battle." His eyes rose to mine—I saw my pain mirrored there. "Should I ask?"

"Probably not, but I didn't lose." I pulled away from Mona's ministrations. Flexing my fingers, I assessed the damage. A manicure was out of the question for a while, but I still had reasonable functionality. "Thanks, Mother."

"They're numb right now, but they are going to hurt like hell later. You never had very dainty hands, and this didn't do them any favors." When Mona giveth, she always taketh away, which at times made me love her, and at other times want to shoot her. Today, it was a toss-up.

Putting an arm around his wife, my father pulled her close to his side. "Now, what is it you're keeping from me?" He held up a finger as she started to shake her head in denial. Batting her lashes, she looked at him with wide-eyed innocence, which he waved away. "Don't play those games with me. I know all your secrets, remember?"

"Perhaps not all." The words were out of my mouth before my minimal filter could kick in.

He gave me an appraising look. "Do I need a drink?"

"Make it a double." I tried to keep my expression neutral, but failed miserably. Mona gave me a cornered-animal look, but I was immune to the plea.

My father switched tactics, now all sweetness and light. "Come, ladies, let's sit by the window while I pour libations." He grabbed Mother's hand. "Remember, confession is good for the soul."

I followed behind. "I'm just glad you don't have a window to throw her out of. Although you share the blame in this one." That sounded harsh, even to me, and I wondered where it came from. To be honest, I was conflicted about having siblings—I was still trying to adjust to having a father to complete the family, and I wasn't sure I wanted to share. Which, of course, was stupid—my father didn't strike me as a stroller-pushing kind of guy, and besides, we'd always have business—it'd be a long time before one of my siblings could wax poetic over the nuances of a balance sheet. And I was all for anything that kept Mona occupied and out of my hair. Irrational, I know, but I felt comfortable being conflicted.

Mona took the couch, burrowing into the soft cushions, then piling pillows around her. She kicked off her ballet flats. Curling her legs to the side, she massaged her swollen feet. Turning my back to her, I faced the view of the Strip—it always took my breath, centering me somehow, as if all those lights were tiny beacons of hope and prosperity . . . signs that everything was right with the world.

Moving my focus in closer, I watched my parents reflected in the large plate glass wall—a reversed, backward image of my life. It reminded me of the first porn movie I saw—the 8 mm film had been spooled backward and upside down. I'd been eight. A couple of the girls at Mona's had shown it to me. Mona was apoplectic. I never saw those girls again. Funny, I hadn't thought of that in decades.

My father handed a glass to my mother. "Fizzy water and lime." Then he stepped in next to me.

I took the proffered tumbler. "101?"

"It's never good to mix one's poisons." My father knew me too well.

"Depends on what kind of forgettin' you're looking for."

He shot me a concerned look, and I smiled and shook my head in reply. He looked relieved. "Have you found Jean-Charles yet?"

"Working on it."

My father shared my view . . . and my love of Vegas. Sin City ran in the Rothstein blood, which was both a curse and a blessing. "This city is a place of redemption, you know."

His observation wasn't what I had expected. "Redemption?"

He shrugged in an embarrassed sort of way. "The Indians believed the desert was a place of rebirth. I've seen it play out enough to feel they were on to something."

I thought about everyone I knew, myself, my parents. Were we all seeking redemption? And what about that Vegas urban legend that said that once you adopted Vegas as your home, you could leave, but you'd never stay gone—was that part of it? I'd certainly seen that play out time and time again. Teddie was the latest example. How I wished he'd stayed gone. But then, I was glad he hadn't. Apparently, conflicted was becoming my normal state. One thing about Teddie, though, he was definitely running from the demons of his past, one in particular: his father. I so got that. Teddie's father pushed me perilously close to thinking that, if I strangled the life out of him, the resulting jail term would be a good trade. "You may be right."

My father took a sip from his drink, an old single malt—I could smell it. "Any theories?"

For a moment, I was lost. "About?"

"Jean-Charles."

"A few. He's leading me on a treasure hunt." I took a sip of corn mash. "At least, I think he's the one leading me around by the nose."

My father stopped gazing out the window, turning a concerned look my way. "Don't you go chasing killers, galloping off on your own like the Lone Ranger. Romeo is with you on this?"

To argue the detective's and my relative abilities to catch the killer and live through it with my father was a no-win situation, so I didn't rise to the bait.

My father didn't seem worried at his inability to prod me to verbal thrust and parry. "Can you trust your chef?"

"Trust. Now there's a word I've tripped over fairly frequently in the last few days." I took a fortifying slug of bourbon. "You're on the list of suspects, by the way."

"Will a noble justification reduce the sentence?" A hint of a twinkle brightened his concerned look. He knew me well enough to know I couldn't hold a grudge for long, especially where he was concerned. As I've said, forgiving is the easy part. Forgetting? Not so much.

"You guys are ignoring me," Mona harrumphed as she patted the pillows around her, building further fortification. "Can't you stop talking shop for even a few minutes? When the two of you put your heads together, I feel left out."

I turned back to my view—this wasn't my show, and I'd probably have a hard time resisting a gloat or two.

Taking his cue, the Big Boss took a seat next to his wife. "I'm sorry, dear. Now, what is it you didn't want to tell me?"

Mona's reflected face clouded, which made me smile. She was the only woman I knew who couldn't multitask. Irritated at being ignored, she'd forgotten the consequences of having the light of my father's attention shining on her. While she worked up the necessary courage, I stepped to the bar and grabbed a bar towel, returning just in time.

"Albert, honey." Mona patted his hand resting on her knee. "You know this baby thing?" Her other hand drifted to settle on her belly, an instinctive protective gesture I found curiously endearing.

My father gave her an amused look as he raised his glass to his lips, seemingly enjoying this whole thing.

"Well—" Mona took a deep breath, then let it rush out, the words tumbling with it. "We're having twins."

My father froze, his glass slipped through his fingers. Hitting the wood, it bounced, but didn't break. I knelt down and began wiping up the mess with the bar towel. My father looked at me— life clearly hadn't registered completely yet. I shot him a smirk. "I'm like a Girl Scout, always prepared."

His eyebrows crinkled. "I think that's the Boy Scouts."

"There's a difference?" I made that sound like benign question.

"You're enjoying this, aren't you?"

"Immensely." I think I even giggled as I finished wiping up and tried not to think of the sacrilege of twenty-five-year-old single malt wasted. Pushing myself to my feet, I felt a huge grin split my face—my father didn't seem to share my mirth. "More than I thought I would. There's some sort of karmic justice in all this that I'm finding fun."

Mona patted my father's knee. "Really, Albert, what's one more?"

A stunned look was all the answer he could muster as he leaned back into the embrace of the soft cushions. His hand shook when I handed him a new glass with a generous splash of scotch. Glazed, her turned to his wife. "Are you okay? Anything the doctor is worried about? Do you need bed rest? What?"

Mona thought for a moment.

I knew she was weighing her options, working the angles. Then she leaned back and patted her husband's hand. "I'm fine, dear." In an unusual show of understanding, my mother didn't push my father further, leaving him time to process. Instead, she turned her smile on me, freezing my blood.

"Oh, Lucky, there's something I've been meaning to talk to you about." Her voice held a normal, everyday chatty tone. Not good.

I eyed her warily. "What?" I stretched the word out.

Mona didn't miss a beat. "Did Miss P. tell you about my political fundraiser? My pack is so excited about it."

"You have a PAC?"

She looked at me as if I'd been lapped in the race of life . . . more than once. "Of course, doesn't everybody?"

"I don't."

Returning to the present, apparently at peace with his wife's latest bombshell—either that, or he was building up a tolerance—my father brushed a strand of hair from her forehead. "Mona, honey, I think you mean your posse."

Confusion flitted across her face—it didn't last long, understanding wasn't something my mother was particularly concerned with. She waved airily. "Whatever they are called, they are happy about it."

"Have you cleared everything with Smokin' Joe and requested the proper permits from the city?" Smokin' Joe owned the largest XXX video emporium this side of Reseda. When she still ran the brothel in Pahrump, Mona had been his best customer. I had been her runner—the glamorous life of a hotel VP. I turned to my father. "Smokin' Joe's place is in the city, right, not the county?"

Back in the day when the mob ran things, rumor had it that they had "influence" with the county commissioners, but less so with the city council. As you can imagine, this didn't sit well with the baseball bat and machine gun crowd. So, in a stunning political move, the mob kept the lower end of the Strip from being annexed to the city. Of course, back then, the lower end was a narrow strip of nothing on the way to California. Now, it was the money end, festooned with megaresorts that channeled the lion's share of tax money to the state. The county still controlled it, along with the Paradise Town Council, technically the "town" that the lower Strip fell within, resulting in the curious situation where the mayor of Las Vegas had no control over the part of the Strip everyone thinks of when they picture Las Vegas.

Visibly more relaxed now, my father pursed his lips as he contemplated my question. For some reason, I got the impression he was working real hard not to smile.

Mona motored on. "We've generated such interest with the girls doing their thing and all that we've changed venues."

"Doing their thing?" I felt panic rising. "Since we're talking working girls from the brothels in Pahrump, could you be more specific?"

"This will be a bake sale, Lucky." She gave me a stern look, which meant only one thing: she was lying.

Before I took up the sword and engaged in battle, I decided to get all the strategic info I could. "A bake sale." I pointed to my father. "You're a witness."

He gave me a noncommittal shrug, which told me where his allegiance lay if push came to shove.

"Traitor," I hissed at him through a tight smile.

"I sleep with her. As history has proven, there are all manner of horrible things a woman can do with sharp instruments while a man is sleeping."

That visual, I could've done without. "Where are you planning on holding this . . . bake sale?" I asked my mother.

She straightened and threw back her shoulders. "Drink and Drag!"

"The drag queen place?" I tried to get my mind around the idea of a political fundraiser in a bar/bowling alley where the servers were men in drag or in their underwear. Frankly, it was one of my favorite places to go, and I didn't want to see it sullied with the stench of political bottom-feeders. "Will they still let me bowl for free if I do it in my underwear?"

"Of course." Mona pshawed. "They do that for everybody, so don't think you're that special."

"I wouldn't dare to presume such a thing."

She frowned slightly at the sarcasm, but it didn't stop her. Clearly warming to her story, Mona tried to lean forward, but was stopped by her burgeoning belly. "There's something even better." She sounded like a co-conspirator planning a daring raid.

I held my breath and waited for impact—I probably even cringed a little.

My father was no help. He couldn't hide his grin now, and his shoulders shook in silent mirth.

Mona clapped her hands like a kid presiding over her birthday cake. "Teddie's going to be the headliner."

My glass hit the floor.

My father burst out laughing. He grabbed the rag and knelt to wipe up the spill.

At a loss, I stared at the liquid spreading across the burnished hardwood. Scotch, then bourbon—I wondered if that would bring out the shine, or kill it. Panic had derailed the logic train.

He looked up at me—a tear rolling down one cheek caught the light. "Still think she's a laugh a minute?"

CHAPTER 16

*F*ORREST RUSHED to greet me when I pushed through the doors of the Presidio. A mountain of a man, he had played defensive end for some Steel Belt football team, I couldn't remember which. Now, he defended the residents of the Presidio against the outside world.

He'd gained a bit of weight in the few months since I'd darkened his doorway. Now, his jacket strained at the seams as it fought to cover the layer of softness over what had been a hard, muscular frame. Any vestige of vanity seemed to have fled—he had given up tending the little hair he had left, preferring to trim it to a short fuzz. His smile was still bright, his skin dark, his presence comforting.

Stopping in front of me, he grabbed my hands in his bear paws. My cringe didn't slow him down. "Miss Lucky, it's been too long. I was so glad when the movers showed up today with your boxes." Concern dimmed his smile as he leaned in, lowering his voice. "You do know Mr. Teddie is back."

"Did you lock up all the sharp knives, just in case?" His eyes widened—I forgot Forrest wasn't used to my snark. I softened it with a smile.

"Oh, you were teasing."

I gave him a noncommittal tilt of my head. "Sort of."

"Broken hearts, they take some time."

I wished people would stop saying that—of course, it was better than the avoidance people often gave someone newly diagnosed with a terminal illness, so I took that as a good sign.

"I had the cleaning crew in this morning. The movers put everything away." Forrest chuckled. "The folks with that damn bird just left. He took a chunk out of one guy's fingers. I think he taught our feathered friend some new words. But everything should be just right for you now."

Just right. Not everything. But I knew what he meant. If only one could quiet the inner turmoil by setting the outer self straight. "It's good to be home." I squeezed his hands, very lightly —mine were still numb, but they'd started to twinge—then let his go as I stepped around him. "Elevators still in the same place?"

"Yes ma'am. If you need anything, I'm here," he called after me.

I waved my thanks as I stepped into the elevator and hit the button. When the doors closed, I sagged against the back wall, assaulted by memories, suddenly unsure about this whole going home thing. Conflicted once more . . . or still. At least I was consistent.

As I ascended, I remembered the first time Teddie and I had known we would have each other. Driven by the heat of anticipation, we'd practically disrobed each other right here in this elevator. Closing my eyes, I could feel his hands on me, insistent, teasing, his kisses taunting, plundering. Driven by desire, neither of us could catch our breath. For a moment, I'd thought I had everything.

What had I missed?

How could I have been so wrong?

Why hadn't I hunted him down and shot him? Men!

The elevator slowed, and I opened my eyes, bracing myself—I

hadn't set foot in the place since right after the night Teddie had left. I had no idea how I would feel. Angry? Hurt? Sad?

I needn't have worried. When the doors opened, and I stepped into my great room with its burnished hardwood floors, stark white walls, bright paintings, and comfortable furniture in a variety of styles, I felt happy. This was *home*, the place where I belonged . . . *my* space. Moving farther into the room, I was enveloped in the comforting hug of peace. I almost didn't recognize the feeling—it had been a while. Yes, my fault, but I always did have to take the long road. For some reason, I just wasn't a shortcut kind of gal.

Drowning in emotion, I hadn't immediately noticed the soft music coming from the kitchen. Nor the aroma of marinara sauce, heavy on the oregano and basil. A loud sound startled me—it sounded curiously like the pop of a Champagne cork. Who would be here?

I narrowed my eyes. Teddie wouldn't dare. . .

Stalking toward the kitchen, by the time I burst through the door I had worked up a pretty good bit of red ass. The sight in front of me stopped me in my tracks and diffused my anger like a swift breeze brightening a stale house.

"Jordan?"

He graced me with one of his best Hollywood-heartthrob grins. In two strides, he was in front of me. Grabbing me, he swept me around, bending me backward in a dip as he kissed me. Our normal greeting, so I was semi-prepared, but he still left me breathless. Putting me back on my now unsteady feet, he grabbed a flute of sparking bubbly off the counter and presented it to me. "Welcome home, sweetie."

I downed the whole thing in one long swallow.

Jordan raised an eyebrow, but refilled my flute when I thrust it at him. "What did you do to those hands?" He grimaced when his eyes found mine.

With his short-cropped black hair running now to salt and

pepper, angular features, strong jaw, bedroom eyes, perpetual tan, and youthful physique, Jordan Marsh was every woman's dream, except for that minor sexual-orientation issue. Just another cruel injustice heaped on the female gender. The thin white tee shirt and fitted European jeans pressed home that point. Even the frilly pink apron didn't dim his masculine appeal.

After I'd consumed half of my second flute, my progress slowed. "It's a long story, and I'll need more to drink to repeat it. What are you doing here? You were on my list of things to do tomorrow."

"Honey, you can do me anytime, but don't put me on a list— my inflated Hollywood ego would be dashed." He turned back to stir a pot simmering on the stove. "I'm underwhelmed by your delight in seeing me."

"Sorry, just momentarily side-tracked by the visual of doing Jordan Marsh."

"You can look, but you can't touch." Rudy Gillespie, Jordan's partner, sailed into the kitchen. Tall, thin, with curly, dark hair and a wicked smile, he grabbed my shoulders from behind and leaned around, planting a kiss on my cheek. Then he joined Jordan at the stove. Individually, they turned every head when they walked into a room, but together, they could stop traffic. "Smells divine. There is just something really sexy about a man who knows his way around a kitchen."

"Tell me about it." I joined them at the stove and peered into the pot. "Is that your famous marinara sauce?"

Jordan dipped a wooden spoon into the thick red slurry, blew on it for a minute, then held it out for me to taste. "Careful, it's hot."

One tiny taste and flavor exploded on my tongue. I groaned in delight. "When's dinner?"

"Soon." He handed me the spoon. "Here, keep stirring for a minute." Thankful that, for once, someone else was making the decisions, I did as asked. "Where's the bird?" I directed the question at Jordan's ass, which was poking out of the open fridge as he gathered ingredients.

"In the pantry."

"You put the bird in the pantry?"

"He's in time-out." Jordan stood, his arms laden with deliciousness, and gave me an accusatory look. He tried to hide his smile, but with little success. "For the record, I am not amused by the recent additions to his vocabulary."

Jordan turned his back and carefully offloaded his armful onto the counter, sorting the items by dish. "A good salad caprese— fresh basil. And the tomatoes!" He bunched his fingers, then put them to his lips and made that exaggerated Italian gesture of fabulousness. "Fresh mozzarella to die for." He held up an elongated bottle. "Twenty-five-year-old balsamic, so thick it pours like molasses. And"—he held up a finger, pausing dramatically —"the pièce de résistance." He reached for plate on the other side of the stove. With a flourish, he removed the light towel covering the contents, then waved the plate first under Rudy's nose, then mine.

My stomach growled. "Yum, prosciutto and figs."

"Not prosciutto, Culatello de Zibello, and not just any fig, fresh Southern Blacks from South Africa."

Rudy snagged a half a fig and its coat of thinly sliced, meticulously cured exotic ham. If I'd tried that, I would've lost a hand. Then he topped Jordan's flute of Champagne. Proffering the bottle in my direction, he raised his eyebrows in a silent question. When I shook my head, he drained the last of it into a flute for himself.

"Keep stirring," Jordan admonished me. "If you let that burn, I will carve out your soul and roast it on a spit."

"I have no soul, haven't you heard?" I risked another taste of the sauce. "Did you bring all this from L.A.?"

"No. Amazingly, I found it here in this horticulturally challenged wasteland."

"Who'd you have to kill?" I cringed at my word choice—somehow, it didn't seem funny anymore.

"Nobody." Jordan took the spoon from me. "You are the worst stirrer."

With Jordan's attention diverted by my woeful lack of kitchen skills, Rudy snagged another fig, making me laugh. Jordan narrowed his eyes at me. "What's so funny?"

I gave him a straight-faced, wide-eyed look of innocence.

He whirled to face Rudy, who managed a similar look, even with his mouth full. Jordan tried to look angry, but he didn't pull it off—so much for his acting skills. "As I was saying." He stopped stirring and focused on another larger pot that was beginning to put off some steam. "I found this little specialty food stall." Measuring out fresh-made whole-wheat tagliatelle, he salted the boiling water and carefully immersed the pasta, checking his watch.

"Food stall?" Since I'd been demoted from head stirrer, I needed something to do, so I went in search of the proper beverage for such a feast. If I recalled correctly, I'd left two bottles of Ribolla Gialla in the wine refrigerator under the bar. The bar was in the great room, so I raised my voice to stay in the conversation. "Where is this purveyor of exotic treats?"

Jordan's voice followed me out of the kitchen. "In the garage."

The wine was where I'd left it.

Returning to the kitchen, a bottle in each hand, I proffered them for Jordan's approval. "Will this do?"

"Impressive."

"I bought it from a lady in Sonoma—a small vineyard. She's cultivating some varietals from her grandfather's hillside in Friuli. A great story." I set about grabbing the right stemware and pouring us each a dose. "This food stall was in a garage?"

Jordan swirled the wine in his glass, then eyed it as he held it to the light. Sniffing deeply, he then took a sip, swishing the liquid around his mouth before swallowing. "Sublime. It should go nicely with the sauce and the subtleties of the appetizer and salad." He lowered the glass and gave me a quizzical look. "Not *a* garage. *The* garage."

"*The* garage? You mean at the Babylon?"

Jordan turned off the heat under the pots, then lifted the pasta pot and poured the contents through a strainer in the sink. "I'm surprised you didn't know about it."

"News to me. Who put you on to it?"

Rudy had set the kitchen table—there were four settings.

I eyed the two men. "Anybody else joining us?"

Rudy wouldn't meet my eyes as he filled an ice bucket and nestled the bottles inside.

Jordan waved airily. "No. Just us three."

Personally, I thought the wine was cool enough, but I didn't feel like trotting out my burgeoning wine snobbishness—a result of spending too much time in the company of a certain French chef who had gone missing. The comfort of good friends dimmed my worry for a moment, but like a bug bite in a place I couldn't scratch, it still tormented me.

Jordan ladled the pasta into a bowl, then topped it with the entire contents of the saucepan. The men brought the food to the table, then Jordan helped me with my chair.

I settled the napkin across my lap. "Why did you set four places if no one else is coming?"

Rudy shot Jordan a glare. "Your friend there thought it would be a good idea to invite Theodore."

I took a deep breath and let it out slowly as I counted to ten . . . then twenty, fingering the knife as I silently tried not to fume.

"Not to worry. He's not coming," Jordan harrumphed as he focused on piling pasta on each plate, reaching for mine, then Rudy's, saving his own for last. "I went up the back stairs, looking for him, but he wasn't home."

"Saving you from a slow and painful death." In my half-starved state, I couldn't resist any longer. The aroma from my plate inciting an irresistible need to feed, I attacked my pasta. "My God, if you ever want to open a restaurant, I'll back you."

"Food is about love. I only cook for people I keep in my heart."

I reached over to squeeze his hand. Remembering the state of my own, I gave his a pat. "I really am glad you're here." I included Rudy with a look. "Jordan, seriously, I thought you were arriving tomorrow—did I screw up?"

Jordan finished his bite and wiped a bit of sauce off the corner of his mouth. "Miss P. called me. Neither one of us thought you should have to come home to an empty house."

Unbelievably touched, I fought down my emotions for a moment—like a cat left out in the rain, Jordan got twitchy when I cried. Clearing my throat, I changed the subject, returning to an unanswered question. "So, tell me about this food stall in the garage."

"It really wasn't a stall per se, more like the back of a panel truck." Jordan sampled a fig. "This really is manna from heaven . . . an amazing find."

"Let me get this straight, some guy is selling foodstuffs in our garage from the back of his truck?"

"They do it all the time in L.A."

I had no idea. "Who put you on to this guy?"

"Brett Baker. I knew him in L.A.—his sushi is positively orgasmic. And he specialized in some of the more exotic stuff—the things that make your lips go numb and can stop your heart. Truly, I remain in awe of what that man can do with eel and urchin."

I knew there was a scathing reply laden with innuendo somewhere in there, but I just wasn't up to the task. "Why would he share that kind of information?"

Jordan gave me his best Hollywood A-Lister smile. "The stuff that people tell me would make you blush."

~

I HAD A RULE IN MY HOME THAT WHOEVER DID THE COOKING WAS exempt from cleaning up. Needing time to think, I'd shooed Rudy out of the kitchen as well. Dinner in the company of good friends was just what the doctor had ordered, and I was feeling a bit more settled, comfortable in my skin and in my space . . . despite Jean-Charles and Teddie and everyone's meddling.

As if on cue, Teddie's voice interrupted my peace and quiet. "Hey, anybody home?"

I didn't need to look to know he stood in the opening to the back stairway we had installed between our apartments—before I minded him popping in unannounced.

With dish towel in hand, drying the last pot, I turned.

When he caught sight of me, his smile fled. "Oh, sorry. I didn't mean to interrupt. Jordan didn't tell me you were back."

"I live here." Of course, that was a recent occurrence.

Teddie was smart enough not to point that out. "I had a note from Jordan inviting me down—his marinara is hard to resist."

"The stuff of legend." Finished, I pulled out the drawer under the counter and put the pot away. "There's leftovers."

"Seriously?"

"Why not?"

Teddie looked at me as if weighing the odds his meal might come laced with poison. "As invitations go, that was one of the least encouraging."

I didn't feel the need to excuse or explain as Teddie took his usual place at the counter while I pulled out the food I'd just put away.

"I wouldn't have come down the stairs unannounced had I known you'd be here. Back at the hotel, I got your message. You need time and space, I get that." He tried to sound sincere, I could see it in his face, but he didn't pull it off.

"The guys killed the wine. How about some Prosecco?"

"I'll get it." Teddie backed off the stool and headed toward the bar with a galling air of familiarity.

Still warm, the pasta only needed a slight bit of reheating. I chose the stove rather than the microwave in deference to Jordan's culinary sensibilities—he'd often complained the microwave toughened pasta. As it warmed, I assembled a small salad—we'd consumed all the figs and culatello—and Teddie popped the cork and poured us each a flute of Italian sparkling wine.

He raised his glass in a toast. "To friends."

Reluctantly, I clinked my glass with his. "In the span of less than twelve hours, I've gone from wanting to shoot you on sight to being able to tolerate your presence without going postal."

With a little less "jaunty" in his stride, Teddie carried his plates to the table. "Not exactly the progress I was hoping for, but I'll take what I can get."

I followed with the bubbly. Awkward would be the word I would've chosen had anyone asked how all this felt.

Teddie attacked the pasta, forking it in without reverence—I was glad Jordan wasn't witnessing. "Amazing stuff. Do you know his secret?"

"Many, but not the one you're looking for. He said it had to do with love."

"Doesn't everything." Pausing with his fork, dripping with pasta, halfway to his mouth, Teddie held my gaze for a moment longer than necessary.

Immune to the BS Teddie ladled with ease, I looked past him through the kitchen window—a different angle of the Vegas Strip, but equally as spectacular as the view from the great room. I fought the pull of the warm familiarity of having Teddie in my kitchen, of sharing my home and my life with the man who had been my very best friend. That's the part I wanted back.

Teddie ate in silence. Consumed by his food, he seemed unaware as I surreptitiously took stock. The few months since I'd last seen him had deepened the worry lines bracketing his mouth and perhaps added a few wrinkles at the corners of his eyes, but overall he looked as delicious as ever.

The movement of his hands drew my attention. Artist's hands, graceful and beautiful, with long fingers to stretch across the keys. I'd loved to sit next to him at the piano while he played. But today, his hands didn't have the beauty they had once held. Red scrapes marred his knuckles, scratches sliced his fingers, a fingernail . . . no, two fingernails were torn, one badly enough to sport a Band-Aid.

When my eyes lifted to his, I caught him staring at me, his fork lifted halfway.

"You were there," I whispered, I don't know why. "Were you following me?"

"I told you I wanted to help. You wouldn't let me go with you." He set his fork down, deliberately placing it just so before he answered. "Two people have died already, Lucky." His eyes had turned a deep, serious blue.

I knew that look. "Learn anything interesting?"

He didn't answer me immediately. And inner battle raged—I could see it in his eyes, in the tautness of his expression.

"Tell me." Propelled by a need to know, I leaned forward. "You have to tell me. As you said, two people have died already—and one almost."

Teddie swallowed hard, a pained look contorted his features. "Your French chef was there."

"Jean-Charles?" Suddenly feeling light-headed, I reached for my flute. As if that was going to help. Without taking a sip, I replaced the glass, forcing a calm tone. "What was he doing?"

"I saw him talking with the scientist who . . . got hurt, then I lost him in the crowd." With his finger, Teddie pushed at a slice of mozzarella. The cheese had a dark slash across it, an angry balsamic stain that looked like dried blood outlining a wound. "I worked my way through the crowd trying to catch sight of him again."

"And did you?" My hand shook, so I placed it palm-down on the table. The other one, I kept in my lap.

Teddie glanced down at my hand. Pain pinched the skin between his eyebrows. His voice faltered.

"Tell me." My voice had gone hard as I braced myself.

His eyes met mine. His face cleared. "I was far away—on the other side of the pit. And the crowd was pressing in, so I could hardly move. But I saw Jean-Charles. Just before the show started, he jumped on the crane and started climbing to the cockpit."

"Did you see him get inside?"

Teddie drew his lips into a thin line and shook his head.

Thinking back, I tried to remember the timing. "The crane's engine, had someone already cranked it over?" Adrenaline blew through my brain, clearing some of the alcohol fuzz.

Teddie furrowed his brows and glanced away. When his eyes returned to mine, they were untroubled. He nodded, slowly at first, then more vigorously, as his lips curled slightly upward. "Yes. Yes, the engine was already running."

"Are you sure?"

This time, his smile broke through. "Absolutely."

"So someone else was in that cab." My heart beat faster with renewed hope. "What did you do then?"

"I fought through the crowd, trying to get to him. I'd almost made it . . ." He stopped.

"What happened?"

He looked at me just like he used to. "I saw you dive into that rock pile."

TEDDIE HAD HUGGED ME LONG AND HARD BEFORE HE'D CLIMBED the stairs back to his place. Several hours later, as I curled under a cashmere throw in the comfort of my winged-back chair in front of the window, I still felt the press of his body against mine. A fire flickered in the fireplace—gas logs, but they provided some heat and a comforting ambience I was grateful for.

Sleep refused to come.

Jordan and Rudy had tiptoed off to their quarters when Teddie had shown up. At first, I'd been peeved, as if the whole thing was a setup. Now, I didn't care. Everyone had been right: dealing with Teddie was something I had to do.

By carrying around the hurt and the anger, I hurt only myself.

My phone, a new one Miss P. had handed me as Mona led me away, sounded at my hip. I had yet to personalize anything, much less the ringtone. So, no more "Lucky for Me." I didn't miss it.

Two a.m. Who could it be?

My heart rate accelerated as I thought of Mona—even though her due date was still weeks away, anything could happen. I pulled the phone from its holster and squinted at the number. No name —I had no idea how to synch my contacts through the cloud, as Brandy had told me to do. I thought the number looked like Romeo's.

I hit the green spot, then pressed the phone to my ear and took a flier that I might just be right. "Hey. You okay?" I whispered, not wanting to awaken my houseguests.

"Sorta." Romeo sounded dog-tired. "Are you still awake?"

For some reason, recognizing his number felt like a small victory. I thought of my normal flip response, but decided this wasn't the time. "Yeah."

"I know this is weird, but can I come up?"

"You know I've moved back to my apartment, right?"

"I'm downstairs."

"I'll send the elevator."

WHEN THE ELEVATOR DOORS OPENED, DISGORGING THE CRUMPLED

detective, I thrust a beverage in his hand—three fingers of single malt in a cut-crystal Steuben tumbler.

"Nice digs." Romeo took a long pull on the scotch as he glanced around the apartment. I'd left the lights dimmed, so the Technicolor reflection of the Strip lights painted the walls in a rainbow of soft colors.

The view beckoning, Romeo walked to the window. Silently, I stepped in beside him. "You'd never been here?" Considering the lifetime of disasters we'd shared over the past year, that seemed impossible.

"Maybe once. I don't remember." He sipped as he drank in the view. "This town . . . ," he started, then quit, shaking his head.

"Is like a good woman—tough on the outside, tender in spots." I crossed my arms to keep myself from hugging him. For some reason, I sensed he needed to stand apart, to find his own strength, to work through whatever had brought him here.

"But all I see is the bad side of human nature, all day, every day."

"That's all you allow yourself to see. Look harder." I risked putting a hand on his arm and giving it a squeeze. "And if that fails, remember you always have me. I mean, how bad can life be with me in your corner? Life has graced you immeasurably, Detective."

He snorted twenty-five-year-old scotch through his nose as he doubled over. Personally, I didn't think my comment was all that funny. When he'd dried his eyes and wiped his face with the napkin I'd handed him, he finally got down to business. "Your hunch about Barrymore was right. The chef had two more RFID chips, and a story about how Jean-Charles had asked him to order some high-end stuff and chip it."

"What kind of stuff?"

"Foie gras, mainly. And some Kobe beef for the hidden menu burger."

I stepped over to the couch and relaxed into its welcoming

embrace. "Tell me about The Barrymore." I pulled the pillows closer, packing them around me—my normal defensive position.

"Not much to tell. Chef fed us, which was . . . amazing. What a romantic place. And the food! An undiscovered gem, if you ask me."

"Yes, it won't be undiscovered for long." I let him enjoy his memory for a moment, then I brought him crashing to earth. "And the murders? Did you find anything new?"

"Just the chips."

"What did you do with them?"

"None of them can be read by a normal RFID reader. Apparently, Mr. Peccorino added some sort of extra hoop to jump through. Curiously, none of the other Berkeley guys knew a work-around, so I handed all the chips to Homeland Security." At my sharp intake of breath, he held up a hand. "Don't worry, I didn't use you to chum the waters. They've got a bunch of scientists working on tracking our food supply—all in the name of national security, or so they say. They're reverse-engineering the thing, but it'll take time."

"And they probably won't share." I thought about Special Agent Stokes . . . Joe. Maybe I had a work-around of my own. "Do you have any new info on Dr. Phelps?"

"Not out of the woods yet, but they're pretty sure he'll make a full recovery." Romeo plopped down next to me. Stretching his legs out, he leaned back and closed his eyes. His hands cradled his glass on his belly.

"Anything interesting on the alibi front?" I asked.

"Looking for easy answers?" The young detective shot me a smirk.

"Any answers." I curled farther into the corner of the couch, tucking my feet underneath me, and pulled even more pillows around me—if we were going to talk murder, I needed my defenses.

Romeo stared at the ceiling. "Alibis. When Fiona was killed, the workday had pretty much started. Practically everyone was wandering around on property at the Babylon. Everyone except Chef Wexler, who said he was off trying to find some interesting things at the Asian market in Korea Town."

"Was Jerry any help?"

Romeo shook his head. "No cameras on the back lot, or in the kitchens at Burger Palais. Everybody still is a suspect."

"And for the time Mr. Peccorino died?"

"Jean-Charles and Teddie were on the Cielo property. As you know, your security system isn't up and running yet. So no video feeds." He raised his head and took a long draw from his glass. "Everybody else was roaming around town, by themselves. Wexler was once again doing his shopping—some of the food vendors remember seeing him, just not exactly when. Gregor was in the hotel, or so he said, checking on the cooking completion setup."

"The doors should have been locked."

Romeo nodded, but didn't look at me. "They were. He had some other song-and-dance. We're checking it out. Chitza said she was with Dr. Phelps, but he's in no condition to say yea or nay."

"No corroboration, then?" I said, thinking out loud.

"Only you." Romeo smiled as he turned his head in my direction. "You were with me."

"Desiree?" I picked at some stuffing poking through a hole in one of the pillows.

"She said she was with her daughter." I started to say something, but Romeo stopped me with a slight gesture with one hand. "I didn't even ask—of course, the girl would support her mother."

I tried to push the stuffing back in the little hole, then decided I was making it worse, so I tossed the offending pillow onto the chair out of reach. "What about Brett Baker?"

Romeo's mouth turned down at the corners. "He drives

around in that dang food truck all day. But some of the workers at Cielo told me he swings by there every day."

"Really?"

"But again, no one remembers exactly the time or date." Romeo undid the top button of his shirt and loosened his tie. "Like Adone as well. No alibi, but no one to place him at the scene, either."

My fingers and hands ached, but I worked the joints slightly, trying to increase range of motion. "I think the whole thing started innocently, whether it was Homeland Security being overzealous, or Jean-Charles being anal about quality, it doesn't matter. What does matter is that somehow, he stumbled onto a scheme involving high-end specialty items."

"Okay." Romeo picked up the thread. "Let's assume you're right. So, your chef steps into a nest of vipers. Now, somebody wants to clean up the mess."

"Exactly." Still flexing my fingers, I uncurled my legs and rose —I did my best thinking when in motion. "So, someone is eliminating loose ends and framing Jean-Charles, or at least putting him in a very bad PR position. And we know, once the public finds a chink in the armor of someone's reputation, they go after it, ripping it to shreds like a pit bull with a play toy."

Romeo's eyes followed me as I paced in front of him. "The person we're looking for has tracks to cover and a bone to pick with Chef Bouclet."

I stopped in front of the detective, my hands on my hips. "That really doesn't help. Just about everyone in this ugly mess holds Jean-Charles accountable for some transgression."

Romeo pursed his lips and gave me a little shrug, then he grabbed the baton. "And the UC-Berkeley guys just got into the mix by sheer dumb luck."

I turned to my view, my hands clasped behind me as I drank in Vegas. "Everyone except Mr. Peccorino, I think. He added a layer of unreadability to the chips. I wonder why?"

"His colleagues are in the dark." Romeo sounded fatalistic. "Here." He rattled the ice in his glass. "Please."

Thankful for a mission, I grabbed the glass and headed to the bar.

He talked as I poured. "I think we're looking for a guy."

"A guy?" I measured two fingers, paused, then added another. "Why?"

Romeo rolled his head back and looked at me over the back of the couch. "It would take a ton of strength to stuff a man, dead-weight, into that oven."

"I've been thinking about that. Initially, I came to the same conclusion."

"But now?"

"The oven wasn't all that high." I returned to stand in front of him and handed him his fresh drink. "Amped on enough adrenaline, and with a bit of leverage, I could probably do it."

"Yeah, but you're not . . ." He eyed me over the rim as he took a sip.

"Careful." I eviscerated the warning with a grin.

Romeo recovered. "You're not average." He seemed pleased with himself, then he shifted gears, almost leaving me flat-footed. "So, I'm siding with you on the theory that Jean-Charles is sending you the pictures, leading you to the RFID chips. It doesn't make sense it would be anyone else. But why? We can't read them, surely he would've known that."

"Unless Peccorino added that little twist all on his own."

Romeo shot me a look as if he hadn't thought of that possibility. "Interesting. But again, why?"

"Hell, I'm making this up as I go, how would I know?" Now, it was my turn to sound frustrated. "But I have a feeling the chips will lead us to a location—the one where shipments are getting tampered with. Somehow, that seems to be the key. And it seems to me that Peccorino must've coded those chips to route all the shipments through one location. That just makes sense—how else would all of them end up flowing through the hands of the person who tampered with them?"

"Good point. But hiding that little scam seems a pretty weak motive for murder."

I gave him a little grin. "I've contemplated it for less."

He conceded the point with a chuckle. "So, if your chef doesn't have all the chips, and he doesn't have the reader, *and* his science guy is dead . . ." Romeo let the thought hang.

I felt hope and fear at the same time. "Then Jean-Charles doesn't know who the killer is, either. He's running, but he doesn't know from whom."

"Then time is short."

I blew out in exasperation. "Of course, it's short. The killer has practically told us he's going to kill again. And if we don't move, then the whole operation that set this killing spree off will move."

"And we'll be back to square one."

"With several dead bodies."

"Okay." Romeo set his glass down on the side table and pushed himself to a more upright position. "So, why do you think Jean-Charles thinks someone is listening in on him?"

I eyed Romeo's drink, suddenly craving one of my own, but I'd already far exceeded my daily allotment. "I know he said that, but I passed it off as overly dramatic. I mean, I know someone could follow him, but listen in on his conversations? Only the government would be able to do that, right?"

"You did say Homeland Security showed up on your doorstep." Romeo ran a hand through his hair. I was going to have to tell him to stop doing that—his cowlick would never remain tamed. "But there's also another way."

"Really? How?"

"Spyware. You can download it. Technically, it's a huge crime to use it against others, but the government hasn't blocked the sale of it because personal use is cool."

"The sanctity of personal privacy resting solely on the exalted character of humankind."

"Look on the positive side." Romeo teased. "But point taken. One would assume that a person who had already shown flagrant disregard for the law, like a killer, would not be put off by a pesky little federal statute, no matter the severity of the penalties for violation."

I mulled over Romeo's theory, trying to shoot holes in it, but I couldn't . . . or didn't want to. "What about the note?"

Romeo mumbled, "Pigs to find a feast so rare. But eat a morsel taking care. A bit is fine but take heed. Death will come to those with greed."

"Pigs to find a feast so rare. Sounds like the truffle to me."

Romeo nodded. "The middle part seems straightforward. But that last part about greed—hell, it could be any one of the current cast of players."

I had to agree—they all seemed to be playing their own angles for personal gain. But really, who in life wasn't? "If you have any theories as to a lead suspect, I'd like to hear them."

"If I was a betting man, I'd say Gregor." Romeo reached to the side and grabbed his glass with his fingers, then wiggled his hand, tinkling the ice in his glass.

Even in my diminished state, I got the hint. "Another dose?"

"Make it a double."

"Grasshopper, do as I say, not as I do."

"Not tonight." Romeo's voice actually had a hard edge that I'd never heard before.

"Okay." I held out my hand. "Give me your car keys."

He hesitated.

"I know your limits."

He opened one eye, then rooted in his pocket. The ring caught on the lining of his pocket, but he yanked the keys loose, ripping a hole, then dropped them into my open palm.

"I'll put these on the hook by the elevator."

When I returned with not only his knockout drink, but also a pillow and blanket, I thought he was already asleep. As I leaned across him to set the glass on the side table, he reached for it. After a sip, he cupped both hands around the glass, holding it in his lap, his eyes still closed, his head back.

I thought he might be drifting off, but I kept talking, it helped to think out loud. "This is like one of those group cluster fucks at that swinger place—everybody here is doing everybody else. We have Chef Wexler, who got his head handed to him by someone who calls himself The Phantom Phoodie. And Gregor beat him out of the restaurant space in the Bazaar . . . the one that is now occupied by Jean-Charles. Chitza DeStefano, Jean-Charles's former lover, is shacking up with the injured Dr. Phelps. Fiona Richards was shacking up with Desiree Bouclet's husband—who has a huge bone to pick with his brother-in-law. And Fiona goes to Gregor with news of the missing truffle, pushing the stone off the cliff, and I'm running all over town collecting RFID chips. Homeland Security is breathing down my neck. Jean-Charles is on the lam." I rubbed my eyes. "My head hurts."

"Don't forget Teddie," Romeo added, surprising me. "He's sure turned up at some interesting places. And him taking the note from the scene of the second murder—that sorta piqued my interest."

Piqued mine, too, but I wasn't going to add fuel to that fire. The thought that practically everyone close to me was working individual angles, that they were being less than forthcoming, shall we say, just hurt my heart too much. "Christ." I glanced at Romeo, who had rotated his head and was watching me. "Jean-Charles is at the center of this whole thing."

"And he's nowhere to be found." Romeo once again closed his eyes. "Even with all that in the hopper, I still think Gregor is the likeliest candidate. He's got a missing truffle, Fiona was right in the middle of that."

"What about the Berkeley guy?"

"If the truffle was chipped, he knew where it went. Maybe he wasn't telling."

"Doesn't really make sense, then, for Gregor to kill him." I tired to figure out where Romeo was going with all of this.

"Maybe he didn't care about finding the truffle." Romeo raised his eyebrows as he raised that question.

"And why wouldn't he want to find it?"

"He had it insured for a huge sum. Without the truffle, he'd get cash, and all of it, as the value of the truffle would be impossible to dicker over."

"So this was just about money?"

"Well, more like life or death, for Gregor." Romeo tried to push himself higher in the chair, then gave up. "I can't prove it...yet... but rumor has it Gregor was in deep to some bad dudes."

"In deep?" That little confusion bomb exploded in my head. Then a thought hit me. "You know, back when he was running the Italian place, a rumor that he had some important friends was making the rounds."

"If he's taking money from those guys, he better be careful," Romeo said needlessly.

"What if he borrowed the money to buy the truffle?" I was plucking at straws, but I'd always been told to follow the money when a crime had been committed. It had worked before.

"I'll check it out, but you'd be better at chasing that lead. You have sketchier friends."

I didn't argue. "I'm sure Gregor could shed some light."

Romeo's eyes shut and remained that way. "We've been looking for him, but can't find him."

I reached over and extricated the young detective's almost empty glass from his loosening grasp. "We both saw him at Dr. Phelps' show."

"Well, he's dropped off the grid since then." There was a hint of fatality in Romeo's voice. "Just once, wouldn't it be fun to have an investigation just sort of come together seamlessly?"

"You have the proverbial smoking gun. What more do you want?" I deadpanned, rather proud of my delivery.

"You're a pain in the ass, you know that?" Romeo said without even a hint of tease.

"You're just figuring that out? We should send you back to detective school."

"Nope." Romeo still stared at the insides of his eyelids—sleep fuzzied his voice. "If I had a do-over, it'd be truck driving school. Then I could get the hell out of here."

This time, when the urge to give him a hug struck me, I didn't stifle it. Amazingly, he gave me an appreciative smile.

Pausing, I touched his face. His skin was hot. Running this long at full throttle on high-octane fuel, he was heading straight for a flameout.

Settling back, I patted my pillows back into place. "When I saw Gregor yesterday, he was all over me about that damned truffle. Got in my face pretty good." I leaned my head to the side, resting it on the back of the couch. Well past tired, I'd been fighting a losing battle with sleep for most of the evening. "It's funny, but at the time, even though he was at full voice, I got the impression he was more scared than angry."

"Fiona was dead. I don't know what he has to be scared of."

"A life sentence?"

"Or his own funeral."

CHAPTER 17

SLEEP HAD finally come, but it had been fitful as murders both real and imagined haunted my dreams. Taking a shower in my own home, then throwing open the doors to my closet, which was large enough to fill Imelda Marcos with envy, provided a positive start to the day, making me feel more like myself than I had in a long time. I chose a pair of black jeans and a cashmere sweater, casual chic, which went with my positive mood. And some ankle boots with low heels that went with my need for comfort these days. Comfort over cool? Did that mean I was becoming sensible?

Not a chance.

The apartment was quiet as I tiptoed toward the kitchen, so I opted to forgo uncovering the bird and punching the coffee machine—the noise generated by both could wake the dead. I stuffed a plastic dish filled with seeds through the door to Newton's cage, affixing it to the bars, then, feeling guilty, I added a couple of slices of apple. One foot tucked under him, Newton gave me a one-eyed look with half-lowered lid—I didn't need to be fluent in parrot to get his meaning.

Before I left, I scrawled a note to Romeo, who still slumbered on the couch, and left it on the coffee table in front of him under a bottle of aspirin. The note suggested he ask Jordan for his famous hangover cure. I had a feeling the kid would appreciate it.

Curiously, when I called the elevator and the doors opened, Teddie wasn't lurking inside. I was a bit surprised—lately he'd been turning up in so many odd places and at awkward times.

The ride down was quicker than I remembered. Forrest nodded and gave me a bright grin, which I returned as I strode through the lobby, then pushed through the doors. Daylight assaulted me. Apparently, even though I was just joining it, the day was well under way.

I'd tossed my replacement phone in my bag and didn't feel like rooting for it, and I hadn't bothered with a watch, so the actual time was anybody's guess. Not that it mattered. If life as we know it teetered precariously over the abyss, Miss P. could find me—she was uncanny that way.

Blinking against the sun, I decided to walk. The Babylon was twenty minutes away if I strolled, ten if I adopted a reasonable pace. I opted for something in between.

A Metro officer was removing the yellow crime scene tape from around Jean-Charles's food truck as I walked by. Hadn't Adone said they were releasing the truck earlier? I waved, but he didn't notice me, or if he did, he didn't respond . . . the more likely scenario. Metro didn't exactly work on engendering warm fuzzies in the population—they turned a blind eye to their employers. I never understood that, but then again, I was in customer service . . . a dying field.

From the angle of the sun and the relative warmth, given that Thanksgiving was looming, I put the hour at just past noon. As I ambled up the curving entrance to the Babylon, a valet or two greeted me as they ran past. Others nodded and smiled.

I loved my job. Oh, it had its moments, all jobs did—at least, that's what I was told. This was the only life I'd ever known, so who was I to say?

Once in the lobby, and before taking the stairs to the mezzanine and my little corner of the universe, I paused under the Chihuly winged creatures arcing across the high ceiling. They settled me, reorienting even my worst fears. They always had. I had no idea why.

Girded for the day, I took a deep breath, then pushed through the door to my office. Brandy skittered back to her desk, and Miss P. studiously ignored me. I decided not to be alarmed. "Why are you sitting out here?" I asked the newly promoted head of customer relations. "You have a very nice office. I should know, it used to be mine."

When Miss P. looked up, her eyes shone and she had a goofy look on her face.

I narrowed my eyes. "What's going on?"

Extending her left hand, she waggled her fingers.

My eyes widened. Grabbing her hand and yanking it toward me, I dislodged her from the chair—she didn't seem to mind. A bright sparkler winked on her ring finger. "Impressive. I want to hear all about it." Ignoring my overflowing message box, I parked one butt cheek across Jeremy's stenciled name on the corner of her desk.

"You know how much I love DW Bistro?" Breathless, she warmed to the story while she kept glancing down at her hand, as if she couldn't quite believe the Beautiful Jeremy Whitlock had indeed come through.

"Great place, but not the most romantic."

"The romance is in the remembering—Jeremy paid attention when I told him about it, and he remembered. Isn't that the best?"

I couldn't help grinning—she looked twenty years younger, like a schoolgirl with her first crush. Maybe Jeremy was the first she'd really fallen for. I'd never thought about it before: why she'd never married. "You've captured the last good man. But he got the better of the deal."

She pshawed, then shared the rest of the story. There'd been

Champagne—from the glazed look in her eyes, I suspected quite a bit. Then the pivotal question on one knee. The whole restaurant had been in on it, and they had partied until the wee hours, ending with a celebratory conga line on the patio.

"This calls for some bubbly."

Miss P. didn't say no, so Brandy fetched a bottle from the fridge in the kitchenette where I kept emergency rations. The three of us stood in a circle as I poured into the proffered flutes, then filled my own. Setting the bottle on the desk, I raised my glass. "A toast. To good friends, good life, good love. Don't waste even one moment."

We clinked, then drank.

I wrapped Miss P. in a hug.

She whispered, "This is the first time. I never thought love would find me."

Filled with joy, I squeezed her tight.

The door behind us burst open. Letting Miss P go, I turned at the intrusion. Amazingly, I didn't spill even one drop of Champagne.

Romeo skidded to a stop, his eyes taking in our glasses. He looked about as I expected: crumpled clothes that he'd slept in, a puffy face, red eyes. He held a hand to one temple, pressing as if afraid his head would explode.

When he looked at me, a chill chased through me.

"We found Gregor."

THE HOME OF MANY PARTIES, EVEN AN ICE CREAM SOCIAL FOR THE young daughter of a famous welterweight, Bungalow 7 had never welcomed death through its doors . . . until now.

Shoulder to shoulder, Romeo and I hurried through the casino and down the long hallway.

"Did you have Jordan fix you his hangover cure?" I asked, avoiding the task in front of us.

"Yeah, took the edge off." He ran his hand through his hair and glanced at me out of the corner of his eye. He looked sheepish. "Sorry about last night. I'm not feeling even half-human these days."

"What are friends for?" I almost slapped him on the shoulder, then thought better of it—his head would probably roll right off its perch.

The officers standing sentry motioned Romeo and me inside. Crime scene techs were already dusting and processing. For some reason, I tested the air for the lingering smell of the room's most recent inhabitant, the truffle pig. Housekeeping had done a stellar job—no porcine perfume. Although I thought I detected a hint of fish. Keeping the bungalows with their in-room kitchens smelling nice was a never-ending battle for our staff. And now, they were going to have a field day with the mess the techs were making. I didn't want to even think about what the caustic black powder would do to the fine finish on the antiques, so I didn't.

My plate was full.

A man with coroner stitched in block letters across the back of his jacket knelt beside the body. Even in death, Gregor looked like the puffed-up pompous ass he had been. Lying on his back, his prodigious stomach popping the buttons on his shirt, eyes open, his skin a bluish tint, his black hair still oiled into place, he looked like he'd just dropped where he fell, overtaken by death.

"Hey, Doc. You know Lucky O'Toole from the hotel, right?" Romeo asked as we stepped behind the coroner.

I bent over him, like a vulture looming over dinner—an analogy that made my stomach turn. "Doc."

"Lucky. Figured you'd show up." Without turning around, he reached into his kit. "You guys sure are keeping me busy. We got another note."

My stomach flipped. "Where?"

Over his shoulder, he handed me a plastic bag with a scrap of white paper in it. "We found it in his jacket pocket . . . with a black Sharpie."

"Really?"

The coroner answered with a nod.

Romeo followed me as I headed toward the bar to lay the note flat on the granite surface.

Staring down at the note, Romeo asked, his voice hushed. "Think he's been writing all these notes?"

"And killing everyone?" I didn't try to hide my disbelief.

"Then who killed him?"

"The killer," I deadpanned.

He didn't appear to appreciate my jocularity as he squinted at me out of one eye.

"Lights too bright in here for you?"

"No, just rethinking why I brought you along," he growled.

We hunched over the note, hoping for a clue. I read the lines out loud. "Mistakes made, nothing new. A gag, a joke, a dream come true. No smiles, just pain. With everything to gain. Why cheat, why steal. A Carnival, a party where no one . . ." I looked up into Romeo's clear blue eyes, rimmed in red. "It stops in the middle."

"So he was writing them?"

I thought about that a moment—conclusions were so easy to jump to, especially when you wanted some answers. "I don't think we can assume anything. We need some proof."

"We'll try to pull some prints." The coroner's voice was muffled as he hunched over the body. He didn't sound hopeful.

"If you could just give us something to go on, some hint of a connection between these three, maybe we could lighten your future workload."

He glanced around, holding my eyes for a moment. I didn't have to explain.

"Any idea what killed him?" Romeo asked, nodding toward the bloated corpse of Chef Gregor.

Turning back to his work, the coroner reached into Gregor's mouth with a pair of forceps. Maneuvering, he squeezed his fingers, and the catch caught with an audible sound. Pulling the forceps free, he held them aloft, rotating them as he eyed the chunk of white flesh held in the instrument's grasp. "Fugu."

"What?" The young detective looked lost at sea.

"Just a guess, mind you. I won't know for certain until we run all the tests. But from the state of the body, the uneaten sushi feast on the counter over there—" He motioned to the dining room table. I hadn't noticed the remains of dinner scattered there, but they explained the smell of fish. "It sure looks like a neurotoxin." The coroner rocked back on his heels, then pushed himself to his feet. He was taller and thinner than I remembered. His eyes looked sad, but his manner was businesslike and perfunctory. Death was an everyday occurrence for him, after all. I'd noticed the same jaded look on Romeo recently. "I'll have to run some tox screens."

"Fugu is a poison?" Romeo tried to catch a thread.

"Technically, a fish," I explained. "A delicacy in Japan, the wild fugu feeds on some sort of plankton or something that in turn ingests a large amount of neurotoxins. The fish eats so much, its flesh becomes saturated with the stuff. Especially its organs."

"Why would anybody eat that?"

"As a stupid show of manhood. Just another of the many curses of the Y-chromosome."

The coroner actually laughed. "And how did you come to hold the male of the species in such high regard?"

"Experience."

He gave me a shrug and a weak smile. "It's the best teacher."

"Apparently, I'm a slow learner." I grabbed Romeo's arm and squeezed as a thought zinged through my synapses. "Pigs find a feast so rare."

His eyes widened. "It wasn't a four-legged pig at all." He looked at the bloated body of Chef Gregor and winced. "The rest of the note makes sense now."

I turned to the coroner, who watched us with interest. "I'm interested in how Chef Gregor came by a lethal dose of fugu, assuming your theory holds up."

Romeo pulled out his tattered note pad and pen from his inside jacket pocket and began taking notes. Odds were, he slept with the thing. Of course, lately he'd been sleeping in his clothes, like a firefighter ready to roll out of bed, step into his boots, then run at the sound of an alarm.

"Surely with all your Japanese clientele, you've had to deal with fugu at some point." The coroner played out the obvious.

"Of course, but the stuff is highly regulated, as you can imagine. Talk about hoops to jump through! And the sushi chef handling the stuff must have been trained by the masters in Japan and certified to work with the fish. Apparently, serving a lethal main course to high-roller clients is considered bad form, not to mention the chilling effect it could have on business."

Romeo looked up from his note taking, his hand poised over the paper. "High rollers?"

"Super pricy stuff," the coroner said.

"Adding insult to injury." I couldn't help myself.

Romeo gave me a wide-eyed look. I shrugged in response.

"You two ought to take your act on the road." The coroner bagged the fish and motioned to his techs, who descended on the body like flies. "But the carton over there says this stuff came from One Fish, Two Fish."

Our eyes wide, Romeo and I looked at each other.

"Bingo," we said in unison.

Brett Baker's Twitter feed indicated his food truck would

be downtown today at the Farmers Market. This being November, the number of farmers there would be few. With the holidays on top of us, the vendors would have mainly packaged goods, maybe even canned cranberry jellies and other traditional fare. Of course, the baked goods would be amazing—I tried to conjure some willpower, but I'd already given it up for Thanksgiving.

Romeo angled his unmarked car across two handicapped spots. Normally, I would've said something, but today, even though he didn't have the sticker, he could probably qualify, so I let him be.

As we stepped out of the car, I motioned him to follow me. "The food trucks will be around on the other side." With the detective on my heels, I strode quickly through the building, past the many stalls, dodging patrons with their reusable bags. California sensibilities leaking into the Consumption Capital of the World? I smiled at the incongruity. The aroma of roasting chestnuts almost brought me up short, but I kept moving.

Bursting through the swinging doors on the far side of the building, I allowed myself a nanosecond of satisfaction. One Fish, Two Fish was the third food truck lined up along the curb, its awing unfurled and its window open for business. A line of people waited while Brett, in his best smile, took orders. Someone I couldn't see plated the orders and stuffed them through the small delivery window to the side. I assumed no one cooked—I didn't know much about sushi, but I felt fairly certain there wasn't much cooking involved.

Romeo shouldered his way to the front the line, then flashed his badge. "May I have a minute of your time?" His tone left no room for refusal.

Brett looked surprised, but not alarmed.

"This won't take long," Romeo assured him with a grim smile.

The sushi man wiped his hands on a white towel hanging from

the apron string at his waist. "Sure. Meet me at the back of the truck."

The crowd muttered a bit, but no one abandoned the line. Their doggedness made me want to try the sushi, but I'd lost my taste for it recently. While both men made their way to the meeting point, I stayed at the order window, inching closer. A head popped into view, stepping in to fill Brett's spot.

Desiree's eyes widened when she saw me. "His help didn't show up. Brett was alone when I arrived with his delivery. I stepped in to help, if you must know."

"I didn't ask."

She gave me a flat stare. "Yes, you did."

"Who was his help?"

She shrugged and shook her head, her curls bouncing.

The first in line, a broad-shouldered man with a scowl, stepped up and barked his order, which Desiree jotted down with a perfunctory smile. She eased back inside and out of view, but given the size of the truck, I felt sure she could still hear me.

"Are you always so hands-on with all your customers?"

The sushi buyer shot me a dirty look. "Leave the woman to work, would you?"

"Women are experts at multitasking. You'll get your food, and I'll have my answers." I stared him down—my patience had evaporated after the last lap of life, which had me running in circles.

He narrowed his eyes, but left me alone.

Desiree reappeared, pushing a Styrofoam container at him. "That'll be twenty dollars. Sauces are over there." She motioned with her chin toward a table set up off to the side.

He handed her the bill, grabbed his loot, and retreated.

"Brett is a friend." Desiree smiled at the next patron as she noted the order, yet talked to me. "He worked for Jean for quite some time." She popped out of sight, then returned quickly, exchanging the container of food for a crisp twenty.

"Does he have any reason to hate your brother?"

She frowned at me. "Of course not."

I lowered my voice, but I needn't have worried. The next in line was still absorbed in the menu. "What about Chitza DeStefano?"

Desiree looked at me coldly, clearly tired of the game. "Who?"

I shrugged off her tone, keeping my voice conversational. "Do you have any fugu on the menu?"

The question stopped her dead. Her eyes widened, and the cool dropped from her tone. "Why?"

"Just curious." I smiled. "Do you?"

Desiree paled. "Not on the menu, no." She turned to the next customer, a well-heeled lady on her cell phone. "Excuse us just a minute, please. I'll only be a moment." The lady seemed unperturbed as she stepped to the side to continue her conversation and stay out of ours. Desiree motioned me closer and lowered her voice. "Why did you mention fugu, specifically? I had an order come in only yesterday."

Now that, I wasn't expecting—I don't know why. Unlike Romeo, to whom everyone was a suspect, I'd granted the Bouclets innocent-until-proven-guilty status. Hopelessly American, I know. "An order for whom?"

"Christian Wexler."

"Did you deliver it?"

"Of course. His paperwork was in order. The fish was superior quality and at the peak of freshness. I had tracked the shipment myself." Her brows crinkled. "There was one odd thing, though."

"Only one?"

She ignored the sarcasm. "*Oui*, the shipment was short several ounces. I have a call into the supplier, but have yet to hear back. I didn't know whether it left the facility that way, or was once again one of the shipments tampered with somewhere along the way."

"My money is on the latter."

She gave me a concerned look. "I do not know. But I will. I kept the chip, and it is one of Jean's."

~

ROMEO AND I RECONVENED INSIDE THE MARKET AWAY FROM
listening ears. "What'd you find out from Brett Baker?" I asked the
detective as he scanned his notes.

He blew out a long breath. "Not much. He had all the right
answers. An alibi, which I will check out. Apparently, he has a
girlfriend."

"Had he noticed any of his containers missing?" I didn't need
to hear his answer, I already knew.

"He said he has thousands of the things. He wouldn't know if a
couple went missing." The detective confirmed my guess.

"Men," I scoffed, but I doubted I'd do any better of a job.
Details weren't my best thing. "Too bad there wasn't some sort of
break-in or something."

Romeo looked at me as if I'd lost my mind, which presupposed
I had one in the first place.

"If his alibi checks out, then someone took those cartons."
Romeo and his everyone-was-guilty attitude. "But since he didn't
notice them missing, he didn't report the theft, and any evidence
we may have found has been lost."

I scoffed again. "Metro wouldn't have worked that scene,
anyway. Small potatoes for your lofty egos."

He didn't argue. "More budgetary constraints than ego
constraints, but you have a valid point."

I thought that a gross understatement, but Romeo was already
well aware of my disdain for those running Metro. "With Fiona...
out of business...did you ask him who supplies him now? How he
comes by such high-quality foodstuffs?"

"Desiree Bouclet services his account personally . . . now."
Romeo kept his voice flat.

"If he's in so tight with the Bouclets, why didn't he just go
through Desiree in the first place?" I started to tell him about
the fugu shipment and the chip Desiree had given to me—she

275

had it in her pocket, intending to give it to Romeo, but had gotten absorbed in helping Brett Baker—when shouts filled the air.

"Stop them, oh, my God, stop them, please!"

Romeo turned to me, his brows crinkled. "That sounds like—"

"Mona." I took off at a run toward the voice. Rounding the corner to turn down the middle aisle, I skidded to a halt and pressed myself against the stall to one side.

A gaggle of angry turkeys, darting from side to side, feathers flying, swarmed in my direction. Behind them, arms akimbo, her hair a mess, came Mona, just as I feared. "Oh, Lucky! Thank God! Stop them!"

For some reason, I did as she asked. Stepping into the fray, I shouted to the people huddling behind me: "Close the doors." I pointed to Romeo: "Come on, you know what to do."

After a fraction of a second of hesitation, he rallied, shouting orders at the other bystanders. Within a few moments, we'd cornered the turkeys, then herded them back into their pen. I have no idea how.

Sure that everything was back to normal, I advanced on Mona. Whatever spark of humanity her cries had appealed to had been effectively extinguished . . . especially when the last large tom bit me in the butt. "May I ask what the hell you are doing?"

The emergency past, Mona gathered her composure, tucking a few stray tendrils back into place as she found her smile. For the first time, I noticed the cameramen . . . from every major station in town. "Great." I offered a few other choice epithets under my breath as I grabbed my mother's arm and propelled her out of the spotlight. Grasping her elbow, holding her tight to my side, I pasted on a fake smile as I leaned down, my mouth close to her ear. "Explain. And it had better be good. You just managed to make fools out of both of us on the nightly news."

"They just got away, that's all." Mona managed not to whine, which meant she would live at least a few more heartbeats.

"What are the turkeys doing here?" I wanted to ask her how she had gotten them here, but the details would be superfluous.

She took a deep breath and puffed out her chest. "You told me the turkeys were my problem, and I quite agree. I've been using you so that I could avoid my messes for far too long."

I narrowed my eyes. "What have you done with my mother? You look like her, you even sound like her, but those words, she would never say them . . . not ever."

"Perhaps you underestimate me." She held me with a steady, serious gaze—I saw maturity, a resolve I'd never seen before.

I let go of her arm and took a step back. "Perhaps." For some reason, I felt like I had just waded into a pool of quicksand.

Relief sparkled in her shy smile.

"Mother, you shouldn't be chasing poultry in your condition. You look ready to pop. Tell me, do you really want to have those twins at the Farmers Market?"

"It'd make a great story." She shot me a jaunty grin. "As they say, any press is good press."

"The jury's still out on that one." I glanced at the cameramen. Still rolling. "But we'll know soon enough. I can't wait to see how they handle this on the evening news. But if I'm to do damage control, perhaps you could give me the rest of the story—short and sweet."

"Well . . ." Mona drew out the intro, sounding proud of herself. "I put out the word that anyone who wanted an all-natural, fresh turkey for Thanksgiving dinner tomorrow could come get one. I hired some butchers to do the deed." At the look on my face, she fluttered a hand, stalling my words. "Don't worry, it's all done out of sight. No one would've known the turkeys were here, had a young boy not gotten away from his mother and decided to set them free."

"Boys, they mess up everything." I couldn't resist swinging at that hanging curve ball.

Mona raised an eyebrow and tried to look serious. "But they

do add some much needed spice. Anyway, if folks can't pay for a dressed bird, they can have one for free. But I encourage those who can give something, to do so. All the proceeds will go to provide the Thanksgiving meal for the homeless tomorrow." She waited, eyes large and round, almost begging for approval.

I couldn't disappoint—not when she was showing so much . . . growth. "Nice thinking. Have at it."

Crossing my arms, I watched Mona, her public persona dropping neatly over her real one as she strode in front of the cameras in full damage-control mode.

Romeo stepped in next to me. "Your mother, she does know how to make an impression."

"Unfortunately, the only way she knows how is to stir things up. I wouldn't be surprised if she let those turkeys go herself."

"Any evidence of that?" Romeo sounded like he could almost believe it.

I watched as she cleverly ushered everyone back toward her stand, where young women in scanty attire waited to relieve them of some money.

"Circumstantial, and a lifetime of anecdotal, but nothing more." I graced the detective with a confused frown. "She always comes out smelling like a rose. I'd sure like to know her secret."

"You." Romeo raised his eyebrows. "You are her secret weapon."

I thought about that for a moment. "Then I need a me."

"But you've got you." Romeo shook his head slowly, but his brightening look indicated his pain might be easing. "I have the oddest conversations with you sometimes. Right now, there's not much I can do about Mona. I can't think of any laws she's broken." Romeo kept the smile off his face, but not out of his voice.

"Such a steward of the public trust you are, leaving her to feast on unsuspecting bystanders."

Romeo squinted down the aisle at Mona's booth, then swallowed hard. "Are those girls . . . ?"

"Working girls? Looks that way." I recognized a couple of them from Mona's Place, the Best Whorehouse in Nevada, to hear Mother tell it. "But today, hopefully, they are more interested in toms than johns, and there isn't a pastry in sight."

"Pastry?" Romeo clearly had not made it onto the party bus.

"I heard rumors of a bake sale."

"Offending Brownies the world over."

"Well." I elbowed him. "You may go sample their wares, but I need to talk to a chef about dinner."

CHEF OMER WAS EXACTLY WHERE I'D HOPED TO FIND HIM—IN THE kitchen at Tigris, going through paperwork, preparing for the day. Tigris didn't open until five o'clock, although the bar opened earlier. Even still, the kitchen staff was busy unloading produce, fish, poultry, and other ingredients for tonight's selected repast. Like most of the top chefs, Chef Omer created a menu each day based on the availability of only the freshest, most succulent foodstuffs.

The aroma of fresh coffee filled the kitchen. Even though I knew his taste ran to thick Turkish coffee whose merits eluded me, I poured myself a thimbleful of the viscous fluid into a mug Desperate for the caffeine hit, any delivery vehicle would do. I did cut it with a serious amount of half-and-half, but I resisted the sugar on principle—drawing lines gave me the illusion of control.

After savoring a java jolt, I straddled a stool across from the chef, then tapped my fingers on the stainless steel countertop before I drew his attention. When he looked at me, his scowl was already in place, and, from the looks of it, well entrenched.

He brightened a bit when he recognized me, but a bit of anger still puckered the skin between his eyebrows. "Lucky. Twice in less than a week.."

"Did I catch you at a bad time? You look preoccupied."

He shook his head, and his readers slipped down on his nose. He fixed his glare over them. "It's nothing, really. The paperwork on my shipments is off—something doesn't add up. Not to mention, the quality is slipping. Trying to provide the best culinary experience in this . . . wasteland . . . is a challenge."

"I think I can explain some of that. But maybe you ought to try the food market in the garage. I've been told they have primo stuff."

That stopped Chef Omer cold. "What?" His tone turned icy.

"The food market in the garage. I'm taking it you don't know about it?"

"Show me," he said with a growl. "And you'd better call Security."

CHAPTER 18

ERRY AND two well-armed guards met us at the garage elevators. As head of Security, Jerry's job was the mirror half of mine, but today, he looked way better than I felt. That struck me as unfair.

Tall and lean, dark skinned, clean-shaven (both cheeks and head), Jerry wore his ubiquitous suit pants, minus the jacket, and a starched button-down—today's was pink. It took a self-assured man to wear pink in Vegas where sexual orientations blended until boundaries were often erased. No socks with the loafers and the normal hunk of Rolex gold on his left wrist completed the picture of perfection.

All business, he flashed me a grim smile. "I checked the video feeds. Apparently, the guy has set up on the seventh floor today. He's quite clever." Jerry punched the up button. "He uses his panel truck to shield his activity from the cameras. We never would've noticed him if you hadn't told us what to look for."

As the elevator dinged and the doors opened, the men motioned me in first, then followed.

I took my spot in the middle of the car, turning to face the doors. "How'd you find him, then?"

"Too hard to explain right now, but we look for patterns."

With the guards positioning themselves behind, Chef Omer and Jerry bracketed me. Chef stared upward, an angry flush climbing his cheeks as his lips moved in silent conversation. Jerry and I stared at each other's reflection in the smooth metal of the elevator doors as we rode up. "Speaking of video, did you have time to check with your contacts at the news stations?"

"After you called me, I hit every one. Even though they were all running footage at the Big Dig, none of them had any angle that showed the cockpit of the crane, before or after the accident. They were focused on the show. Just like they told Romeo."

"I thought maybe one of them might have been running some B-roll. It was a long shot."

The elevator dinged our arrival. Tapping my thigh, coiled like a racehorse poised to leap out of the starting gate, I waited for the elevator doors to open.

As I moved to slip through the opening, a meaty hand from behind stopped me. "Let us handle this, Ms. O'Toole. It's our job."

"Our job," Jerry scoffed. "Hell, it's our asses. I don't want to be the one who lets you get perforated—the Big Boss would give me a pair of cement boots and toss me into Lake Mead." Jerry, with the guards on his heels, bolted though the widening opening and ran.

"Not to worry," I shouted after him. "After ten years of serious drought, the lake is probably only waist-deep."

Red-faced, Omer glanced at me. Bowing slightly, he motioned for me to precede him. I gladly obliged. In light of his bulk and already elevated blood pressure, I followed the security trio, but set a more sedate pace.

Up ahead of us, around the corner out of sight, an engine revved. Gears ground. Shouts. Jerry's voice. "Stop."

Tires squealed. A shot. Then another.

I pressed Omer in between two parked cars. "Get down," I

barked, then paused to make sure he would do as I said. Then I ran.

The truck careened around the corner. Going too fast, the top-heavy cargo van listed sideways, caught by centrifugal force. Time slowed. For a moment, it looked like force would win, but at the last moment, when the truck had tipped to an almost impossible angle, the tires grabbed. The truck settled back onto all fours with a lurch and a bounce. The driver overcompensated. Swerving, he glanced off several cars on the far side with an ear-splitting screech of metal on metal. The acrid smell of burned rubber billowed with the smoke from the spinning tires. The impact slowed the truck, steadying it. The driver regained control.

The engine whined as he stepped on it.

The truck heading down the ramp. Me heading up.

We met halfway.

Dead center, I stood my ground.

Several heart-stopping moments. Narrowing my eyes, I stared through the windshield. I never thought he would stop—I just hoped for a glance.

At the last minute, I dove to the left.

I landed on the hood of a Mercedes Roadster, then rolled off. Landing with a thud, I felt my breath rush out of me as I absorbed the blow. Gasping for air, I saw stars as I fought to regain composure.

The sound of the engine still screamed, tires squealed, but the noise faded. Voices, shouts filtered in. Tinged with panic, they called my name. Slowly, the world came back, my sight, which had pinpointed, broadened to full spectrum.

"Over here." I struggled to stand.

Jerry and the guards, running out of control down the ramp, veered in my direction. They gathered around me. "Are you all right?" Jerry asked. Smoothing the hair out of my face, he took a good look.

"Pissed as hell, but otherwise fine." I whirled around to look behind me. "Chef Omer?" I put a bracing hand out as my world spun. Adrenaline surged, bringing the world into focus. "Chef Omer?"

No answer. Jerry and I locked eyes, then we both took off. A little slower, I was on his heels.

We met Chef Omer huffing and puffing back up the ramp on the floor below. He mopped his face with a soggy handkerchief.

"Thank God." I slowed to a walk.

Relief flooded his face. Pausing, he leaned against a car and waited for us. "I tried, but I couldn't see a face."

"Me, either." I shook my head as I stopped in front of him. "I got a clear look, but couldn't make anything out. Damn."

Looking angry, but unruffled, Jerry pulled out his push-to-talk and keyed Security. He barked some orders, then waited. I worked to get my heart rate under control and assess the damage. Not too bad—only a smudge on my pants, but they were dark enough to hide it well.

Chef Omer looked a bit ragged. Despite his dabbing with the cloth in his hand, water ran in rivulets down his face, disappearing into the folds of his jowls and neck, then reappearing as a growing stain on his collar.

Jerry muttered an epithet, then said, "Thank you." He looked at me and shook his head as he put his phone away in its sleeve at his waist. "Cameras didn't get a good angle on the driver's face, either. There may be something I can play with, but I'll have to get up to Security to see. But I did see the plates were covered, so that's a dead end."

The three of us worked our way back up the ramp—this time, at a more sedate pace. I was glad to see the color in Chef Omer's face lightening with each passing minute.

The two guards waited for us at the elevators. Some help they had been. I started to voice my displeasure when the vision in front of me brought me up short.

Three people waited. The two guards and Christian Wexler.

The chef held a box—from the strain on his face, it must've been heavy.

"This guy was just paying for his stuff, when the other guy jumped into the truck and took off." The guard who had spoken before explained.

"Who was selling you this stuff?" I asked the chef, who had put the box down.

Chef Omer squatted and started through the contents.

"First, it was Fiona," Chef Wexler answered. "And now, who the hell cares?"

"Ah-ha!" Chef Omer held a tin aloft. "My caviar." He set it down and rooted some more, pulling out tins as he ticked them off. "My saffron. My piment d'Espelette." He hoisted the small container skyward. "Thank God, I do not want to anger the Basques, they get pretty nasty." He pounced again, giggling in delight. "And the black garlic." When he looked at me, his face held a kid's delight at Christmas. "This explains a lot of things." He rose and turned on Wexler, wagging a meaty finger in the younger man's face. "You should be ashamed, stealing these things."

Wexler paled. "I didn't steal them, I swear. I just bought them."

"And turned a blind eye."

Wexler vacillated. "Yeah, yeah, you're right. At first I thought it was all black market stuff, but Fiona was behind it, so I figured it was just part of her business model, know what I'm saying? Since everyone else was buying the good stuff, I had to, too. How else could I compete?"

"That argument didn't get Barry Bonds very far with Bud Selig."

"Yeah, well, when Desiree showed up today—I sorta figured it was all legit."

"Desiree? Bouclet?"

"How many Desirees do you know?" Chef Wexler gave me a

condescending look, which I though pretty bold, or foolhardy. "She was the one driving the truck."

~

DESIREE BOUCLET. WHAT THE HELL WAS SHE UP TO? I FELT somewhat homicidal—my natural reaction when someone tried to kill me. And I felt a bit sad—how I'd wanted to believe the Bouclets were aboveboard. I should've known better, though. No one is what they seem—Jean-Charles had told me that himself, the last time we talked.

Anger propelled me through the casino. The open door to Teddie's theatre stopped me in my tracks. Open only a crack, it was enough to attract my attention. No one should be in there— the set for the Last Chef Standing competition had been set, Brandy told me so herself. The theatre should've been locked up tight.

Without easing the door open much farther, I squeezed through.

Kliegs on the tracks overhead bathed the stage in bright light, accentuating the darkness of the seating area. In the small arc from the edge of the stage back to the maze of prep tables, cook-tops, and ovens, two men stood side-by-side facing an unnoticed audience of one—me.

Of course, Teddie would have a key.

Jordan had joined him.

The two of them were a study in contrasts: Jordan dark and steamy, Teddie blond and All-American. Both buff, with pelvises thrust forward, one hand on a hip, shoulders back, pouty faces—a gay sashay.

"Okay," Teddie explained. "There are six main drag queen moves."

As quietly as I could, I settled into the nearest seat, and leaned back. As shows go, this one had great potential—if I could score a beverage with a small umbrella, life would be perfect.

"The first one is pick-the-grapes." With palm facing downward, hand cupped, Teddie lifted one arm in front of him, then at the top of the stroke, he turned his hand over as if plucking a grape from a tall vine. "You have to exaggerate it. Like this." He gave a hip tilt, more bend and movement to his arm, a snap at the top. Jordan mimicked him. The man was a natural—not that I was surprised, or anything.

Where was a video camera when I needed one? This would go viral on YouTube.

The two of them worked through the rest of the moves. There was pull-back-the-drapes and pass-the-plate, which were variations of the arm extended, swiping dramatically across the body. Next came a finger-wagging get-off-my-lawn, as if scolding a child. Then churn-the-butter: the men clasped their hands in front of them and moved every part they could in a circular motion. That one had potential in a slightly different venue, I thought. This was followed closely by the pièce de résistance and my personal favorite, toss-the-condom. With thumb and forefinger on one hand pressed together, the other hand placed back on the hip, they made a flicking motion over one shoulder as if flinging away something distasteful.

I clamped a hand over my mouth to keep the laughter bottled up inside. The men moved through the series several times until Jordan could follow along without a hitch.

"Okay, now we put it to music." Teddie glanced into the crow's nest above my head and gave a curt nod. "The Diana Ross, please," he called. Then he glanced at Jordan and gave him a huge smile. "You ready?"

Jordan gave a little laugh. "Here goes nothing."

When the first strains of music hit through the speakers, I about choked. "'I'm Coming Out'? Seriously?" I said, unable to stifle myself any longer.

Teddie laughed as he shielded his eyes with one hand and searched the room, finding me at the top. He didn't seem surprised. He gave me a grin. Both men waved. And the two of them didn't miss a beat, bobbing their heads to the music, then stepping into their routine.

Watching two incredibly handsome, virile, masculine men mince and prance their way through the song helped me find my smile. Life had been a bit of a drag lately—I smiled at the pun, of course. I'm easily amused. To be honest, lately, I'd taken to whining a bit too much—I was boring myself. It dawned on me that I was *sooo* over me. Time to move on, kick butt if I had to.

And live.

When the song wound down, Teddie and Jordan glanced at each other, then burst out laughing as I clapped wildly. They took rather dramatic bows.

"You guys are almost as good as Bing Crosby and Danny Kaye and their 'Sisters' act in *White Christmas*."

Teddie gave me an interesting look—I wasn't sure how to read it. We had reprised that scene a hundred times as we giggled our way through a bucket of popcorn and a bottle of meaty Petit Syrah each Christmas Eve for the past couple of years, at least.

Good memories.

Teddie. I wanted my best friend back. Could we once again find our center? Was it really possible to go back like he said?

All I knew was: if he wanted to regain my trust, he'd have to earn it.

"Let's do it again." Teddie gave a signal to cue the music again.

Jordan proved to be a quick study, and soon the men had the beginnings of a worthy act. I moved closer, landing in the center of the fourth row—as the only fan in the audience, I couldn't think of a reason why I shouldn't try out the primo seats. As an executive at the hotel, I never found my ass in this kind of class during a real show—the seats went to our most important guests.

When the song ended, they both looked satisfied with the

progress they'd made—and like they were having fun. "Jordan, Teddie hasn't talked you into joining his show, has he?"

Jordan gave me a tilt of his head and a slight shrug. "I might do a guest appearance, I don't really know. We'll see." Since coming out a few months ago, confirming the whispers about his sexual orientation, Jordan seemed so much calmer, his true personality shining through. If the admission had any impact on his film career, I couldn't see it. Rumors had abounded for years, so the revelation had been met with pretty much a collective yawn. That said as much about Jordan as it did about how we as humans had grown in understanding and acceptance. Somehow, that gave me hope.

Teddie picked up where Jordan left off. "I think I have him convinced that a limited run would be a great way to start." Teddie looked happy, at home.

"Perhaps you should run it by his lawyer first?" Rudy's voice boomed from the rectangle of light that opened at the top of the stairs.

"Leave it to a lawyer to throw water on the creative fires," Jordan joked as he squatted and eased himself down from the stage. As he passed me, he gave me a wink, then grabbed me by both shoulders and gave me a lingering kiss on the cheek. Jordan lived with passion—I loved that about him. He hooked his arm through Rudy's, and I watched them climb the stairs, then disappear through the door, leaving Teddie and me alone.

Teddie gazed down on me with a look I remembered well, and the time and distance fell away.

I raised an eyebrow at him, and tried, mostly unsuccessfully, to hide my smile. "We've just been set up."

His grin blossomed. "Looks that way." He glanced at his cluttered stage. "Where's a baby grand when a guy needs one?" Taking a seat on the edge of the stage, letting his legs dangle, he patted the spot beside him. "Join me?"

He didn't have to ask twice. Settled beside him, I leaned

forward, anchoring myself by grabbing the edge of the stage, a hand on either side of my thighs. Our shoulders touched as I swung my legs. I didn't mind. Soon, our legs swung in the same rhythm.

If Teddie noticed, he didn't let on. "Any closer to catching the killer?"

I thought it funny he considered that a safe topic to open the conversation. "I feel like the answers are there, just out of reach. Too many pieces to see the whole puzzle just yet, though."

"You'll figure it out, I have faith. Just be careful, okay?"

"You know me." I shrugged and thought about the many layers to that simple comment.

"That's what scares me." Teddie stilled his legs, and mine followed suit, as if tethered. "Want to talk about it?"

"What?"

"Anything."

I gazed out at the empty rows in the darkened theatre. Tomorrow was Thanksgiving. Mona had some big shindig planned, but I was still in the dark as to exactly what—and how exactly she planned to feed the homeless without all the turkeys. Oddly, I didn't care. Not about not feeding the homeless, but about how and what my mother had up her sleeve. Funny, as I looked back on it, despite some false steps along the way, she usually accomplished her goals . . . and rarely got arrested.

I mentally worked through some topics to broach with Teddie, safe and not so safe. Before I got the chance to open even one can of worms, the door at the top of the stairs burst open.

A thin man rushed through, silhouetted by the light behind, his features shaded in the darkness. "There you are! I've been looking all over!" The voice of Adone Giovanni sounded brittle enough to break with a high note. "You must come quickly, this terrible thing has happened."

I launched myself off the stage, my heart rate spiking with a huge shot of adrenaline. "Not another body?"

"They have arrested Desiree."

~

ALONG WITH THE HOSPITAL, THE CLARK COUNTY DETENTION Center was one of my least favorite places. Lately, though, I'd been getting to know both of them well. Especially since, due to an odd quirk of corruption and influence peddling, the Strip, and thus the Babylon, were not in the City of Las Vegas, but rather in unincorporated Clark County. As government buildings went, the detention center had at least a modicum of style, stuccoed and painted in colors of the desert. Of course, it was relatively new and had yet to acquire the patina of despair most jails wore. During the ride from the Babylon, Adone had chattered endlessly, saying nothing other than, "I do not think it is what you think."

Exasperated, I had fired back, "Why don't you tell me what *it* is, then I will tell you if it is what I think it is."

Looking like a schoolboy who had spoken out of turn, he had spent the rest of the ride with his arms crossed in sullen silence. Now, he dogged my heels through the metal detectors and incriminating stares of bored officers.

Stopping in the middle of the atrium, I put a hand in the center of his chest. Amazingly, this got his attention. "Sit over there." I motioned to some uncomfortable-looking plastic chairs strewn haphazardly around wobbly tables. "Wait."

I didn't give him a chance to argue as I turned on my heels and approached the desk. The officer sitting behind a clear, bullet-proof wall buzzed me through the locked doors to the side of the desk.

Romeo met me on the other side. Turning, he fell into step—we both knew where we were going. "She's not talking."

"So why am I here?"

"To make her talk." He actually sounded serious.

I did not answer in the same tone. "Well, in that case, you should've told me to bring the thumbscrews and my sadistic side."

"I thought you'd know to do that by now." Romeo didn't even smile. As I suspected, he was growing into my snark.

Side-by-side, we strode briskly down the hallway, through a couple of sets of security doors, then stopped in front of a door with a mirrored glass window marked interrogation room two. Through the window, I could see Desiree sitting at the metal table, hands crossed primly, looking very composed. "I want to be the good cop this time. Okay? You always get to play nice and expect me to be the heavy, breaking kneecaps and all."

Romeo rolled his eyes as he turned the knob and opened the door.

Desiree turned worried, angry eyes to me as I sat opposite her. The room was small, the space tight for three adults. "I am not who you are looking for."

A rather odd opening, but I went with it. "Who should we be looking for?"

"They say I am driving a truck? That I tried to kill you." In an aggressive move, she stood abruptly, propelling her chair backward.

Romeo moved to intervene, but I put out a hand, stopping him.

Desiree whirled and paced, her agitation propelling her from one side of the small room to the other.

Worn out, I stayed where I was. "So you were not in the garage at the Babylon. You were not selling stolen foodstuffs out of a truck?"

She stopped. Placing both hands on the table between us, she leaned into me.

"Why would I do these things? Selling things I stole from myself? It makes no sense. My products are good. If I wish more money, I raise the prices. Few complain."

I held her gaze. I could smell her cologne. Chanel No. 5, I

thought . . . but of course, what else would it be? "Chef Wexler? Did he complain?"

A flicker of surprise. "He tried to play me against Fiona." Desiree looked insulted at the thought. "He was not successful."

"I see."

"You cannot compromise on quality." Desiree's voice held an air of finality.

"Agreed. Did Chef Wexler try again to buy from you?"

Her eyes drifted from mine, focusing instead on Romeo, who stood guard behind me. "Yes, but I would not give him credit. After the bad review, I did not trust his business anymore. It is obvious I don't trust his judgment, so on what basis would I sell to him?"

Using emotion to counter logic was not my strong suit, so I conceded the point.

"So, he has reason to be angry with you," Romeo stated.

Desire looked askance. "It is business."

As if that explained it all. "And ego," I added.

"He is"—she paused, searching for words—"how do you say it? A small fish?"

I felt like saying that so are piranha, but I had a feeling that she'd feel this little bite Christian Wexler took out of her ass for some time to come. Getting her arrested, even if briefly, was a nice stroke of revenge, if you asked me. I'm sure Romeo would have something to say to Chef Wexler about lying to the police and making false accusations, but perhaps the chef's revenge was worth the price.

Desiree started pacing again, but this time, with less enthusiasm. "When was I to be doing these things?" She threw the question out, not looking at Romeo or me.

"An hour or two ago."

"Impossible." She paused, throwing the word down between us like a gauntlet. "I was teaching a class at the Culinary Institute all day." She lasered Romeo with a stare. "You must check. You will see I am telling the truth."

"And," I turned to Romeo, "while you're at it, you might want to round up Chef Wexler and find out why he lied, and who really was driving that truck."

Behind me, there was a rustle of clothing. The door opened, then closed. Desiree and I were alone.

As the sole target, I absorbed her ire. "You are fools. Who says these things about me?"

"Where did the police find you?"

"At Jean's. I had just arrived home. The Culinary Institute is five minutes away."

"When the police came to arrest you, did you tell them where you had been?"

"*Non.*" Desiree gave me an imperious look. "They are thugs, putting on the . . ."

"Handcuffs?"

"Yes, these." She rubbed her wrists and deflated a little, her bombast leaving as quickly as it had come. "I am scared, so I say nothing until I have a friend." Her eyes darted to mine. "Tell me, who says these things about me?"

Was she playing me? Who knew? I decided to take a flier and tell her the truth. "Christian Wexler."

Romeo walked back in just in time to hear me give her the goods. I didn't look at him, but I heard his sharp intake.

Desiree's brows knit as she slowly reached for her chair. Pulling it under her, she lowered herself to her original position. "Why would he say this?"

"Oh, I can think of several reasons." I didn't try to hide my sarcasm.

Desiree's brows knitted in confusion. "What have I done to him?"

"Put his business on the ropes."

Incomprehension colored her complexion. "But it is only business."

"Is that how you feel about Fiona? And Adone?"

Her cheeks flushed angry red. "That is different."

"Only difference is that you are on the receiving end. It was done to you."

She righted her chair, then sank slowly into it as realization dawned. "I see."

"Reputation is all we have." I threw her words back at her.

They hit with the force of a slap. "He was angry, yes. But he understood . . . I think."

"When his restaurant got trashed, did he blame you?"

When she looked at me, her face was clear. "No, he blamed you."

～

"HER STORY PANS OUT." ROMEO CONFIRMED WHAT I FIGURED would be true as he walked me out. "I'll get her things, then take her where she wants to go."

Lost in thought, I didn't feel the need to respond. "And Wexler?"

"We're looking for him."

Romeo trotted to keep up with me. "Any idea why that chef has it in for you?"

"Sure. He was in the running for the space I gave to Gregor."

Romeo whistled. "So, Wexler could've had a primo spot at the most important Strip property, when the eyes of the world turned in that direction. Most folks I know would kill for that."

"Apparently." I did not like where this was going.

"Which spot was it?"

"Where the Burger Palais is now."

Romeo grabbed my arm, bringing me to an abrupt halt. "Jean-Charles's place?"

I swallowed hard as I nodded. "Wexler could be behind this whole stunt, setting up Jean-Charles."

"Your lover." Romeo's eyes widened. "Lucky no more."

I grabbed Romeo and squeezed his arm so hard, he winced—of course, he was down to bone and sinew. "Find Chef Wexler. But don't kill him until I get my shot."

CHAPTER 19

*a*DONE SNAGGED me as I strode through the atrium, lost in thought. "She okay?"

"What?" I tried to focus on him. To be honest, I'd forgotten all about him.

The kohl around his eyes had smudged underneath, giving him a Halloween haunted look. "Is Desiree okay? Did they arrest her?"

I appraised him out of the corner of my eye—to me, his question held a hint of hopefulness.

I gave him the short version, leaving out the important parts.

He looked relieved as we burst through the doors into the fading sunlight—maybe I had been wrong about the hope thing.

The halogens flickered as they fired up. The day had disappeared.

I paused with my hand on the Ferrari's handle. "I'll take you back to the hotel."

He didn't argue as he followed my lead and folded himself into the car. "This your ride?"

"Only when I'm good." With the push of a button, the engine growled to life. A flick of my right hand, easy pressure on the accelerator, and we roared out of the parking lot. Heads turned, tracking our progress. A bright red Ferrari lacked even a hint of subtle—I liked that.

"And I bet you are very, very good."

With a glance, I confirmed he intended the innuendo, which creeped me out. Tatted prima donnas with an attitude—to the extent one didn't always beget the other—rarely hit my radar. Add the fact that Adone was technically married, and his mistress wasn't even in the ground yet, gelled the creeping out into a gross-out. What do you know; my libido had developed a bit of discernment. That fact alone gave me hope."And I'm taken."

He didn't seem broken up about that as he turned to stare out the side window, leaving me to the business at hand. I think I probably set a land-speed record getting back to the hotel.

Our good-byes were brief, then I headed for my office—my port in a storm.

I called the Beautiful Jeremy Whitlock on the way. Ideally, he could get some answers from Wexler before Romeo found him. The ante had been upped several times, and I could no longer afford to play by the rules. Besides, I didn't have the patience for it.

With my serious authority issues, rules weren't my best thing.

THE BEAUTIFUL JEREMY WHITLOCK MET ME AT THE ELEVATORS.

"Are you telepathic?" I asked before he had a chance to say anything.

"Just think about me and I appear." Once again, he shot me those dimples. He should be required to have a license, or at least a concealed carry permit for those things.

Curiously, while I could appreciate, it seemed I'd developed an immunity, another good sign. Perhaps, just perhaps, I was actually growing up and into my own skin.

The doors opened and we stepped inside, then turned to face out as the doors slid shut. "I'll show you mine if you show me yours." I grinned at his reflection.

"I'm getting the short end," Jeremy groused with a smile as he held back the door for me—the ride up one floor to the mezzanine didn't allow even enough time for good repartee.

"I wouldn't have it any other way." I fumbled for a key, then remembered my office was still a war zone with a hole in the wall that rendered keys superfluous. "I hope you've got something good."

At my sidelong look, he swallowed the quip I'd known would follow. "I did some poking around on that guy, Livermore."

I flicked the switch, juicing the single bulb that hung on a wire over my desk. The weak circle of light pushed back the darkness enough to leave me wondering what lurked in the corners. I assumed my normal position leaning back in my desk chair, my feet propped on an open lower drawer. Resting my head, I stared at the ceiling. "I've forgotten my manners—can I get you anything?" I raised my head and opened one eye. "Champagne, perhaps?"

He gave me a grin of true contentment.

"Well done, by the way."

"I'm a lucky guy." He bowed his head briefly, then his smile turned all business. "Livermore. It was sheer dumb luck I found out who he was. That bad rug he was wearing made him hard to identify—especially from my grainy photos."

"It's funny how hair changes a look. I assume he was using an alias."

Jeremy rubbed his chin and looked a bit chagrined. "I assumed so as well—a stupid, greenhorn mistake."

"Never assume," we both said in unison.

"Hiding in plain sight, was he?"

Jeremy nodded. "Dane actually was the one to put me onto the bloke."

I pretended I didn't see his worried glance in my direction. "How's Dane doing?"

"Good days and bad. His ego and his heart took a huge hit when he lost Sylvie."

He actually hadn't lost Sylvie—she had died, and he hadn't been able to save her. Ego-induced blindness had been partially at fault, but I didn't think it appropriate or necessary to point that out—beating a dead horse.

"Turns out Livermore's a PI—gives my profession a bad name. He mostly stakes out cheating spouses, that sort of thing. Word on the street is, he'll do pretty much anything for a buck."

"Dane's kind of guy." That was snarky, not sure why. Okay, I knew why—Dane had been a huge disappointment as a friend . . . huge. Disappointment. Trust. People being less than they could be . . . or should be. Maybe I was just a victim of my own optimism . . . and arrogance. Who was I to think others should live up to my expectations? "Where does he hang his shingle? Livermore, I mean."

Jeremy gave me a grin with a bit of wicked in it. "The low rent district."

"Let me guess, Naked City." A section of town straddling Las Vegas Boulevard just north of Sahara and extending almost to downtown—its exact limits depended on who you talked to— Naked City had been home to a bunch of the showgirls back in the heyday. They had taken to sunbathing nude on the rooftops of their apartment buildings, hence the name. When I was a kid, I thought living there would be the best, but, when I discovered that 'Naked City' would not be part of the official address, I lost interest.

"You got it." Jeremy smiled. "And he's expecting us."

～

THE FERRARI STILL WAITED IN THE VALET, ITS ENGINE NOT yet cool.

Jeremy paused when he saw the car. "Maybe we should take mine."

I stepped around him, then raised a questioning eyebrow. "A Hummer is so much more understated."

"Good point." He joined me in the car and gave me the address as I started off.

"He's expecting us?" I asked. If I was to play a part, I needed to know what part. At the end of the driveway, I took a right, heading north, away from the glitz and glamour.

"Yes. I told him it was about a job." Jeremy seemed to be enjoying this. "He said he'd wait. I got the impression he's pretty hard up."

"There's no telling what people will do when their backs are against the wall."

Naked City began where the sexy, high-end part of Las Vegas Boulevard ended. Over time, the showgirls had filtered away—the lucky ones wedding mobsters and moving to estates in one of the elite enclaves off Rancho. Cheap motels replaced the apartments. Pushers and pimps moved in.

In recent years, signs of new life energized the law-abiding residents. They had rallied together to clean up their neighborhood. Still a rougher section, Naked City showed a bit of renovation, refurbishment . . . even gentrification. With the resurgence of development in downtown, that would continue. If someone wanted to speculate on real estate, this wasn't a bad section of town to focus on.

"Take the next right." Jeremy's voice cracked the silence.

I downshifted, using the engine to slow us, then accelerated through the turn.

Jeremy scanned the street numbers. "There. Third one down."

I killed the lights as I eased to the curb, then shut the engine down. A look-at-me car by design, the Ferrari attracted attention, which we didn't need right now. Of course, I'm sure I wasn't the first person with a fancy car to troll the street looking for a low-rent PI. Vegas was that kind of town.

Two cinder-block boxes stacked one atop the other housed the yin and yang of Mr. Livermore's existence—eat and sleep upstairs, work downstairs. The upper windows were dark, but light shown in the one on the right downstairs. The thin curtain diffused the figure of a man standing in front of the desk. Short, hunched shoulders as if hiding from attention, a quick glance toward the window . . . Livermore.

I met Jeremy in front of the car, then turned and followed him up the broken concrete sidewalk. "When he sees me, he'll smell a rat."

"We just need to get him to open the door, not that that will be a problem."

"No need to alert him any sooner than necessary." I used Jeremy as a shield, keeping him between me and the window in case Livermore decided to take a peek.

Behind me, a car roared around the corner, tires squealing, engine whining at a high pitch.

A loud pop.

A backfire?

Before I could move, Jeremy grabbed me. Throwing me to the ground, he covered my body with his. "Stay down." His voice was an angry whisper.

In the shadow, out of the rectangle of light cast by the office lights, we didn't move. Holding my breath, I was afraid to breathe.

More pops. Bullets pinged off the building, ricocheting into the darkness. Several hit the lawn near us. The ground absorbed them with a wet sucking sound. Glass broke.

The car slowed. The bullets stopped.

My heart hammered even though my chest was squeezed tight by fear. I could almost feel the shooter's eyes moving, looking for a hint of movement, anything to give away our position.

Sweat trickled under my blouse. Adrenaline surged. I couldn't move.

"Stay here," Jeremy's voice sounded hoarse in my ear. In the blink of an eye, he rolled off me. As he rolled, he reached for the gun he kept in a holster in the small of his back. Using momentum to bring his feet under him, he stopped in a crouch. Gun at the ready, held tight in both hands, he squeezed off a few rounds.

Metal thunked into sheet metal as he laced the side of the car.

The driver, shrouded in darkness, stepped on the accelerator, gunning the engine. Tires whined, rubber shredded, then caught. The car fishtailed as the driver struggled for control. I sat, mesmerized. Waiting. The car straightened and accelerated down the street. The brakes glowed red, then the car turned right at the far corner.

Jeremy glanced at me.

"Go!" I tossed him the keys.

He snagged them midair, then ran. In a nanosecond, he had the Ferrari at full growl. He floored it. The taillights blinked once, then he, too, turned out of sight.

Silence closed around me. My heartbeat thrummed in my ears. It was the only discernible sound. Slowly, I peeled myself off the ground. Searching for balance, I rose to my full height, unsteady and shaking, wobbling like an old tree in a savage wind. I brushed down my sweater and jeans and took my bearings.

This was the sort of neighborhood where the sound of gunfire made people stay indoors, so I wasn't surprised to find myself alone. Livermore's office still stood, the light shining.

But Mr. Livermore had disappeared.

Worse, the glass window was shattered.

Willing my legs to obey, I bolted up the walkway. The door was unlocked. "Mr. Livermore?" I tried to keep my voice calm, but I couldn't. The volume too high, the tone too tight, it shook with fear and an overdose of excitement. I didn't care. "Mr. Livermore?"

I darted into the front room. It was empty. The cool night breeze blowing through the broken window billowed the thread-bare sheers inward. A siren sounded in the distance. I paused. Bending at the waist with my hands on my knees, I pulled in deep lungfuls of air. The siren grew louder.

A scuffling sound came from behind the desk—a massive oak monstrosity, its varnish yellowed and peeling. Someone had carved names into the wood—Jessie loves Darryl.

Narrowing my eyes, I moved closer. "Mr. Livermore?" My voice was calmer now.

"Don't shoot." The little man rose from behind his wooden fortress. Hands held high, he was as pale as Casper. He shook like a dog on his way to the vet, his whole body racked with tremors. Confusion creased his brows, then the light dawned. "Ms. O'Toole?" Slowly, he lowered his hands. Wide-eyed, he took a step back. "Were you shooting at me?"

I gave him the special look I reserve for a few select morons . . . and Mona, on occasion. "Really?" I held up my hands, palms out. "Do I look like I've been shooting at you?"

"Who, then?"

"I don't know." The siren had faded—I could barely distinguish it from the sounds of the city.

"Why would someone shoot at me?"

Considering his profession, I thought the question a bit naïve. "Cleaning up loose ends, if I may hazard a guess."

Livermore swallowed hard as he sank into his desk chair.

I don't know what it was, a near-death experience, an over-dose of jump start, or an exhaustion of patience and energy, but suddenly, a few things fell into place. I advanced on Mr. Liver-more. Placing my hands on the desk, scattering the few files and at least a day's worth of mail, I leaned into him, towering above him. "Why did Jean-Charles hire you?"

He cowered back as if I were an avenging angel. "Why do you think Chef Bouclet hired me?" He tried to sound strong, tough.

He didn't scare me. "You fabricated a whole story to get into my office to see me. Then you made a point to provide the whole paperweight Internet photo scenario to put me on the scent. You were most helpful. It seemed a bit odd to me at the time that you just sauntered in and had the answer."

He tried to smile—a wan stretching of his lips that made him look like he had gas.

"You made sure your story had just enough holes and inconsistencies to hit my radar." I stepped next to the shattered window, using the wall to shield my body as I took a peek up and down the street. Quiet had once again settled over the neighborhood. Nothing moved. "It was a bit of a gamble, expecting me to put a tail on you."

"Word on the street is, you got some smarts."

Personally, I thought that an exaggeration. "Glad I didn't disappoint."

"Jeremy Whitlock is the best." Livermore's voice steadied.

"Then, when you were sure you had a tail, you left my office and went running to Wexler." I leaned in, getting as close as I could without cringing. "Why?"

"Chef Bouclet knew something was going on with the shipments. He also knew Wexler couldn't pay his bills. Initially, Chef Bouclet suspected Wexler was behind all of this. It was my intent to put him on your radar."

"You did, but that just added him to a cast of characters." Satisfied the shooters weren't easing down the street to finish the job, I stepped away from the window. With the excitement over, I let my eyes roam around the office, taking a measure of Mr. Livermore's life. A spring poked through a hole in the fabric covering the love seat in the corner. The wallpaper, peeling in spots and faded in others, showed the neglect of time. The floors, splintered by sun and use, had once been a beautiful burnished wood still evident in the untrafficked corners. Livermore's desk held a few thin files, each marked with the initials JCB in black marker—

Jean-Charles Bouclet. The shelves behind were bare—no photos of loved ones. "But you don't think Chef Wexler had anything to do with whatever it is that's going on?"

"No." Livermore put his hands on the arms of his chair as if clinging to the sides of a storm-tossed dingy. The chair swallowed him, making him look like a kid playing grown-up. "He's a desperate man, which makes him look guilty. But as far as I could find, he's just a guy trying to make a buck and keep his business afloat."

"Do you know where Jean-Charles is?" I felt the flicker of hope.

"He moves around." Livermore paled, if that was even possible, but it seemed like he lost color. "When we first started poking around, he got sorta spooked. It just seemed like whoever is behind all of this was always, if not one step ahead, they at least knew our every move." Livermore glanced at the window. "Apparently, they still are tapping into our phone calls, or something."

I grudgingly conceded that point. "They found you."

He leveled his gaze at me. "And they knew you were coming here."

I pulled my phone out of the holster at my hip. "This is a new phone."

"If they know what they're doing, they can capture the signal—they don't even need the phone. They need to be pretty savvy, though."

"And pretty amoral."

He gave me a look that wasn't hard to read.

"Yeah, that's a given, I know." I sighed as the weight of disillusionment landed on my shoulders. "It's just that people are so disappointing sometimes."

Livermore didn't say anything. He didn't have to. It didn't take a rocket scientist to see disappointment and disillusion were his constant companions. And desperation could prod even the most reluctant to do a lot of things they never would have considered doing. Even in my diminished state, I realized that Livermore himself could have squealed us out to the bad guys and was deflecting suspicion by pointing to someone else. I hated games—especially when I was the one being played. Romeo's theory that everyone is guilty until proven innocent was looking better and better—particularly for those of us with a clear self-preservation goal.

"Well, it seems my ride is not coming back." I gave him an appraising stare. I could take him, if I had to. So, why not play him a little longer, see what I could ferret out. I gave him my most benign smile, which I had a feeling wasn't all that good. "I sure could use a lift back to the Babylon."

Livermore looked relieved at having something to do. "My car is in back."

Probably not the wisest move to go with the guy—he was as slimy as a snake-oil salesman and, although I felt for him, I still didn't trust him.

"Okay." I stared Livermore down until he curled in on himself like a scolded puppy. I used my height to full advantage, towering over him. "But you pull any fast ones, and I'll break every bone in your body . . . one at a time."

He looked like he believed me. It was a proud moment.

Livermore motioned for me to follow him down a narrow hallway. When he turned, I grabbed the thin files on his desk and stuffed them in the back of my sweater, then tucked a bit of the soft fabric into the back of my jeans, making a pocket. As an afterthought, I grabbed the mail, too, stuffing it in with the files.

The hallway was longer than I'd thought, and harder to navigate with the carpet bunched and torn beneath our feet. The smell of rancid grease, reheated frozen dinners, and hopelessness permeated the stale air, leaking from the walls and drifting down the stairs.

"The garage is this way." Livermore confirmed my presence with a quick glance over his shoulder, then he pushed through a door that looked like it had been salvaged from a long forgotten restaurant—the greasy handprints embedded in the bubbled paint were there to stay.

The kitchen reeked of abandonment—the electric coiled burners on the cooktop were bent and sprung, the oven door hung on one hinge. From the last century, the refrigerator was one of those things the guys hoped to find in that storage unit reality show—refurbished, it would bring a mint. We followed the furrow in the linoleum, the pattern long faded by decades of trudging.

"Will we need to hand crank your ride to get it started?" I muttered, half joking, half dreading the answer.

He took that question straight up, without a smile, which gave me pause. "I keep it on a trickle charger, it should be fine."

The garage consisted of four poles topped with corrugated fiberglass, now opaque and cracked, desiccated by the desert sun. And his ride, a thirty-year-old Caddie, red with a white convertible top, actually looked fine, as he had said. Not a speck of dirt or mold marred the cloth surface of the top. The paint, as vibrant as the day the car rolled off the showroom floor, showed no signs of oxidation. The metal of the doors, smooth as a baby's butt, hinted at what part of the parking lot Livermore frequented. I opened the passenger door—the interior smelled like glycerin. I smoothed my hand over the soft leather seats as I slid in. Livermore obviously lavished all his love on this grand car, and it made me feel a bit sad for him.

Livermore disconnected the battery, then took his place behind the wheel. The engine fired after only one anguished turn, and he shot me a grin. "She's a grand old gal." He swiveled, his elbow thrown over the back of the bench seat as he concentrated on backing out. A tight fit for the huge car, he had to maneuver back, then forward twice, before he got us clear. With the bow of the car pointed down the alley, Livermore accelerated slowly.

Once I was assured he headed in the right direction, I settled back. "How did Jean-Charles get caught up in this?"

"It's pretty benign, really." Livermore glanced out of the corner of his eye at me. Behind the wheel of the huge Caddy, he looked liked a teenager taking the family car for a joy ride, his feet barely touching the pedals. I fought complacency—God help me, I felt my fondness for him growing. The bond of shared disappointments was insidious.

"You know about the tracking chips and all," he said, then confirmed my answer with a quick glance.

I nodded, even though his statement wasn't a question—I was pretty sure he had a better idea of what I knew than I did. "Jean-Charles and Mr. Peccorino were testing the chips," I said, giving him a foothold in the conversation.

Livermore spun the steering wheel like a captain at the helm of a sailing ship, turning us onto the Strip, heading south toward the lights and out of the darkness. "Everything was going great until Desiree started having trouble with her shipments."

"Is there really a truffle that has gone missing?"

Livermore looked at me a bit longer than I was comfortable with, considering he held my life in his hands. "I saw the truffle. It is a thing of beauty." He said the words with a surprising reverence.

"Who stole it, then?"

He waved away my question. "We tried to read the truffle chip. When we couldn't, we realized Mr. Peccorino might be playing a game of his own—perhaps playing both ends against the middle. Or perhaps he was using this opportunity to prove his chips really were brilliant. Dr. Phelps had indicated there was some issue with funding the project going forward. Chef Bouclet had arranged to meet Mr. Peccorino at Cielo that day, intending to hold his feet to the fire." He winced. "Bad choice of words. Sorry."

First Romeo, now Livermore. Was everyone stealing my lines, or was I just slow on the uptake?

"When Chef Bouclet arrived, Mr. Peccorino was dead in the oven."

"That scared him underground."

"Yes, the evidence against him, while circumstantial, was fairly incriminating. And Jean-Charles knew he couldn't chase a killer from a jail cell."

We both lapsed into silence for the rest of the ride. If Livermore had any more answers, he'd decided he's shared enough.

Fifteen minutes later, swearing Livermore had the best red light karma I'd ever witnessed, he eased the big car into the queue snaking up the drive to the Babylon. My notoriously thin patience completely worn through, I stepped out of the car before we had a chance to make much progress. "Thanks." I tossed the word at him as I shut the door carefully—old gals should be treated with care.

I should know.

~

THE LIGHTS WERE OFF, THE OUTER OFFICE EMPTY, WHEN I PUSHED through the door. Relieved, I left the lights off, using the light filtering in through the large window overlooking the lobby to navigate back to the construction project I called home.

Pausing in the doorway, I pulled the files from their hiding place nestled against my back. Using the weak ambient light, I quickly perused the first file. Nothing Livermore hadn't told me. The second wasn't any more enlightening. I'd about given up when I flipped through the mail I'd grabbed. Mostly bills and junk mail, it seemed benign. Except for the last envelope. Wedged in a flier—a contest promotion at one of the local watering holes . . . the grand prize was a boob job. Tired and distracted as I was, I almost missed the letter. Pulling it free, my heart rate accelerated. White, legal-sized, no postmark, with only Livermore's name scrawled in black marker. It had been torn open, a single sheet stuffed quickly back inside. I pulled out the folded piece of paper. Flapping it open, I held it up to the light as I read the short paragraph. "Holy shit!"

The puzzle fell into place as the pieces aligned. A picture of revenge, it wasn't pretty . . . but it made sense. I still needed proof. But how to get it? I needed to think.

I staggered to my desk chair and fell into it. Tossing the files and the mail on my desk where they blended with the pile of papers already there, I grabbed my phone and started to dial Romeo.

"Lucky?" A soft voice from the dark stopped me cold.

Instantly, my heart rate redlined.

"Who's there?" The soft light in here did little to brighten the corners. I squinted and could just make out a small form seated on the couch.

"Chantal." The girl leaned forward until I could just see her features, her curls. Her voice shook.

"Why are you hiding in here, in the dark?" I leaned back, my heart still hammered in my ears, but I was no longer in danger of stroking out.

"I need your help. Oh, please, you must come with me."

"Where is your mother?"

"She is doing what she does." Even though I could barely make out her shrug of insouciance, I got the message: she wasn't telling me the whole truth.

I started to respond with a less-than-kind retort when she stopped me cold.

"Uncle needs your help. He asked me to bring you."

"You're in touch with your uncle? You know where he is?"

She nodded. "He's found something. You must come. It is important."

I let that sink in for a moment. "You stole my cockroach paperweight, didn't you?" My eyes were adjusting to the darkness —details came into focus. The girl's face looked pinched with fear.

"I am sorry for that." She reached into the hobo bag at her feet and pulled something out. She rose and extended it to me across the desk. "Here."

My cockroach.

"I know how fond of it you are." It was clear she didn't understand my attachment.

I didn't feel the need to explain. "You gave your uncle the idea for the photos to help with the clues."

Chantal returned to the couch, settling on the edge like a bird on a perch. "He does not know much about the Internet. I maintain all of his websites." She pulled her shoulders back. "I even write his blogs about food. This is how I got interested in studying to be a chef, myself."

"Where is he?"

The girl blinked rapidly. "He is okay, for now, but you must come with me."

CHAPTER 20

CHANTAL'S HEAD bent over the smartphone she held in both hands, her thumbs flying. With my hand on her elbow, I steered her through the thickening crowd to the garage elevators.

"Are you texting your uncle?" After the quick trip to the third floor where my car hunkered in my very own parking space, I ushered her out of the elevator and down the ramp. "Here we are."

Finishing with a flurry, she pocketed the phone. The car, a thirty-year-old Porsche 911 in mint condition, actually got her attention. "Wow, this is a classic."

She was right, but I wasn't exactly thrilled—me and the Porsche, we shared a birth year. While I considered myself pretty classic, it was for different reasons. And I liked to think the car was much more temperamental than I, which wasn't always true. "Where are we going?" I asked, as if I knew the car would actually start.

"A warehouse in Henderson." She gave me the address.

I raised an eyebrow, but for some reason, I wasn't as surprised as I should have been. I turned the key and held my breath. After a pause long enough to make me appreciate the effort, the engine turned over, then caught with that patented Porsche low growl. What was it about cars that made me smile? A serious personality defect or a life off-kilter, I suspected, but I didn't care. Some things just were.

The traffic was heavy, the residue of rush hour, as we made our way east. Nervous, I drummed my fingers on the paddle shifters. Chantal said nothing. She didn't look happy.

As we drove east, the cityscape changed, the warmth and comfort of the residential streets with their sidewalks, street lights illuminating cozy homes with the occasional bicycle strewn on the lawn, or a basketball hoop hanging above the garage, giving way to dark, hulking, dimly lit warehouses.

My senses switched to high alert as I killed the high beams and eased in next to the galvanized tin building Chantal wordlessly pointed out. In front of us, a series of five steps provided transition to a concrete landing perhaps three to four feet above the ground. Several delivery trucks, their rear panels rolled up leaving the enclosed bed of the truck open, backed to the landing. The corresponding bay door on the building had also been furled so that small forklifts and men wheeling dollies could load the trucks with goods from inside the warehouse. Business was light—a few men worked, but no more than two or three. In Vegas, most of the restocking took place in the wee hours, so I assumed business would crank up as the night deepened. Our best odds were right now.

Chantal pocketed her phone. The light inside the car winked on as she opened her door. "Come on. I know a side entrance. I won't raise any alarm—the men are used to me hanging around. But you . . ." The youngster cocked an eyebrow in my direction.

I wasn't exactly sure what she meant by that. The comment seemed odd, wrong somehow.

Chantal looked at me, her eyes dark and serious. "Please. We need your help. You can help, can't you?"

There was something in her eyes, in the weight of her words, her cadence. Before I could figure it out, the light winked out as the girl stepped out and shut the door behind her, plunging me once again into darkness as I weighed my options.

Which would it be, fold, or go all in? Something didn't feel right. I couldn't put my finger on it. But my inner me screamed a warning. Which I ignored.

Pansy-ass. She was just a teenager doing what her uncle asked. What could go wrong?

Besides, I had to find out what was going on.

Before a killer killed again.

The slip of a girl eased away from the car. The night quickly swallowed her until she looked like a wraith flowing through the shadows.

Pushing aside my doubts, I did what anyone would do: I followed her.

I couldn't just sit there, could I? Even though our brief relationship had been founded on the soggy bog of teenage distrust, I had to make a move. Of course, I could've called the cops, but what would I have told them? Granted, I had every reason to believe they might be interested in what was going on inside the building, but I had no proof of connection to any crime.

Time to find some.

Chantal walked boldly. Her presence didn't attract any attention from the workers, except for a lone wolf whistle, which she ignored. While they might be accustomed to her presence, I doubted mine would go as unnoticed. Timing my moves so as not to attract attention as the workers came and went from the trucks, I worked my way through the shadows. I caught Chantal at the side door, her hand on the knob. With a finger to her lips, she quieted me, which seemed out of place if we were expected. Before I could tell her exactly how I felt and ask what the hell was going on, she opened the door and slipped through, leaving me once again alone and in the dark.

This had to stop. Taking a deep, bracing breath, I turned the handle and followed her. Blinking against the brightness from the overhead halogens, it took me a moment to get my bearings. Although it looked much larger from the outside, the interior warehouse was actually quite small, partitioned into a dry goods section and a refrigerated area. The sweet aroma of ripening fruit masked the rotten smell underneath. The forklifts must run on electricity, as there was no exhaust to add to the bilious mix.

My pupils cranked down, bringing a man into focus—Adone Giovanni.

I scanned the space. "Where is Jean-Charles?"

He raised the gun he held in his hand, pointing it at my chest. "I'm afraid you've been misled."

"Apparently." I flicked my eyes to Chantal, who watched me intently. From her posture and her wide eyes, I got the impression she was trying to tell me something, but what? My eyes drifted back to Adone. "A gun. Really? You expect me to believe all of this was your idea?"

He bristled and waggled the gun at me. "Always a laugh from you. I really hate you women who think you run the show."

"Well, you seem to think you need a gun to even the playing field."

He shrugged, not taking the bait. "Expedient."

"Getting rid of me will make everything better?" Sarcasm probably wouldn't improve my situation, either, but I couldn't help myself. Looking into the pointy end of the gun, I should've been scared, but I was just mad.

"Where is Jean-Charles?" Clenching my fists at my sides, I took a menacing step toward him.

He raised the gun higher, pointing it at my head. "Stop."

The chances of him hitting such a small target were slim, but fresh out of original ideas, I decided to string this along a bit longer.

Looking smug, Adone opened his arm, inviting Chantal into his embrace.

She stepped in, allowing him to pull her close. Without shifting his gaze from me, Adone bent and kissed the top of her head. "Thank you, daughter."

Daughter? I hadn't given their relationship any thought. Why, I assumed he was too young to be her father . . . perhaps because he lacked any hint of fatherly affection.

The girl glanced up at him. "Stepfather," she corrected, her voice holding a hard edge that caught my attention. When she saw he wasn't looking, she gave me a stare. Placing her elbow in line with his stomach, she bent that arm and put her fisted hand in the other for leverage, then cocked her eyebrow at me.

I gave her a subtle nod—no one would've noticed if they hadn't been looking for it. Thankfully, Chantal was paying attention.

My attention swiveled to Adone when he spoke—he hadn't noticed my interchange with Chantal. Men, they rarely anticipated the resiliency of women.

"That's why I brought you here." His voice was cold, his eyes dark slits of hate.

"I don't know where he . . ." Then the light dawned. "Ah, I'm to be bait."

Adone shrugged. "I have not been able to find him. He will come for you."

That made me feel both good and terrified. Adone's tone conveyed his conviction, and his hate, so I tried a different tack, turning my attention to the girl. "Chantal, why are you doing this? You know he's just using you. He killed Mr. Peccorino."

"You do not know this," Adone mocked.

"Oh, but I do." I narrowed my eyes. "When you rushed into the kitchen at Cielo, you mentioned the oven had been set to broil. No one told you that."

Adone paused, thinking, then he shrugged. "But you will not be around to remind anyone of that."

I turned to the girl. "Why are you helping him? Look at what he has done."

Chantal gave a noncommittal head tilt, her eyes holding mine in a steady, angry gaze. "He has been kind to me," she said without conviction.

Adone didn't seem to notice. His focus remained on me. His smile grew wider as he shrugged. "The girl has impeccable taste. Her mother and her uncle do not." His face shut down into a hard mask.

Chantal cuddled in, selling her ruse, but her face remained stern, angry, her eyes cold. Moving her outside foot slightly farther away, she subtly gained leverage, coiling herself to react—at least, that's what I was counting on. But, a good salesman, she could be selling me . . .

Turning my attention back to Adone, I tried to buy some time while I thought this through. We were outnumbered. Our only advantage was surprise . . . and the depth of our anger. That should even the odds.

I swept my arm in a half-circle, focusing attention on the half-dozen men who had paused in their work and now looked at the little farce unfolding. "With all these witnesses?"

Disinterest reigned as they turned their backs. Moving away, they got back to business. Even better.

I knew what I had to do.

With a quick nod, I gave Chantal her cue. Despite her slight frame, she uncoiled on Adone with the full force of a grown woman protecting her own. Her elbow hit him firmly just below the sternum. I launched myself into the fight.

With a whoosh of breath, Adone collapsed to his knees, clutching his stomach. Chantal fell back. I stepped in like David Beckham readying a shot on goal. With as much force as I dared, I kicked Adone, my instep connecting with his jaw. It only hurt a little, okay, a lot. But Adone dropped like a stone.

Reaching down, I grabbed Chantal's hand, pulling her to her

feet and propelling her in front of me. I swooped and grabbed the gun Adone had dropped, then limped after her. A nine-millimeter. I popped the clip as I ran. It was full. I slammed it back home, chambered a round, flicked on the safety, then stuck it in the waistband of my jeans at the small of my back.

The girl glanced over her shoulder, questioning.

"Into the shelving. Quickly."

We raced through rows of dry goods higher than our heads. Finally, I saw what I was looking for: a tight space tucked between fifty-pound bags of flour stacked at least twenty bags high. I grabbed her shirt, stopping her, then pushed her into the space. For once, she did as I said without any lip. I knelt down in front of her as she worked herself backwards, out of sight. "Why didn't you tell me?"

"Adone, he has my mother. He told me he would kill me if I didn't come get you. Had I told you, you might not have come, insisting instead to go to the police. I could not take that risk." Her voice hitched. "I knew you would help."

"Where is your mother?" I wheezed, my breathing accelerated from an adrenaline overload.

"The office." She gestured with her chin, her eyes round saucers of hate. "Far corner in the back."

I pulled the gun from my waist and thumbed off the safety. "Promise. You will stay here."

She wavered for a moment, then gave me a curt nod. Her eyes widened when I growled, "I will dismember you if you defy me."

That took the last hint of defiance out of her, at least as far as I could tell.

Crunching myself into a crouch, I eased down the row to the end. Peeking around, my heart fell.

Adone was gone.

Raising myself to my full height, I leaned back against the rows of boxes, my gun held in both hands chest-high, at the ready. I closed my eyes for a moment, steadying myself.

Chantal had said the office was in the back. Adone would head there—a hostage would give him an advantage. And he had a head start, so I eased my way, taking my time, keeping myself hidden.

His raised voice stopped me halfway there, shattering the quiet and jangling my nerves. "Lucky. You cannot save them all. Not by yourself."

His voice came from behind me, but not close. I pivoted, my gun in front of me. Careful not to make any noise, I retraced my steps back to the end of the row, then eased my head around.

Once again in the open, Adone faced the other way. He had Desiree. Holding her by the elbow, he kept her close to his side. Though her hands were cuffed behind her, she resisted as much as she could. The gun pressed to her temple probably took a bit of the stuffing out of her as well.

Christ, another gun. How many did he have?

"Show yourself," he demanded. Slowly, he turned in a circle, scanning.

I didn't move. Like an anchor, Desiree hung back, forcing Adone to yank her around with each step.

Scanning the boxes, I had an idea. Quickly, careful to make as little noise as possible, I pried a can from the container closest to me. The box ripped with an audible tear. I froze.

Adone paused, cocking his head to listen.

My hand closed around a can; the heft of it felt good as I tossed it a couple of inches, gauging weight, trajectory, and force. Rearing back, I threw my considerable weight behind my throw, hurling the can. Arcing over the heads of Desiree and Adone, it clattered into the shadows on the far side.

Adone whirled toward the sound. As he did, Desiree brought the heel of her shoe down on his foot. Leaning into it, she drove the spike down into soft flesh.

Adone yelped. His gun shifted lower, his attention drawn to Desire. But he was seconds too late.

Desiree swung around, whipping her leg into his knees from

the rear, buckling them. At a dead run, I tucked my gun back in the waistband of my jeans. Several strides, no more than three, and then I launched myself like a pro NFL safety into his back. The collision jarred my teeth. Anger kept me focused. Rolling off him, I propelled myself to my feet. With a look, I held Desiree back as Adone staggered to his feet. Before he regained his balance completely, I stepped into him. This time, I used my elbow.

His eyes rolled back as he crumpled.

This time, I made sure he'd be out for a while.

I kicked his gun into the shadows.

When I looked around again, I caught movement in the stacks on the far side. I squinted into the shadow.

Oh, thank God! The Beautiful Jeremy Whitlock, his head on a swivel, taking stock. On his second sweep of the space, I moved just enough to catch his eye. He gave me a jaunty grin.

The sound of voices, raised slightly to be heard above the whine of electric engines as the forklifts strained, solidified my plan. The workmen. I didn't need them to join the fight. I pantomimed my thoughts to Jeremy. He frowned his disapproval, but knowing me well, he finally ceded defeat. With a nod, he drifted back, and the shadows swallowed him.

Desiree stood, bent at the waist, hands on her knees, drawing deep breaths.

Placing my hand on her back, I leaned over. "Are you okay?"

With a growl, she raised herself, then took a kick at Adone's inert body. She connected with his stomach. Air left him in a whoosh, but he didn't stir.

Grabbing her arm with both hands, I pulled her away.

When I was sure she wouldn't attack him again, I stepped back, taking a deep breath, steadying myself. I couldn't shake the sense that danger lurked. Turning a full 360 degrees, I couldn't see anything, but the frisson of fear tickled my nerve endings, telegraphing a feeling someone watched us from the shadows.

Someone evil. Someone with nothing to lose. The hairs on the back of my neck stood up.

With a feral sound, Chantal bolted out of the shadows toward her mother.

"No," I shouted, and raised a hand trying to hold her back, make her stop. "There is another . . ." But I was too late.

I felt her presence before I turned, pulling myself to my full height. I knew this foe. "Chitza. So good of you to join us."

I turned, then wilted. My smartass fled.

Chitza DeStefano held Christophe in one arm, balanced on her hip. In the other, she held a gun.

Clutching a teddy bear, the boy looked calm, disbelieving, wide-eyed, but only a bit frightened.

With a low growl, Desiree started toward her nephew. Chitza raised the gun and narrowed her eyes.

I grabbed Desiree, pulling her back. She and Chantal closed ranks beside me, one on each shoulder. Christophe extended his arms toward us, breaking my heart. Emotions assaulted me. Fear. Anger. My eyes got all slitty. I gave the boy a smile, and with one hand, I motioned for him to be patient.

Chitza laughed. "Lucky, you of all people, I thought you would be a more worthy opponent. But you are like the others, so easy to manipulate."

"When it comes to kids and animals, people with a heart have the disadvantage."

"Ah, you think I am cold-hearted. You are wrong. My heart, it is big. But I believe in a life for a life." She eyed me coldly, but she didn't look alarmed. She glanced at Adone's inert form crumpled on the ground.

"Several lives," I corrected. Needing time to think, I tried to draw her out.

"I killed no one. But they are a fitting price for several hearts broken." Chitza cocked her chin at me.

"Hearts heal." Time and healing hearts, an adage with a grain of truth, but not the whole truth. "The hurt leaves us changed, but life goes on."

"Not always." Chitza took a ragged breath as she seemed to turn inward. "My mother, she died from a broken heart." In her voice, I heard the lingering whisper of an old pain.

"I am sorry. And I am sure Jean-Charles is sorry, too. He very nearly died as well. The boy saved him."

"Perhaps the boy could have saved my mother, too. But his father . . ." Chitza spat the last words. With renewed fire, she waggled the gun at me and shifted Christophe higher on her hip.

"You were quite clever, I will admit." With a hidden tug on the women flanking me, I pulled Desiree and Chantal closer until they pressed in tight next to me. "Knowing that eventually, the Bouclets would gather and give you an opportunity."

Desiree vibrated with anger. "What is she talking about?" she hissed at me out of the side of her mouth.

I kept my left hand on her arm, holding tight. "Stay calm," I hissed in reply. It took all the willpower I had left to move slowly, to keep my voice calm, appropriately angry. I didn't want to admit just how long it had taken to see through her plot. "It was all there, just took me a while to see it."

"Really?" Chitza shifted Christophe—holding fifty pounds of unwilling boy sapped arm strength. That much I knew.

Leaving my arms hanging at my sides, I shielded any movement with the women on either side as I talked. "Fiona came to you. She needed an entry into the high-end distribution business—she needed someone who could make the introductions necessary to get her supply chain in order. That would've been you."

"Me?" Chitza looked askance. "I'm just a middle-grade chef working my way up. Who would I know?"

"Everyone. Through your family in Venezuela—your mother and father moved back after you left home. They aren't just farmers, they control much of the agricultural production out of a large part of South America. You would be the perfect point man for Fiona Richards, wouldn't you?"

"But why would I make those introductions?" When Chitza looked at me, her eyes shone. With interest or with madness, I couldn't tell.

"Because you needed her."

She gave a derisive laugh. "For what?"

"Revenge. That's what we've been talking about, isn't it?" Desiree glanced sideways at me. I didn't look at her.

"If Fiona was helping me, why would I kill her?" As Chitza's arm tired, Christophe sagged lower, the space between their bodies growing. With the gun in the other hand and three women ready to pounce, she couldn't risk lowering the gun to move Christophe.

Time worked in my favor.

Adone twitched, showing the first signs of coming to.

Okay, time might be on my side, but it was running short.

The voices of the workmen had quieted. I assumed Jeremy had something to do with that.

"The distribution business is hard work, the relationships can take a lifetime to fully cultivate. Fiona wasn't a hard-work kind of gal. She wanted more, and she wanted it fast, so she started taking some of the shipments, lining her own pockets." I had Chitza's attention, so I kept going. "Then she discovered you had started tagging all the shipments. She knew the gig was up. I don't know how she forced your hand, or if you just convinced Adone that you needed to be rid of her—either way, the result was the same. You tried to put the blame on Jean-Charles." I marveled at her coldness, the cool, unflustered thinking of a natural predator. "You knew you had a bit of time, as you had Mr. Peccorino doctor the chips so they couldn't be read by a normal reader."

Chitza leveled her gaze. "Anything else?" she asked with murder in her tone.

"No, other than that you killed him, too."

"Adone. The poor boy, I tried to stop him, you see. But he is so in love with me, he would do anything." She seemed nonplussed.

That wasn't a good sign—once a person had nothing to lose, they became even more dangerous.

"Oh, it wasn't Adone. It was you. You drove this whole sick scheme. And just to see Jean-Charles suffer."

"Why would I care about Jean-Charles?" She grimaced as she shifted the boy's weight. He was getting heavy.

I kept my face blank, my voice calm. "You blame him for the death of your sister."

Chitza reared back with a sharp intake of breath. Desiree's head swiveled in my direction. I kept my eyes on Chitza while I worked my right arm slightly behind me, using Chantal as cover.

Desiree whirled back to Chitza. "Is this true?"

Chitza's eyes flashed, her mouth hardened into a thin line. "His wife, she was my younger sister. She, too, wanted to be a chef. And she was good, much better than me. And much better than *him*." She hurled the word like an epithet. "My family sends her to Paris to study. She meets Jean-Charles, and the next thing we hear, she is dead."

"But that was an accident. A blood vessel inside her shredded. . . ." Desiree seemed saddened at the memory. "Surely, you can't blame my brother."

Unmoved, Chitza continued, "My family, we had no time to get there for the funeral. He would not wait to bury her. Then he kept the child from us."

When she raised her eyes once again to mine, they looked haunted. "How did you know?"

"I didn't, not for sure—not until a little while ago, when I read a letter that wasn't meant for me. But I suspected something. First, there was a rumor of a fight between you and Jean-Charles —an affair gone bad. But I couldn't find any evidence that you and he had even worked in the same city at the same time. And

Desiree didn't know you at all—she and her brother are close, so that was odd."

"Anything else?"

Desiree stirred beside me, clearly on the verge of losing control. I gripped her wrist and squeezed as I continued, "One night, you stopped to talk to Christophe. I saw you, but you didn't see me. When the boy came to me, he told me that you said he looked like his mother. Jean-Charles caught on more quickly. He didn't know you were his sister-in-law, did he?"

"No." A look passed over Chitza's features.

"Your sister. You were not close."

Anger flushed her cheeks . . . or perhaps shame. "We had a fight. We were young, so young. Stupid. We did not talk again. For many, many years. Now, I will never get the chance. *He* took that from me."

With my right arm safely behind me, and Chitza seemingly unaware, I bent it at the elbow. My hand closed around the gun tucked into the small of my back. I hadn't fired it; a round was still chambered. With my thumb, I checked to make sure the safety was off as I eased the weapon free and held it by my side.

Wide-eyed, Chantal glanced at me. I shut her down with an almost imperceptible nod. She returned her eyes to Chitza, a stoic expression falling over her features, but I felt her attention on me.

Somewhere to my left, a door banged open. All heads turned, including mine . . . briefly. Then I refocused on Chitza, waiting, watching. Out of the corner of my eye, I caught a body hurtling into the open space, then skidding to a stop. I didn't look. It didn't matter.

Christophe twisted to look behind him at the figure. "Papa!" he squealed. Wiggling and pushing at Chitza's arm, he worked himself down a bit, and distracted his captor.

I had one shot.

I took it. Raising the gun, I stroked the trigger. The gun jerked in my hand, but I heard nothing. Fear shut down my senses until all I could focus on was my target.

I'd aimed for Chitza's free shoulder. I hit it.

The force of the shot spun her back. Christophe landed on his feet, his hands barely grazing the floor for balance. His legs already churning, he propelled himself toward his father.

Chitza grabbed her shoulder, then staggered back into the shadowed safety of the shelves. Adone rolled—he'd been playing possum. He pushed himself to his feet.

Surprised, I squeezed off a quick round. Too quick. It hit the metal shelving to his right as he disappeared into the dark safety of the rows of shelved goods.

I gave a quick command, my voice low, but insistent. "Desiree, take your family outside." I pressed my gun into her hand. "It's ready to fire. Adone, Chitza, anyone who poses a threat, shoot first." She shook her head and refused to take the gun. "You have the children."

Our eyes met. "Do not let your brother follow me."

After a moment of hesitation, she did as I said.

I ran after Chitza, leaving the light, hiding in the shadows.

Jean-Charles barked a quick _"Non!"_

I ignored him.

I should have stopped to find Adone's gun that I had kicked into the shadows.

I wasn't that smart.

CHAPTER 21

*N*O GUN. Short on ideas. Not good . . . but normal.

I paused in the shadows, letting my heart rate slow and my mind clear. I heard a door slam somewhere in the distance, then quiet closed around me. Ahead, somewhere in the darkness, Chitza moved quietly, Adone helping her.

If I had this figured right, I had two people and one gun to deal with.

Scanning the shelves, I found sacks of beans and peas, boxes of canned goods, but no effective weapons. The cans had come in handy, so I grabbed one. Not much of a weapon compared to their gun, but it made me feel good. Self-delusion, I can do.

I inched my way down the aisle, pressing into the shadows on either side as much as I could. One white sack of flour held a red smudge. I tested it.

Blood.

Energy coursed through me. I could find her. I hoped I could surprise her. Easing my way along, I looked for blood. Drops on the floor, a swipe across a box or bag, Chitza's trail wasn't hard to follow.

After several turns, weaving my way through the maze of

foodstuffs, I reached the end. The trail of dark red drops led across an open area to the door to the freezer. Water droplets smeared in a damp arc across the concrete bore evidence of a recent opening. Glancing to either side, I didn't see anyone—that didn't mean someone wasn't there. I weighed my options and decided to take my chances. I bolted across the open space, then pressed against the door before opening it. The metal was cold; the small window at eye level frosted over. Shielding myself behind the wall to the side, I pulled the heavy latch as quietly as I could. The door moved soundlessly on its hinges, so I yanked it open, letting it fly.

Waiting. Breathing. Nothing happened—no shots, no nothing.

Hitting the rubber stops, the door sprung back. Slipping through the opening, I paused, catching the door before it slammed. I left it ajar. Still in a crouch, I ran behind the nearest pallet, using it for cover. My breath fogged. My eyes worked to adjust to the dim blue light. The cold felt refreshing, bracing, at first. But within moments, it permeated my clothing and pricked my exposed skin like hot needles. Each breath became more difficult, painful. I turned the can in my hand with periodic flips, the metal conducting the cold through my thin skin. Pushing my discomfort away, I concentrated, listening, focusing, reaching for the slightest sound. The heavy, cold air muffled the noise: the sound of the freezing unit kicking on, the fan, the crackle as things expanded as they froze, or adjusted to a subtle change in the temperature—three bodies at 98.6 could raise the ambient temps enough, I bet—but no sound of movement.

Either Chitza and Adone had stopped and were hidden now, lying in wait, or they had run through the freezer section and out the door to docks in the back. Crouching, I peeked around. Nothing moved. So I zigzagged from one pallet to another. Pausing, listening, waiting, then bolting to another covered position.

Finally, I reached the end.

Either the two of them had left, or they had doubled back and gone out the entrance. I didn't think that likely—the freezer was small, the pallets stacked close to the sides.

Cold now, shivering, I felt my skin might stick to the surface of the can, but I clung to it like a lifeline. When faced with danger, even a bad plan was better than none. Feeling my fingers numbing, I pushed the emergency release on the door.

It came off in my hand. The latch remained closed; the door locked.

Balling my fists, I banged on the door, knowing it was hopeless. The thing was as thick as the vault walls at Fort Knox.

The door behind me was my only way out. I whirled, fear pushing me. If they got to the door first . . .

A few strides, and I skidded to a stop. A man blocked my path.

Adone. An ugly look on his face, he raised the gun—Chitza's gun—leveling it at my heart.

I hurled the can at him. He dodged it easily. Cold muscles were slow to react.

He gave a lopsided grin devoid of humor. His eyes stayed hard and cold. Placing his other hand to steady the gun, he closed one eye, taking aim.

Dropping my hands to my sides, I squared my shoulders and stared him down. "You don't have the nerve." I'd heard folks on TV say that when in the same situation. I'd thought it seemed classy. Now it just seemed . . . inadequate.

Adone's forearms bunched, tightening his hold. His finger curled around the trigger.

I braced.

The freezer exploded with sound. The gunshot reverberated, echoing waves of pummeling sound.

Instinctively, I curled in on myself. Flexing muscles in self-protection. Anticipating the hit, the pain. But there was none. No pain. I looked down at myself. No blood. Nothing. Maybe it was the cold. Looking up, I stared in disbelief at Adone.

His eyes glazed. His expression slackened. The gun slowly

slipped from his hand as he looked down. A red stain ballooned on his shirt. He fell to his knees. A quizzical expression glanced across his features. Then he fell forward on his face.

Back in the shadows, a man stood behind him.

Romeo. A gun in his hand.

I couldn't move.

Romeo tucked his gun back in his shoulder harness as he strode toward me. He paused to check Adone's pulse. After a moment, Romeo stepped over him. "Don't grow roots. It's cold as Hell in here. You gotta be half-frozen by now." Turning, he grabbed my arm, pulling me with him as he babbled. "Thank God you left the door open. I had one heck of a time finding you."

My teeth chattered as he pulled me out into the warmth and light. Blinking, I tried to regain my composure as Romeo rubbed my arms, trying to generate heat. "Thank you."

The kid grinned. "Just repaying the favor. I owed you a rescue or two, as I recall."

"Next time, don't cut it so darn close. Okay?" Keeping the mood light chased away the horror of the what-ifs I saw in Romeo's eyes. A second or two later . . . "Chitza?"

"In custody. She'll be fine. You are going to help me connect all the dots, right? I've got some of them, but the whos and the whys are a bit murky yet."

"We'll tie it up tight."

Romeo raised an eyebrow in a perfect mimic. "How you figured it out before me . . . it's really irritating. You've got to teach me how you put all the pieces together so easily."

Before I had to admit luck was the glue to my puzzle, the sound of running feet heading in our direction had Romeo reaching for his gun. He pushed me behind him as he turned toward the sound. Unarmed, I let him.

Special Agent Stokes burst into the opening first, followed by Jean-Charles and the Beautiful Jeremy Whitlock. They managed to brake to a stop in front of us—I have no idea how. Jean-Charles grabbed me in a bear hug. My emotions spilling over, I returned it in spades. Tucking my face into the warm curve of his neck, I didn't let go.

Neither did he.

"Is everyone okay?" I mumbled against his skin, absorbing his warmth.

"Yes. The police have Chitza." He pulled back so he could see my face. "You must believe I didn't know."

I nodded. "You had your suspicions, but you didn't know until Livermore came for you this evening. That's how you got here, isn't it?"

"*Oui.*" A chuckle rumbled, low and deep, in his chest. "Livermore told me you had been at his office. I knew you would find this place somehow. I wanted to shoot him for not bringing you to me." His lips close to my ear, he whispered the words. "You were not wise to come here alone."

I felt the warmth of his breath. He didn't sound angry, so I didn't bore him with the details. In good time, he'd learn them all from his sister and niece. Everyone was safe. Chitza in custody. Adone dead. For the first time in days, I could finally breathe without the steel bands of emotion cinching my chest.

Freedom. Peace in the quiet center of my soul.

I had seized my life from the demons of fear and hurt.

I raided my head and eased out of Jean-Charles's embrace. I could stand on my own two feet just fine.

A few days had taught me a lifetime of lessons.

Jeremy shot me a grin.

I gave him a halfhearted smirk. "You took my ride."

He took me with a grain of salt, as always. "I'm thinking of keeping it. Adone did the shooting. I followed him, but . . ." Looking sheepish, he let the implication hang.

"You lost him in the warehouses." Personally, I thought that was inevitable—the place was a maze—but I didn't feel like letting Jeremy off that easy.

"I was trolling around when I saw your car—it's hard to miss. Sorry I was late to the party."

"You came at just the right time."

Romeo moved away and spoke in a low tone into his shoulder radio.

Special Agent Stokes . . . Joe . . . cleared his throat. "I'd like to hear your part of this story."

"Sure, but I'd like to check on the kids." I hooked my arm through Jean-Charles's and let him lead me in the right direction. With a quick look over my shoulder, I made sure the others followed. I waited for Romeo to catch up before I spoke. "Adone and Chitza—they both had huge bones to pick with Jean-Charles. They met on the set of that cooking show." I tugged on Jean-Charles's arm. "Remember?"

"Yes, they were contestants. I remember. Desiree supplied the food, but she did not come to the set." He nodded, then sighed as realization dawned. "Fiona worked as the set sous chef."

"Right. That's where it all started." Adrenaline still thumped through my veins, scattering my thoughts, but the whole plot was coming together bit by bit as I talked. "Fiona approached Chitza about getting into the food supply business. Chitza saw a way to stick it to at least one of the Bouclets. Adone wanted in; his feud with Jean-Charles and estrangement from Desiree was pretty public."

"The stage was set." Joe stated the obvious. Thinking out loud —I recognized the method. In fact, I could almost hear the grinding of his mental gears. "But where did the plan go off-track?"

"When Fiona double-crossed everyone, rerouting the ship-ments. It only takes one bad apple." What was it with me and all the adages lately? And here, I thought that character flaw was limited to clichés.

"Choosing your partner is critical to success." Jean-Charles gave me a grin with the tidbit, leaving me with the impression he was talking about more than business.

"How did Chitza discover the duplicity?" Joe asked.

"She was smart. She didn't trust Fiona, so she used her relationship with Dr. Phelps and his gang to put the extra bit of code into the chips so only she could read them. That way, she kept tabs on her partners, and no one else was the wiser."

"Clever." Joe sounded impressed. "Worked like a charm too, until Chef Bouclet here got us involved."

"How did you stumble onto the scheme?" Jeremy directed the question to Jean-Charles.

"Some of my sister's shipments started going awry. They would leave the suppliers with the appropriate quality goods, but when they arrived at their destinations, lesser quality goods would have been substituted. Smelling a dog, I went to Agent Stokes."

"A rat." Correcting his idioms had become knee-jerk with me. I needed to stop.

"Yes, this is it." Jean-Charles squeezed my arm. "I will learn this."

Agent Stokes picked up the thread. "So, I went to Mr. Peccorino, the guy's the expert in the RFID field. I used my position to scare him a bit, so he wouldn't tell anyone he was working with us on this."

"But he had to clear the project with the head, Dr. Phelps," I said, as another connection fell into place.

Joe confirmed my suspicion. "In a university setting, resources are limited, data is critical. And in this case, the chip prototypes are carefully controlled and monitored. Especially since the program has national security uses."

"And Dr. Phelps, being a bit of a showman and proud of his work, most likely bragged to his bedmate." I completed the circle.

Jeremy put the exclamation point on it. "Chitza. So, why didn't she sound a general alarm?"

"Oh, I think she saw the end coming, but she had some time if she could keep the key to reading her chips hidden until she could clean up loose ends. She used Adone to do that."

"Chitza was very clever, showing Adone how he could get rid of the three loose ends, as you put it." Romeo chimed in.

I'd almost forgotten he was back there, he'd been so quiet, letting the others do the asking. "Yes. He could do the deeds, and the two of them could frame Jean-Charles for it. And he almost got Dr. Phelps as well."

"How did he play into all of this?"

"Innocent braggart. He knew of Chitza's involvement."

"It almost worked," Jean-Charles whispered, pulling me tighter to him. "Except for you."

I leaned away from him so I could get a good look at his face. "Now, about that truffle."

He eyed me with a bland look. "Yes?"

"First, let's talk about the fake truffle. Let's trace its path to see how it got Fiona killed."

"It is not fake." Jean-Charles's narrowed his eyes at me.

I gave him an exasperated look.

He got my meaning. "The truffle, the *real* truffle, was in my walk-in. I had seen it there when I opened the restaurant early to check in the shipment. That was the day you took Christophe to your office, yes?"

I nodded. "Who helped you check all the items in and put them away?"

Jean-Charles thought for a moment. "Rinaldo, of course. My other two sous chefs, the pastry sous chef." His eyes widened. "And Adone, he came to stock my truck."

"He stole the truffle. When he jimmied the box, the real truffle wasn't there. You had substituted the lesser one. He alerted Chitza. They both thought Fiona had switched the truffles. She'd been tampering with shipments all along, so it seemed logical. But she hadn't messed with this one."

Jean-Charles shook his head. "I was trying to keep the truffle safe—it is a special truffle." When he looked up at me, his eyes were sad. "You must believe me, I had no idea anyone would get killed."

"Of course." I put my head back on his shoulder. "How could you have known?"

"Okay." Romeo stepped in. "I buy Fiona, the truffle thing, and Peccorino, but why Gregor?"

"That's easy," Jeremy stepped in. He gave me a glance. "Allow me?"

"The floor is yours."

"He made too much of a stink. He wouldn't let the truffle thing go. He filed an insurance claim, thereby triggering another investigation—the insurance blokes would never pay that kind of money without their own investigator looking into the theft."

"And Chitza couldn't risk someone else poking around. Her deception was wearing thin, anyway."

"And he made a good patsy. But I also suspect, though I can't prove it yet, that she lent him the money to buy the truffle, knowing Fiona and Adone wouldn't be able to resist taking it, leaving Jean-Charles in a very public predicament," I said, and gave Jean-Charles a look. "But you were working with Homeland Security all along, weren't you?"

"Not at first. Then I was more under suspicion. And the police, I am not too sure how they will react if they have the chips. I didn't trust them, but I knew some answers were there. That's why I had to get Chantal to help . . . to get the chips in your hands. Once there, I knew they'd get to Homeland Security or the police, you would know what to do. We were able to triangulate this location, once we got past Mr. Peccorino's lock."

I looked at Jean-Charles for a moment and then asked the last question I was pretty sure I knew the answer to. "And the original truffle?"

He gave me one of his patented Gallic shrugs. "Under lock and key."

"It never left your walk-in, did it?"

"*Non.*"

We stepped to one side to let a phalanx of Metro officers through. Romeo peeled off, joining them. My story was done—the rest was up to the white hats to prove.

But, there'd be no more murders tonight.

"Shoot." I slid to a stop, jerking Jean-Charles to a stop as well. The men behind us managed to avoid a collision, but I don't know how. "What time is it?"

"Sevenish. A bit after." Jeremy looked at me liked I'd lost it. "Why?"

"There'll be one more murder if I don't get to Drink and Drag in a hurry."

CHAPTER 22

THE FERRARI turned heads even in Vegas. Even in downtown Vegas under the canopy of lights on Fremont Street.

With minutes to spare—the traffic had been as thick as one of the shakes at Heart Attack Grill—I slid to a stop in front of Neonopolis, a previously ill-advised commercial real estate project that was undergoing a resurgence. A surprised valet leaped out of the way.

"What a wuss," I remarked to Jean-Charles, who still held on to the handhold with a white-knuckled grip. "I would've missed him by a couple of inches, at least."

Opening the door, I unfolded myself from the car. For a moment, I thought Jean-Charles would remain, transfixed by fear, and I'd have to pry his fingers from the grip. But he followed me out of the car. Crisis averted.

I tossed the valet the keys with a smile. "Keep it out front, okay?" I didn't wait for an answer. Instead, with Jean-Charles on my heels, I bolted for the stairs.

Some sort of evangelical spiritual thing was going on in the courtyard, which somehow seemed appropriate. Everybody could find what they were looking for in Vegas—the trick was knowing where to look.

Drink and Drag was up three flights of stairs on the top floor.

On the brink of apoplexy at the top of the stairs, I smiled at the lady at the door. "Hey, Julius, how're they hangin'?"

"Tucked tight, Lucky." With long, black hair, unmarred olive skin, and eyes that tilted up at the corners, in her white tank top and tiny short-shorts, she was the envy of females far and wide. But *she* wasn't . . . female, that is. "Her" name was Julius Green and he held a management position at one of the larger Strip properties.

I shot Julius an appreciative glance. "Tucked tight? So I see. What I would do to have your ass."

"Honey, you can have my ass anytime." Julius gave me a provocative waggle of his perfectly plucked and arched eyebrows. "And any other body part you might find intriguing."

Unsure of the appropriate response, I laughed. Safer that way. A man whose manhood was not compromised by wearing women's clothing had none of the familiar inhibitions. I didn't see any upside in testing the boundaries.

"You two be safe in there—the place is jammed with all manner of nasties." Julius shot me a beatific smile.

He waved us inside, past the sign that said closed for a political private party. Yes, Mona was holding what I surmised just might be the very first fundraiser at a drag venue. And, going with my whole everyone-has-a-place-in-Vegas philosophy, this seemed appropriate, too.

Vegas not only tolerated nonconformists, we welcomed them with open arms. Considering my lineage, I thought that a good thing.

Pushing my way into the darkness, I realized just how right Julius was. People, in every sort of dress-up and dress-down, packed the large space. Spotlights highlighted young men in very brief boxer briefs dancing on several raised platforms dividing the area to the right. Clusters gathered at each platform like supplicants bowing to a god. The thirsty gathered three-deep around the U-shaped bar. The bartenders were either dancers awaiting their turn under the lights, or men in drag, slender, beautiful . . . feminine, prettier women than most of us born with our plumbing on the inside.

As I scanned the crowd looking for my parents, I realized I had lost Jean-Charles—he had not followed me. Across the crowd, I saw he was still deep in conversation with Julius. Backtracking, I grabbed his hand. "I'm sorry, Julius, for dragging him away. Pun intended."

Julius groaned, which made me proud. "Honey, you need to work on your material. But your guy here is a hottie." He gave Jean-Charles a lascivious look. "And that accent! You better watch him inside." While most drag queens weren't gay, they just liked wearing women's clothing, Drink and Drag welcomed one and all, so Julius's warning was not to be ignored. However, I felt sure Jean-Charles didn't need my protection.

I pulled my chef's hand. "Come on, the show's about to start. And if I'm to live to see tomorrow, I better make my presence known to my mother." I raised my voice to be heard over the music booming from the rear of the space where the dance floor was open to any and all—even those of us not dressed only in underwear. Of course, if patrons stripped down to their skivvies, they could bowl for free in the bowling alley along the far wall, to the left of the bar.

This place was such a metaphor for Vegas: if you couldn't find something to suit your fancy, then . . . well, you were to be pitied.

Hand in hand, as we wormed our way through the throng toward the front, my normal height advantage dwindled to none. Me in flats in a sea of men wearing five-inch stilettos had me feeling positively Lilliputian. Okay, overstatement—but I felt normal. For a moment, considering the crowd, I wondered what feeling normal here meant, but I really didn't think I should overthink it. So I went with it—sort of like accepting that, in Vegas, the land of tiny blond women, I had to shop for clothing in the transvestite section—they had my size, but finding my style was problematic. One of life's little challenges.

Tonight, the challenge was proving to be a bit larger. The people were packed in like cattle off to the processing plant—an uncomfortable analogy that was probably more appropriate than I liked. Mona, the Pied Piper of Las Vegas. She crooked her finger, and we all did her bidding. Too bad that wasn't part of the gene sequence she contributed to my DNA. She'd be up front, near the narrow raised walkway used as a stage between the bar and the bowling alley.

We'd made it halfway when the few lights dimmed, and the dancers stopped and jumped down from their platforms as the intro to "Coming Out" blared through the speakers.

"Hurry," I shouted to Jean-Charles as I tugged on his hand. We arrived at my mother's side as Teddie and Jordan sashayed onto the stage. Teddie scanned the crowd. Catching my eye, he gave me a look that was easy to read. Warm, inviting, a shy smile.

My heart tripped.

Mona reached over and squeezed my hand as wolf whistles and cheers greeted our performers. She was decked out in the only thing that still fit—a flowing white peasant skirt and a large pink caftan—her jewels, and a look of peace and joy that was transcendent. My father, casual in pleated slacks and a button-down, leaned around his wife and gave me a thumbs-up.

Our performers, in full makeup, styled coiffures, jewelry gaudy enough to make Elizabeth Taylor drool, and beaded gowns —Teddie's was his Cher dress, an off-the-shoulder, silver-sequined sheath with an indecent slit up one side—bowed low, as the crowd went wild. I glanced around. Everyone knew Teddie—I could see they were happy to have him home and back in a dress —personally, I had mixed emotions about the dress part.

As recognition dawned that Teddie's partner was none other

than Jordan Marsh, the place erupted. Joining in, I gave Jean-Charles a wicked grin, then stuck my two little fingers in my mouth and whistled as loud as I could.

His reaction to the show was a bit less enthusiastic. "Is that the man who used to be your lover?" he shouted in my ear. "The one who made the ass of himself in my kitchen?"

I shrugged and nodded.

Jean-Charles turned back to the show with renewed interest. I wondered what was going through his head, but I figured it really wasn't my business. Life would be what it would be. I needed to let go and let it happen.

I turned back to the show. Teddie and Jordan were a great team—the Dream Team of Female Impersonation, God help them both. And God help *me*—I had to negotiate the deal to bring Teddie back to the Babylon and to convince Jordan to join him. What a coup that would be! And after tonight, I had a feeling their price just skyrocketed. Ah, the thrill of the chase! I could pull it off, I knew I could . . . and wouldn't it be fun?

Bucked with life. Cheering and laughing from the sheer joy of being alive, I hooked my arm through Jean-Charles's—I'd been doing that a lot this evening. He squeezed my hand, and his smile warmed my heart.

Turning to my mother, I gave her a grin. But the stricken look on her face froze the blood in my veins.

"What?" I mouthed to her.

Her eyes as big as saucers, she looked down.

I followed her gaze.

A pool of liquid between her feet.

I looked up into her eyes, realization dawning.

She held her belly with both hands and smiled. "The babies are coming."

A NEW BEGINNING...

THE END

Thank you so much for going on a Lucky adventure with me. I hope you enjoyed the ride.

As you may know, reviews are SUPER helpful. They not only help potential readers make a choice, but they also help me win coveted spots on various advertising platforms.

So, if you would please, do me the favor of leaving a review at the outlet of your choice.

Read a short excerpt below

CHAPTER ONE

Me, getting married. I still couldn't believe it. We hadn't set a date, but still... married!

When Jean-Charles asked me to marry him, I had said yes.

One simple word. I'd said it a million different times, in a thousand different contexts, with no life-altering consequences ... well, except for the whole Teddie thing. That hadn't worked out quite as I'd hoped, but about like I'd feared.

He'd loved me and left. If I'd listened to more country music, maybe I could've avoided that.

For good or for ill, I paused one last time in front of the full-length mirrors in my closet that caught all sides. Normally, I avoided the things like I avoided my mother, both for good reason. At six feet and, shall we say it, fully fleshed-out, I fell far short of my mother's dream that I would become a dancer on the

Vegas Strip. Alas, I became something much worse, a hotel executive, specifically the Vice President of Customer Relations at the Babylon, Vegas's premier Strip property. But, despite my lofty rung on the corporate ladder, Mona still made me feel guilty that I didn't live down to her expectations.

Why is it we all want what we can't have?

Teddie.

As if hearing her lead-in or something, Mona breezed into my boudoir. "Well, don't you look every inch the virginal bride?" Mona said with her barbed tongue planted firmly in her cheek.

Resplendent in a rich shade of burnt orange organza that darkened and lightened as she moved, one shoulder bare, the bodice fitted, the skirt flowing, she looked every inch the hotel magnate's wife. To further fill her days, she also was the mother of month-old twins and a candidate for public office—the County Commission—if the voters didn't wise up soon. With the vote almost a year away, she was ahead in the polls, which frightened the hell out of me, but also made me grudgingly proud. My 24/7 job would never allow the time for a family and a job as servant of the people—I don't know how she did it. The wear-and-tear showed in added crow's feet and a subtle weariness dimming her normal wattage. Her brown hair was pulled into a chignon with tendrils of hair left to softly frame her face. The baby weight had almost disappeared. What was left softened her angular features and rounded her in an appealing, maternal way. Recent motherhood had made her even more stunning, a cross I bore. Her blue eyes, round with hurt and accentuated with black liner, put me on guard. "Red does suit you," she added as she eyed me with the calculation of a children's beauty pageant momzilla.

I'd chosen a strapless sheath of fire engine red with tiny gold threads running through the bodice just in case the red was too subtle. The five-carat emerald-cut diamond sparkled on the ring finger of my left hand. Every now and again I'd look at it just to make sure. Still, I couldn't believe it.

Me. Getting married.

Holding onto my mother's shoulder, I used her to steady myself as I donned first one low-heeled strappy Jimmy Choo, then the other. "Is this a social call?" I asked my mother, knowing her wounded doe-eyes provided the answer, but hoping just this once she'd let her bet ride. But she'd gone out of her way, making the trip from the Babylon, so the odds were against me.

"What?" She feigned offense. "Lucky, you act as if I don't want to check on my daughter every now and again."

Yes, my name is Lucky. Last name O'Toole, and, to be honest, I have no idea where either name came from and I'm too scared of the answer to ask. "Well, since this is your first visit in ages, it does make me wonder." I leaned close to the mirror to check my make-up one last time. I still wasn't used to the whole lipstick, powder, blush routine, but I did like the result. Especially the shadow and eyeliner that accentuated my blue eyes—even if they still carried a hint of shell-shock in them. I applied one more swipe of pink gloss, then pressed my lips together. "I know you well enough to see an ulterior motive lurking behind your innocent act."

She gave me a hint of a smile, a kid caught with Black Cats at school. "I want to talk to you about Jean-Charles."

"None of your business."

She ignored my frosty tone and eyes that had gone all squinty. "Are you sure about this? Are you sure Jean-Charles isn't one of those boomerang things?"

"Boomerang?" The visual was interesting. "You mean rebound things?" I corrected before my brain kicked in, shutting down my mouth. She knew perfectly well what she meant—and she misspoke to get me to engage. Would I never learn?

"Exactly. You're not over Teddie and what he did."

"So you don't want to talk about Jean-Charles; you really want to talk about Teddie."

"And your father."

That one whirled in out of left field, tripping my heart. "The Big Boss? He's okay, right?" Ever since he had that heart scare not too long ago, I hadn't been able to shake a feeling of impending doom. A dose of mortality to puncture his Mount Olympus aura.

"Of course, he's fine." Mona shrugged that suggestion away, a horse shaking off a fly. "It's what he's doing to Teddie."

Teddie.

This was my night, Jean-Charles's night. Tonight's party celebrating the opening of Jean-Charles's restaurant, J-C Vegas, would be the kickoff to a ten-day celebration of the grand opening of my very own hotel, Cielo. And she had to bring Teddie into it. I gave her a look that I hoped would instill terror. "Curiously, Mother, when Teddie left he ceased being my problem."

Mona rolled her eyes.

"Did you just roll your eyes at me?" A hand on my hip, I felt like the parent here. "Really? Keep doing that and maybe you'll find a brain in there somewhere."

I grabbed my purse, a sweet little evening bag in red and gold to match my dress—who knew love could turn this tomboy all girly-girly? If I started giggling, I'd hate myself. Mona dogged my heels as I strode through my bedroom and into the main room of my apartment. "Now where did I put my wrap?"

Mona's voice held the tinny notes of a whine fraying my already on-edge nerves. "Lucky, you have to deal with Teddie."

Taking a deep breath, I counted to ten … twice. My gaze wandered around the room as I drank it all in: the view of the Strip through the wall of windows, the white walls, the burnished wood floor, the white leather furniture and the splashes of color on the walls—original paintings depicting the glory of the Mojave. My home. My sanctuary. Me. "I have dealt with Teddie, Mother. Done. Over. Finished."

"But your father." Mona trotted after me breathless. "He's cancelling Teddie's contract." My father had offered Teddie his former theater to develop and stage a new show—one based on

Teddie as a singer rather than The Great Teddie Divine, Vegas's foremost female impersonator, his previous gig. I was glad that was behind him. I'd tired of him rooting in my closet for "costumes" and stretching out my shoes. Especially my shoes.

When my father had invited Teddie back into the fold, he hadn't consulted me. Both of my parents considered it their duty to meddle in my life. Up to now, they'd been irritating but not hurtful. Jerking the contract out from under Teddie, that was a knife to the heart. Teddie would wither and die without his audience. And, no matter what he'd done, how much he'd disappointed me, I didn't want to see him broken. Punishment, like revenge, wouldn't ease the pain. Oh, maybe in the short term ... but I didn't want my future to be burdened with guilt. *The high road, Lucky. The high road.*

I stopped and whirled on Mona, almost meeting her nose-to-nose. "What do you mean 'cancelled his contract'?"

She drew up, shoulders back, chin at a defiant angle, the look in her eyes a slap—a trait she'd taken from my father. He wore it better and could back it up. "Teddie's out with no place to go, and it's all your fault."

This time *I* rolled my eyes. And I knew that no matter how many times I did it, I wouldn't find a brain in my hollow head. "Of course it's not my fault. I don't know anything about it. So, stop doing that." Wow! Apparently I had shucked some emotional armor and exposed a backbone.

"You have to fix it." Mona wrung her hands. She used to campaign against Teddie, telling me he'd leave me for a life on the road. She'd been right. He'd broken my heart. And now he and my mother were best friends? Unlike her daughter, *he* had lived down to her expectations, so I guessed she had a soft spot. There was all sorts of wrong in that. "Without you and Teddie being an item," her eyes slipped to the ring on my finger and then back to mine, "your father has less incentive to keep him around."

"Don't be silly, Mother. This is *all* about money. You know the

Big Boss." With a hand on one hip, I eyed Mona, as I plotted my battle strategy. Brush her off or look into the problem? Which would be the least painful path? To ignore her would bring out her inner piranha. She'd keep biting off chunks of my resolve until I finally caved. Easier to get it over with. "I'll look into it, Mother. First, I have to know what the deal is and why the Big Boss is cancelling it."

Mona opened her mouth, but I heard Teddie's voice.

"He got a better offer." Teddie strolled in from the kitchen looking like a million bucks before taxes. Spiky blond hair, blue eyes rimmed with lashes most women would sacrifice body parts for, broad where he should be, trim where he shouldn't, a tight ass, and a voice like honey, the guy was a walking, talking, singing pheromone.

I whirled on my mother. "You asked Teddie down? So you two could gang up on me? Tonight?" Teddie's apartment connected to mine through a back staircase, which used to be convenient. Now it was a violation ... and a betrayal. I narrowed my eyes at my mother and wondered what the punishment for matricide was these days. If everyone's mother was like Mona, it couldn't be that bad. But everyone couldn't be so lucky.

Mona didn't look sorry. "A stacked deck is the best kind," she said, parroting her husband.

"In business."

She met me glare-to-glare. "This *is* business."

"My business, I should think," Teddie said. "Look, if it's any consolation, I didn't want to mention this at all. My presence here is as much a part of Mona's set-up as your help is. But, here it is, short and sweet. Your father cancelled my contract because Holt Box said he'd do thirty weeks a year for five years, coup of epic proportions getting him to come out of retirement. He'll be a huge draw for the Babylon, much more than I would." Although Teddie adopted a casual air, he was angry. It boiled just below the surface. His smile was taut with the effort to cover it.

I was blindsided. Ten years ago Holt had left country music at the peak of his career, devastating his legions of female fans and making himself into the stuff of legend.

And now the Babylon was hosting his coming-out-of-retirement tour? How could the Big Boss have inked such a deal without me being in on it? Considering my parents made me and my life their business, I didn't have to think on it too hard. In a way, Mona had been right. It was my fault, of a sort. Business and pleasure, almost impossible to separate, and my father didn't have enough confidence in me to do so.

Grudgingly I admitted, in this case, he was probably right. If I'd been left to negotiate the Holt Box deal, I would've been hard-pressed to do so. But that wouldn't stop me from letting my father know how I felt ... about all of it.

Promises were promises.

And when it came to love, I didn't need him riding in on his white horse to vanquish the unworthy. Or to save me from my own mistakes.

Teddie.

Teddie had a lot riding on his new show; he'd put his heart and soul into it. And he'd given up his spot on his newly rejuvenated tour. Finally, the rage burbled to the surface, coloring his face and hardening his voice. Holding up his hand, he stopped the platitudes I was going to offer—I didn't have anything else, and he knew me well enough to know it.

"Don't fret, not that you would. Your father had the legal right to do what he did."

"Being legal doesn't make it right."

Teddie's anger cooled. "You always tilt at windmills, don't you? One of the things I love about you. In a gray world you see black and white."

"Principles."

I left it to the Harvard boy to fill in all the rest. Principles applied to life and love.

Hiking up the flaps of his tux jacket, he stuffed his hands in his pockets. "This whole thing is my own damned fault. In such a hurry to get back here, back to—" He gave me an open, vulnerable look that tore at my heart. "But that was a pipe dream. In my haste, I agreed to stuff Rudy went apoplectic over." Rudy Gillespie was his entertainment lawyer, one of my good friends, and married to an even better friend, Jordan Marsh—the Hollywood heartthrob who had finally come out, dashing hopes of young women worldwide.

I knew what Teddie had left out, what he wanted to say: He'd been in a hurry to get back to me. Back to us. After having thrown me over for a line-up of groupies.

Trust, an emotional Humpty-Dumpty.

"Don't forget Holt Box had a hand in all of this," added Mona.

Teddie's anger sizzled as it flared anew. His shoulders rose toward his ears, as his face closed. "Yeah, that dude is on the top of my hit list."

"If you want to kill him, don't do it tonight. Murder has such a chilling effect on fun and frivolity." I spied my gold pashmina on the couch. Grabbing it in one swoop, I headed for the elevator. One advantage of having one of the top floors was a private elevator that fetched me from the middle of my great room. "I'm late. And, Teddie, I'm sorry. I really am. I'll see what I can find out. But right now I need to go. You two have a fine time. It's well past pumpkin time and I've got to hurry."

"Holt Box will be there tonight?" Teddie's voice lost any hint of nice.

"What rock have you been living under?" I wrapped the pashmina around my shoulders—Decembers could be cool in Vegas. "He's cooking with Jean-Charles. Apparently he loves to cook, has a cookbook out or something, I don't know." In my world of late nights and early mornings finding a meal involved finding the time to grab something quick and convenient. "Holt asked to assist. Jean-Charles said yes."

"And you went along with it?"

"Not my purview. And, trust me, having him in the kitchen during the opening might sound like a great media play, but it's been a nightmare of epic proportions. For weeks, gaggles of female predators looking for their hunk of country music flesh have been stalking the well-guarded perimeter of the Cielo property."

Too late, I realized I'd added fuel, igniting Teddie's slow burn into a raging inferno. Hate flushed his face, a new look. I didn't like it, but I got it.

Mona chose that moment to wade back in. "I have Paolo waiting downstairs." She studiously analyzed her fingernails as she dropped that little bombshell.

"But, I have Paolo waiting downstairs," I said as the realization that my mother could now overrule me at the hotel hit me like a bucket of ice water. I jabbed at the elevator button. Thankfully, the thing was waiting.

The doors opened and I stepped inside, followed by Mona and Teddie, rounding out our awkward trio.

When the doors closed, Teddie's reflection half-smiled at mine, an appreciated effort to cut through the ugliness. Still, I felt he was contemplating burying a knife in my back. How fun to have all of the blame and none of the authority.

In the closed space, the subtle aroma of very good Scotch, or very bad bourbon, competed with his Old Spice cologne. Apparently he'd gotten a head start—some joy juice to deaden the downside.

From the look on his face, I could tell he wanted to change the subject as much as I did.

"Now, *that* is a dress," he said, a hint of warmth melting the ice in his tone.

While he looked appreciative of the wrapping, I knew he liked the package as well. A bit of sad longing brushed over my heart. We'd been so good together. Until we weren't. His smile dimmed when he caught the flash of my ring. He reached around my shoulder, pulling me close, shoulder-to-shoulder in a one-arm embrace. Catching me off guard, I fell into him. My hand braced against his chest; the other grabbed his waist as I struggled to get my feet back underneath myself.

"Sorry," Teddie said, not sounding the least bit as he helped me right myself.

Mona, looking a bit uncomfortable, had put as much space as possible between her and me, which wasn't much given we were in an elevator. Teddie stood close enough that I could feel the heat radiating off of him. Anger? Passion? Didn't know and didn't care. Straightening my gown and my thoughts, ordering the outside to cover the muddle inside, I focused on the party ahead and ignored both of them as the elevator whisked us downstairs. As we pushed into the night, Paolo was indeed waiting by one of the Babylon's limos wringing his hands.

He snapped to attention when he caught sight of me. A small man with jet-black hair slicked back, an always-impeccable uniform, a normally ready smile, and enough energy to light Vegas for a year, tonight Paolo looked uneasy. Another hapless male fallen prey to Mona's charms, and I'm sure her veiled threats. He rushed to open the back door for me. "Oh, Miss Lucky, Paolo is so very sorry. Mrs. Rothstein …"

"I know, threatened to boil you in oil or something. Don't worry. It's fine." I stopped before I disappeared into the dark confines of the car. "Just ignore them," I whispered. "Maybe they'll go away."

Paolo nodded, his smile forced, terror in his eyes.

He situated Mona next to me and Teddie in front, then slid behind the wheel, I checked the clock. Ten minutes until a press conference my father had arranged. If I wasn't there, heads would roll.

I toggled the switch that would allow Paolo to hear despite the glass window raised to cocoon the back. "Paolo, the time."

"Yes, Miss." Paolo pressed his cap on tight as he gripped the wheel, his knuckles white. "Hold on."

I reached for the looped strap near my left ear and held on.

Mona tapped me on the leg to get my attention, like we'd been having a nice conversation and I'd gotten distracted. She recoiled when I looked at her with my not-so-happy face.

"This is my night, Mother. How dare you?"

She looked crestfallen, her best gambit. I didn't cave.

Teddie lowered the window separating the front seat from the rear compartment. "Lucky, I'm sorry. Mona said—"

I held up my hand, cutting him off. "Playing the hapless stooge in a game run by women is getting old, and it is not attractive. You know Mona. And you know our rules. We are friends, but you are not allowed in my apartment unless you have a specific invitation from me."

"At least you're talking," Mona said with more than a little gloat. "This is wonderful," she said with bright eyes.

A bit late to wise-up, Teddie ignored her. "Mona said you'd be okay with it."

"Mona lies," I said, transfixing my mother with a stare. But Teddie knew that already. "Paolo, step on it before I kill somebody."

Tires squealed as he did as I asked, fishtailing the big car onto Koval, then accelerating south. The forward momentum of the large car pressed me back in my seat and scared Mona into quiet.

In less than five minutes, with several tourists terrified but still breathing, Paolo turned up the grand drive to Cielo. Huge trees lined the curved entrance, giving the hotel a secretive feel, as if one had to be in the know to find the place. Like The Mansion at MGM, Cielo was a decadent hideaway for those who valued their privacy or just needed a respite from the constant pulsing energy of the Strip. The front entrance, normally protected by large gates and armed security, stood open, ready to receive all tonight. Protected under a copper porte cochere, and softened with pots of riotous flowering plants, the entrance was welcoming and warm with understated elegance. The architects had bent under my supervision and used rock, wood and other natural building materials where possible. The effect was stunning, warm and welcoming like a Japanese sanctuary. Frosted glass with images of reeds etched into them separated the large space into smaller vestibules. When the hotel officially opened, hosts would greet each guest, escorting them to a desk where the registration process would be handled with a glass of Champagne. The water-fall on the far wall lent a comforting sound as well as humidity, to the parched desert air. Yes, the place had turned out exactly as I'd hoped.

When the Big Boss and I had bought the property out of fore-closure, I had imagined this, dreamt of it, but never really thought I'd pull it off. The building, which we'd taken down to the bare bones, then built out, adding on where we could, had housed one of the grand dames of Vegas past, The Athena. Irv Gittings, the former owner, would never recognize what had been the diamond in his crown. Life had taken a hard turn for Ol' Irv. The rest of us moved on, and he went to jail.

Through the glass, I could see Jean-Charles just inside the front entrance talking to a group of reporters. Resplendent in his chef's whites, the trousers black-and-white striped, he looked at ease amid the well-liveried crowd milling about the lobby in their formal dress. His brown hair curled softly over the collar of his jacket. Trim, with broad shoulders and a slightly formal bearing, he made my heart melt.

When the limo eased in next to the curb, he moved to meet us as if he'd been watching, which he probably had. He opened the door, extended a hand, and pulled me into his embrace. Flash bulbs popped as I lost myself in his kiss. For a moment the world disappeared, and it was just the two of us. "You are late," he whispered against my cheek. "I was worried."

I kept my arms looped around his neck. "Shanghaied by my mother. I'm sorry. Shouldn't you be upstairs?"

He gave me a Gallic shrug and an irresistible smile that lit his robin's-egg-blue eyes. "This is more important."

"There's just something about the French. Romance oozing out of every pore," Mona cooed.

Even though her words sounded benign, I felt the prick of her jab. Apparently, Jean-Charles didn't; his eyes warm, never drifted from mine. "You look good enough to eat. This is right, *non?*" On a never-ending quest to learn American idioms, Jean-Charles never missed a chance to trot one out. Tonight, he got it right. Most of the time, not so much, with charming consequences.

"High praise indeed from a master chef."

He beamed, until he caught sight of Teddie with Mona now leaning possessively on his arm, claiming her horse in this race. "Your mother and her games." While the words were light, his tone was not. "Mona, how good to see you," he said, slipping into a well-honed insincerity.

Mona smiled, unaware of the frost chilling his words.

"Theodore, I didn't know you were attending." Jean-Charles acknowledged Teddie but didn't extend a hand as he ushered us all inside. "Your father is waiting. He is a bit angry."

"Why?"

"The reporters, they only want to talk to you." He led me to the half-circle of chairs bookending a couch and lighted for the media. "I will be upstairs. The food ..."

"Needs your attention." I gave him a quick kiss. "Go. I'll be there as soon as I can."

I watched him as he worked his way toward the elevators, admiring the ease with which he made each person he spoke with shine ... like they felt like the most important person in the world. Where did sincerity end and civility begin? With the French, it was hard to tell. So polished. So smooth.

"Lucky?" A light touch on my arm rescued me just before I slipped into insecurity.

Kimberly Cho, one of the P.R. people who had been helping me with a sticky problem at the Big Boss's Macau property, looked up at me, her eyes a bit too wide, her normal polished perfection a bit ruffled. "Do you have a moment? It's important. I won't take much of your time." Her black hair drawn back in a soft chignon, her porcelain skin lightly blushed, her eyes kohled, she'd chosen a one-shoulder sheath of exquisitely embroidered Asian silk in turquoise. I envied the ease with which she carried her elegance. Although short and trim, she had the presence of someone much taller. "You know I wouldn't ask unless it was important."

"I know." I checked the time. I glanced at my father, a light sheen on his face from the heat of the kliegs. The interviewer and her attendants shifted nervously—everyone waiting on yours truly. "Will it wait until after my interview? Everyone is waiting."

Her hand shook as she tucked in a strand of hair that had the audacity to wander loose. "There's this man. A very bad man. You must be careful."

"What? Who?"

"I knew him. From before." Her eyes stared past me. Her face went slack.

"Kimberly, what is it?"

When her eyes again shifted to mine, they looked dead. "Be careful." With a nod, she backed away.

"Find security, then meet me at the elevator," I called after her. "We'll ride up alone. You'll have my undivided attention, and we'll have some privacy."

I turned to go. Something in the way she looked bothered me. The paleness of her skin, the slight haunted look in her eyes. She wasn't scared; she was terrified. Why did I let her go? I whirled around to call her back.

She was gone.

I scanned the crowd. Nothing.

I couldn't wait any longer. Kimberly would be waiting at the elevator, I told myself as I painted on a smile and mentally shifted, grinding a few gears and threatening to throw the transmission.

My father waited, his smile firmly in place, his eyes questioning. "You look like you've seen a ghost," he said, half-joking.

"Once-removed." At his confused look, I said, "A friend, she looked troubled."

"You can help her." My father stated that like a certainty.

Helping people, solving problems, was a yin and yang kind of thing. Sort of like the push and pull of life. I loved helping people, then I resented them for needing too much. Drawing boundaries was not a tool in my toolbox.

"I'm sorry I cut it rather close," I said, settling myself. A perfunctory peace offering as a young man worked to find a place for the mic on my minimal bodice.

Seated next to my father, with Teddie and Mona stashed somewhere in the back of the crowd, the lights hot and unforgiving, I felt like a captive awaiting interrogation. While I was often the spokesperson for the Babylon, I wasn't used to having the spotlight turned on me, on my personal life. Everyone wanted to see my ring, which I thought odd, and an invasion of a sort.

My father chuckled at my discomfort. Tonight, sharp in his tux, his salt-and-pepper hair perfectly groomed, his square jaw thrust slightly out as if begging for a fight, my father looked every inch the hardscrabble hotel magnate he was.

"Throwing me to the wolves, how ungallant of you," I pretended to grouse.

"It's your show, kid. I'm old news."

According to those present, I had managed to sidestep the most invasive questions, keeping the interview on topic, and I didn't offend anyone in the process. A clear win in my book, but I didn't remember much of it. Panic derails any ability I might have to remember clearly. The pain was so great, if I remembered it I'd never do it again.

Like love.

Pain and pleasure—emotional triggers separated by perception.

Having Teddie around scratched at the thin scab over the tear in my heart. I wished he'd leave, which, had I chosen to listen, should've told me something. But I didn't.

I paused to speak with a few colleagues and old friends. Even though two million people lived in Vegas, in many ways it still was a small town. The power elite, the casino owners and representatives, the few local professionals peddling regulatory connections or perhaps insight earned from years in the business, and the requisite attorneys to create messes where there were none and the P.R. people to repair the damage—it was a small group. We hung out at the same parties, knew the same people, fought the same battles, often on opposite sides. But if one of us succeeded, Vegas succeeded. So, when the contests were over, the winner declared, we all settled back into being wary combatants always looking to realign allegiances to better our positions. Nerve-wracking and exhausting. The Big Boss was a pro, I an unwilling acolyte, strictly third-string.

At the elevator, I waited, surprised Kimberly wasn't lurking close by. Since we'd talked, I couldn't shake the feeling that she was in some sort of trouble. Silly, I kept telling myself. But I'd seen enough trouble to know how it looked, and how it felt, worming its way inside, coiling, cold and dreadful in the pit of your stomach.

I'd seen it, felt it, when I'd talked to Kimberly.

She didn't show. *Get a grip, Lucky.* As I stepped into the cab of the elevator, I shook off the odd feeling. Okay, I pushed it aside and tried to ignore it.

I had a party to work and a man's arm to grace. So nice for once not to be in charge, to be able to relax and enjoy the fruits of someone else's labor.

Amazingly, no one pushed in with me and I had the elevator to myself as I rode to the top floor. Teddie and Mona had left me to the media wolves, preferring to be early at the party. Mona loved to stake out the best spot in a room. From there she would work the party like a well-seasoned debutante. The thought of Mona with the high-society crowd made me smile. Teddie's parents wore the blue-blood taint, and Mona had put them where they belonged. I wished that kind of moxie, that ability to dissect someone without them realizing it, was genetically transferred, but no such luck. Either that or it had skipped my generation. Either way, I came out on the short end.

Pressing my back to the cool metal at the back of the elevator car, I let it hold some of my weight as the doors slid shut, cocooning me inside.

I used the quiet to breathe, the smooth ride to make a mental transition from being the lead dancer to a member of the corps. As the elevator slowed, I brushed down my dress, arranged my hair, wiped under my eyes, and relaxed ... ready to enjoy the part of the evening where Jean-Charles could showcase his brilliance and I could stay out of the limelight. The doors opened. My luck held—the hall to the restaurant was empty.

Visible through the glass doors, a Van Gogh hung on the wall, spotlighted perfectly, the personification of perfection and elegance of execution—like Jean-Charles and his cuisine. Jean-Charles and I had had a bit of a tiff over the painting—actually, it was the ace up my sleeve that I held until Jean-Charles had capitulated on a few expensive requests. He'd been played, and he'd handled it well.

Somehow we'd managed to be business partners as well as a team in life. I had no idea how we'd dodged the bullets that flew at us from every direction, but we had.

The noise of a party in full swing buffeted me as I pushed through the double glass doors fronting the elegant foyer. A few steps to the right and around a corner, then I stepped into the crowd. I loved seeing the Vegas glitterati turned out for a formal gathering. A quick scan of the room confirmed everyone who was anyone or who thought they were someone was here, including the political contingent. Not the governor, but some Gaming Commission members, as well as the mayor of Las Vegas and a few local politicos. If I remembered correctly, the lieutenant governor had hinted at putting in an appearance. With campaigns ramping up toward next year's elections, he just might. That would make sure we got some press in Carson City and Reno, never a bad thing. Even though the northern part of the state was further from Vegas than L.A., San Diego, and Phoenix, those folks still popped down for a taste of the bright lights.

The men looked brilliant in their fitted formal wear. The women, many of them powerful businesspeople in their own right, dressed to showcase figures and surgery, rather than their innate loveliness and quiet competence that made them truly interesting and set them apart. Superficiality—a Vegas thing that didn't make me proud.

Most days I felt like I waded alone in my quest for something a bit more solid than pretty outsides and relationships measured in hours. As Teddie had likened it, Don Quixote and his windmills, considering this was Vegas, where one could try on a different life for the weekend.

Excited voices competed with lively tunes from a quartet in the corner. Sinatra. *My Way.* Perfect. Mouth-watering aromas drifted from the kitchen each time a waiter pushed through the swinging doors. The tables and chairs had been hidden away, leaving the expanse of wooden floor open for gathering, dancing, and whatever. Bar tables with high stools ringed the floor, except that the far wall of windows overlooking the glory of the Strip was left unobstructed. The dark green walls, the wooden beams overhead, the brass sconces casting a warm glow, and the wrought-iron light fixtures above, each with a tiny flame in glass where a light should be, gave the space the comfort of a French country house, just as Jean-Charles had wanted.

"Food is pleasure," he told me, "to be enjoyed and shared with good friends. I want my customers to feel like friends here."

From the looks of it, he'd accomplished that in spades.

Many turned to greet me as I worked my way across the room. Mona and my father were encircled against the far wall of windows, the multicolored lights of the Strip backlighting them. My former assistant and now the Head of Customer Relations at the Babylon, Miss P, nuzzled her intended, the Beautiful Jeremy Whitlock at a table in the corner. Their wedding was set for Christmas Eve, only a few days from now, it would be the first to be performed at Cielo. Brandy, my assistant, had corralled a few important media-types, presumably stroking their egos as she spoon-fed them the story we'd like to see printed.

Still no Kimberly Cho. I tried not to be worried. But, no matter how hard I tried, I couldn't shake the feeling that tonight was going to be anything but routine.

Waiters passed trays of delectables, which I waved away for the moment. Me? Passing up a feeding opportunity? I was either sick or the apocalypse was imminent. I should wear tight clothes more often. Perhaps one day I'd fit comfortably in them and pigs would fly.

The Babylon's head bartender, Sean, appeared at my elbow with a flute of bubbly. "Schramsberg rosé. Medicinal. Chef's orders."

That I didn't wave away, thanking him with a smile as he stepped back behind the bar. I spied Jean-Charles across the room and began working my way toward him.

The back of a man walking away from me caught my eye. For a brief moment my heart went cold.

Irv Gittings? It couldn't be. An old, old flame, back when I was young and stupid, the thought of him usually had me reaching for a deadly weapon. One of my proudest accomplishments had been to play a large role in seeing him put behind bars a few months ago. There were nights I fell asleep picturing the problems he would be having in the general prison population. He'd tried to frame the Big Boss for murder, and then steal the Babylon from him. A capital offense in my book. And this was Nevada, one of the last outposts of the Wild West, where the death penalty was considered fitting punishment.

The guy easing out of the kitchen and striding away from me was dressed like Irv used to: a white dinner jacket with the crested gold buttons glinting on the sleeve as he raised his hand and a red tie that I could just catch a corner of as he angled away. The cut of the jaw, the arrogance in the exaggerated shoulder-back posture … I narrowed my eyes. No, not Irv. Shorter, maybe. And hair more pepper and less salt than Irv's. But close enough to be spooky. I got ahold of myself. Irv couldn't be here. He was playing games with the inmates at Indian Springs.

Jean-Charles was engaged in animated conversation with a couple I didn't recognize when I stepped in next to him. Without missing a beat, he snaked an arm around my waist and pulled me close. Pausing, he introduced me. His fiancée! I never tired of hearing it, and, to be honest, it still shocked and delighted me each time he referred to me that way. With the pleasantries over, he picked up the conversation where he'd left off. Parking my head lightly near his, I let the words recede and my thoughts wander.

Just the nearness of him tingled me in places long dormant if not near dead.

Teddie was nowhere to be found. A minor blessing, all things considered. I didn't know why he came anyway. Nothing but bad for him here. He'd left this life. We'd moved on. I'd moved on, despite what my mother said.

The unease from my brief talk with Kimberly Cho had lessened to a low thrum, like distant traffic, my joy eclipsing that niggling feeling that something was off. Of course, being bush-whacked by Mona and Teddie hadn't exactly started my evening down a smooth path. Swaying to the music just a bit, making Jean-Charles grin as he tried to concentrate on the people in front of him, sipping my Champagne, I began to relax into the joy of life.

Big mistake. Tempting Fate had never worked out well for me.

Detective Romeo materialized at my elbow. Nodding to the others, he leaned in close to my ear. "We have a problem."

"Nope," I said, enjoying the happy bubbles that tickled my nose as I took a big sip of my Schramsberg. Then they tickled and warmed all the way down, settling into a nice pillow of content-ment somewhere deep inside. "No, Romeo, we do not have a problem."

"Lucky, this is serious. And yes, we have a problem." He tugged on my arm, sloshing a bit of my Champagne. After counting to ten, twice, I gave him my full attention.

Even though spit-and-polished in a slim-cut dark suit and Hermès tie, his sandy hair cut and combed, even his recalcitrant cowlick bending to propriety, he looked a little ragged around the edges. His blue eyes dark, his smile absent, a frown puckering the skin between his eyes, he looked at me as a friend, which doused that warmth I'd been enjoying.

This was personal.

Brandy, my assistant and his girl, squeezed his arm. Her eyes big as saucers, she remained mute. Not good.

As I disengaged from my chef, handing him my glass of Cham-pagne, I gave him a reassuring smile. This was his party, his time to shine, and whatever it was Romeo was dragging me into, I'd keep it to myself.

Yeah, I'm a dreamer.

Weaving through the crowd, I noticed security was guarding the exits. At this point, I doubted anyone wanted to leave as the party was just getting started, so the fact that they couldn't hadn't yet caused any alarm.

"Lucky. Come on." Romeo, one hand on the kitchen door, motioned to me with the other.

I joined him. "What's going on?"

"You are not going to like this."

"You always say that." I followed him into the kitchen.

Two steps inside, I stopped in my tracks. "And you're always right."

Holt Box lay on the floor, a red stain spreading across his chest, soaking his chef's whites. His face, slack. His eyes, sightless. His skin losing the ruddy flush of oxygenated blood.

Teddie stood over the body, holding a knife.

My father pressed to his side, blood on his hands.

End of Sample
To continue reading, be sure to pick up *Lucky Break* at your favorite retailer.

THE LUCKY O'TOOLE VEGAS ADVENTURE SERIES

WANNA GET LUCKY?

A woman falls from a tour helicopter to the horror of the 8:30 Pirate show crowd.

Was it suicide? An accident? Could she have been pushed?

Lucky's day began with the invasion of the Adult Video Awards and Trade show convention, then got more hectic when the spouse-swapping annual event checked in.

And if adding a body to the mix wasn't enough, Lucky's got a new suitor. Her best friend, Teddie, a female impersonator who is pressing to take their relationship to the next level.

Can she really date a man who looks better in a dress?

What happened to the woman over the pirate show?

Will her sleuthing skills catch the killer and save her job?

LUCKY STIFF

Someone fed Numbers Neidermeyer to the tiger shark in the tank at Mandalay Bay resort.

Lucky's friend, the Beautiful Jeremy Whitlock, is suspect Numero Uno.

Miss P, Jeremy's squeeze and Lucky's partner in crime, is in a tailspin.

A tractor-trailer full of honeybees jackknifes on the Strip in front of the Babylon, spilling its load.

The district attorney—apparently the odd man out in a threesome—is hiding in the buff in a laundry room.

And Lucky's mother decides to auction a young woman's virginity.

Can Lucky get Jeremy out of the hot seat, handle the new hot French chef and her mother…and restore order in her life?

SO DAMN LUCKY

Lucky O'Toole is good at murder…solving it, but tonight she feels like committing it.

Her live-in lover, Teddie, has rock-starred out and taken his show on the road.

Her mother is a pregnant hormonal weapon of mass destruction.

Renowned magician, Dimitri Fortunoff apparently dies while trying to pull a Houdini.

Then his body actually disappears.

Lucky is less than amused. She has enough problems already.

Paxton Dane, a handsome Texan long on charisma, short on history, is pressing for an opening.

And the new French chef is equal parts charm and venom, seasoned with a dash of irresistible.

But Lucky can't shake the question: did Fortunoff really die or is this some elaborate hoax?

With his connections to the UFO convention in town, outlandish theories abound.

Love, laughter, and a few evil spirits from the Great Beyond or the Great Void—

LUCKY BASTARD

As the Chief Problem Solver for the Babylon, Las Vegas's most over-the-top destination, solving the occasional murder is in Lucky's job description.

A rapier wit, her weapon of choice.

Tonight, someone turned a young woman, a Jimmy Choo embedded in her carotid, into a hood ornament for the latest Ferrari in the Babylon's dealership.

And one of the big-name players in a huge poker tournament ends up dead.

Are the two deaths related?

Lucky starts making connections putting her in the crosshairs of a killer.

Her former lover, Teddie, comes back from his rock tour to deliver a bombshell.

Then life deals another major complication to her personal life…and it's not going to be pretty.

Can Lucky handle the fallout and catch a killer?

LUCKY CATCH

Lucky's former lover, Teddie, shows up, hat in hand.

A gaggle of egomaniacal chefs appear for a televised cook-off.

And Lucky's current lover, Jean-Charles stops answering his phone.

Since trouble comes in threes, Lucky is sure this is the extent of tonight's trouble.

As usual, she's a tad optimistic.

A prized Alba truffle disappears from Jean-Charles's restaurant.

A young chef is murdered in Jean-Charles's food truck.

Jean-Charles still isn't answering his phone.

And when Lucky's path crosses the killer's will her goose be cooked?

LUCKY BREAK

Some People Never Catch a Break

For Lucky O'Toole it's a break from murder.

As the Chief Problem Solver for the Babylon, Las Vegas's most over-the-top destination, Lucky is used to cracking heads and cracking jokes.

Besides, it's Christmas.

But even Santa can't give Lucky what she wishes for.

Holt Box, a beloved country singer on the comeback trail is killed in Lucky's lover, Jean-Charles's, kitchen.

Mr. Box dies in Lucky's father's arms.

Her former lover, Teddie, is accused of the murder.

A heavy-hitter in the Macanese underworld is working over Lucky's father.

An old nemesis salivating for revenge gets out of jail on a technicality.

Lucky's mother is ramping up an ill-advised political campaign.

And the holidays are racing to a crescendo.

And then things get really messy...

LUCKY THE HARD WAY

For Lucky O'Toole, living with murder is, well...murder.

As the Chief Problem Solver for the Babylon, Las Vegas's most over-the-top destination, mischief is in her job description, but murder? Not so much...until recently...

Fleeing a murder indictment, Lucky's first love, Teddie, flies to Macau on the heels of the real killer.

A powerful figure in the Macanese underworld has Lucky's father and his empire over a barrel.

Lucky's own hotel is days away from opening.

And her engagement is very new.

So, there's only one thing for Lucky to do...

Take a trip to Macau.

She has five days to catch a killer, save Teddie, and rescue her empire from financial ruin.

Piece of cake for someone with Lucky's superpowers...

Right?

LUCKY RIDE

Who would want to kill a clown?

Lucky O'Toole, chief problem solver for the Babylon Hotel, the primo property on the Las Vegas Strip, isn't in any mood to find out.

For one, it's New Year's Day and Lucky's birthday.

And she hasn't caught her breath after a chase to the death in Hong Kong and Macau.

Her French chef is pushing to set the wedding date.

Her former lover, wounded in the China chase, needs TLC.

A young woman, in town with the rodeo, shows up at her office with a secret that could blow the lid off Lucky's life as she knows it.

And Lucky's mother starts acting like the secret could be true.

Could it?

LUCKY NOVELLAS:

LUCKY IN LOVE

Lucky is seriously regretting booking a reality television show, *The Forever Game*, into the small theater at her hotel. Vegas does NOT need a dose of reality.

The four couples competing in *The Forever Game* add their own mischief to the incendiary mix normally available in Sin City while competing for a Las Vegas wedding extravaganza.

The host of the show, Trey Gold, appears interested only in keeping the spotlight on himself while the contestants run-wild sampling all Vegas has to offer, threatening to blow the whole show out of the water.

Teddie, her live-in lover is chasing a new dream as a singer, and leaving Vegas…and Lucky behind.

A new French chef seems determined to muddy the murky waters of love even further.

Then there's Lucky's mother, Mona, who never could leave well enough alone…

LUCKY BANG

Having a blast on the 4th of July in Vegas takes on a whole new meaning for Lucky when she discovers a bomb in a friend's restaurant and narrowly escapes becoming part of the "explosive entertainment."

And this wasn't the first time.

Years ago she'd had another narrow escape.

Could the two be related?

Missing dynamite, an old grudge, whispers from the past, force Lucky to delve into dark secrets best left alone.

And when her father disappears, things become personal.

LUCKY NOW AND THEN

Las Vegas, the City of Reinvention.

No one knows this better than Lucky.

So, when the time comes to implode her father's first hotel, The Lucky Aces, she feels the angst, but moves on.

Until skeletal remains are found in the foundation and her father is implicated in a murder.

Then it is a race to uncover the long-buried past. Lucky must unravel the twisted knot of lies, Mob hits, Vegas power plays, passions, and corruption.

Her father's life hangs in the balance.

And when Lucky discovers a key to the puzzle is locked in her own memory, she becomes a target herself.

LUCKY FLASH

Johnny Pismo, a washed-up-never-been singer shows up at the Babylon singing a song about a ring of thieves stealing Vegas' music memorabilia. Pismo even claims to have the prize piece in Lucky's father's collection—a large diamond ring given to the Big Boss by Liberace himself.

Lucky is shocked to learn he's telling the truth.

Lucky sends her down-and-dirty best friend, investigative reporter "Flash" Gordon on the trail of Johnny Pismo.

Teddie, Lucky's former lover, offers a few choice pieces of his memorabilia collection as bait. Of course, Lucky must join the chase to protect Teddie's treasures.

But can she protect her heart from him in the process?

AFTER ME

"**Fantastic!** Coonts combines her trademark strong characters and clever plotting with one of the freshest concepts in suspense--a heroine with early onset Alzheimer's who literally can't remember why everyone wants her dead. **Buckle your seatbelt for a wild ride!**"

— LISA GARDNER, #1 NEW YORK TIMES
BESTSELLING CRIME AUTHOR

"*After Me* hooked me from page one. *After Me* **is the hallmark of a great thriller**: strong voice, twisting mystery, and a compelling heroine."

Twenty million in diamonds missing.

Kate Sawyer, a cop in witness protection, holds the key.

If she could only remember.

Early-onset Alzheimer's clouds the past. Stem cell therapy is working to clear it.

But time is running out for Kate.

One night finds a dead man in her bathtub with a note stuck in his pocket.

I know what you've done.

Her cover blown, Kate runs, the clock is ticking. People close to her are being killed. Shadowy memories tease her. Some she recognizes. Others don't seem familiar at all.

Running from people she can't remember, dogged by a past lost in the haze, Kate discovers no one is who they appear to be, perhaps not even herself.

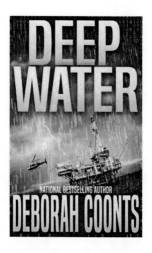

DEEP WATER

"**Thrilling, explosive suspense, a wonderful romance,** *Deep Water* **has it all**. So many twists and turns. I loved it."

OIL, THE KEY TO WORLD POWER

Patrick Donovan, Texas wildcatter, has tapped into a vast reservoir.

A senior Senator from Texas is presumed dead.

Sam Donovan, Patrick's daughter, finds herself in the bullseye of a world scramble to gain control of her father's well. A helicopter pilot operating between the rigs in the Gulf of Mexico, Sam knows how the game is played.

But this time, the stakes are life and death.

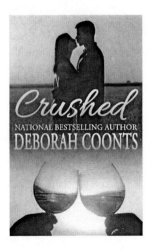

CRUSHED

In Napa Valley, he who has the best grapes wins.

And in the pursuit of perfection, dreams and hearts can be crushed.

Sophia Stone is a widow on the brink of an empty nest, stuck in an unsatisfying job managing the vineyard for a mediocre Napa vintner.

Faced with an uncertain future she wonders how do you choose between making a living and making a life? Between protecting your heart and sharing it? Five years ago, after her husband was killed in an accident, Sophia put her heart and dreams on ice to care for those around her. Now her home, her dreams, and her family's legacy grapes are threatened by the greed of the new money moving into the Valley. Sophia has a choice—give up and let them take what is hers, or risk everything fighting a battle everyone says she can't win.

Nico Treviani has one goal in life: make brilliant wine. A woman would be an unwanted distraction. So, while recognized as one of Napa's premier vintners, Nico finds himself alone… until his brother's death drops not one, but two women into his life—his thirteen-year-old twin nieces. In an instant, Nico gains a family and loses his best friend and partner. Struggling to care for his nieces, Nico accepts a job as head winemaker for Avery Specter, one of the new-money crowd. And he learns the hard way that new money doesn't stick to the old rules.

ABOUT THE AUTHOR

Deborah Coonts swears she was switched at birth. Coming from a family of homebodies, Deborah is the odd women out, happiest with a passport, a high-limit credit card, her computer, and changing scenery outside her window. Goaded by an insatiable curiosity, she flies airplanes, rides motorcycles, travels the world, and pretends to be more of a badass than she probably is. Deborah is the author of the Lucky O'Toole Vegas Adventure series, a romantic mystery romp through Sin City. *Wanna Get Lucky?*, the first in the series, was a *New York Times* Notable Crime Novel and a double RITA™ Award Finalist. She has also penned a few standalone novels; *After Me*, a medical thriller, *Deep Water*, a romantic suspense, and *Crushed*, a contemporary romance set in

Napa. Although rarely there, Deborah calls Houston home. You can always track her down at:

www.deborahcoonts.com
deborah@deborahcoonts.com

Published by Chestnut Street Press

eBook ISBN: 978-0-9857925-5-8
Paperback ISBN-13: 978-0-9857925-9-6
Hardcover ISBN-13: 978-1-944831-86-8

V100617

Cover design by Streetlight Graphics
(www.streetlightgraphics.com)

Digital formatting by Austin Brown (www.cheapebookformatting.com)

CPSIA information can be obtained
at www.ICGtesting.com
Printed in the USA
LVOW12s1307060318
568839LV00001B/36/P